RACE AGAINST TIME

Next Time Book 3

...UNTIL NEXT TIME

RACE AGAINST TIME

Next Time Book 3

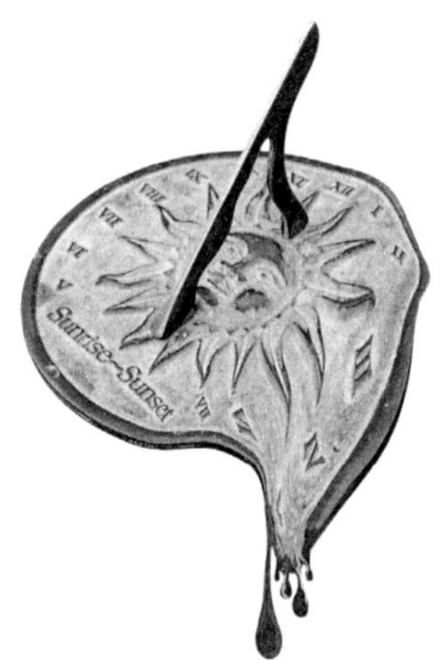

W.M. WILTSHIRE

NEXT TIME SERIES: RACE AGAINST TIME
First Edition

This book is a fictional dramatization based on true stories and real events and was drawn from a variety of sources, including published materials and interviews. For dramatic and narrative purposes the novel contains fictionalized scenes, composite and representative characters and dialogue, and time compression. The views and opinions expressed in this book are those of the characters only and do not necessarily reflect or represent the views and opinions held by individuals on which those characters are based. Errors, misinterpretations, and sheer liberties with the facts contained in the book are solely the responsibility of the author.

Book Cover Design and Interior Formatting by Melissa Williams Design

Edited by Hugh Willis and Susan Strecker

ISBN: 978-1-9991134-4-5

To Keiko, a.k.a. Bear—"*nobody can fully understand love unless they are owned by a dog.*"

Thank you for being a part of my life.

(quote by Gene Hill, The Dog Man)

Part VI

Race Against Time

Present Day—Wednesday NZ

1

QUINN SLOWLY OPENED his eyes. Except for a sliver of light filtering through a crack in the cavern wall, there was only pitch black. He began to pull himself up, but immediately regretted it. His head throbbed incessantly. "Oww," he moaned. He figured he must have been struck by a piece of stalactite loosened by the tremor they had felt moments ago. He called out. "Richard?" And again, he regretted it.

"This is worse than a hangover," Quinn groaned, reaching up to hold his aching head. He felt something moist and sticky. "Richard, are you okay?"

Quinn felt the ground around him until his hand recognized the shape of his dive light. He clicked it on and quickly scanned the cavern. Richard was gone. And so was Richard's equipment.

"The coward," Quinn muttered. "A little tremor and he runs for the hills."

Quinn pulled his hand away from his head and noticed blood on his fingers. He looked down and saw the large chunk of stalactite lying close by. "No wonder my head hurts," he grunted.

Quinn went to retrieve the piece of chronizium he had spotted before the tremor, but it was gone. "I didn't come all this way to go back empty-handed," he muttered. "Okay, Quinn, start looking. You need to get out of here, too, before something else falls on you."

Quinn, on his hands and knees, searched the area where he had found the first shard, when the beam from his dive light bounced off something shiny. He reached over and picked it up. "That's it!" he exclaimed, as he examined the mineral. This piece was larger than the first one he had found and subsequently lost.

Quinn tucked the chronizium into his utility pocket. "Time to get out of here," he said, making his way over to his equipment. He checked the gauge on his rebreather unit.

"You bastard!" Quinn shouted in the empty cavern. "Richard! How could you?"

Quinn now realized he had been duped. He hadn't been struck by any falling object. Richard had clobbered him over the head when his back was turned and had taken the chronizium and left after bleeding Quinn's air supply. With no air in his rebreather unit, there was no way Quinn could get out of the cavern, definitely not the same way he had come in. And who knew how long it would be before someone would stumble upon this cavern . . . days, months, even years. He didn't have that kind of time to wait. He had to find a way out.

2

QUINN CHECKED HIS equipment over to see whether there was anything he could use to help get him out of this death trap. He picked up his mask and put it on.

"Richard? What do you think you're doing?" Quinn shouted into the mask's communication system. He waited a few moments. He didn't really expect a reply, but he had to try. Quinn checked his dive computer and realized that too much time had passed since the tremor. Richard would be out of range of the communication system by now.

"Damn!" Quinn tried changing the frequency on the mask's communication system and called out to anyone who might be within range, but the only reply he received was static.

Quinn took off his mask and set it down beside him. He reached for his rebreather unit. As he had noted earlier, the gauge's needle was showing "empty"; even so, he remained hopeful. The two tanks on the Poseidon Discovery MKVI Rebreather unit, which he had specifically asked for when he was renting his diving equipment, were independent of each other. Richard, who had never used a rebreather unit before, would have been unaware of the backup air supply, so when he opened the valve to empty the tanks, he had only emptied one tank before leaving the cavern. Unfortunately, when Quinn checked the second tank, there wasn't enough air for him to get back to the surface. "Another dead end," he muttered.

Quinn took stock of his drysuit. His five-inch titanium dive knife was still strapped to his right leg. In his utility pockets, besides the piece of chronizium, were a spare dive light, two flares, and a handful of glow sticks.

On his left wrist, Quinn had his two dive computers. One contained a virtual dive map he had preloaded prior to their dive. It had a backlit display specifically for cave diving and a built-in digital compass that could be used both during a dive and on the surface. His other dive computer was a redundant system, but it also functioned as a watch.

Quinn never went on a dive without packing his dive tool pack. It was like a Swiss army knife, with multiple stainless steel hinged tools, only they were designed for repairing dive equipment.

Having taken stock of his meager resources, Quinn focussed his attention on the rebreather unit. He removed the two tanks from their harness and pulled off whatever rubber hoses and nylon straps he could; they weren't cumbersome to carry and might come in handy if he ever got out of here.

Sitting with his salvaged gear beside him, Quinn tried to stay calm and come up with a plan on how to get out of the cavern and get back to the surface. As he considered the number of discouragingly unworkable ideas that came to him, he turned off his dive light to conserve its batteries. In the total darkness, he saw a sliver of light coming through a crack in the back wall of the cavern. He stood up and moved slowly and carefully toward the light. "Could I be so lucky?" he wondered aloud.

3

AS QUINN CAUTIOUSLY made his way to the back of the cavern, he was guided by the thin shaft of light seeping through the crack in the wall. "I don't remember any light in here before, other than from a dive light," he said out loud, in a futile attempt to break the eerie silence that engulfed him. "Maybe the tremor caused the crack."

The crack was only a few inches wide, not nearly wide enough for Quinn to squeeze through. He placed his face against the wall and gazed through the opening. The light was coming from the other side of the cavern wall, but he couldn't identify its source. "I'm too far underground for that to be daylight," he reasoned. He tried to squeeze his arm through the crack to determine how thick the wall was, but the opening was just not wide enough. He took another look through the crack and tried to estimate the wall's thickness.

"Maybe, just maybe," Quinn said with a hint of optimism. As he headed back over to his meager collection of supplies, he checked his dive computer on his wrist. Enough time had passed for the oxygen that Richard had released into the cavern to dissipate, most likely through the same crack that was now offering Quinn at least a glimmer of hope.

As Quinn stood contemplating his next step, a rough plan began to form in his mind. “This might just work.”

Quinn turned on his dive light and set to work. He collected scattered chunks of stalactite from the cavern’s floor and piled them in an area as far from the cavern’s back wall as possible. When satisfied with his small barricade, he returned to his supplies. He picked up the back-up cylinder and headed once again toward the fissure in the wall, stooping to pick up a piece of stalactite on his way.

At the fissure, Quinn placed the cylinder gently on the sandy ground and started to pound the wall around the crack with the piece of stalactite. He succeeded in chipping away a few chunks of limestone from the crack, creating a small cradle that could hold the cylinder.

Quinn picked up the cylinder. He paused for a moment to check his dive computer again. Still okay, he confirmed. He slowly opened the air valve and then wedged the cylinder into the newly formed cradle. He hurried away from the tank and crouched behind his barricade.

“Okay, Quinn, you’ve got only two shots at this. Let’s make the first one count,” he muttered, trying to give himself some much needed encouragement. If this doesn’t work, he would have only one flare left for a second and final attempt. He just hoped that he didn’t blow himself up in the process. He pulled a flare out of his utility pocket and examined it. It looked okay. He took one deep breath, pulled the cap off, and ignited it. He immediately tossed it at the oxygen tank and took cover. There was a deafening explosion and a blinding flash of light, followed immediately by complete silence and total darkness.

Unknown—Day 1

4

"BEAR!" DANI SCREAMED, as the black before her eyes slowly ebbed to grey and light finally filtered through.

"Dani?" Daric called, alarmed by his sister's cry.

"Bear! Where's Bear?" Dani's voice projected a tone of panic, as she jumped to her feet, looking around in desperation.

"Dani, remember our last jump? Bear appeared after we did. Maybe we just have to give her more time," Daric offered, getting to his feet.

"The last thing I saw was that guy's knife slashing down at Bear," Dani moaned. "What if he killed her?"

"Let's not jump to any conclusions just yet," Daric encouraged, as he placed a calming hand on her shoulder. "Why don't we look around and try to figure out where we are? Maybe Bear will surprise us like she did last time."

"Yeah, maybe you're right." Dani replied hesitantly. She was still worried about her dog, but she thought, *Might as well put this time to good use, at least until we know for sure what happened to Bear.*

"So, tell me, what were you thinking just before the bands

touched?" Dani asked, as she bent down to examine a stone.

"Huh?" Daric spun to look at her. "Are you sure you're all right?"

"Look, Dad's note said that travel is determined by thought waves. So what were you thinking?" Dani asked again, hoping to figure out how the travel bands worked. She thought if she and Daric made an effort, they could maybe direct their next jump; with any luck, they might land back home.

"I don't know, exactly. Everything happened so fast. It was all kind of hectic, if you recall," Daric muttered, wiping a bead of sweat from his brow.

"Try! We need to figure out why we ended up here, wherever here is. It might just help us with our next jump through time."

"All right," Daric grunted, trying to think back to what was actually only a few moments ago. "We were running, trying to get out of the city of Cuzco. There was chaos everywhere. I remember saying something like we were stuck in the middle of a bloody war while we were darting in and out of doorways trying to avoid being captured. And that's when we bumped into Caso. Next, he grabbed you and held a knife to your throat."

"I remember all that, but what were you thinking when you yanked me out of Caso's grasp and touched our bands together?" Dani prodded. "At that precise moment, what were you thinking?"

"Uh, the only thing I can remember is I was trying to come up with an answer to your dumb question of what could be worse than being caught in the middle of a civil war," Daric replied. "But, I don't think that helps us much, does it?"

"No, not really," Dani said disappointedly, as she looked around their new surroundings. "But, then again, we were in the middle of a civil war, like you said, and we did see a lot of death, which might explain why we've ended up in the middle of a graveyard."

"I suppose," Daric mumbled, as he scanned the area, looking for some clue as to where they were.

Dani examined a few more stones. "And by the writing on these tombs, I'd say we're somewhere in Italy, ancient Italy, so you better brush up on your Latin."

"Great, one of my favorite languages," Daric grumbled. He had realized before now that their parents' insistence on having them learn about other countries and cultures had served them well on their travels through time.

"This must be the southern part of Italy, because it's stifling out here. I'd also hazard a guess that we're not far from the sea: I smell salt water, or is that fish?" Daric added, wrinkling his nose up and brushing aside another drop of perspiration.

"I guess I don't need to ask you what happened to Titu Cusi, because the Incas were basically wiped out of existence by the Spaniards," Daric said, encouraging a bit of small talk while they scouted the immediate area.

"Titu Cusi was one of the last Inca rulers to hold out against the invaders," Dani answered. "History, as we know it, is written by the victors, who usually glorify their cause and mock their beaten foes. But what is truly unique is that Titu Cusi actually documented a firsthand account of the Spanish invasion, offering the world a unique Inca perspective on the Spanish conquest of Peru. Something unheard of in times past."

Just then Dani picked up on a strange sound, not an unnatural one, but definitely one that was out of place. She started walking toward it.

"Hey! Where are you going?" Daric yelled, as Dani disappeared around a large stone monument. Without receiving a reply, Daric reluctantly followed.

5

THE TOMBS IN the necropolis or cemetery ranged in size and shape, from statues and portraits eloquently crafted from marble to simple fieldstone grave markers. Some were adorned with fresh flowers and trays of food, recent offerings from family members. Interspersed among them were mausoleums, some the size of small houses. On the side of one of these structures, Dani found some graffiti: AMIBTIONE TOT FRAUDES. She translated: 'So many lies for the sake of ambition!' Must be a politician, she ventured to guess.

"Hey, wait up," Daric yelled, from somewhere behind a large monument. "A person could get lost in this maze."

Dani turned the corner of the mausoleum and came to an abrupt halt; Daric ran right into her.

"Hey, give a guy a warning before you stop next time," Daric snapped, rubbing his nose, as he peered over Dani's shoulder.

"Roooo," Bear yowled joyfully, her wagging tail raising small billows of dust.

"Bear! It's good to see you. Whatcha got there?" Daric asked, as he bent down to affectionately greet his beloved dog.

"Hey, hey, it's all right," Dani purred softly, as she slowly sat down on the mausoleum step to get a closer look at what Bear seemed to be protecting.

"She can't be more than a few hours old," Dani said, reaching out to check whether she was injured. "Daric, rip a strip off your cape, will ya. This sun can't be good for her delicate skin."

Daric did as he was told and handed Dani the material.

"Thanks," Dani said, taking the material and wrapping it around the precious bundle. She picked up her swaddled, fussing package.

"What are you doing?" Daric asked nervously.

"We can't just leave her here," Dani snapped.

"I don't think we should get involved. What if we're suddenly whisked away to another time or maybe even back home?"

"Then she'll be no worse off than she is right now," Dani reasoned. "But, while we have the time, we need to find her mother."

"Do you think that's such a good idea? She was abandoned, at birth, by the looks of it," Daric countered.

"I'm not leaving her here to die," Dani announced firmly. "Come on, Bear."

Bear got up and eagerly followed Dani, who was carrying her new-found treasure.

6

DANI LED THE way, trying to go back by the same route they had come. She didn't want to admit it out loud, but Daric was right; this place was like a maze. And some of the taller monuments were obstructing her view.

Daric quickly realized that Dani's "storming out" of the cemetery wasn't proving as effective as she would have liked. He also knew that she was too proud and stubborn to admit she was lost and could use some help. So, he climbed up onto one of the more ostentatious monuments. "If we bear to the right . . ."

Bear glanced up at Daric upon hearing her name.

"Not you, Bear," Daric said, as he jumped down and reached over to give her head a gentle pat. "As I was saying, if we stay to the right, we'll come out onto a road. It's about forty feet in front of us. Farther to the right, there's a town. We could start looking for the baby's mother there."

"Thanks." Dani's eyes smiled with affection and gratitude. Daric had always been a great ally. She remembered when they were in grade five and she had come across a schoolyard brawl. Dani had hated to see arguments settled with fists, so she had tried to break it up. She had not been having much success, that is, until Daric had stepped in after one combatant had shoved her a little too hard. She peered over at her brother, who was now walking a few paces ahead of her. They would do this together.

"I don't know how anyone could abandon their own child," Daric growled angrily under his breath.

"There had better be a damn good reason," Dani snarled. She stopped abruptly when they came to the road. "Come here a minute," she said, as she ducked back behind a large tombstone.

"What? Is something wrong?" Daric asked anxiously as he stepped into the shadow of the monument.

"Look at us," Dani said bluntly. "We're screaming to anyone we come across, 'Mug us!'"

The problem was that Dani and Daric were still wearing the elegant clothing that Manco Inca had had made specifically for them, including all the pure gold jewelry he had bestowed upon them for saving his son, Titu Cusi.

Daric looked at his sister's attire and then down at himself. "Yeah, you're right. We don't know what we'll be walking into and there's no sense putting a target on our backs. Let's stash some of this stuff," Daric suggested, as he held out his arms. "Here, I'll hold the baby, while you pull off your jewelry."

Dani placed the crying baby in Daric's care. She unfastened the large gold pin that held her mantle around her shoulders. She folded the cape, placed it on the ground, and put the pin in the center. Methodically, starting from the top, she removed the three bands of braided gold from her head.

"Hurry up, will ya," Daric urged. He was very uncomfortable. *How do mothers put up with this screaming?* he wondered. He had no idea what to do with the crying baby; his first thought was to get rid of it. *Okay, Daric, think; what would Mom do?* Then he had an idea. He started to gently rock the baby while he softly hummed a lullaby.

Dani removed her gold necklace. She was working on removing her intricately crafted gold cuff-bracelet from her right wrist when she froze. She listened intently. She looked at Daric. She had recognized that tune. It was a lullaby their mom used to sing to them, called 'hush little baby'. And it seemed to be working; the baby had stopped crying.

"Genius," Dani whispered.

"Don't get any ideas," Daric whispered back. "Just hurry up."

Dani finished removing the last pieces of finery from her body, but she couldn't do much to conceal the gold embroidery on her garments. *Maybe it will pass as yellow thread,* she thought, before quickly concluding, 'Not likely'.

When Dani had finished placing all of her jewelry on the cape, she suddenly remembered the knife that Titu Cusi had given her. She pulled it from the folds of her garment and extended her hand to Daric. "Here, you take this, but conceal it. We're not looking for any trouble, but it always seems to find us."

Daric took the elegantly carved bone knife as he handed the baby to Dani, being careful not to wake her. Daric quickly removed his cape and gold accessories and placed them with Dani's. Then he put the two capes together and started to tie them, when Dani asked, "Wait, what about Bear?"

The two of them looked down at their patiently waiting pet, who perked up upon hearing her name, her tail wagging in earnest.

"We can unthread the yarn from the gold-link chain of Bear's leash and just use the yarn instead," Daric suggested.

"And we can tear another strip off your cape and fashion a collar for her," Dani offered. "We can't be seen walking into town with a dog wearing a gold collar. What would the neighbours think?" Dani teased.

Once Dani and Daric had altered Bear's accessories, Daric tied their belongings inside the two capes. He made sure the precious-metal items contained within didn't make a sound when the bundle was jostled; any sound would be a sure give away as to what was concealed inside. They were hoping their parcel would pass as the personal luggage of simple travellers, containing clothing and some baby items.

Dani and Daric checked each other over. When satisfied with their appearance, they stepped back out onto the road, turned to the right, and headed toward the town.

Present Day—Wednesday NZ

7

QUINN SPUTTERED AND coughed through the settling cloud of dust. He had no idea whether his plan had worked; he sure hoped so because now he had nothing left for a second attempt to blow a hole in the cavern wall.

Slowly, light filtered through the still-floating particles. Quinn could swear that the cavern was getting brighter. After a few minutes, he ventured out from his sheltered location and began to investigate the effects of the explosion.

Quinn was right. The cavern was getting brighter. What had been a narrow crack was now a three-foot-by two-foot hole, exactly where he had placed the cylinder in the cradle. "Hot damn, it worked."

Quinn cautiously checked the hole for any loose rock fragments before sticking his head through the opening to see what was on the other side.

"Well, hello there," Quinn said, feeling like an intruder to the party. He was looking into another cavern. Its vaulted limestone ceiling was covered with an incalculable number of glowworms, the source of the twinkling bluish-green light.

On Quinn's previous visit to New Zealand, his family had enjoyed touring the Waitomo Glowworm Caves on the North Island. They had learned that the glowworm was the only creature, apart from humans, to bring their own light underground. They had also learned that the glowworm wasn't really a worm; it was the larva of a small fly and had no eyes to see its own light. It fed on insects that normally live in the wetlands on the ground's surface but, while in their larvae form, they were swept by flowing water into the cave. The larvae, attracted to the glowworm's light, quickly fell victim to the glowworm's sticky fishing lines. Through the resulting vibrations in it glowing lines, the glowworm learned of its successful catch.

Helped by the light emitted by the glowworms, Quinn saw that this new cavern was much more spacious than the cavern in which Richard had left him for dead. He could only hope that it would lead to passages that would eventually take him to the surface.

Quinn hurried back to collect his meager supplies of straps and hoses. He was anxious to confront Richard, but his first priority was to find a way to the surface. "Let's get out of here," he told himself. He was feeling hopeful he might actually make it.

Quinn carefully climbed through the ragged opening and entered the cavern beyond.

8

QUINN PAUSED FOR a moment to survey his new surroundings. He recalled what the tour guide at the Waitomo Glowworm Caves had told them: the limestone caves were formed by a combination of tectonic uplifting and pressure that resulted when the Pacific and Indo-Australian Plates along the western coast of New Zealand collided over thirty-million years ago. An active fault still ran over four-hundred miles along New Zealand's Southern Alps and was believed to move every one-hundred to three-hundred years. Quinn did a quick calculation, based on the guide having said that the fault last moved in 1717. "That could explain the earlier tremor in the cavern," he reasoned.

The tour guide had explained that limestone isn't actually a stone, but rather a composition of fossilized corals, seashells, fish skeletons, and many other small marine organisms on the sea floor. Over a period of millions of years, these fossilized rocks layered upon each other and compressed to create limestone. In some areas, the limestone can be over six-hundred feet thick. Quinn was grateful that the wall separating the two caverns wasn't anywhere near that thickness.

The guide had said the earth's movement caused the hard limestone to bend and buckle under the ocean and to rise above the sea floor. As the rock became exposed to the air, it cracked and separated, allowing for water to flow through it. Over millions of years, the water flowing through the cracks dissolved the limestone and the caves were eventually formed.

The guide had further explained that the continuous action of water dripping from the ceiling or flowing over the walls left behind limestone deposits. When the deposits grow downward from the cavern's ceiling, they're called stalactites; when they grow upward from the floor, they're called stalagmites. When a stalactite and a stalagmite connect, they're referred to as a pillar or column, taking millions of years to form.

Although awed by what was in front of him, Quinn hadn't forgotten his priority. He knew he had to concentrate on what he was doing; if he didn't, he could be lost for ever in the bowels of the Southern Alps, which covered two-thirds of the island and were the backbone of the South Island. "Enough gawking. It's time to press on," he scolded himself.

Quinn looked at the virtual map on his dive computer in an effort to retrace the route that Richard and he had followed into the cavern. He knew he had to move along a northerly heading to come out somewhere near where they had started. He noted the time and started walking, looking for a passage that might take him in the right direction.

Preserving the batteries in his dive light, Quinn used the illumination from the glowworms to guide him through to the new cavern. The only sound he heard, other than his own breathing, was dripping water.

The cavern abruptly ended at the mouth of a tunnel. Quinn could no longer rely on the glowworms' light to safely guide his way, prompting him to turn on his dive light. He cast the beam directly ahead of him. As far as the light could penetrate, he could see that there were no obstructions in the tunnel ahead. So before proceeding he switched off his light and pulled a glow stick from his utility pocket. He snapped the stick, causing an eerie green glow that cast a bit of light into the claustrophobic blackness that engulfed him. “My own glowworm,” he quipped, nervously, as he continued forward.

Quinn walked five minutes and then turned on his dive light again. It looked as though he had walked into a dead-end; all around him was solid rock, or so he thought. He pushed forward slowly. The closer he got to what he had first assumed to be a back wall, the more he thought he might be mistaken. There was a turn in the tunnel; it headed west. “Not really the direction I want to go, but then again I have no choice,” he said aloud, just so he could hear something other than the persistent sound of dripping water.

The farther along the tunnel Quinn went, the narrower it became. He was glad he had on his drysuit; it protected him as he squirmed through the passage that was barely big enough for him to pass without getting stuck. He had no idea what was at the end of the tunnel. Was it a dead end? Was the passage going to get smaller, tighter? He continued into the unknown.

Quinn was driven purely by the urgency of getting to the surface and getting back home. He had to bring his kids back and he couldn’t do that so long as he was stuck underground half a world away. Just as that thought crossed his mind, Quinn found he could no longer move forward. “Great, just great,” he grunted.

Unknown—Day 1

9

DANI AND DARIC had crossed a bridge over a river that bordered the western edge of the town. Daric took a moment to work his way down to the water's edge, with Bear close on his heels. Daric needed to dunk his head to try to cool himself off. The sun was well passed its zenith, making it, in Daric's opinion, the hottest part of the day.

When Daric pulled his head out of the water, he noticed that the river was well below its regular level. The barren space between the current water line and where the surrounding vegetation stopped along the bank spanned at least two-and-a-half feet. He figured that the region had seen no rain in quite a while; that, and the fact that, they had been raising dust clouds off the stone-paved road with every step they took.

Daric scooped up a couple handfuls of water when he caught Bear, just out of the corner of his eye, struggling to reach the water for a drink. "Here, Bear," he said, moving his cupped hands, full of water, over to Bear, who lapped at it greedily. "Dani, do you need some water?"

"I can wait until we reach town. Besides, I don't want to wake the baby," she replied quietly, as Daric and Bear scrambled up from the ravine.

As they continued along the road, to their right loomed an enormous mountain, perfectly shaped like a pyramid. A patchwork of pastureland ran along its lower slopes, dotted with the occasional farmhouse. Dani could just make out the sound of a sheep's bell somewhere off in the distance.

A flock of wood pigeons feeding in a nearby field took to flight as they approached. One of the more irate birds voiced its displeasure with its guttural hooting call.

Elegant estates were perched on the flanks of the mountain, with row upon row of green vines, laden with plump purple grapes ready to harvest.

The pastureland on the lower slopes ended about halfway up the mountain where the dark green forest began. Dani could just make out alders, with their triangular shape, amongst the beech, oak and pine trees.

The tapered peak of the mountain was dark with no hint of the lush green vegetation that blanketed its fertile slopes. A few wispy clouds floated aimlessly above its summit.

The route they had travelled lay among vines and olive groves and, thankfully, it had been flat. As they approached the edge of the town, they walked alongside a low parapet made of river-washed boulders. They soon found themselves standing at the town's highest vantage point; they had arrived at a little hilltop town, set on a peninsula that jutted out into the sea. Dani and Daric paused briefly, soaking in the beautiful scenery around them.

They were looking over terracotta-tiled roofs atop ochre-colored buildings that gradually sloped down toward a sparkling deep blue sea. From this distance, there appeared to be small toy boats bobbing in the water; some fishing boats, others luxury yachts.

At the mouth of the bay, there was another outcropping of land; off its point were several small islands. It was almost impossible to determine the horizon because the blue of the cloudless sky melted into the blue of the sea.

Daric detected a pattern in the town's layout. Streets ran from the top of the town down to the water; north to south. There were several narrower streets running at right-angles to them, making a grid of rectangular blocks.

"Beautiful," Dani murmured.

"And damn hot," Daric grumbled. "Let's get out of the sun, so we can cool off and try to figure out our next steps."

"We should be able to barter some of this gold for lodgings and what supplies we might need," Dani speculated.

"Some lighter clothes would be my first priority," Daric moaned, wiping sweat from his forehead, yet again. "But let's play it cool and keep our hand close to our chest. We don't know what we'll run into."

"Good idea."

"Come on."

10

JUST INSIDE THE town gate was a hostelry or inn. Travellers often stopped there before journeying farther along the road that hugged the coastline as it wended its way to the larger and more celebrated city on the bay.

Daric led the way, with Bear close at his heels, as he entered the inn. He had to squeeze past the patrons standing at the L-shaped masonry counter by the front door. The counter was conveniently equipped with embedded containers that stored hot and cold food to be served to passersby. Patrons wishing to dine longer used the marble tables and benches farther inside the inn. The stuccoed walls were painted a banana yellow and, at various points around the room, were decorated by imaginative and colorful frescos. There was a large wooden rack on the back wall, stacked with amphorae containing wine. Through a rear doorway, Daric could see a set of stairs leading, most likely, to rentable rooms on the upper floor. He also noticed a young man sitting alone at a table facing the entrance as if he were waiting for someone. Their eyes met and held for just a moment.

Dani made her way past the busy counter and farther into the interior. She couldn't help but notice a number of patrons were staring at them. She had thought she and Daric wouldn't stand out from the locals, but she had been wrong. Dani looked down at her attire and then over at Daric's. *Damn*, she thought. They definitely looked out of place. Most of these people were in travelling clothes, by comparison, Dani and Daric looked like they were about to meet royalty. Furthermore, Dani was showing much more leg than any other woman in the room; all their dresses reached down to their ankles.

Dani moved closer to Daric and whispered nervously, "We need to find a place to stay while we look for the baby's mother, and I don't think this place is such a good idea."

"You may be right," Daric replied, just now becoming aware of all the attention they were drawing, including the curiosity from the young man. "Look, why don't you see if you can get something for the baby. And make sure you get some water for yourself. I'll see if I can find us a place where we can stay."

"You know finding her mother could take a while," Dani whispered uneasily.

"Yeah, I know," Daric admitted, glancing over at the young man, who had signalled that he wished for Daric to join him. "I'll be back in a minute," he said, handing Bear's leash to Dani.

The young man stood when Daric approached. "Please, join me," he invited, gesturing for Daric to take the bench opposite him. "My name is Gaius Caecilius Cilo; Cilo, if you please. And you're definitely not from around here."

"That obvious?" Daric remarked, extending his hand in greeting. "I'm Daric; just Daric," he said. He was caught off guard when Cilo responded by reaching out and firmly clasping his forearm. Daric quickly followed suit, remembering this gesture from an old movie; *Troy*.

Daric figured Gaius Caecilius Cilo was a bit younger than he, maybe late teens, and was definitely on the slight side. He was dressed in fresh clothes, compared to the other dust-covered patrons. He was clean shaven, with wavy reddish-brown hair cut about half-way down his ears.

While Daric had been approaching the table, Cilo had signalled a waitress to bring another cup. “Thanks,” Cilo said, as he accepted the cup, grinning at the pretty young girl. He watched her blush, then turn and scurry away. Cilo poured some wine for Daric and pushed the cup across the table. “Looks like you could use a refreshment,” he observed. They raised their cups, touched the rims and took a drink.

“That’s very good,” Daric murmured, as he took another drink from his cup.

11

THE INNKEEPER'S WIFE had spotted Dani, Bear, and the baby and slowly made her way toward them. She was a buxom woman in her late thirties. She was wearing a dark brown tunic whose color, Dani was sure, had been chosen to hide the filth. She had a scarf tied around her head to keep her hair out of her eyes and, no doubt, out of the food as well. Her smudged face peered down at the fussing baby in Dani's arms, then up at Dani. There was a curious look in her eye.

Dani caught the peculiar look and chose to ignore it. She hoped that they wouldn't be staying long and figured the less interaction she had, the better. "I was wondering if you might have some milk," Dani asked pleasantly.

"Just donkey's milk, if that'll suit ya?" the innkeeper's wife rasped.

"That'll be fine, thank you. And a clean rag if you have one," Dani called after her, as she disappeared through the rear doorway.

The innkeeper had been watching Dani closely. He was no fool, at least as far as he was concerned. He knew others in town would disagree with him, but what did he care? He could smell money when he saw it, and these two new strangers were reeking of it. He could tell by their clothes that they had money; maybe in the satchel that guy had placed on the table and thrown his arm over.

The innkeeper weighed well over two-hundred-and-fifty pounds. In his youth, most of that would have been muscle. In his later years, however, a lot of that muscle had turned to fat, judging by his flabby bare arms and the paunch that sagged over his belt, nearly covering a set of keys hanging there. He wore an apron that at one time might have been white, but was now more on the grey side. Part of his business was to be aware of the comings and goings in this town and to report the arrival of apparently wealthy strangers to his benefactor.

"Agatha, I'm going out; mind the inn," the innkeeper shouted at his wife, as he dropped his keys on the shelf behind the counter and hurried out the door.

"Festus! No drinkin', do you hear? You get back before dark! You know how busy it gets after dark, and I'll not be run ragged because you're out somewhere drinkin'!" Agatha yelled at her departed husband. "Worthless oaf," she muttered, as she placed a half-filled bowl of milk and an old rag on the counter.

"Thank you," Dani said, as she accepted the "clean" rag. She was sure the rag hadn't seen a bar of soap in years, but she had no other options at the moment. She dipped the least filthy corner of the rag into the milk and brought it to the baby's lips. The newborn latched onto it like it was a lifeline, and no doubt it was. Dani guessed that the baby had been abandoned for only an hour, two tops, but it could have been longer. And she knew that if she and Daric had not stumbled upon her, the baby would never have lived to see tomorrow.

"What kind of animal is that?" Agatha asked skeptically. "Is it a fox? We don't allow wild animals in here."

"She's not a wild animal; she's my dog," Dani said, as she dunked the rag again and placed it to the eagerly awaiting lips. "Bear, say hi."

Bear's head lifted off the floor. She looked up at Agatha, for only a moment, then looked over at Dani. Bear was satisfied that Dani still had Bear's treasure, and that's all that mattered to her; so Bear put her head back down on the floor and let out a deep sigh.

"It's not a fox, but it's a dog you call Bear," Agatha uttered. "You people really are strange, I'll give you that." She turned and walked away to wait on other patrons.

12

"AGATHA, BE A dear, and bring some more wine; the Vesuviana, not the Pompeiana," Cilo called, holding up the empty jug. Agatha collected the jug as she passed the table.

"I'm a great admirer of the wines of Campania, and the Vesuviana wines are among my favorites. Legend has it that the god of wine won a great victory over the god of grain. But I believe that the rich fertile soil in this area produces a much superior grape.

"This is very good," Daric acknowledged, as he drained his cup.

"The Pompeiana wines are, by far, inferior wines, because they have a lifespan of only ten years. And in my personal experience, they produce the most brutal of hangovers." Cilo finished his dissertation just as a new jug of wine arrived at the table.

Cilo poured the wine, set down the jug, and then leaned forward. "So, Daric, tell me your story," Cilo encouraged as he looked across the table to the tall athletic young man with piercing blue eyes, even features, all framed by wavy, sand-colored hair.

"Well, as you've already surmised, we're not from around here," Daric said cautiously, trying to gauge Cilo's intentions for calling him over to the table. "We're going to be here for only a short period, while we transact some business."

"I see," Cilo said guardedly. "And what business might that be?"

"Uh," Daric stalled. He wasn't as good at thinking on his feet as his sister. After only a moment's hesitation, he offered up the truth. What could be the harm, he thought. His mom had told him, when he was a little boy, that it was always better to tell the truth. So, here goes.

"See that baby over there?" Daric asked awkwardly.

"Of course," Cilo replied.

Daric leaned in and whispered, "We found her."

Cilo's eyebrows shot up into his curly bangs. "Seriously? Where?"

"In the cemetery outside town. My sister refused to leave her behind, even though it's quite apparent that someone had abandoned her," Daric murmured, before taking another gulp of wine.

"So, what are you going to do?" Cilo asked, his curiosity piqued. *His sister?* Cilo puzzled.

"That's the business I was referring to. We're going to try to track down the mother," Daric explained. "But we're going to need a place to stay while we do it, and Dani, that's my sister, doesn't think this place is right for us."

Cilo glanced at Dani. He was enthralled by her beauty and had been from the moment she had walked through the door. She was a real goddess in his eyes. Her beauty and athletic grace reminded him of Diana, the goddess of the hunt who was usually accompanied by a hunting dog. Even their names were similar! Regretfully, however, Cilo recognized that the goddess at the counter was out of his league.

"Well, I do have a friend who lets out rooms in her house," Cilo replied with a smiled. He liked this young man, and he liked what they were trying to do. And he had judged, from the moment they had entered the inn, that they were honorable people.

"We don't need a handout. We can pay our own way, if that helps," Daric offered.

"It does," Cilo grinned. "Come on, I'll take you there. It's on my way. I was about to leave to collect my uncle when you arrived and curiosity got the better of me. Come, we must hurry. I promised my mother we'd be home before dark."

13

CILO AND DARIC got up from the table and walked over to the counter. Dani had just finished giving the last of the milk to the now-contented baby.

"Dani, this is Cilo," Daric said. "He knows of a place where we can stay. He's offered to take us there, now."

"Hi," Dani said to Cilo. She couldn't offer her hand, because she was busy rocking the baby, trying to get her to go to sleep.

Dani had noticed Cilo was dressed in a tan-colored, short-sleeved tunic, trimmed in green, with leather sandals on his feet. Around his waist was a leather girdle or belt. He wore a golden-colored cape fastened at his left shoulder with a fibula or clasp, which sparkled with emeralds. He was a delicate-looking young man, maybe a scholar, she speculated.

"You're really good at that," Cilo said shyly. He was drawn into Dani's captivating, azure eyes. He gulped audibly. *Definitely a goddess,* he thought. She was taller than he; in fact, she was taller than all the women in the room and taller than most of the men, too. She had a well-proportioned physique with exquisite features, framed by flowing honey-blond hair.

"Pardon me for staring," Cilo said, realizing that he had been doing just that while lost in his own thoughts. “I didn’t catch what you said.”

Dani smiled disarmingly. “I said it’s kind of you to show us where we can stay.”

“It’s on my way,” Cilo stammered, returning the friendly smile. He reached into his belt and withdrew some coins that he placed on the counter in front of Agatha. “For the milk, too.”

Agatha did a quick count and was satisfied with the payment, which she slipped into the pocket of her apron.

“Let’s go,” Cilo said, as he pushed his way through the growing throng of people around the counter. Dani was directly behind Cilo, with Daric and Bear bringing up the rear.

Once they were outside, Daric remarked to Cilo, “You mentioned you had to get home before dark. Where’s home?”

“My mother and I live with my uncle in Misenum. It’s just across the bay. We sailed over here this morning,” Cilo explained, catching the disapproving glares from the townsfolk they passed.

“I don’t mean to sound disrespectful, but your clothes are attracting a lot of attention,” Cilo said to Dani, referring to her short tunic that came just to her knees. “Women around here don’t usually show that much of themselves in public,” he went on. “We’ll try to stick to some less travelled streets. It’s just a short distance from here,” he assured them.

“There seems to be a lot of repair work going on in the town,” Daric remarked, as they passed the third shop in a row, on this street alone, that was under construction. They had already come across a home being painted, a bakery having finishing touches applied to a new layer of plaster, and a bar or tavern with some pronounced cracks being patched with cement.

“Most of the town sustained damage during the big earthquake of ‘62 and repairs are still being made, even seventeen years later. But some repairs have led to significant improvements, which are most welcomed,” Cilo explained.

Dani was doing a quick calculation when . . .

“Look out!” Cilo yelled, as he threw a protective arm in front of

Dani. She narrowly missed being knocked over by a body, thrown out onto the street, directly in front of them.

14

THE MAN ON the ground was slow to get up. He wiped his arm across his mouth; it came away streaked with a trail of blood. When he realised people were standing behind him, he spun around, with his right hand quickly drawing the pugio, or dagger, from its sheath, ready to protect himself.

Dani gasped. Bear let out a "Roooooo."

"What are you staring at?" he growled at them, revealing two missing front teeth. He secured his dagger once he saw the people were no threat to him. He grasped the ornately decorated capulus, or knobbed hilt, of his gladius and, then stormed off down the street. They still heard the iron hobnails on the soles of his military sandals on the stone-paved street, even after he had turned the corner and was no longer in sight.

Dani and Daric stared at each other.

"Who was that?" Daric asked anxiously, trying to mask his and Dani's shocked behaviour.

"Oh, that's Ricardus Barak Casus," Cilo replied. "He's harmless, if you stay out of his way."

Dani and Daric exchanged looks of disbelief; both were thinking, *'how is this possible?'*

"Sad story, really," Cilo continued. As they walked farther

down the narrow street, Cilo deliberately said nothing about Dani and Daric's peculiar reaction to their brief encounter with Casus. But he couldn't help but wondered whether their paths had crossed before.

"How so?" Daric encouraged, wanting to learn as much as possible about Ricardus Barak Casus, otherwise known to them as Uncle Richard. Remove a few of the facial scars and the man was definitely Uncle Richard.

"Casus was a career soldier; he joined after his father was killed at sea. He wanted nothing to do with the navy, whom he blamed for his father's death, so he joined the army. He trained hard and worked his way up to the rank of centurion of the Gallic Sixteenth Legion. What little money he had earned with the army, he periodically sent home to his mother and sister. He did that for over fifteen years until he learned that his mother and sister had died of pneumonia eight years earlier."

"That's terrible. Where did his money go if his family was dead?" Dani asked sombrely.

"Their master kept it as payment for his lost property. You see, Casus's family were all slaves, Casus had a different master than his mother and his sister. Before Casus's master died when Casus was twelve years old, he granted Casus his freedom. Since Casus was no longer a slave, he joined the army. His goal was to complete his twenty-five years of service and be granted Roman citizenship. He would then return home and buy his family's freedom. But that never happened," Cilo explained sadly.

"Casus fought in many battles. He was usually the first one to cross enemy lines. No one ever said he was bright. But he truly wanted to be a hero like his father. What generally happened was Casus would be struck down earlier in the fighting. He never saw the end of any battle; so he got none of the spoils of war or any of the glory he so desperately coveted. What he got was so many scars they covered most of his body, and some of those old wounds still give him grief to this day. To hear him tell his stories, he's lucky to be alive," Cilo said pensively.

"So what happened?" Daric asked impatiently. "How did he end up here?"

"Well, when he received the news of his family's death, Casus lost his reason for fighting, namely to buy his family's freedom. So, now his goal was to survive, to one day retire from the army. Around that same time, however, another Roman solider, named Gaius Julius Civilis, who commanded the Batavian auxiliary troops in the Rhine, led a rebellion against Rome in '69," Cilo explained.

"During months of intense fighting, Casus watched the odds slowly shift in favor of the rebels. Eventually, he was persuaded to align his Gallic Sixteenth Legion with the rebels, as was the Germanica First Legion. Soon afterwards, however, the situation changed. Vespasian became emperor and assembled an enormous army which he immediately dispatched to Germania. Upon receiving news of the approaching army, both Casus's Gallic Sixteenth Legion and the Germanica First Legion surrendered to Rome. The Gallic Sixteenth Legion was disbanded in disgrace and Casus lost his entitlement to become a Roman citizen," Cilo concluded.

"That is sad," Dani echoed.

Daric could appreciate Casus's story: the wannabe hero who always fell short. Sort of reminded him of himself. Daric was in a family of geniuses. His father a brilliant physicist who just so happened to have invent time travel. His mother was head of Emergency Services and an esteemed surgeon at Mount Albert Hospital. And his twin sister, who got the lion's share of the brains between them, never forgot anything she read, heard or saw. And then there was Daric; he had always been the screw-up.

"So what's he doing here, now?" Dani inquired.

"Herculaneum is Casus's hometown," Cilo said.

"What?" Dani blurted out.

Cilo stopped in mid-step and spun around on hearing Dani's outburst. He watched as Dani scanned the area as if in search for something or someone. But there wasn't much to see past the buildings that lined the narrow street.

"Herculaneum, it's Casus's hometown," Cilo repeated calmly,

not understanding what had so agitated Dani. "He came back home out of some need to prove his worth to the townsfolk, in hopes of not being remembered for his transgressions."

Daric looked at Dani. He was confused and, to be honest, a little unnerved by her panicked expression.

"Are you all right?" Cilo asked.

"I'm fine. Just getting a little tired," Dani lied. *Let's not jump to any conclusions,* she scolded herself.

"Well, it just so happens that we're finally here," Cilo announced.

Present Day—Wednesday NZ

15

QUINN WAS NOW wedged into the tunnel he had followed and had squirmed through for the past ten minutes, only to find it was a dead end. "Now what?" he grumbled.

He reached for his dive light and turned it on. There was definitely no way of going forward and going back the way he had just come wasn't an option. He shone his beam around the tight enclosure. With his face inches away from the tunnel walls, Quinn saw fossils embedded in the limestone. One looked like a huge oyster, about eight inches long. "To be served only in the finest restaurants," he joked, trying to make light of his dire situation and, then, wished he hadn't. The mention of food was causing his empty stomach to rumble.

Quinn cast his light upwards. There was his answer. Directly above his head was another opening, about ten feet straight up. "All I have to do is get up there, somehow. It shouldn't be too hard. Considering I'm tightly wedged in here, there won't be much of a chance of falling back down. I'll just wriggle my way up the wall."

It took more effort than Quinn had expected. By the time he

reached the top, he was exhausted and his chest felt like he had been imitating Tarzan for hours. He was certain his body was covered with bruises.

Quinn popped his head through the opening. He suddenly heard the shifting of fine grains of sand right beside his left ear. He redirected his light and saw many tiny legs scurrying away, desperately trying to evade the light. They belonged to a giant cave spider, whose legs spanned six inches. "Glad you don't live near me," Quinn said to the elusive arachnid. "Dock spiders are bad enough." He couldn't help but wonder what other strange creatures were living secluded lives here in the darkness.

Quinn's beam revealed another large cavern. When he had fully emerged through the opening and got to his feet, he scanned the entire room. He felt like he had wandered into the ruins of an ancient castle. There were massive columns or pillars stretching up to the vaulted cathedral ceiling. Stalactites dangled from the ceiling and stalagmites rose like fingers from the ground.

Quinn was also witnessing something miraculous, something many had never seen and never would: the birth and early stages of life of a stalactite. They begin as slender crystal straws where each drop of water leaves behind a rim of limestone, slowly building slender tubes of crystal through which the water flows. It is when the water begins to run down the outside of the straw that the straw fattens and becomes the classic conical stalactite. In its crystalized form, the sight reminded Quinn of fireworks, just at the time of the explosion.

Quinn also noticed some tiny, exotically curled helicities that seemed to defy gravity as they reached out from the cavern walls, looking like twisted icicles. The helicities are similar to the stalactites, but they change their axis from vertical at one or more stages during their growth. They have a curving or angular form that looks as if they were grown in zero gravity.

Despite his precarious predicament, Quinn couldn't help but pause and marvel at all the spectacular decorations that adorned the cavern. And to think they were all the product of the special chemistry between water and limestone.

The spectacular decorations weren't the cavern's only feature. Huge piles of shattered rock lay scattered around the cavern's floor, evoking the image of a castle in decay. The image was reinforced when the beam from Quinn's light revealed a skeleton.

Quinn investigated. It was an animal of some sort, an accidental visitor from the world outside. It reminded him that forest floors can have treacherous and unseen dangers, such as holes and shafts that open into hidden caverns and act as natural pitfall traps for unsuspecting surface dwellers of all sizes. Quinn shone his light overhead, looking for this poor stiff's entrance to its early grave, but there was no discernible opening. He only hoped that his stumbling across this skeleton was a good sign and that he was getting closer to the surface and to finding a way out of this crypt.

Right now, however, Quinn was faced with a dilemma: which of the three passageways leading out of the cavern and into the darkness should he take? He checked his trusty dive computer and decided to take the one with the most northerly bearing. He noted the time and, then, headed toward the passageway.

Quinn followed the passageway for twenty minutes; he stumbled often over the uneven cavern floor, but always able to catch himself before he fell. Now, directly ahead of him was a rockfall. The amount of loose rock wasn't massive, so he went to work clearing the rubble. After several minutes, he had dug an opening big enough to crawl through. Once through the opening, he directed his beam into the new passageway. It was just high enough for him to walk upright. After checking his compass, he set off.

This new part of the passageway was narrower than the last. He just hoped it led somewhere. Quinn suddenly stumbled, but caught himself before falling. Something had caught him about shin high. When he looked back to see what it was, he saw a bone. From its sheer size, Quinn thought it was the backbone of a whale or some prehistoric marine specimen. It must have been buried beneath the sea in sediment and have eventually become limestone. It had remained undisturbed in its stone crypt until water had hollowed out a cavern around it. Now it was bridging the narrow passageway, its head and tail still buried deep within the stone walls of the tunnel.

Quinn pressed forward, until he came to another cavern. This one had two tunnels leading out of it. He checked his dive computer once again and took the left-hand tunnel.

After an hour, he came to another cave-in. There was no way he could get past or through it. The boulders were too big; the pile of debris too high. He would have to go back and try the other tunnel; unfortunately it was blocked, too.

As Quinn retraced his steps, his mind kept coming back to the fact that his selection of this passageway had resulted in a useless detour that wasted two hours . . . an hour to the cave-in and an hour back to his starting point.

When Quinn reached his starting point in the cavern, he wanted to give more thought to which of the two untried passageways he should try next, but it was a crap shoot, either way. He consulted his dive computer and decided he would follow the passageway to his right. It was a little off the northerly bearing he was aiming for, but it was better than the alternative. He headed for his chosen route, praying it would not prove to be another dead end.

16

QUINN HAD SPENT hours squeezing through tubes, wading through underground rivers, and walking wonderstruck through cathedral-like spaces, with ceilings, walls, and floors covered in spires.

He had scaled several vertical shafts. In one particular shaft, he had had to fashion footholds, using the nylon strapping he had stripped earlier from his rebreather unit. He had pounded his dive knife and tool-pack into the wall at staggered heights and had slowly ascended. He prayed that one of the shafts would take him to the surface. But he had discovered only more corridors, chambers, and shafts that intersected in bewildering complexity. All were a reflection of the changing course the water followed when it created them, producing an incomprehensible labyrinth of criss-crossing tube-shaped passages, each looking very much like the next. But Quinn possessed a stubbornness that would keep him going until he dropped.

As Quinn pondered his situation, he was grateful for all the hard physical labour he had done around the estate, even if he had balked at times. Cutting and splitting firewood, building decks and docks, and constructing stone cribs along the shoreline had kept him in peak physical condition, just what he needed if he was going to survive his current predicament.

A new sound, not the incessant sound of dripping water, but water nonetheless interrupted Quinn's thoughts. It was more like the sound of rushing water. Quinn headed in that direction. As he drew closer, the sound grew louder. "Keep your fingers crossed, Quinn, my boy. This could be your ticket out of here," Quinn muttered as he increased his pace.

Quinn turned a corner. Opening up in a corridor before him was a twenty-foot waterfall. *Must be coming from a melting snowcap,* he surmised. There was a river at the base of the waterfall, flowing past him, following along another passageway that ran off to his right. "And this has to be going somewhere, because it's not flowing into the caverns I've travelled for the past . . ." Quinn checked his dive computer . . . "Ugh, six hours. So hopefully it's flowing outside. Guess there's only one way to find out."

Just then Quinn's dive light flickered. "Damn," he cursed. This was his backup light; the other had died long ago. How he wished he had put new batteries into his dive lights before leaving home. But, then again, he could never have imagined that he would need the lights for more than an hour, two tops.

"Guess there's no time to waste," Quinn murmured, as he turned off his light and slipped into the icy river. He drifted away on the current, wishing he hadn't discarded his torn thermal gloves; even a little protection against the frigid water would have been better than none.

The river had carried Quinn through a number of caverns when he suddenly realized that the current had picked up speed. He turned on his dive light.

"Oh, shit," he groaned, staring at a solid wall of rock in front of him. The current was too strong for him to pull himself out of the racing river; besides, there was no time. He took a couple deep breaths, pocketed his light, and was yanked under water.

Quinn felt the current increasing as he was propelled faster and faster along the narrow passage, his hands clasped above his head to protect it from slamming into anything. Losing consciousness would be a death sentence.

Quinn's lungs ached, screaming for air. He prayed that the river would break from its underground world before long. As if in answer to his plea, he saw the water ahead of him becoming brighter. *Could it be?* he wondered. He thrust his arms out in front of him, looking a lot like Superman in flight. He didn't know what to expect, but he knew he would need to react quickly to whatever happened next.

Quinn continued to be propelled forward. Suddenly, the river exited the cavern and almost immediately plummeted down a fifty-foot chasm. Quinn reached out in desperation and grabbed onto an outcropping of rock as his legs were swept over the edge. As he hung on, he pulled his dangling legs out of the rushing water and hauled himself onto a ledge.

Quinn had no idea where he was. All he knew was that he was perched halfway up the side of a mountain, but he didn't know which one. His dive computer showed that he was, in fact, on the north side of whatever mountain it was.

It was after sunset and it was raining; there were no stars or moon to help guide Quinn on his way. Even so, one thing was certain: he wasn't staying there until daybreak. So, he pulled out his last glow stick and snapped it. "Something is better than nothing," he said. The eerie green glow didn't provide much in the way of a navigational aid, but he would have to make do.

Quinn carefully made his way off the ledge. Checking his dive computer, he slowly headed in a northerly direction.

Herculaneum—Day 1

17

RICARDUS BARAK CASUS made a right turn and rounded the corner. He walked past a few shops where women sat on stools fanning themselves in the oppressive late summer heat. He heard men talking and laughing at the bar on the next corner. Before he reached the bar, he turned down an alley.

Casus shuffled up the creaking back staircase, unconsciously pressing his hand on the small of his back. It had been giving him more grief than usual, lately. He chalked it up to old age. After all, he was almost thirty-eight. He knew that if he were still in his prime, he would have won that bar fight. Upon reflection, he realized that that was the second fight he had lost in as many days. If he kept this up, he would run out of teeth, he mused, as he looked down at the tooth in his large calloused palm, before irritably tossing it aside.

Casus's room was at the far end of the floor. He unlocked his door and then entered. The room was dark; only a thin beam of light penetrated the closed wooden shutters. He cautiously walked across the room, without stumbling into any of its furnishings, and flung open the shutters. The day's waning sunlight filled the room, bouncing off dust particles floating in the stale air.

The room was sparsely furnished. There was a bed with a thin horsehair mattress, a pillow, and a coarse grey blanket. Against the far wall was a chest for storing what little clothing he possessed; he didn't need, and never had, much in the way of clothes. On top of the chest sat a ceramic bowl and a pitcher containing water for washing. The only other furniture in the room was a rickety three-legged table and two wooden stools, which he rarely used, because he preferred to go out to eat his meals.

Casus removed his sword, pausing momentarily to study the ornamental rings on its scabbard, which depicted figures in erotic positions. He grinned devilishly as he hung the sword on a peg, next to a red woollen cape. With the oppressive heat and the unusually dry spell the region had been experiencing over the past several weeks, a layer of dust had accumulated on his unused cape. He withdrew his dagger from its metal sheath and held up its highly polished surface so he could inspect the most recent damage to his face.

"By Pollux," Casus cursed under his breath, his wide-set cold brown eyes staring back at him. He was deemed to be rather tall at just around six feet since the average male stood about five-foot-three. With his height and sinewy build, he had never had any problems getting what he wanted out of life. His steely dark eyes, over a broad nose, pinched lips and pointed jaw, gave him the appearance of having a permanent scowl; so who would want to mess with him? Maybe it was his receding hairline that led others to think he was old and weak. Evidently, in the last little while, he had been on the losing end of these bar fights. He bared his teeth to expose two gaping holes.

Casus walked to the chest. As he was about to put his hands into the wash basin to splash water on his face, he felt something. He looked down into the basin and saw tiny rings radiating out from the centre, like the ripples caused by a pebble dropped into a pond. The surface of the water was vibrating. He wasn't unaccustomed to tremors; they happened all the time. They were a routine occurrence for the residents of town and for the Roman elite who vacationed at their exclusive resorts around the bay. But the tremors seemed to be occurring more often.

Casus shrugged, knowing there was nothing he could do. He splashed water on his face to wash away the last traces of blood. He removed his balteus, or belt, which was covered with ornately stamped bronze plates. Attached to it was the sporran, or apron, which consisted of eight leather straps, decorated with bronze plates with dangling terminals. The sporran protected the groin area during battle. Also attached to the belt was his dagger's metal scabbard on the left-hand side. Finally, he removed his brown leather jerkin and draped it over the small table.

Casus moved toward the bed, picking up his dagger on the way. He placed it just under the edge of his mattress, within easy reach, a long-time habit he wasn't willing to relinquish. He stretched out on the lumpy mattress to catch a quick nap before he headed out for a bite to eat and some much needed companionship.

18

FESTUS WAS OUT of breath by the time he reached the front door. He slumped over, placing his hands on his knees. He had tried to get there as fast as he could, but all that extra weight and his aging years were not in his favor. After taking a second to catch his breath, he banged on the large wooden door.

A moment later, the door opened a couple inches. Tucked behind the door was the porter, who cautiously assessed the visitor. The porter recognized him as the innkeeper, whose inn was at the north edge of town and who was a frequent visitor to the house.

"I need to see your master immediately," Festus huffed.

"The master is entertaining some very special guests and will not be disturbed," the porter replied, as he had been previously instructed.

"Clitus, tell him it's very important and that he will definitely be interested in what I have to say," Festus persisted.

"As I said, he does not wish to be disturbed," Clitus repeated. Then he proceeded to shut the door, but Festus had shoved his foot forward, preventing the door from closing.

"Look, if your master finds out you refused to let me in and he hears of my news from someone else, he'll throw you to the eels," Festus threatened. "Now, let me in!"

Clitus knew what a horrific death that would be, being slowly eaten alive. He had seen it firsthand. Actually, all the master's slaves had been forced to watch. He was sending them all a message. Clitus had learned early on that the most inhumane master was an ex-slave. So, reluctantly he opened the door. He stood aside as Festus entered.

Clitus wore a sleeveless, knee-length crimson tunic tied at the waist. He wasn't a tall man, but he had a sturdy build, and enough bulk to turn away unwanted callers. He figured that, if there were consequences to be paid for this infraction, they would most likely be in the form of a whipping, which was far better than being the featured course at a moray banquet.

Clitus escorted Festus through the corridor into the atrium. "Wait here," Clitus directed, as he went grudgingly to inform his master he had an unexpected visitor.

Festus knew this house well. As a former slave, he had lived there for twenty-two years. The house was a fine aristocratic villa, whose main entrance faced the town's main street. It had an L-shaped plan, the result of an expansion into some properties to the rear, providing additional space for the colonnaded garden. By joining the two properties, the house had gained a second entrance off one of the narrower side streets. The house was again modified after the earthquake of '62 when the two street-facing rooms were turned into shops.

The entrance passageway opened onto a square atrium where Festus was now biding his time. In the center of the atrium was a marble-lined impluvium, or reservoir, sunken in the floor. Above the impluvium was a square aperture in the roof that funnelled in rainwater, which drained into an underground cistern. The last rays of sunlight were reflecting off the far edge of the water's surface. The walls, like the impluvium, were covered with polished marble. The floor was lavishly decorated with an intricate mosaic of small black-and-white tiles.

The household shrine, before which the family and slaves gathered every morning to pray to the gods, stood to the left of the atrium's entrance. The upper part of the shrine was a miniature model of a temple, supported by carved ivory columns with Corinthian capitals; the model's small doors opened to a tiny decorated interior. The lower portion was a cupboard where small statues of the gods were stored. Festus knew them well even though they weren't currently on display. There was the bronze statue of Jupiter, the spirit of the sky and the father of all gods, holding a thunderbolt. There was a matching pair of Lares, two young men representing the spirits of the dead ancestors; one with his right hand, the other with his left, raised to hold aloft drinking horns. There was Vesta, the spirit of the hearth, and Mercury, the merchants' god. And last, but not least, there was the elegantly crafted statue of Hercules, the patron god of the town.

In the corners of the atrium were bronze and marble statues, the original and very expensive Greek statues, not the replicas that some so-called wealthy Roman citizens displayed. The furniture in the atrium was minimal, but designed to impress visitors, fashioned as it was out of bronze and marble and embellished with gold and silver. Placed about the atrium were bronze oil lamps and large potted ferns.

Directly off the atrium and in alignment with the entranceway was the tablinum, an office on a raised platform. This was where the master greeted his clients and conducted his daily business. It was also where his money was kept, in a locked strong box bolted to the floor. The lower part of the walls were decorated with alternating red and blue panels, divided by painted vertical ornamental bands. On the upper portion there was a complex series of frescos depicting buildings, statues and stretched animal skins.

After what seemed to Festus to have been a long time, the master of the house entered the atrium. He did not look pleased. Festus braced himself.

"This had better be worth my while or by the gods . . . Festus, you, of all people, should know better than to disturb me while I'm entertaining guests," Primus barked.

19

LUCIUS COMINIUS PRIMUS was a loud, obnoxious man of fifty-three years, who had gained at least fifty pounds since obtaining his freedom twenty-three years ago. After having spent most of his life in servitude, Primus was determined to live the life of the rich and famous. His business as a moneylender had started out small, but had become lucrative and had allowed him to amass a considerable fortune. He owned this house. He had a very large profitable vineyard on the outskirts of town. And he owned a luxury yacht which was berthed at the pier in the harbour.

Primus was dressed in one of his finest togas, decorated with lilac bands and embellished with decorative silver figures. His preference would have been a toga with purple bands, but that would have been sacrilege, since only Roman nobility were allowed to wear purple.

Although not part of Roman nobility, Primus considered himself a member of Herculaneum's nobility. As a freed slave, however, he had no official recognition in the town; he couldn't even run for office, the stigma of slavery having relegated him to the sidelines. But such obstacles had never deterred him. He had his hand in everything that was going on in Herculaneum. He was the heart of this little town, and everyone knew it. If he couldn't hold office, he would control those who did. And that brought him back to this untimely interruption.

"Master," Festus muttered, as he bowed humbly. Festus had once been Primus's slave, one of many. As a domestic slave, he had earned a small wage, called a peculium which he had eventually used to buy his freedom from Primus. On becoming free, slaves commonly took on the name of their owners; in Festus's case, he had become Lucius Cominius Festus. It was also common for ex-slaves to be beholden to their previous master and to continue to serving them in one way or another, but now as a client.

"I'm no longer your master, Festus. I am your employer. Speak. What have you to tell me?"

"There are strangers at my inn, a young couple with a baby and a fox," Festus started excitedly.

"A what?" Primus snapped.

"Well, it looked like a fox to me, and it was on a leash," Festus explained. "Anyway, they clearly don't come from anywhere in these parts, of that I'm sure."

"How can you be sure?" Primus pressed. He was convinced he was wasting his time. He had more urgent matters to attend to. But then again, Festus had been a valuable resource in the past; so, for now, Primus gave him the benefit of the doubt.

"For one, their clothing. It wasn't just trimmed with golden thread; it had thin strands of real gold woven into it," Festus assured him. "And hers was something you'd see no respectable woman wear."

"How so?"

"Her dress came only to her knees; her legs were showing!" Festus exclaimed. "And her hair hung down loosely, not up like everyone does here."

Primus pondered a moment. He would say one thing for Festus: he was very observant.

"The man with her, most likely her husband, was carrying a satchel. By my account, it's really a cape he's using to keep whatever's in there out of sight."

"What makes you think that?" Primus's curiosity had been piqued.

"The fabric was the same as the fox's collar and leash. It looks like he ripped the material off his cape, so they could bring the fox into town. I know they're hiding something, something of great value. I'd stake my reputation on it."

Primus grunted; Festus made a worthless bet; he didn't have an esteemed reputation to lose.

"Where are they now?" Primus asked distractedly. He had snatched a fig off the tray as he had passed the kitchen on his way to the atrium; he was now trying to dislodge a seed from between his teeth with a manicured finger nail. In the process, he flashed a large gold ring on his index finger.

"I don't know. They were still at my inn when I left to come here," Festus replied sheepishly.

"You fool!" Primus roared. "You should have seen where they were going, before coming here. They could be anywhere by now."

"Excuse me, master, your guests," Clitus said cautiously, regretting he had walked in on an explosive moment. He hated to be around his master when he was the least bit irritated because he tended to take out his anger and frustration on whoever was close by.

"By Jupiter, I'll . . ." Primus paused briefly. A simply delicious idea was brewing in his head. "My guests . . ." he purred.

"I thought you'd want to know right away, so I came as fast as I could," Festus replied nervously, bowing his head in shame.

"Get your carcass back to the inn and find out where they went. I want to know if they're staying in town or moving on," Primus barked his order.

"Right away," Festus snapped firmly, and then he scurried out of the atrium, down the corridor and out the door.

Primus had an idea. He would have to position it just right so that his guests would think it was their idea. He walked back to the dining room, stopping suddenly beside the pool in the impluvium. Primus peered at the water's surface and could see ripples.

He looked up through the aperture in the roof. There wasn't a cloud in the sky, so it couldn't have been rain that had disturbed the pool's surface. As a matter of fact, he had seen no rain in weeks. He shrugged and made his way back to his guests in the triclinium, or dining room.

20

PRIMUS WALKED PAST the oecus, which served as the family's winter dining room—red and mustard-yellow panels on each wall. The upper portions portrayed buildings and figures on a white background.

A corridor ran between the office and the winter dining room that led through to the peristyle, or open courtyard, which was surrounded by a colonnade. The courtyard contained several fig and olive trees, intermingled with manicured evergreen shrubs.

A flight of stairs off the northeast corner of the courtyard led to an upper floor apartment. At the west end of the courtyard were three bedrooms.

On the north side of the courtyard was the triclinium, or dining room, where Primus was headed. He flinched momentarily when a small lizard darted out from under one of the bushes and sought shelter deeper within the garden.

The large dining room was decorated in the same color scheme as the winter one; this one, however, had elaborate decorations including figures of Bacchus, Apollo, and floating cherubs over a lower black frieze. The room was furnished with three lounges arranged in a U-shape and in front of each one was a table with intricately sculpted bronze legs and a polished marble top. The lounges were covered with overly stuffed cushions and pillows. The room opened on to the spacious courtyard where diners could hear birds chirping in the background.

"It's about time you got back. We were going to eat without you," a guest grumbled.

"And you're out of wine," complained another, tipping a jug, from which only a couple of drops trickled out onto the table.

"Not to worry. I have plenty of wine," Primus grinned evilly, as he entered the dining room. "Andreas, more wine," Primus bellowed to one of his slaves. "And bring on the feast, I'm starving."

21

THE HOUSE OF Julia Felix was on the north side of the main street, not far from the Forum and the Theatre. The house occupied one entire block, making it one of the largest villas in Herculaneum.

"After the earthquake in '62, Julia decided to rent out part of her home to those who had lost theirs. She also opened her private baths to the general public," Cilo explained as he hammered with his fist on the large wooden double-door. They waited less than a minute, before the heavy door swung open and a stocky man appeared, dressed in a sleeveless glacier-blue tunic. Dani figured he had to be the porter or bouncer, just by his muscular build. "Cyrus, my good man, please tell your mistress I have some people interested in renting a room."

Cyrus opened the door wider and gestured the visitors to enter the house. "Please wait here," he said, as he closed the door, then quickly disappeared from view.

Daric cast an eye around the entranceway. Almost immediately, he snatched Bear up into his arms when he noticed on the floor the image of a fierce dog with the words 'cave canem' next to it in a black and white mosaic. He feared that there was a larger watch dog on-site and didn't know how it would react to Bear. *Better to be on the safe side,* he thought.

"Good idea," Dani whispered.

The entranceway in which Dani and Daric found themselves differed from that in most Roman houses. The entranceway in most houses was joined directly to a long narrow corridor designed to protect the family, who lived farther within, from intruders. In contrast, this entranceway opened onto a large rectangular atrium. An atrium was considered the most important part of the house where visitors were received. Dani realized how quiet the interior of the house was; the noise of the bustling streets outside had vanished completely.

At the far end of the atrium, Dani saw two passages leading farther into the house. One emptied into what appeared to be a colonnaded garden; lush greenery beyond a row of stuccoed columns. That was the direction in which Cyrus had gone. The other passageway was dark and narrow. She also noted there was a doorway to her left, however, from where she was standing, she couldn't see where it led. In the middle of the atrium's floor was a shallow impluvium. The walls were decorated in red and yellow frescos, depicting, Dani assumed, everyday life in the market and forum. Several large statues were placed around the sparsely furnished room and a small household shrine positioned against the wall next to the entrance. Several potted exotic plants dispersed throughout the room, gave the windowless atrium a somewhat tropical feel.

Suddenly Dani felt the floor vibrating. Alarmed, she looked at Daric. She couldn't help but notice Bear's ears were twitching and her head was cocked to one side; she had sensed something, too. Dani then glanced at Cilo.

"It's nothing," Cilo assured her. "We get tremors like this quite often around here. There's nothing to worry about. Isn't that right, Julia?"

Dani directed her attention to the passageway in front of her, the one that led into what she had earlier assumed was an interior garden. There, in the doorway, stood a matronly woman in her late forties. Her face lit up when she recognized who had come calling. Her soft hazel eyes seemed to dance with excitement.

"You're right, Gaius. It's so good to see you," she said cheerfully. "Come and give this old woman a hug."

"My dear Julia, you are anything but an old woman," Gaius replied, as he threw his arms around his dear friend. Julia used Cilo's praenomen, or personal name, which was fine by him.

Julia pushed him back at arm's length and looked him over; a scowl graced her oval face. "Don't be such a stranger. I haven't seen you in months. And now look at me, I must look a fright. I wasn't expecting any guests today," Julia apologized, as she glanced down at her attire and worriedly fussed with her long brown hair. It was pulled back and tied into a bun that nestled casually at the base of her neck. She was wearing a cobalt-blue dress, or stola that reached down to her ankles, which were laced in delicate leather sandals accented with sapphire ornaments. She wore a gold sculpted bangle on her right wrist, and a string of pearls hung elegantly from her neck.

"Julia, you look as beautiful as ever," Gaius remarked gaily.

Julia looked past the strangers standing in her atrium, ignoring them for the moment, as if she was expecting the door to open. Clearly disappointed, she asked, "Where's that handsome uncle of yours?"

Gaius couldn't help but see her displeasure. "Uncle is visiting Rectina, or more correctly, her library. I'm on my way there now to collect him. We have to get back to Misenum before dark. You know how my mother gets when we're late."

"You must give Plinia my best and tell her it's been much too long since last we met," Julia replied. Changing her focus to the handsome couple, she asked, "And who do we have here?"

That name, Dani puzzled internally. She had heard it or read it somewhere before.

"Forgive me, Julia. This nice couple just arrived in town and are looking for a place to stay. I hope you don't mind that I brought them here," Gaius explained, purposely omitting that they were siblings and not a married couple; he would let them explain all that to Julia later.

"Nonsense, of course I don't mind," Julia replied, making her way toward the couple standing just inside her door. "Welcome to my home. And you are . . ." she asked looking at Daric, then Dani, and then down at the sleeping baby.

"I'm Dani." She couldn't understand why she was so nervous. It may have been the look that Julia had given her that had unsettled her. "This is Daric," Dani continued, referring to the man standing to her left. "And this little one has not reached the day of lustration," Dani said, recalling that a baby girl is given a personal name on the eighth day after her birth, and a boy on the ninth day.

"So I see," Julia replied skeptically. She knew she wasn't getting the entire picture, but she completely trusted that Gaius would never bring to her home anyone who was of an unsavory nature. "And who's that you're holding?"

"This is Bear," Daric answered, as he shifted Bear in his arms. "I noticed the 'beware of dog' sign. Do you have a watch dog?"

"No," Julia chuckled, "that's just to keep trouble at bay. I actually like dogs, and this one's a beauty," she said, scratching Bear behind an ear before Daric put her down on the floor.

"Julia, I must bid you farewell. I'm sorry that our visit was so short. You can help my new friends here, right?" Gaius asked hopefully.

"Of course," Julia affirmed. "Next time, make your visit sooner and the duration longer, and I will not take no for an answer."

Gaius leaned over and kissed Julia on each cheek. "I promise, next time I'm in town, I'll stop by for a proper visit." He then showed himself out.

22

"I'LL TAKE YOU to your rooms, and then we'll get to know each other a little better," Julia said, as she led the way. She walked through the doorway from whence she appeared. The portico's walkway ran along the right side of a large central garden framed by elegant stuccoed columns, which Dani had glimpsed earlier from the atrium. A long narrow water channel, with three stone bridges equally spaced along its length, ran through the center of the garden. A variety of fruit-bearing trees were scattered throughout providing much needed shade. The chirping song of birds drifted in the humid air while butterflies flitted among the delicate flowers planted in decorative pots.

Julia and her guests walked past an open room that faced out into the garden. "We'll come back here and talk once you get settled," Julia said, referring to her summer dining room.

At the far end of the walkway, they came to another atrium. "This is where my rooms are," Julia informed them. "It's like a house within a house. And I can come and go as I please," Julia said, indicating the thick studded wooden door hung on brass hinges to her right. "It's also much quieter back here. I have rooms upstairs you can use."

This atrium, like the other, had a central marble-lined pool.

There were rooms off all four sides. Like the other atrium Dani and Daric had seen, the walls were ornamentally decorated in reds, with a black lower band.

From one of the rooms off the atrium, a young girl scurried out and bowed in front of Julia. "Narissa, take the baby and make sure she is bathed, dressed and fed."

"Yes, Domina," Narissa replied humbly. She couldn't have been more than a child herself. Dani figured she was in her early teens. As Narissa reached for the baby, Dani pulled back.

"It's okay; she has the experience," Julia reassured her.

Dani reluctantly relinquished the baby.

"Now, let's see to your needs, shall we?" Julia pronounced. "Nneka! Tobius!"

No sooner had Julia said their names than two individuals emerged as if out of thin air.

"Take Dani and Daric upstairs and show them to the two rooms at the back. After they unpack their belongings, take them to the baths and see that they have some fresh clothes to wear. You must be sweltering in those," Julia remarked, indicating the heavy garments they were wearing. She saw that the couple carried few possessions, particularly considering they had a new baby.

"But . . ." Dani started to say.

"I'll meet you in the dining room in an hour and then we'll talk." And with that, Julia walked out into the garden, across one of the bridges, and entered a doorway on the opposite side of the garden.

"This way, please," Tobius said, as he ascended the staircase outside the back wall of the atrium. Daric shrugged and followed. On his heels were Dani, Bear and Nneka.

When the group had reached the upper floor, Nneka walked into one of the rooms and opened the wooden shutters to allow in what little breeze there was. Dani glanced around the room and then looked out the open window. "Oh my god!"

23

PRIMUS RESUMED HIS place in the dining room beside his wife, Aquilina. He rarely included his wife or daughter when he had business matters to discuss with the leading local citizens of the town. But his guests tonight were his usual leeches. They called about once a week for a free meal and to put a gaping hole in his wine cellar. However, having the female members of his family at the banquet tonight guaranteed an early end to the evening, which suited him just fine.

Sitting around his table were the local town officials: the two aediles and the duumviri. The town aediles were responsible for keeping the water flowing and keeping the streets clean. They took care of the town's sacred and public buildings, issued all the business licenses, and sponsored the town's spectacles. The duumviri were the magistrates; the two men who presided over local squabbles and tried cases of crime against the state. They were also responsible for dispensing justice by levying fines, imposing whippings, or ordering executions by means of crucifixion or combat in the games. Primus needed to keep these men contented so they would remain receptive to his propositions. They might hold official positions and status in this town, but Primus had dominion over them; as a result, he was the one running the town, and most of the citizens knew it.

Marcus Rufellius Robia had just recently been elected as an aedile in the March election. He was a young, ambitious man who preferred to do things the easy way, not necessarily the right way. He was hoping to marry Cominia, Primus's daughter; doing so would see to all his future needs in life. Consequently, Primus had easy sway over this young man; he just had to threaten that he would give his daughter's hand to another. All Robia really wanted was Primus's fortune and he would marry the homely-looking Cominia to get it.

Then there was the other aedile Aulua Tetteius Severus, a man in his early forties, with little ambition or aspiration. He came from a long line of wealth. He had barely lifted a finger his entire life. Anything Primus suggested, Severus agreed to, providing it didn't involve a lot of effort.

Tiberius Crassius Firmus, one of the duumviri, was the most honorable one of the four officials at the table. He often argued for the greater good, usually finding himself at odds with his peers. Eventually, he would be forced to concede reluctantly to the majority, even though a ruling was unjust according to his beliefs. Primus had to keep a tight rein on this one.

And then there was Arlus Marius Celus, the other duumvir. A man of aging years, he was extremely overweight and had difficulty participating in the town's public functions, which of course, he was obliged to attend. His weight, however, wasn't his only problem. He also had a gambling problem and had nearly lost his entire fortune. If it hadn't been for Primus, some plebeian would have found Celus dead in a back alley for failure to pay his creditors.

Primus's guests were all dressed in their formal attire: long white togas with Tyrian purple stripes. His wife and daughter were both dressed in the finest silk stolas, or ankle-length dresses, that money could buy. They were adorned with expensive gold jewelry including necklaces, bracelets and dangling earrings encrusted with fine gem stones.

Primus clapped his hands twice and three slaves immediately

appeared. They all wore crimson tunics, similar to the porter's. They carried silver serving trays, which they placed on the individual tables in front of the three dining lounges. The trays were heaped with oysters.

"These aren't just any oysters," Primus boasted. "These are Brundisium oysters. They have been fed in Lake Avernus and in Lake Lucrinus, combining the flavours of the two regions."

Primus reached over, picked up an oyster, and slurped it down. He then pointed to the edge of the empty shell in his hand. "See that purple line encircling the edge of the shell? The experts have marked these oysters to be of a nobler variety, known as the 'beautifully eye-browed'. No supper in Rome is complete without them."

After Primus and his guests had devoured the oysters, the slaves removed the shell-laden trays and then brought in silver bowls containing olives, pomegranate seeds and sardines. They also brought in a silver platter with dormice rolled in honey and sprinkled with poppy seeds.

"I sure hope that sign we posted works," Severus griped, referring to the actions he and Robia had taken earlier in the day. "I'm sick and tired of hearing complaints about the quality of the town's water."

"We threatened that if anyone was caught dumping rubbish near the town's public fountains, they would either be fined or flogged. We won't have any more complaints, trust me," Robia said confidently, as he held his glass aloft. Andreas, acting as wine steward, had already walked around the dining room for a third time, refilling everyone's glasses.

"So, Primus, what business took you from our table?" Celus boldly asked as he reluctantly picked up one of the honeyed rodents. He knew it was impolite to turn down what had been offered.

"Well, as a matter of fact, I just learned that there are two new visitors in our town," Primus replied loftily.

"So," Robia grunted. "We get visitors every day. What makes these two so special?" Robia had picked a sardine out of the dish and held it over Cominia's head. When she tilted her head back and parted her ruby lips, Robia slipped the tiny fish into her mouth. He held his hand there momentarily as she sensuously licked the oil from his fingers.

"They appear to be very wealthy, so I'm told, and young, too," Primus announced, planting a tiny seed.

"Maybe they're here to visit a relative," Firmus said flatly. "Why should we care?"

"Apparently they carry with them one satchel, always in the young man's possession. Travelling light for two people with a baby and a fox, don't you think?" Primus opined.

"A fox?" Firmus spat, almost choking on the olive pit in his mouth.

"I'm sure it's a dog with the same coloring as a fox," Primus responded indifferently.

"You're right; that does seem strange," Celus agreed; but then again, he usually agreed with almost anything Primus said.

"What if that satchel is full of stolen items, like gold or silver?" Primus asked, planting another seed. "What if they've come to Herculaneum to rob some of our fine citizens?"

"That would explain the loot they are carrying," Robia mumbled, pulling a small bone out of his mouth and placing it on the table. Without realizing it, he was jumping to conclusions, the ones that Primus hoped and knew he would. "We'd better keep a close eye on those two."

"I agree," Primus encouraged. "It strikes me odd that someone so young should carry around that kind of wealth."

"I think we should spread the word to our people to be on the lookout for them," Celus urged nervously.

Primus grinned, it had worked. He knew these newcomers were here for something and he wanted to know what. And now he had the officials of the town doing his work for him. That's not to say Primus wouldn't have his own people keeping an eye out, too.

"I'm glad that's settled," Primus announced, as he clapped his hands twice.

24

TWO MALE SLAVES quickly appeared and swiftly cleared away the empty bowls and trays. They were followed by three female slaves, who entered carrying large brass bowls, with towels draped over their arms. They knelt down in front of each of the guests, who dipped their hands into the bowls, cleaned off the residue from the earlier course and then drying them with the towels offered by the slaves.

The two male slaves returned, after the females had left, to rearrange the dining tables for the main course. Moments later, four kitchen slaves carried in a roasted Trojan pig on a large wooden plank, which they placed in the center of the dining table for all to see. Served standing upright on its four feet, the pig was stuffed with sausages and fruit, rather like the Trojan horse that had been filled with Greek soldiers. A large red ruby was jammed in the pig's mouth.

Just another gaudy display of Primus's wealth, Firmus seethed internally.

"Marvelous," Celus exclaimed, as he applauded the presentation. The other diners joined in the accolades. "Simply marvelous."

The chef entered the dining room carrying a large kitchen knife. He bent over and sliced open the belly of the pig; the sausages and fruits spilled out onto the table.

Primus sat patiently over dinner and listened to the officials talk about mundane topics, such as Gullus's porter being caught screwing Gullus's wife and how Gullus had the porter condemned to fight in the games.

Sad really, how a slave could be condemned for simply obeying orders, Firmus thought.

After the main course had been cleared away, trays of figs, plums and grapes were presented for dessert. At the final course's arrival, Primus clapped his hands three times, signalling for the entertainment to start. He had been waiting in anticipation all evening for this moment.

A hunched-back, gray-haired old man appeared, carrying papyrus scrolls.

"Where's the entertainment? Where's Nais?" Primus bellowed.

"She's not well, father," Cominia explained. "We gave her the day off. This is Myron, a Greek poet. He's going to recite some poetry."

"Get Nais, now!" Primus bellowed angrily.

"Father, she can't perform tonight. She can hardly keep her feet under her; there's no way she could possibly dance tonight," Cominia pleaded. She and Nais had become close during the fifteen months that Nais had been in their home and she knew Nais wasn't comfortable with the arrangements. Cominia had heard rumors, but she refused to believe them, choosing to treat them as wicked gossip among idle slaves. Then she recalled something her father had once said, 'slaves know every secret of the household'.

"By Pollux," Primus cursed under his breath. He had been waiting all night for Nais to grace his presence with her fluid movements as she floated across the floor in her rhythmic dance.

Primus had acquired Nais as security against a loan he had made to Marcus Nonius Fuscus. That was over a year ago and Primus had been enjoying Nais's company ever since. He had no intentions of ever giving her back. Fuscus had tried to repay his debt, but Primus would not attend him.

Primus had long since lost interest in sleeping with his wife; Nais, on the other hand, had put the spark back into his life. A few years older than his daughter, she was about five-foot-three and had a slim build. Her features were like those seen on a finely sculpted Greek statue. Her eyes were sad, but warm. Her brown hair shone like the moon reflecting off the midnight water and her skin was a tawny brown. Primus figured she was of Egyptian decent. Just thinking about her got him aroused.

She better get well soon, Primus thought angrily, resigning himself to the fact he would not have her company this evening. Come to think of it, she had been sick quite a bit lately. He thought back to the time several years ago when he had lost another fantastic body slave, along with the slave's mother; he didn't want to lose this one, too. Maybe he would have a doctor look at her tomorrow.

Primus glanced up when he realized that the room had gone silent; he had been lost in his own musings. "Well, what are you waiting for? Get on with it, then," he barked, ordering the evening's boring entertainment to continue.

25

TOBIUS HAD LED Daric to a room right next to the one to which Nneka had escorted Dani. "This is where you will stay," Tobius said, as he lifted a silver chain from around his neck. He held it out for Daric to take; there was a key dangling at the end.

"The key opens the strong box," Tobius said, pointing to the metal-studded wooden box bolted to the floor in the corner of the room. "You must keep the key with you at all times. You lock your valuables in the box."

Bear had entered the room and started to investigate every corner, just like she had in Dani's room, where she had found nothing of interest.

Daric took the chain and walked across the small room. He knelt by the box, took the lock in his hand, and inserted the key, then froze.

"Oh, my god!" Daric heard Dani cry out. He bolted into the next room, with Bear right behind him. Dani was kneeling on the floor, her legs bent under her, as if they had just given out. Nneka moved quickly away from Dani.

"Dani?" Daric asked nervously, as he knelt by his sister. He looked at her closely; her eyes seemed vacant as if she were in a trance. He reached for her hand; it was ice cold. "Dani?" he whispered again. He was concerned; he had never seen her like this before.

"Master, she just slumped to the floor. I did nothing," Nneka explained, hoping she wouldn't be blamed for whatever was happening. Her domina was a reasonable mistress, but she didn't know if the newcomers would be as understanding.

"Dani?" Daric whispered yet again. This time Dani's head turned. She looked directly at him. *Is that fear is see?* Daric thought. Dani seemed to snap out of whatever had traumatized her, as she threw her arm around Bear's neck, who had been whimpering beside her. "What is it? Are you all right?" Daric asked anxiously.

"Yes, I'm fine," Dani replied, her voice a little shaky. "I guess the heat finally got to me," she lied.

"I'll fetch some honey water," Nneka offered, as she darted from the room.

With Tobius standing in the doorway, just out of earshot, Dani whispered, "We'll talk in private."

Daric realized that something must have caused Dani's outburst; he would have to be patient and wait for Dani to explain. *Hopefully it won't be too long in coming,* he thought. The suspense was killing him.

26

DANI WAS SITTING on the edge of the small bed, with Bear glued to her side. She was trying to pull herself together when Nneka returned and handed her a goblet. After Dani downed the honey water and calmed her nerves somewhat, Nneka handed her a white toga. "Please, put on," she directed.

Nneka stood by patiently as Dani removed her garments. "Where's the baby?" Dani asked, as she slipped into the fresh toga.

"She is being looked after," Nneka assured her, noting with interest that Dani had said 'the' baby.

"Follow me, please," Nneka said, once Dani was dressed. Nneka took a metal ring which held a flask and some utensils, off a peg on the wall, before she walked out of the room. Dani followed, holding onto Bear's leash. Standing in the hallway, waiting for them, were Daric and Tobius. Daric was wearing the same attire as Dani, and Tobius was carrying a ring similar to the one Nneka carried.

Tobius and Nneka led the guests down the back staircase, through the small atrium, and out into the open courtyard. They crossed over one of the bridges that spanned the long narrow water channel in the center of the garden. Daric took notice of how low the water was in the channel. *Same as the river,* he thought. *Must be from lack of rain.*

The foursome walked past a series of fig, olive, and lemon trees. Dani spotted the red heads of a few goldfinches among the branches when she searched for the source of the high-pitched chirping.

Tobius and Nneka stopped at the baths' latrine and waited while Dani and Daric relieved themselves. "Well, that was interesting," Dani muttered, as the group proceeded toward the changing rooms.

"Domina has closed the baths to the public for thirty minutes," Tobius announced. "She felt you would be more comfortable, seeing that you are not from around here and may be unaccustomed to our ways."

"That was very thoughtful of her," Dani replied.

The changing room opened off the back of a square courtyard. The room had red panels with decorative borders above a black frieze. The floor was paved in a black and white mosaic incorporating large white circles. A broad band of white framed the mosaic.

When Nneka reached from behind Dani to pull her toga off her shoulders, Dani grasped her hands. Dani recalled that slaves helped with the daily bathing ritual, but she preferred, for now, to do it herself. Nneka held up the ring, which Dani took from her. Hanging from the metal ring or handle were the necessary bathing instruments. There was no soap; instead bathers rubbed oil, contained in the flask, onto their bodies and, then, used curved metal utensils, called strigils, to scrape the oil, sweat and dirt from the skin.

"This doorway," Tobius said, pointing to the west side of the changing room, "leads through to the warm room."

"I'm warm enough, as it is," Daric grumbled. "Where's the cold water? As you said, we have only thirty minutes, no time to waste."

Tobius pointed to the south wall where, recessed in the middle, was a cold plunge pool, lit by small windows on three sides. An arch decorated with stucco framed the entrance to the pool; the lower parts of the walls were painted light blue.

"There is also a larger open air pool off the east side of the court," Tobius explained.

"That'll be perfect. Thank you," Dani said, as she made her way to the outdoor pool, with Bear in tow. Daric followed, after getting his bathing instruments from Tobius.

Tobius and Nneka just stared at each other, not knowing what to do next. Tobius opted to stay while Nneka returned to their mistress.

"We might as well get used to this," Dani said. "There's no room for modesty in ancient Rome, but, for now, turn your head while I slip into the water." Daric did what he was asked, and Dani reciprocated.

Now that they were finally alone, they could talk freely. But not for long. They needed to be dressed and ready for dinner in about twenty minutes.

"Okay, give," Daric started. "What happened to you in that room?"

27

"REMEMBER, WHEN WE first arrived here, I asked you what you had been thinking just before the bands touched?" Dani whispered.

"Yeah, we already talked about that. I said I was trying to come up with an answer to your question. What does that have to do with your screaming?" Daric grumbled impatiently.

"And my question was; what could possibly be worse than being caught in the middle of civil war?" Dani recalled perfectly, referring to their past situation. "Well, how about being caught in the middle of a natural disaster that claimed thousands of lives? Isn't that far worse than a civil war?"

"Huh?" Daric grunted, as he kept an eye on Bear as she went exploring.

"When I entered that room and Nneka opened the shutters, my darkest fears were confirmed," Dani said, as she splashed cool water on the nape of her neck.

"You'll have to be more specific than that," Daric urged restlessly.

"When Cilo or Gaius . . . damned if I know what to call him now. Anyway, when he was bringing us here, he mentioned an earthquake in '62 and that repairs were still being made seventeen years later. I was trying to do the math when Uncle Richard or

Casus stumbled into our path," Dani said. "Once I got a look out of that window, I realized exactly where we are and I have a good idea when."

"Well, we already knew we're in Herculaneum; Cilo mentioned that," Daric stated. "Come to think of it, you had a strange reaction to that news, too."

"And for good reason, because outside that window, I got all the confirmation I needed," Dani asserted. "Sixty-two plus seventeen is seventy-nine, as in AD 79, and that mountain outside the city is Mount Vesuvius."

"Are you telling me that that mountain is about to go ballistic?" Daric blurted out.

"Keep it down, will ya," Dani whispered, scanning the immediate area for anyone who might have overheard them.

"Why did it take you this long to figure it out?" Daric asked warily. "We had that mountain in full view while we were walking toward the town."

"I didn't recognize the mountain as Vesuvius, because it doesn't look anything like that today, or should I say in our time? The shape is completely different; this one has a peak," Dani explained.

"So how much time do we have?" Daric asked anxiously. Even knowing that their travel bands would offer immediate escape when the time came, he was still nervous being this close to what would be the equivalent of an explosion of 100,000 atomic bombs. The sooner and the farther they were away from here, the happier he would be.

"I don't know, but what I do know is that the eruption happened on August 24, AD79," Dani said. "We need to find out today's date."

"Then what are we going to do?" Daric wondered aloud.

"We still need to find the baby's mother, if we have enough time. After that, I don't know," Dani moaned. "We can't interfere with the timeline; we can't alter history."

"I understand that, but what do we know about the eruption and Herculaneum?" Daric asked, hoping that there was something they could do to help these people.

"Herculaneum was believed to have had a population of about four-thousand people," Dani informed him. "In 1982, during the excavations, three-hundred skeletons were found in and around the boat sheds down at the beach."

"Then that means that most of the population had fled," Daric speculated.

"We don't know that," Dani said depressingly. "Only part of the city has been excavated; a large part of it is still buried under the current city of Ercolano."

"But maybe the three-hundred were the only casualties," Daric said wishfully.

"I guess that could be true. Even with the skeletons found in a few of the houses, the total would have been nowhere near the population of four-thousand," Dani whispered.

"Then we have our work cut out for us, and it would appear that time is not on our side," Daric said. He wasn't feeling or sounding very optimistic, but he knew he would think of something; he had to. "Come on, we don't want to be later for dinner."

Present Day—Wednesday NZ

28

HIKING THE NARROW trail that ran along the side of the mountain, Quinn thought that he must have been quite the peculiar sight in his drysuit and dive boots, his knife still strapped tightly around his right leg. "Not your basic gear for trekking, I must admit," he mumbled. "But it's keeping me relatively dry and warm."

Quinn cautiously moved along the side of a saddle that passed between two massifs. Earlier, on his descent, he had passed a series of rock cairns, which he assumed led uphill to the summit. But since then, there had been no markers or signposts. He realised he was blazing his own trail, which wasn't the ideal situation, especially in the dark.

Suddenly, Quinn's left leg went out from under him, pitching him forward. He instinctively reached for whatever hold was within his grasp as visions of falling through one of the pitfalls and plummeting down into the caverns below flashed through his mind. He didn't want to become another pile of bones in the bowels of the Southern Alps.

Quinn had grabbed onto a sapling, praying that its roots

wouldn't give way. He was hanging, waist-up, over a hole, his legs dangling below him. He had no idea, and at this moment, wasn't the least bit interested in finding out how deep the hole was. Slowly, he pulled himself out of the hole and rolled over onto his back. "That was too close," Quinn groaned. "I could have been right back where I started, if I had survived the fall."

He got to his feet. As he did so, he felt a sharp pain in his left ankle. He collapsed on the ground again. "Great; just great." Quinn reached down and gently probed his left ankle. He realised that it was sprained. "At least it's not broken."

Quinn searched the ground with his hands. He was thankful that the rain had stopped a while ago, but even so, everything was still soaking wet. His right hand stumbled upon an old stick, about eight feet long and it seemed thick enough to be of use. "Can't hang around here till daylight," he muttered, as he used the stick to push himself to his feet. He slowly hobbled forward, but this time he used the stick, not only as a crutch but also as a probe to test the ground in front of him. He wanted to avoid any further mishaps.

Quinn moved past several small tarns, or ponds, and stayed to the east of another peak. He paused for a moment on a large area of tussock grassland. Ahead of him, he noticed a tiny speck. He could swear it was a light in the distance. "In the middle of nowhere, be serious," he scolded himself. Still, what did he have to lose? So, he headed for what he hoped was a light, and possibly a way back to civilization.

As Quinn continued his slow trek, he could gradually make out the shape of a building. There was a small light coming from inside. As he approached, he heard a faint musical sound, a guitar maybe. He gingerly stepped onto the wrap-around deck and cautiously drew close to a grimy window. He leaned forward and peered into the hut. "Well, I'll be," he mumbled.

He limped across the deck toward the door, passing two large black rain catchers just off the front edge. *Well, at least there's fresh water,* he thought. Stepping up to the door, he knocked, announcing himself to the lone occupant. "Jaclynn, it's Quinn. May I come in?"

The music stopped. A few seconds later, the door flew open. Jaclynn took an involuntary step back. She had recognized the friendly voice, but not the lacerated drysuit and debris-covered body standing in front of her. This wasn't the handsome man she had met in town earlier.

"You look like you've been to hell and back," Jaclynn said, stepping aside to allow Quinn to enter. "What are you doing way up here?" She looked over his shoulder. "And where's your friend?"

"It's a long story," Quinn grunted, as he shuffled into the hut. He slowly made his way over to a picnic table and sat down on its bench. "I thought you weren't coming up here because the ford was flooded."

"Well, a woman is allowed to change her mind," Jaclynn bantered, closing the door. "Besides, it turned into a beautiful day; it started to rain again when I got up here. But the next couple of days are supposed to be gorgeous. I just couldn't let them go to waste."

Jaclynn put her ukulele down on one of the twelve bunks in the sparsely furnished hut and walked toward Quinn. "Let me take a look at that foot," she said, as she knelt on the floor in front of Quinn. She carefully removed his left boot.

"It's just a little sprain," Quinn assured her. He suddenly tensed and gritted his teeth as soon as Jaclynn touched a very tender area.

"I can see that," Jaclynn jibed. "Give me a sec. I have a tensor bandage in my gear." She walked to one of the bunks and rummaged through her belongings she had scattered on the bed. She quickly found what she was looking for.

"Look, I've got to get back home as quickly as possible. Can you give me a lift back to Tapawera?" Quinn asked, as Jaclynn returned and handed him a container of water. She knelt down in front of him.

"Sure, but not until morning. It's much too dangerous to travel these trails at night, even if you know them as well as I do. It's a wonder you even got here in the dark." Quinn knew she was right.

Jaclynn placed a half-inch, U-shaped pad around each ankle

bone. "Hold these," Jaclynn instructed Quinn. She began wrapping the ankle, starting at the arch of the foot and working her way up, making figure eights around the ankle and foot.

"I'd say you've done this before," Quinn remarked, impressed by her proficiency.

"I've had a sprain or two in the past. I always pack a sprain kit, just in case. It helps to be prepared since there usually isn't anyone around to help you if you get into trouble. I learned early on to be very self-sufficient," Jaclynn admitted. "There, that should do it. Is that too tight?"

"No, it's perfect, thank you," Quinn replied gratefully.

"Try to stay off it for a while. We'll head out tomorrow, at first light," Jaclynn assured him, patting him on the knee as she got up off the floor.

Quinn glanced around the fairly spacious hut. He figured it had probably been built within the last five years, because the pine walls were still pale in color, not yet darkened with age. There was no electricity. The light he had spotted was an oil lantern hanging from the ceiling. He had passed a small outbuilding as he approached the hut; he assumed it was an outdoor toilet.

When Jaclynn opened the back door, Quinn got a sudden whiff of burning charcoal. He hobbled to the door and looked onto the back porch. Under the eaves by the back stairs, there was a small portable hibachi. Without warning, his stomach grumbled, reminding him he hadn't eaten in over eleven hours.

"Don't worry, I have enough for both of us; remember, I packed for a few days." Jaclynn chuckled, as she finished checking the coals. She pulled out a package of lamb chops from the cooler section of her backpack. "I was just waiting for the coals to be ready." She reached once again into her pack and pulled out a small box of red wine and handed it to Quinn. "Why don't you pour while I grill?"

Quinn gave Jaclynn a quizzical look. "What?" she remarked. "I enjoy my creature comforts. 'Roughing it' doesn't have to mean going without, in my book, anyway." Jaclynn had pulled out some tubers she had collected on her trek up to the hut and was preparing a foil wrap to cook them in while Quinn poured the wine.

During the delicious meal, Quinn filled Jaclynn in on his ordeal. She knew she didn't like Quinn's so-called friend for a reason. She had never liked the look of him, not even during the few brief moments when they first met.

Present Day—Friday

29

EARLY FRIDAY MORNING, Richard entered his study. He was smartly dressed in black dress pants, a black brushed-suede sports coat, with a slate-grey open-collar dress shirt and black leather shoes. He removed the picture of his great-great-grandfather from the wall, revealing a small safe. Richard put his eye up close to the retina scanner. When the green light came on, he turned the safe's handle and pulled open the three-inch-thick steel door. Sitting on top of several bundles of cash was a M1911 single-action, semi-automatic, 45-caliber handgun; it had been in the family for years. Richard tucked the two-and-a-half-pound, eight-inch gun into the inside pocket of his sports coat.

It was the same gun that Richard had given to Harry Bennett ten years ago to eliminate one of Richard's 'problems'. He had told Harry that the gun was covered with his prints and that Harry could be forever linked to the murder; with Harry's checkered past, he would likely never see the light of day again. It was the one thing that Richard could hold over Harry to ensure his loyalty. Unfortunately, Harry didn't know that Richard's prints had long since obliterated his. As far as Harry knew, Richard had the gun under lock and key. He figured it would stay there until he slipped up and Richard had no more use for him.

After leaving the study, Richard collected Eddie from his locked room. Eddie was in navy blue Docker pants, an indigo long-sleeve Henley shirt under a navy blazer, with casual tan loafers. The two men exited the mansion and headed for the garage. Harry, in his chauffeur's uniform, was standing at attention beside the fully fueled Audi Q7 SUV.

Eddie silently acknowledged Harry, who returned the nod. They didn't want Richard to notice the friendly exchange for fear of reprisal.

"Is the equipment I asked for loaded?" Richard asked bluntly.

"Yes, sir," Harry replied smartly, as he moved toward the back of the SUV. He opened the hatch, reached in, and extracted a small case. Opening it, Harry revealed three small audio transmitters, also known as bugs. Harry didn't take the time to explain how they worked to Richard, because Richard had used them many times in the past when dealing with companies, most of which Richard had wanted to put out of business, permanently.

Richard looked at the transmitters only long enough to confirm they were what he had told Harry to pack: three bugs that would broadcast five watts of power output, enough to cover the Delaneys' vast acreage. He nodded to indicate that he was satisfied. Harry closed the case and returned it to the back of the SUV.

Harry turned his attention to a much large case. He dragged it toward him and opened it. Inside, was a professional grade ultra-high-definition surveillance camera with digital zoom and zero-light night vision.

"Good," Richard said. "And the last piece of equipment I asked for?"

Harry pulled out yet another case; it looked like it had come from a fine jeweller. He opened it, tilting the case so it was directly in front of Richard, out of Eddie's line of sight. Richard reached for the case. Holding it, he nodded to Harry, who immediately removed the contents then spun around and snapped the collar around Eddie's neck.

"Hey!" Eddie bellowed, as he reached for the collar, staring coldly at Harry. Harry shrank back with an apologetic shrug. He had no choice. He had to follow Richard's orders.

"It's a perimeter collar," Richard said callously. "It will keep you within a half a mile of me; any farther and the collar will emit an electrical charge, which, in effect, will arrest your heart."

"So much for being partners," Eddie shot back.

"I have trust issues," Richard replied. "Get in," he ordered, as he climbed into the SUV. Eddie climbed into the passenger side while Harry closed the rear hatch.

Richard pulled out of the estate and was heading for the Delaneys' and some unfinished business.

Herculaneum—AD 79–Day 1

30

DANI AND DARIC were sitting in Dani's room, waiting to be taken down to dinner. They were both dressed in glacier-blue tunics, the same ones that all of Julia's slaves wore. Dani figured they had a supply handy, but, regardless, the tunic was comfortable and of lighter material than the clothes they had been wearing.

"I think she senses something," Dani whispered to Daric, as she scratched behind Bear's ear, who had refused to leave Dani's side since her outburst.

"Who?" Daric asked, looking around for whoever Dani was referring to.

"Julia. I think she suspects we aren't a couple with a newborn baby," Dani clarified.

"What makes you say that?" Daric inquired.

"I just have a feeling." Dani couldn't offer a more concrete explanation.

Their discussion was interrupted when Tobius appeared to take them to dinner. He escorted them to the dining room Julia, precisely one hour earlier, had indicated they would meet. The room contained three couches, which were veneered in marble, as were the three surrounding walls up to the level of a broad molded rail. A grotto in the back wall was also finished in marble, with cascading rungs which a small stream of water flowed down, like a brook tumbles over rocks. The water seemed to vanish behind the wall. There were two framed niches on either side of the grotto, each containing a marble statuette.

"Punctual, I like that," Julia said, entering the dining room. "Please, come in and make yourselves comfortable." She took the lounge on the right side of the room. Dani took the one by the grotto. And Daric took the one on the left, with Bear sitting at his feet. The U-shaped dining lounges were covered with cushions and pillows. Below where the diners would lounge was a marble ledge which usually served as the individual diner's table. For tonight's informal dinner, however, a wooden table had been placed in the center space for everyone's convenience.

"I hope you don't mind, but I'm not one for extravagance. I asked the kitchen to make a little more of my usual repast," Julia said, just as Tobius and Nneka entered. Tobius was carrying a tray that held a jug and three goblets, while on Nneka's large silver tray there were oysters, olives, a fresh loaf of bread, and seasoned oil for dipping. They placed the two trays on the table.

"The wine is sweet Lyttian wine from Crete, refreshing, yet not heady," Julia informed them while Tobius poured the wine and placed a full goblet in front of each diner. He also poured some wine into a small goblet that had been sitting next to a small porcelain bowl on the table.

Unsure of the customs, Dani and Daric had earlier agreed to wait and take their lead from Julia, even if Daric's stomach was protesting loudly.

Julia reached over and tore a piece off the loaf of bread. She dipped the piece into the oil and raised it high. "To Vesta, goddess of hearth and home." She lowered the piece of bread and placed it in the small porcelain bowl. She leaned over and picked up the small goblet which she held aloft. "To Bacchus, god of wine and fertility."

She bowed her head for a moment as did Nneka and Tobius. Dani and Daric followed suit.

"Now, let's put that beast in Daric's stomach to rest, shall we?" Julia laughed, as she tore off another piece of bread, dunked it in the oil; this time, however, she put it into her mouth.

Dani and Daric sampled the items before them while they enjoyed the light conversation. "So, what breed is Bear?" Julia asked, as she reached down and scratched behind Bear's ear. Bear had moved over to sit next to Julia because Bear knew she wouldn't get any table scraps from her two favorite humans; she never did. She always had to wait until her family had finished their meal before she tasted any of the night's leftovers.

"Bear is a Shiba Inu, a breed originating from . . ." Daric said, before being interrupted.

"Wa. It's a small country of islands, not very well known," Dani jumped in. Japan wasn't yet the recognized name of the country. She also recalled from her studies that, during this era, the country was being ruled by Emperor Keiko. *Sometimes it helps to have hypermnesia,* she thought; her being able to recall facts she had once read had certainly helped them more than once. "The Shiba Inu was originally bred to flush out birds and small game and was also used to hunt wild boar. But Bear's just our family pet; she's not the hunter that her ancestors were."

"Why the name Bear?" Julia asked, looking down at the fox-like dog, who had cocked her head to the right on hearing her name.

"When we first got her, she looked like a little bear cub, with a short black muzzle, rounded ears and a stubby tail. It wasn't until she started to mature that she lost those features and came to look more like a fox," Daric said, cautiously looking over at his sister, hoping he had said nothing wrong.

Tobius and Nneka had finished clearing the first course dishes and had returned with bowls of warm water so that the diners could wash their hands.

"Now, then, tell me, how do you come to be in Herculaneum?" Julia questioned, as she dried her hands.

After Dani and Daric exchanged a brief glance, Dani began to spin her tale. "We were on a ship heading toward Ostia, when we encountered a storm. Our mast broke, leaving us at the mercy of the winds. We drifted for what seemed like weeks. By the way, what's the date today?"

The twins had used a shipwreck excuse in the previous time period. It had worked then, so why should it not work now? Besides, it gave Dani the perfect segue to ask about today's date without raising any suspicion as to their story.

"Why, it's August 19th," Julia replied.

"Oh my god," Dani muttered.

"What did you say?" Julia asked.

"I said, by the gods. I didn't realize that we had been adrift for six days," she lied cleverly.

Julia knew that they were hiding the truth from her, but for the life of her she couldn't understand why. If they had been adrift as they said, they would have come aground on the outer coastline, not inside the Bay of Neapolis.

Dani and Daric now knew they had four days, four and a half max, to find the baby's mother and to get out of Herculaneum.

"And whose baby do you have with you? Another ship passenger's?" Julia asked, warily.

Herculaneum—August 19, AD 79

31

"WHAT MAKES YOU think she's not ours?" Dani responded warily. "By the way, where is she?"

"Narissa is taking good care of her. She has seen to her bath, has taken her to the wet-nurse on the next block, and we have sufficient milk on hand for the rest of the night and into the morning. She's now sleeping in a crib in Narissa's room. So don't fret about the baby," Julia said coolly.

"And as for why I think she's not yours, well, for starters, you two are both fair-haired; that baby has a mop of thick brown hair. Second, your eyes are both blue; hers are brown. And last, she has the skin tone of an Egyptian whereas both of you are of white descent," Julia concluded. "Not to mention the shape of her nose, a sure giveaway, even at her young age." In addition, Julia had been told earlier by Nneka that Dani had said 'the' baby instead of the more obvious 'my' baby.

Dani sensed that Julia wasn't buying their story, and she was hesitant to push the lie any further. Before she could continue, Daric jumped in.

"Okay, we found the baby in the cemetery just outside town," Daric stated candidly, staring boldly at Dani. "Well, we did, and you refused to leave her behind to die. And we've already told Cilo or is it Gaius; so don't give me that glare. And we're not husband and wife, we're brother and sister."

"That was kind of you," Julia remarked dryly.

"Look, he's right. I wasn't walking away and leaving the baby to die. I figured she had to be only a couple of hours old when we found her and the logical place to look for the mother was the nearest town, which was Herculaneum," Dani explained. "I'm sorry if we've upset you, but we could really use your help. Because, you see, we have to get back on our way to Ostia and must leave here in a couple of days." Dani couldn't tell Julia that she, too, needed to leave town, even though her heart was screaming to.

"What makes you think the mother wants the baby?" Julia asked flatly. "She was abandoned, as you said."

"See, I told you. That's exactly what I said," Daric snorted.

"If the mother wanted the baby dead, why didn't she kill her after giving birth? Why leave her alive and crying for someone else to find?" Dani countered.

"Good point," Julia conceded.

Tobius and Nneka came into the dining room, halting the conversation momentarily while the main course was set on the table. It was roasted quail arranged on a circular platter. Between each tiny bird were tips of asparagus and, in the center of the platter, were quail eggs. Everything was nestled in an asparagus sauce.

"This looks delicious," Daric mumbled.

"I think I may be able to help you with your search," Julia said. "I don't know what you expect to happen when you find the mother, but don't be surprised if she rejects the baby. What then?"

"I don't know," Dani said miserably. "I just couldn't leave her out there to die."

"This town isn't very big and I have a very large and respectable network of friends. I'll host a party tomorrow and enlist the help of my friends. We'll find the mother and, then, we'll find out why she abandoned her little girl," Julia said resolutely.

"Do you really think we can find her?" Dani asked eagerly.

"I know we can. But first we need to get you two looking like respectable citizens of Herculaneum. Do you have any money with you to buy what we'll need?" Julia asked, even though she felt awkward about doing so. It wasn't polite to inquire about another's wealth, but she felt that the circumstances warranted it.

"Not money, per se, but we do have valuables we can sell," Daric offered.

"Great, then we'll get started first thing in the morning. You did say you have to be on your way in a few days, so that doesn't leave us much time," Julia concluded enthusiastically.

32

THROUGHOUT THE MAIN course, Julia had been pulling tiny pieces of meat off the quail bones and slipping the tender morsels to Bear, who had devoured them eagerly. When Nneka brought in the dessert tray, Julia asked her to bring a bowl of water for Bear.

The dessert tray contained grapes, figs, plums and cheese. As soon as Bear got a whiff of her favorite treat, all her manners went by the wayside.

"Bear loves cheese," Dani said, grinning at the happy canine who quickly took the offered piece from Julia's fingers. "She's been getting a piece as a bedtime treat ever since she was a pup. At times, she'll even urge you to go to bed early just so she can have her treat."

"Well, then, we'll just have to make sure we pick up more at the market tomorrow, won't we? Can't have this little one going without her bedtime treat," Julia said cheerfully.

"I'd like to check on the baby before I turn in for the night," Dani voiced.

"I'll take you there," Julia offered, as she got up from her lounge. "We're finished here, and it is getting rather late. Sorry, Bear, no more."

Bear looked up at Julia with those sad brown eyes and Julia

melted. She snatched one more piece of cheese from the passing tray on its way back to the kitchen. Julia held it out for Bear. "Now, that's definitely the last piece."

Julia led Dani across the courtyard, over one of the small bridges. They walked past a small shrine to the Egyptian goddess, Isis, and past several marble statues and fountains scattered throughout the garden.

"This is beautiful," Dani said in awe, as they passed several large ceramic pots, overflowing with beautiful flowers, placed close to the walkways where passersby could appreciate their aroma.

"Why, thank you, my dear," Julia responded, her face beaming with pride. "We also have a fruit orchard, vegetable garden and stable out back. We grow almost everything we need."

They walked along a porticoed ambulatory, or walkway, until they came to a small wooden door. Without knocking, Julia quietly opened the door. Dani wondered whether Julia's failure to knock resulted from her not wanting to wake the baby or from the fact that Julia owned the house and could come and go as she pleased. Dani didn't know, nor did she want to. She was having enough difficulty pretending that slavery was okay and a natural way of life in Herculaneum. In fact, most ancient Romans believed it was a birthright to own slaves.

When Julia and Dani entered the room, Narissa was sleeping on a tiny bed. She immediately sprang to her feet, an instinctive reaction in the presences of her mistress. "Be at ease, Narissa. We came to check on the baby," Julia said quietly.

"She is resting peacefully, Domina, and has been for a few hours," Narissa told Julia.

Dani reached into the small wooden cradle and lifted the baby out without waking her. "May I?" Dani asked, gesturing toward Narissa's bed.

Narissa nodded and stepped aside. "Did you notice anything unusual about the baby when you gave her a bath?"

Narissa looked confused; she wasn't sure what Dani was asking.

"Did she have any marks on her body? Does she have five

fingers, five toes, that sort of thing?"

"I saw nothing unusual. The baby looks fine," Narissa replied nervously, wanting to please her mistress.

"What are you looking for?" Julia questioned, watching Dani feel along the baby's limbs as she started her examination.

"I'm feeling for lumps, bone structure, things that might indicate that there's a problem. I learned this from my mother," Dani explained as she finished her examination. She thought it wise not to go into detail about her mother's profession. It would only raise more questions.

"Well, she looks fine to me, too," Dani agreed, as she placed the sleeping baby back into her cradle. "I don't see any deformities that might have led the mother to abandon her child."

"That's good to hear. Good night, Narissa," Julia said, as she and Dani left the room. "We'll meet in the dining room in the morning for breakfast and to plan our day. Please ask Daric to bring some of your valuables so I can see what we can barter."

"I will. See you in the morning, and thank you, Julia, for everything," Dani said sincerely, as they parted ways.

"You're welcome, my dear; good night," Julia replied, before turning and walking through the doorway opposite the shallow central impluvium.

Dani headed up the back stairs. She continued past her room and went into Daric's. He was stretched out on the small bed with his feet hanging over the end and an arm draped over his eyes. He was still awake.

Since the room had no chair, Dani sat on the small wooden table in the room. It was sturdy and low and, Dani assumed, intended to serve a dual purpose. She cast an eye around the room. It was identical to hers, except for the strong box. Each room had a small bed with a thin mattress, a blanket and a pillow. There was also a chest, most likely for storing clothes. On top sat a full water pitcher, a wash basin, and a small oil lamp for light.

"I checked out the baby, and she seems to be fine," Dani reported. "At least we now know she wasn't abandoned because she was imperfect."

"That's good to hear," Daric mumbled.

"Julia wants us to meet her in the dining room in the morning and she wants you to bring some of our valuables so she can figure out what we can exchange for some money."

"Okay," Daric uttered, half listening to what Dani was saying.

"What's with you?" Dani asked bluntly. Daric hadn't moved since she entered the room.

"I've been thinking," Daric said, as he sat up, slowly. "How many times in our travels have we run into Uncle Richard?"

"Every time we've jumped, if you're talking about our encounters with his ancestors."

"And how many times has he tried to kill us?"

"Let's see. There was the traitor in 1937, the detective in 1888, the zealot in 1692, and the murderer in 1537. By my count, he's tried to kill us three out of the four times."

"So, what is he now: friend or foe?" Daric pouted.

"Odds favor foe." Dani sighed.

"Let's just watch ourselves," Daric cautioned.

"Sounds like a good plan. Good night, Daric."

"Night, Dani."

33

CASUS HAD AWAKENED from his nap. He was feeling refreshed and was looking forward to a hot meal, followed by a night of good companionship. While he donned his uniform, he recalled how grateful he had been when Tiberius Crassius Firmus, one of the duumviri had persuaded the other duumviri, Arlus Marius Celus, to enlist Casus's skills to help keep order in the town. What Firmus hadn't realized at the time he recruited Casus was that Casus had a short fuse. Firmus had been able to rein Casus in, but not before some damage had been done.

Casus had overstepped his authority when he interfered in a squabble between two homeowners who had been arguing over the boundary between their two properties. The homeowners had wanted to press charges against Casus. They had relented only after Firmus reprimanded them, advising that they should have brought the boundary dispute before the courts instead of arguing it in the streets. Once the dispute had been settled, Firmus ordered that a marble plaque be fastened on the wall at the boundary point of the adjoining properties.

There was also some bad blood between Casus and Lucius Cominius Primus. Casus still blamed Primus for the deaths of his sister and mother. There was also the large sum of money that Primus owed Casus and Casus was determined to get it back. Needless to say, Primus vehemently objected to the town's hiring of Casus.

Casus fastened his balteus, or belt, with the leather sporran, or apron. He retrieved his pugio, or dagger, from under his mattress and sheathed it in the metal scabbard attached to his belt; the metal of the dagger's handle and that of the scabbard matched. He finished by fastening his gladius, or sword, before walking out the door, locking it behind him.

Casus descended the wooden staircase, walked along the narrow alley, and soon turned right onto via Neptunia, the next street down from the main street that ran east to west. He was heading in the direction of the noise coming from a local tavern. As he strode along, he came to one of the city's many public fountains, each distinguished by a different deity. The fountain now in front of him displayed the sculptured portrait of Neptune, god of the sea and of earthquakes. He paused for a moment to stare at the bearded figure from whose mouth flowed a constant stream of water. Casus knew that the god was reputed to have a violent temper, but he wondered what had so vexed the god that he felt it necessary to torment the mortals with tremors. Lately, tremors had been happening far too frequently.

Casus said a silent prayer hoping to ease Neptune's ire and then continued down the street. He entered the tavern that was on the corner of via Neptunia and via Herculia.

The tavern had an L-shaped masonry counter. The shorter section was along the street front, to allow for serving passersby, the forerunner to our fast-food outlets of today. The longer section was inside the tavern and contained embedded terra cotta containers, called dolia, which contained food items for sale. Behind the counter, on a rack, were a number of amphorae containing a variety of wines from throughout the region; hanging from the rack were drying herbs and spices. Also behind the counter were marble shelves holding a number of eating and drinking vessels. On the back wall was a fresco depicting Mercury, god of commerce, and Bacchus, god of wine. The remaining walls were painted ochre with a dark red upper and lower band.

The tavern's main room included a few brass tables and chairs for those who wanted to enjoy a meal. Along the room's right wall were stone lounges for those who wanted to sit, drink, and talk. In the back of the tavern was the kitchen and rooms for the owner and his family. Under the stairs was the latrine. Upstairs, there were six bedrooms, each with a stone bed and mattress. Frescos on the upper storey wall depicted the different sexual activities offered, the prostitutes' names, and the prices; usually six-hundred sesterces were sufficient.

The tavern didn't seem to be as busy as it normally was on a Saturday night. *Maybe the tremors have scared patrons away,* Casus thought. That meant he could spend more time with Kallisto. He scanned the interior looking for her. There she was, serving drinks to a small group gathered at a back table.

Kallisto was a slender woman in her late twenties. She had soft wavy chestnut hair and warm hazel eyes. Casus had fallen in love with her the moment the barmaid had walked into his life, but she belonged to another, for Kallisto was a slave. It had taken Casus a few years to convince her, but the time and the effort had paid off. He had finally had his love reciprocated.

Kallisto walked to the counter when her eyes fell upon Casus. Her delicate eyebrows furrowed. She hurried over, grabbed his chin and turned his face to the left, to the right and back again. "What happened to you?" she asked worriedly.

"Just a little misunderstanding," Casus said nonchalantly, taking her hand from his chin and kissing it tenderly.

"You seem to be having a lot of misunderstandings lately," Kallisto scolded.

"It's nothing I can't handle. Now, give us a proper kiss and then fetch me some dinner; I'm starving. And maybe afterwards, I can have you for dessert," Casus teased.

"Cad," Kallisto taunted, before leaning over and planting a long, passionate kiss on his eagerly awaiting lips.

"Well, that's more like it," Casus sighed deeply, as Kallisto turned and walked through the back doorway toward the kitchen. She returned a moment later with a large bowl of stew and a loaf of bread.

"Thanks, love," Casus said as he dug into the stew heartily. Kallisto returned with a mug of wine and placed it on the table in front of him. "I'll come back after I serve these other customers," she said as she went back to waiting on the other patrons.

Casus ate in silence as he watched his sweetheart work her way around the room. Casus had been working hard and had been saving his money so one day he could afford to buy Kallisto's freedom and then they could get married and start a family. *If that cursed Primus would return my money, I could buy Kallisto's freedom now,* he seethed internally. He would pay Firmus a visit tomorrow. He would try to get Firmus to persuade Primus to return Casus's money. Casus wasn't holding out for a favourable outcome, but what did he have to lose by trying?

Casus and Kallisto had talked about starting a family and about him getting a job as a carpenter, a trade he had learned, in secret, at a very young age, from one of his father's slaves. His father had been of the belief that having to perform menial tasks was no better than being a slave. But Casus had figured that knowing a trade would be to his advantage and would give him a means of supporting a family once he had left the army. And, as a carpenter, he wouldn't be subjected to the unrelenting ridicule that usually ended with him in a fight.

Kallisto walked over to clear the dishes in front of Casus. He noticed that she looked awfully pale. "Are you okay? You don't look so good," Casus remarked anxiously.

"I don't know. I was sick to my stomach this morning, but then I felt fine," Kallisto explained. "Now, I feel ill again."

"Here, sit down for a minute, maybe it will pass," Casus said, as he took Kallisto's hand and gently pulled her down on the seat beside him. "Maybe you're working too hard."

"No, it's been fairly quiet tonight; even the girls aren't busy," Kallisto said.

The mention of 'the girls' made the hairs on Casus's neck stand erect. Marcus Livius Alcimus, the owner of the tavern, also ran a brothel upstairs. Besides these two businesses, Alcimus had a wine shop across the street; the shop of course, supplied his tavern.

Alcimus was a money miser and out for every coin he could make. When one of his 'girls' was sick, and he had customers who needed attention, he would call on Kallisto to provide it and *that* infuriated Casus. On more than one occasion when Casus had been in the tavern for his evening meal, Alcimus had ordered Kallisto to satisfy one of his patrons. Casus wanted to be the only man whom Kallisto made love to and according to Kallisto, he was. The others were just business; there was no passion involved, definitely not like what they shared. Casus was thankful that Kallisto hadn't been called upon in over the past two months.

"Since it's not busy, why don't I ask Alcimus to give you the rest of the night off; it's only a couple more hours," Casus said, as he got up from his seat.

"I don't want to get into any trouble," Kallisto whispered weakly.

"Trust me; I've got this," Casus replied over his shoulder, as he made his way toward the counter.

Alcimus was an elderly man of fifty-plus years and had seen the bottom of one too many wine amphorae. He was wiping around the edges of the terra cotta containers when he noticed Casus approach. "Casus, what can I get for you?" he asked cordially, acknowledging that Casus was a frequent and good paying customer.

"Kallisto isn't feeling well. I was wondering if you could give her the rest of the night off," Casus asked respectfully.

"No! Who would take care of the tables?" Alcimus snapped.

"Look, there's only a couple of hours left before you close up shop and, besides, how would it look if she vomited on your clients? If word got around . . ." Casus never finished relaying his thought.

"Okay, okay; just get her upstairs before she makes a mess of herself," Alcimus barked.

"Thanks," Casus muttered. He walked back to his table and

gently lifted Kallisto in his powerful arms. “Come on, I’ll take you up to your room.” He walked through the tavern with Kallisto cradled in his arms, her head resting against his strong shoulder.

So much for my dessert, Casus thought.

Herculaneum—August 20, 79 AD

34

CASUS HAD SPENT the entire night holding Kallisto while she slept. She had awakened about an hour ago and had been throwing up ever since. Casus was on his third trip downstairs to empty the wash basin when he noticed Alcimus in the kitchen. Casus approached. Alcimus was preparing a batch of conditum. It was a mixture of wine, honey, pepper, dates, laurel, saffron, and mastic that was cooked and left to mature over time.

"Morning, Alcimus," Casus greeted.

"Morning, Casus," he replied, as he stirred the liquid on the portable stove.

"Kallisto is still sick this morning. I don't think she should work today."

"Fine! I don't like it, but what choice do I have?" Alcimus groaned grudgingly, without taking his eyes from his task at hand. He had been awake all night worrying that Kallisto might have food poisoning. If word got out, he would lose customers. More importantly, he would lose money. Then he had worried that she might be coming down with something really serious, like the plague; he could be shut down permanently. So he had decided it would be best to keep her away from his paying customers until she got better. He just hoped she would recover soon.

"That's great. I'll tell her," Casus said. As he turned away, he had an afterthought. "Would you mind checking on her a couple of times? I have an important meeting this morning, and I won't be back until later in the day."

"You want me to be a nursemaid, too?" Alcimus grunted. "Fine, I'll check on her, if it's not too busy in here. But from a safe distance."

After taking a pitcher of fresh water and a loaf of bread from a table in the kitchen, Casus went back to Kallisto's room. She was resting comfortably, lying on her side, with her legs drawn up into her torso.

Casus placed the pitcher of water and the loaf of bread on the room's small table. He knelt beside Kallisto's bed and placed his large callused hand on her forehead. It wasn't hot; that, at least, was a good sign. "How are you feeling?" he whispered.

"A bit better, but I should get up and get dressed for work," Kallisto mumbled half-heartedly. When she tried to push herself up, she was gently, but firmly encouraged to lie down.

"I've already cleared it with Alcimus; you have the day off," Casus informed her. He immediately noticed a wave of relief wash over her body. "I've brought you some bread and water. You need to keep hydrated in this heat and putting something bland, like Alcimus's bread, in your stomach might help, too. I have to go out for a little while, but Alcimus said he'd check on you. Okay?"

"Thanks," Kallisto mumbled, as she closed her eyes and tried desperately to settle her stomach. She didn't understand what was wrong with her. She had never been sick, for as long as she could remember. She had to admit that she was a little scared. One minute she felt fine; the next she felt like her insides were trying to get out.

Casus let Kallisto rest while he washed and shaved and finished getting dressed in his uniform. He walked over to the bed, bent over and kissed Kallisto on her forehead. "I'll be back before you know it. You need to drink some water and try to eat a little, if you can."

"I'll try," Kallisto replied weakly, seemingly too exhausted to say anything else. *Maybe I have been working too hard,* she thought.

35

PRIMUS WAS IN his tablinum, or office, ready to conduct his first ritual of the day: the salutatio, the ritual of meeting with his clients. The room was sparsely furnished, save for the throne-like chair that he sat upon, perched on a raised platform in the center of the room. The only other item in the room was a large strong box, bolted to the floor; it contained his wealth and his important papers. The walls were decorated with red and blue panels, divided by vertical ornamental bands and accented by a number of ornate elements, such as statues and stretched animal skins.

Primus was dressed in his finest white toga, with broad lilac bands, adorned with gold decorative trim. A large gold cuff on each wrist was intricately sculpted to represent the gods that Primus worshipped, the same ones to which he had just paid homage to at his household shrine. On his right index finger Primus sported a large gold signet ring, with a carved ruby at its center. Primus used the ring to sign and seal important papers.

Standing behind Primus's right shoulder was his slave and bodyguard, Ferox. Being a powerful man in Herculaneum, Primus was often unpopular with some of its citizens and needed the protection that Ferox could provide.

Ferox had been a gladiator in the games in Rome. After receiving a serious injury, however, his next fight would have meant certain death. Primus had seized the opportunity and had bought Ferox for a very reasonable price. By doing so, he had literally saved Ferox's life.

Ferox had loved his life as a gladiator. He had soaked up the celebrity status that his long and victorious career had earned him. Although he now sported several noticeable scars, he had been a rather handsome man in his youth. He had also been an extremely clever combatant, assessing his opponents and looking for the slightest weaknesses he could exploit.

In the world of gladiators, few reached the age of thirty; Ferox, however, had done so. If he had had his choice, he would have preferred to have died an honorable death in the Colosseum, as the gladiator, rather than become the muscle for this despicable character. But the choice wasn't his to make. He stood there quietly, as he did every morning, looking stoic and menacing.

The first client with whom Primus met was his debt collector, Lucius Cominius Tiro, one of Primus's ex-slaves. Tiro had previously been Primus's personal secretary and had become well educated in Primus's business affairs. As a result, he was the perfect successor to Primus's previous debt collector, who had just vanished one day.

Tiro was a small man with a slim build and a calm demeanor, hardly the image of the stereotypical debt collector. His approach was to keep his hands clean and to rely on a group of men, whom he referred to as 'the enforcers', to do the collecting. He simply kept the books.

Tiro advanced toward the raised platform, bowed his head and said, "Morning, Master."

"What do you have to report today, Tiro?" Primus asked, tired of correcting his ex-slaves when they insisted on still referring to him as 'master'.

"I regret to report that business is slow," Tiro said reluctantly.

"And why is that?"

"We have competition: Lucius Venidius Ennychus. His rates

are much lower than yours and citizens are going to him for loans instead of to you," Tiro explained.

"So, what do you suggest we do about that?" he asked, curious to see what Tiro would recommend.

"We could cut our rates," Tiro suggested humbly.

"Fool! Why would I do that?" Primus snapped, disappointed with Tiro's lack of vision. "I want you to teach Ennychus that lending money in this town is not good for his health." Primus paused for emphasis. "Do you understand me?"

"Yes, Master," Tiro replied timidly.

"Good. Now take your place while I finish with today's business," Primus instructed. Tiro took his usual seat below the raised platform, with his ledger in his lap and stylus in his hand, and waited.

36

PRIMUS'S SECOND MEETING of the morning was with Lucius Cominius Festus, the innkeeper who approached the raised platform and bowed, as Tiro had done. Eager for news about the strangers, Primus dispensed with the usual formalities of a greeting. "Well, have you found them?"

"No," Festus replied anxiously. "I've looked everywhere and there's no sign of them. Maybe they went farther down the coast. Maybe they went to . . ."

"I don't want to hear your excuses! I want to know where they are. Now, go and start spreading the word. If what you told me yesterday was correct that woman would have caused quite a stir if she had walked through town. So ask around; someone must have seen them."

"Yes, Master," Festus replied humbly. He bowed and turned when Primus called after him.

"And spread the word that I want my people to continue to harass Casus."

Festus acknowledged the order and left to carry out Primus's bidding.

"Why would you do that, Master?" Tiro asked cautiously. He knew it wasn't his place to question Primus's orders, but he was curious nonetheless.

"Because it gives me great pleasure every time I hear that Casus got kicked, punched, or got his teeth knocked out," Primus sneered evilly.

Primus met with several more clients. Some had come simply to pay their respects and ask about his well-being. Others had come to grovel for leniency for overdue debts, which Tiro confirmed were still outstanding in his ledger. The clients who impressed Primus were sent to the dining room to enjoy the leftovers from last night's feast. The clients who failed to impress Primus were instructed to return the next day with more encouraging news.

When the last of his clients had been heard and attended to, Primus got up from his over-sized chair and walked to the strong box. He lifted a chain from around his neck and used the key dangling from the end to unlock the box. He removed his large gold cuffs and placed them in the box, locking it afterwards. He would soon be going into town, where it wasn't fashionable for men to be seen in public flaunting jewelry, except perhaps, a large ring to reflect a man's financial status in the community. His first stop would be the Basilica to see Firmus about some business matters. His second stop would be the Forum.

37

"BEAR!" DARIC SCREAMED in a panic, when he woke up and found her missing.

"She's with me, Daric," Julia replied calmly from below. Julia was sitting on a bench in the garden, with Bear dozing in the sun at her feet. Julia reached down and scratched Bear's head when it popped up at the mention of her name. "It's okay, Bear, he'll be down in a minute."

"That was one hell of a wake-up call," Dani complained, as she walked into Daric's room. He was still sitting on the edge of his bed.

"Sorry, I didn't know where she was. She was with me all night and when I woke up, she was gone."

"How'd you sleep?" Dani asked, placing her hands at the small of her back.

"It's not the most comfortable bed," Daric complained.

"Yeah, but it's better than the straw mats we were sleeping on in the last time period," Dani countered.

"I really miss my own bed," Daric moaned.

"Me too; my memory-foam king-size mattress, my down-filled duvet, my 600-thread-count Egyptian cotton sheets, all in a thermostatically controlled environment . . ."

"Stop," Daric interjected. "You're making me homesick. I hope I never forget how lucky I am to live at the time that I do, with all the modern luxuries and conveniences. I don't want to ever take those things for granted."

"Ditto," Dani agreed. "We best get dressed and head downstairs to see what's in store for today. It sounds like Julia's been up for a while."

"I'll be ready in a minute," Daric assured her.

Once washed and dressed, Dani and Daric went downstairs and found Julia in the garden. Bear rushed over to greet her two favorite humans. "Have you been a good girl?" Dani asked affectionately, giving Bear a kiss on the top of her head.

"She's been good company," Julia replied, as she finished signing and folding a letter-size piece of papyrus. She picked up a nearby candle and dribbled some liquid wax onto the edge of the papyrus. She pressed her small gold ring into the hot wax and waited a few seconds before lifted the ring; the resulting seal depicted a bird on a branch. A small pile of similarly sealed documents was next to Julia on the bench.

"What are those?" Dani asked.

"These are the invitations to a party here tonight," Julia explained. "I've asked some of my influential friends to dinner, where we will enlist their assistance in locating the baby's mother."

"Do you think it'll work?" Daric asked skeptically.

"It's a small town. Someone will know something and these ladies, though I love them all dearly, are quite the gossips. They'll know what's going on or will know someone who does. Trust me," Julia assured them.

"But first, we need to get you two looking like respectable citizens, not house slaves," Julia announced. "Daric, you said you had some valuables. Can you bring a few down? I'd like to see what you have that we might be able to sell."

"Sure," Daric replied, as he turned to go back up to his room.

"We'll meet you in the dining room," Julia called after him. "We have a lot to do today before the party."

"I'd like to see the baby," Dani said.

"I checked on her when I awoke this morning. She had already been bathed and fed and was sound asleep. I've made Narissa her surrogate mother until we can find her real one. She's in good hands," Julia assured her.

38

WHEN DANI AND Julia entered the dining room, Julia sat in the seat she had occupied the previous night.

"Do you have other tenants?" Dani asked, while waiting for Daric to return. She took a seat opposite to Julia.

"I have a few," Julia replied, as she offered a piece of cold fish to Bear, who took it delicately from her fingers. Julia smiled, delighted with Bear's manners.

"They don't dine with you?" Dani questioned, curious why them and not the other tenants.

"I'm usually a very private person. Even though, you might not think so because I've opened my house to renters. But, normally, I keep to myself. That's why I have the entire back section of the house for myself," Julia explained.

"But why are we here, then and not your other tenants?"

"Gaius brought you to me personally and I trust his judgement in people."

"But we only just met him. How could either of you be so trusting?"

"Two young people who find an abandoned baby and venture into a strange town to search for her mother, how bad could those two people be," Julia replied genially.

"Okay, I see your point. And again, thank you for taking us in and helping us in our search. I don't think we could have done this without you," Dani said warmly.

"Do you think these would do?" Daric asked, entering the room and handing the items to Julia. Daric had chosen only a few of their valuables. He was hesitant to reveal their entire wealth at this time, just in case.

Julia examined the exquisitely intricate details on the large gold pin. "We can use this to fasten your palla over your stola." She handed the pin to Dani, who knew that Julia was referring to the cape worn over the dress.

"And this would look lovely around your neck at dinner tonight," Julia said, handing the gold necklace over to Dani.

"Now, these we could sell," Julia said, referring to two gold cuffs she was holding in her hands. She had noticed the bands on Dani and Daric's wrists, and thought it odd that Bear was sporting bracelets, too. She wondered why she never thought to ask about them before now. "What about selling the ones you're wearing? And what about Bear's; why does she wear bracelets, too? They look like miniature copies of yours."

"No, we can't sell these," Dani blurted nervously. "Uh, they're a long-standing tradition in our family. They symbolize that the family is linked together. They must never be removed for fear of severing that link." Not that she was telling a lie because they were linked; she just didn't disclose how. Without the bracelets, there would be no hope of Dani, Daric and Bear ever returning home.

"All right," Julia agreed skeptically. "I was going to suggest you leave the bracelets here when we go to the market, but I know now not to bother. Just be watchful of thieves. So, we'll sell these two cuffs and a couple of these braided bands of gold. Keep this one for tonight," Julia said, as she handed it to Dani. The three braided bands were the ones that Dani had previously worn around her head.

"That should get us started," Julia concluded, indicating the two cuffs and two bands of braided gold. "We'll see what they fetch, and then go from there," she added, returning to Daric the other valuables he had brought to the dining room.

Nneka and Tobius carried in a couple of trays with grapes, figs, pears and apples. Nneka removed the empty tray which had been laden with an assortment of cold fish and poultry.

"Nneka, when you're finished in the kitchen, there's a pile of invitations in the garden I'd like you to deliver, the earlier the better," Julia instructed. "Have to give these women time to prepare," she said gaily to Dani. "And, Tobius, I want you to take these to the gem-cutter and exchange them for coin. See that you get a fair price."

"Yes, Domina," Tobius replied, as he took the cuffs and braided bands from Julia and tucked them inside his tunic, ready to depart.

"But, before you go, Tobius, I want you to help Daric get ready for the market. It's not fashionable around here for men to sport facial hair; only barbarians have facial hair," Julia explained, noticing that Daric had not shaved before he came to dine. Even though his stubble was fair, it was still noticeable, and Julia knew appearances were everything.

Daric, embarrassed by this slight to ethics and culture, welcomed Tobius's help. He followed Tobius upstairs, carrying the balance of his valuables he would return to the strong box.

Bear suddenly leapt up and raced into the garden to investigate some movement.

"Bear?" Dani called, as she got up to go see what had caught the dog's attention. Dani couldn't help but notice that the peristyle was like a tranquil oasis in the middle of a busy town; it was like living in the country. Dani took in the fresh aromatic air, the bird songs among the trees and bushes, and the sound of the fountains in the distance.

"The Romans have a phrase; it's 'Rus in urbe', meaning countryside in the city," Julia commented casually, as if she had read Dani's mind. Julia had followed Dani into the garden, wondering what Bear had discovered.

They found Bear with her nose pressed against a hard shell.

"That tortoise has been here longer than I have," Julia said. "Don't tease the old girl, Bear," Julia said jovially. "Come on, Dani, we need to get ready. We have a very busy day."

39

DANI WAS WEARING one of Julia's stolas. The pale blue silk dress with multiple folds decorated with gold trim was a little on the short side for Dani, but it flowed effortlessly when she walked and would do nicely for now. Overtop of the dress was a blush-colored palla, or cape, pinned over her right shoulder. Opting to stay away from the elaborate coiffured hairstyle adopted by Julia, Dani had arranged her hair in soft ringlets that framed her lovely face. She had also shied away from wearing makeup, letting her natural beauty shine forth. Her accessories included a gold necklace, as suggested by Julia, but Dani had decided to refrain from wearing the braided gold band. She, of course, also wore her travel band. On her feet, she wore sandals.

Julia was similarly dressed, with a long flowing silk cobalt-blue dress under an amber palla. She had a plaited gold wire necklace with a gold crescent-shaped pendant hanging from the middle.

Unfortunately, Julia had nothing appropriate for Daric to wear to proclaim his status. He would have to go on wearing the tunic he had been wearing. "We'll get you something more suitable to your station when we're at the market," Julia assured him.

"Actually, I don't mind this at all; it's comfortable and a lot cooler than what I was wearing," Daric reflected.

"Then we're all set," Julia announced, nodding for Cyrus to open the door. Waiting outside was a litter, with the curtain drawn open on the side closest to the house. One slave stood at each corner, as it rested on its four legs, waiting for the mistress of the house to climb on top.

"No, Bear," Daric said, as he pushed Bear back inside the house. "You have to stay here. We won't be long."

"Yes, we will," Julia corrected him.

"It's just something we always say when we leave her at home," Dani explained. "I don't know if she understands exactly what we mean; I guess it's just a habit."

"Maybe just saying it makes you feel better, when you have to leave her behind," Julia speculated.

"You may be right." Dani laughed.

"We won't be using the litter, today," Julia said to the attendants, as she dismissed them. Turning to Dani and Daric, she continued, "The market is just around the corner and we'll have plenty of hands to help us carry our purchases." Julia was referring to the household slaves who were standing in the street waiting, to accompanying them.

"Besides shopping for some clothing, we'll also be picking up the food for the party tonight," Julia announced, as they set off for the market.

"Roooo!"

"What's that?" Julia asked in alarm as she came to an abrupt halt.

"That's Bear protesting being left behind. She'll stop soon," Dani said.

As Julia and her two guests walked along the length of the block that Julia's house occupied, they came across a grand doorway, framed by brick half columns, which were attached to the wall. On top of the two columns was a triangular brick pediment.

"That's the public entrance to the baths complex," Julia explained, as she caught Dani staring. "It opens onto the square courtyard."

A little farther up the street, the trio passed two open doorways. "That's where we serve hot and cold food and drinks to the patrons of the baths," Julia said. "It's also where my other tenants dine."

Daric noted the familiar L-shaped marble-topped counter with insets for food; the same layout he had seen earlier at the inn. In the northwest corner, there was a small oven and, next to it, a window linking the shop to the baths' courtyard, allowing food to be served to the waiting patrons. The adjoining shop had a series of masonry benches and tables along the south side of the room where diners were served their meals. Occupying most of the north side were three large banqueting couches, arranged as they would be in a traditional Roman dining room. *Impressive*, he thought.

40

CASUS WALKED OUT of the tavern, he was satisfied that he was leaving Kallisto in good hands. Alcimus's wife, Nona, and their six-year-old son, Livius, had said they would regularly check in on Kallisto. They had a real fondness for Kallisto, because, in her spare time, she was teaching Livius how to read and write. Kallisto sometimes lost her patience with her young pupil, who was too easily distracted by his playful dog, Titan. But Kallisto persevered and Livius was making real progress, to the delight of his parents. Casus felt better leaving Kallisto in their hands, rather than depending on Alcimus, whose only concern was to make some coin, not tend to a sick slave.

Casus turned left and proceeded along via Neptunia. It was exceptionally hot for this early in the day, and it appeared from the clear blue sky above that it would be another day without rain. "Great," he mumbled. He knew that water levels in the region were low, but posed no immediate threat to the town's water supply. He also knew, however, that the crops were suffering during this unusual dry spell.

Casus turned up via Veneria, heading toward the main street. He passed several shop fronts with their colored awnings extended, providing the weary with limited shade and shelter from the blazing sun. There were benches placed outside some shops hoping passersby might rest long enough to buy something from the shopkeepers or snack houses.

At the junction of the main street and via Veneria there was another public fountain and a water tower. The fountain had the sculpted image of the goddess Venus, washing her hair. Casus noticed a new sign. He approached it and read it. Its message was clear: 'No dumping: freeman will be fined if caught, slave will be flogged.'

Casus turned left onto the main street which led to the Forum. He passed under the triumphal arches that spanned from one side of the street to the other.

On the next corner, on the south side of the street, sat the building known as the Curia, where the local senate met. The exterior was entirely covered in plaster that had been painted white. Casus hoped to find Firmus here before he was called to the Basilica.

The Curia was a rectangular building with two entrances: a side entrance off via Jupitinius and the main entrance off the main street. Casus entered by the latter entrance and walked through a narrow corridor that took him directly into the main hall.

The interior of the hall consisted of one large room, divided into three naves, or aisles, by four central Tuscan columns that support the roof, with light entering through a skylight. Behind the central columns was a roofless shrine. The floor of this room was raised above the level of the main floor. On the back wall of the shrine, there was a pedestal which displayed a bust of Emperor Augustus. There was a wreath painted on the wall above the bust.

The shrine's side walls were divided into three panels. The central panel fresco on the left wall pictured Hercules sitting next to Juno, with a rainbow, and Minerva, with her helmet. A fresco on the right wall portrayed Hercules fighting Achelous.

Casus was familiar with the story of Hercules and Achelous, having heard it often in his youth. Achelous kidnapped Deianira, who was Hercules's wife. A prolonged struggle between Achelous and Hercules resulted. Despite assuming many forms, including that of a monstrous bull, Achelous was eventually defeated. During the struggle, however, Hercules broke off one of the bull's horns, which the nymphs later fashioned into the cornucopia, the horn of plenty.

A separate room had been created at the end of the right aisle, by using a partition wall made from a wooden frame that had been filled in with small stones and overlaid with mortar. The room contained one bed, that of the porter, who happened to be standing by the secondary entrance, with a broom in his hand, staring at Casus.

Spurius Subinus was an elderly man of frail stature. He had been the porter at the Curia for more years than he could recall. The job didn't pay much, but at least it put a roof over his head and gave him a place to rest his weary bones at night. In addition, it was basically across the street from the market, which saw to his every need. What more could he ask for?

"I'm looking for duumvir Tiberius Crassius Firmus. Do you know where I might find him?" Casus asked cordially.

Subinus looked up at the sun to gauge its position and determine the time of day. "He will be at the Basilica. Can one of the aediles assist you? I'm expecting them soon," Subinus offered upon seeing Casus's disappointment.

"No, thank you," Casus replied as he turned and walked back along the corridor. He exited onto the main street, turned left and headed for the Basilica.

41

EVEN THOUGH THE Forum was on the next block down from where Primus lived, he insisted on taking his entire entourage with him, and why not, he had earned it. The size of a man's retinue announced to others the station of that man.

Primus bid farewell to the Lares, the spirits of his dead ancestors, and left the house, making sure he set off with his right foot first. Emperor Augustus had been very superstitious about this point because it was believed to be unlucky to enter or leave a house on your left foot. It was also believed to symbolize that a man's first duty was reverence to the gods. Either way, Primus wouldn't tempt the Fates.

Outside, waiting for Primus, were all of his clients, who had paid homage to him that morning and who were obliged to escort him to the Forum. But, first, Primus had to stop at the Basilica for some crazy nonsense that duumvir Firmus wanted to talk to him about. No matter, it was on his way and he knew it wouldn't take long.

A half dozen of Primus's slaves led the way down the street, clearing a path for him as nervous citizens jumped clear. Ferox walked directly in front of Primus, ready to intervene should some ugly pleb try to reach his master. The rest of Primus's retinue tagged along behind at a respectful distance; they realized it would be a very long and extremely hot day to be agreeing to Primus's every whim, laughing at his every joke, and supporting his every decision.

Primus and his entourage walked under the triumphal arches and passed the entrance to the Forum on their right. To their left, at the intersection of via Jupitinius, and just below the main street, was a small shrine. On top of the shrine was an elegant bronze statue of Hercules, standing naked with a lion's skin draped over his left arm. With the shrine at the end of Jupitinius and the triumphal arches spanning the main street by the Forum, it was physically impossible for wagons or carts carrying supplies to shops or private houses to pass through this area.

The Basilica was one-hundred-twenty-five-feet wide and two-hundred-feet long. Its primary entrance was off the main street on the short side of the building overlooking the entrance to the Forum. The Basilica entrance had five doorways: one at either side of the portico, or covered entranceway, and one between each pair of columns. On the top of the arch, above the entrance was a marble statue of an emperor riding in a four-horse chariot. In addition to its primary entrance, the Basilica also had a side entrance off via Jupitinius.

The Basilica was used for conducting commercial transactions and for administering justice. The records of all the citizens of the town were officially stored here, including all the legal documents, because this was the place where the local court proceedings were held.

Inside the Basilica, there was a long central hall, with a colonnaded aisle or arcaded space on each side. At the far end of the hall was an apse or semi-circle recess, with a slightly raised dais and a curved vaulted ceiling. This area was known as the tribunal where the magistrates sat when fulling their official duties.

The Basilica was donated to Herculaneum by Marcus Nonius Balbus, the greatest benefactor of the town, one who rose to the rank of praetor in Rome and to the governorship of Crete and

Cyrene. In the year 32 BC, the pact between Marc Antony and Gaius Octavian for governing the Roman Republic was disintegrating; each blaming the other of being the obstacle to achieve peace and, therefore, to returning the Republic to a normal life. At the beginning of the year's senate proceedings, the two Republics consuls supported Antony. When one of the consuls was about to introduce measures against Octavian, Balbus, one of the ten tribunes of the people, used his power of veto to block him. His intervention at that critical moment won the future emperor's gratitude, and he was rewarded with a promotion and governorship of a province.

The wealth that Balbus acquired over the following years, he directed back to his beloved seaside town. On pedestals around the central aisle were exquisitely crafted marble statues of Balbus, as well as of his father, his mother, his wife, and his daughters. Statues of the Imperial family were also scattered in recesses around the room.

Primus hoped that one day Herculaneum would recognize him, too, as one of their benefactors and would bestow upon him the honors he felt he rightly deserved, even though he had done nothing for his town.

Primus stood just inside the entrance with his multitude of supporters around him. He saw the duumviri seated on the raised dais, with a toga-clad man adamantly gesturing in front of them. Firmus looked up and, recognizing Primus, motioned for him to come forward. "Wait here, I'll be only a minute," Primus told the others, as he walked forward. Ferox followed dutifully behind.

When Primus got closer, he recognized the man standing in front of the duumviri; he owned the vineyard next to Primus's property outside town. *What's that old buzzard up to?* Primus wondered. He had an inkling.

"Primus, Proculus here is accusing you of moving three-hundred-six fence poles from the boundary line of his estate, thereby expanding your property in the process," Firmus stated.

"That's nonsense," Primus rebuffed.

"I can prove it!" Proculus fired back. "I can show you where the original holes for the poles were, even though they now appear to be on Primus's property. No doubt the holes have been covered over already, but the ground will have fresh soil. And that soil will follow the original property line."

Lucius Appuleius Proculus owned a large vineyard on the lower slopes of the mountain. It had been in his family for years and he planned to leave it to his sons when he died. In the meantime, its grapes were some of the best, if not the best, in Campania.

Proculus and Primus had been rivals for over ten years, right from the time Primus had bought the property (more like had stolen it, Proculus believed) from the estate of its previous owner. He was opposed to the way Primus ran his business and to the way he treated his slaves, but there was nothing Proculus could do about that. He could, however, make sure he wasn't, like most of the people in town, bullied or pushed around by Primus. He knew his rights, and he was going to make sure Primus didn't get away with stealing his property.

Arlus Marius Celus slouched in his chair, completely disinterested in the proceedings. He was confident that Primus would talk his way out of this accusation made by Proculus. *Or he would signal me and Firmus to throw the case out on some trumped up grounds,* Celus mused.

"Primus, you will remove those three-hundred-six fence poles," Firmus instructed. He paused for a moment to consider who was in attendance. He recognized a disinterested party who didn't live far from the properties in question. "You will give them to Marcus Nonius Primigenius for safekeeping, until this dispute can be settled. You will have all three-hundred-six fence poles in Primigenius's custody before the end of day tomorrow."

Celus bolted upright in his seat and stared at Firmus in disbelief as thoughts raced through his mind. *What had Firmus just done? Had he gone up against Primus? Was he siding with Proculus? Was he crazy?*

Primus glared at Firmus, seething under his skin. Then Primus glared at Celus, hiking an eyebrow, as if to say, “Do something!”

Celus leaned and whispered so only Firmus could hear. “Do you think that’s wise?”

“It’s the right thing to do,” Firmus whispered back.

“Next!” Firmus yelled, as he dismissed the claimants in front of him. He was ready to hear the next case.

42

MOMENTS EARLIER, CASUS had entered the Basilica and had pushed his way through the mob gathered by the entrance. Once clear, he recognized Primus at the tribunal talking with Firmus. *There goes any hope of getting Firmus's help*, Casus thought. He perceived that Primus and Firmus were conversing amiably, but he couldn't have been more wrong. Casus, disheartened, left the Basilica.

Primus, after having been summarily dismissed, stormed out of the Basilica; he was fuming. "How dare he?" he bellowed, as he turned the corner and plowed directly into Julia.

"Hey, watch where you're going," Julia objected. "Oh, it's you."

"Out of my way, woman," Primus ordered, and then froze in his tracks.

Standing beside Julia was one of the most beautiful women he had ever laid eyes on. The blush-colored palla brought out the natural hue of her cheeks. The pale blue dress accentuated her lovely eyes. Her honey-blond hair and sun-kissed skin gave her a youthful glow. He was awestruck. Pulling himself together, he said, "Pardon me. And who is this lovely creature?"

Julia glared at Primus, *the degenerate*. "This is my friend, Dani."

"A pleasure to meet you, Dani," Primus said softly, as he bowed his head slightly.

Dani looked into the cold glacier-blue eyes. She felt an instant dislike for the man now standing in front of her, pretending to be gracious. Dani wondered why she was so quick to judge this book by its cover; she had never done anything like that before. Nevertheless, her first impressions were not favorable.

Daric was standing close by. Julia hadn't introduced him. He suspected there was a reason. So, he kept silent, pretending to be a slave. Just from the looks of the man, Daric could tell he was trouble. Daric glanced at Dani and sensed she felt the same.

"Dani, this is Lucius Cominius Primus . . ." Julia started to say.

"One of the more notable citizens of this town," Primus finished.

"Notable, in more ways than one," Julia murmured.

"Why, thank you," Primus acknowledged and then wondered whether she was being facetious. He chose to ignore it. "I assume she is staying with you?"

"Yes, she is," Julia replied, not giving away any details.

"When did you arrive in town?" Primus asked Dani, who had been standing by quietly, but who had also been picking up on the tension in the air.

"Yesterday," Dani replied, following Julia's lead of supplying a minimum of information.

"How long will you be staying?" Primus probed.

"A few days," Dani responded aloofly.

"Well, enjoy your stay," Primus said, as he turned and left, heading for the Forum.

"Who was that guy?" Daric asked when he was out of earshot.

"Someone who thinks he runs this town, and, unfortunately, he does," Julia said coldly. "He's nothing but trouble. You need to stay clear of him."

"You don't have to tell me twice," Dani muttered.

"Daric, I hope you don't mind that I didn't introduce you, too," Julia said apologetically.

"Not at all. Although, I was wondering why not," Daric confessed.

"I just don't trust that man," Julia warned. "The less he knows the better."

Present Day—Friday

43

FORTY-FIVE MINUTES later, Richard pulled into the Delaneys' driveway, parking far enough away from the house to not awaken Sandra. He had given her enough sleeping pills the night before to keep her out for a few more hours, but he wanted to err on the side of caution.

Richard and Eddie got out of the SUV and walked around to the back. Richard popped the hatch and looked coldly at Eddie. "Mount the camera on the garage roof and direct it at the house," Richard instructed. "I'll be back in a few minutes."

Eddie glared at him. He was no fool. There was no way Richard would keep his side of the bargain. The only way Eddie was going to see his parents again was on the other side.

It was almost is if Richard could see the wheels turning in Eddie's head. "And in case you're planning on giving me the slip, the collar has a tracking device, not that you'd want to wander too far." Richard pulled a device from his coat pocket and pressed the little red button. Eddie immediately fell to his knees.

"Oh, and I forgot to mention, it also has a little persuasion feature, in case you get any crazy ideas. Now, mount that camera," Richard ordered.

Leaving Eddie to complete his task, Richard headed off on his own mission. He needed to keep tabs on Sandra while he was working in the lab. He was very thorough in everything he did, planning for every contingency. The camera would tell him whether Sandra received any visitors and the bugs would allow him to eavesdrop on any conversation she might have. Being in the know would give him a strategic advantage.

Richard entered the house through the kitchen door, using the key he had taken on his last visit. He attached the first bug to the underside of the slate-grey granite countertop of the island that divided the casual eating area from the rest of the kitchen. Any visitors to the house would normally congregate here. He recalled having had a number of casual meals here with the Delaney family around the large maple table with its upholstered benches. He had had lunch at this very place only a few days ago with Sandra and Quinn while discussing plans for their trip to New Zealand. *That was only a few days ago; seems like a lifetime,* he thought, shaking off the unpleasant image of Quinn in his head.

Richard went to the living room, across the hardwood floor, to the coffee table where he secured his second bug to its underside. And lastly, he crept up the varnished oak staircase and into the master bedroom.

There, on the king-sized bed, was Sandra, sound asleep. The floor-to-ceiling windows were covered with sunshades, blocking out the daylight and giving the room a warm gentle hue. The fireplace on the wall opposite the bed was stone cold. A rocking chair, draped with a hand-knitted afghan, sat vacant in the corner.

Richard walked quietly to the edge of the bed, tripping on the oriental rug. He regained his balance and froze, motionless, for a moment. Sandra didn't stir. He looked at her longingly. If it hadn't been for Quinn, Sandra would have been his. But when Quinn had entered the picture, it was as if Richard had never existed. Richard had always dreamt of making Sandra his wife. He had been so close to asking for her hand in marriage; then his world came crashing down when Quinn transferred in from out of state. But now that Quinn was out of the picture, Sandra was his again, and only his.

Richard wanted so badly to climb into that comfortable bed and hold Sandra in his loving arms, but now wasn't the time. He took a few moments to drink in the beautiful woman before him. Then he reached down and planted his last bug, on the inside of the lamp shade sitting on the bedside table. He cautiously turned, not wanting to catch his toe on the rug again. He walked out of the bedroom, down the stairs and through the kitchen door, locking it behind him.

The time had come for Richard to take his plan to its conclusion. He had just a few more details to work out, and, then, Sandra would be forever indebted to him for bringing back her children. He would have everything he desired. Nothing could stop him now.

44

EDDIE SLOWLY PULLED himself up off the ground, his hands instinctively reaching for the source of his pain: the collar. He fumbled around the edges, looking for the locking mechanism, but couldn't find one. *It must be a magnetic lock*, he thought.

Disgruntled and having no other viable options at the moment, Eddie reluctantly pulled the cumbersome camera case from the back of the SUV and carried it to the corner of the four-car garage. He stood for a moment, looking up at the roof. He needed a ladder and some tools.

Eddie entered the garage and started sorting through an abundant supply of well-cared-for tools. He knew what he needed for mounting the camera, but that wasn't his first priority. He was searching for anything that would untether him from Richard's torture device.

Five minutes swiftly passed and Eddie was no closer to finding a solution to his dilemma. Out of sheer frustration, he snatched up a hammer off the workbench, spun around and hurled it against the back wall. It smashed against one of the storage lockers, scarring the door and leaving a wicked dent. Eddie tossed, in rapid succession, whatever was within arm's reach–wrenches, pliers, and screwdrivers–before he had finished venting his anger.

It wasn't only the collar that had irked Eddie. It was everything around him. There was no way he could overlook the size of the estate as they drove in, or the large private peninsula that the beautiful home sat on. Or the many expensive 'toys' housed in this very garage. Or the very pricey craft moored at the dock; what he wouldn't give for a boat like that one.

Eddie didn't have to be a mathematical genius, even though he was, to recognize that the family was financially well-off. "Just another 'privileged' family," he grumbled. He thought, just maybe, this could have been all his. Maybe he could have been enjoying this lifestyle, too, had his parents not been killed in a car accident when he was just five years old. Instead of bouncing between foster homes, he could have had a stable, loving family, who would have spoiled him rotten. He would have had the finest clothes and the newest gadgets. Instead, he was trapped in a nightmare. He was being forced to do the bidding of a billionaire lunatic, whose endgame would, now more than ever, mean Eddie's certain death.

Eddie glanced at his watch, the one that had belonged to his father, the only possession that Eddie could call his own. Time was passing quickly. If he didn't have the camera installed before Richard got back, he could expect another jolt, of that he had no doubt. The sadistic look in Richard's eyes, when he pushed that little red button for the first time, had conveyed to Eddie that he would do it again, just for the hell of it. Eddie didn't want to provoke him.

Eddie grabbed an extension ladder off the mounted hooks on the side wall and carried it outside where he propped it up against the side of the garage. Eddie went back to gather up the tools he needed to secure the mounting bracket to the roof.

After installing and ensuring the camera was pointed at the house as instructed, Eddie tossed the tools onto the grass below. He was descending the ladder just as Richard appeared. "Is it done?" Richard grunted.

"Just need to put this stuff away," Eddie replied, as he slung his right arm between two of the ladder's rungs and walked it back into the garage. He soon reappeared to retrieve the tools he had tossed on the ground. While doing so, he said, "I can remotely access the camera and audio transmitters to any computer you want. It'll just take me a couple of minutes to set it all up."

"Good," Richard said. "Let's go."

Richard started walking toward the gazebo at the end of the peninsula. He was getting closer to fulfilling his destiny, to righting an injustice inflicted upon his family.

Eddie followed Richard. An overwhelming sense of hopelessness weighed heavily on his shoulders. He would have to bide his time and watch for an opportunity to get out of this situation before it was too late.

Herculaneum—August 20, 79 AD

45

JULIA AND HER party, small compared to Primus's entourage, crossed the main street and walked under the archway entering the Forum. Dani and Daric stopped and stood in awe and marveled at what was before them: an actual, functioning Forum, the heart of every Roman town or city. It was a gathering place to conduct business, elect their magistrates, host religious ceremonies, discuss politics, and argue judicial decisions.

The Forum was a large, open, rectangular space, flanked on all sides by porticos, or covered colonnaded ambulatories. It was surrounded by public buildings, such as the Curia and the Basilica, and by temples dedicated to the most revered gods.

On their right, just inside the entrance, was the Capitolium, the temple to Jupiter, perched high on a raised platform and decorated with magnificent Corinthian columns.

Julia looked at her young guests and was a little surprised by their reaction. *Maybe they come from a small town and have never seen a Forum before,* she mused. "Come on, you two."

With Julia in the lead, they walked past dozens of statues, some bronze, others marble. Dani recognized most as portraying members of the imperial family. However, there was a noticeable absence of Nero, most likely because it was torn down after his death.

Impressive frescos of mythological heroes occupied the end walls. One showed Theseus and the dead Minotaur. Another portrayed Hercules and his son Telephus, suckling a hind in Arcadia. And a third presented the young Achilles learning the lyre from the centaur, Chiron.

In a few of the side niches, before the scenes of these heroes of old, were the new heroes. There was a bronze statue of Augustus and a statue of Claudius as Jupiter, holding a thunderbolt.

The noises of the Forum seemed to bounce off its porticos and remain trapped within the confines of its walls. Loud, animated conversations blended with diverse sounds of busy hawkers, beggars, buskers and musicians. The smells of fish cooking on portable open ranges and of exotic spices permeated the air. A few merchants with amphorae full of wine to sell were doing a brisk business with Herculaneum's thirsty citizens.

They passed another temple, this one to Augustus. It was similar in design to that of Jupiter, but, of course, was on a smaller scale; after all, Augustus was only a mortal god. Near the base of the steps, a schoolmaster was trying to explain something to his inattentive class.

Julia set a brisk pace, with Dani and Daric close behind. Their progress was suddenly interrupted when they had to step out of the way for a group of men, all dressed in long white togas, who were in a hurry to get somewhere. "Priests," Julia explained a tinge of sarcasm in her voice.

As soon as the priests had passed, Julia and her party were once again on the move. Their destination was the Macellum, or public market, situated off the north-east corner of the Forum.

46

THE MACELLUM WAS bustling with activity and was much louder and smellier than the Forum. The market was a square building with a central courtyard. In the middle of the courtyard was a tholos, a round structure, built up on a couple of steps, with a ring of columns supporting a domed roof. This was where fish were sold, scaled, and cleaned. And it was Julia's first stop.

"Nikanor, what are you selling today?" Julia asked her regular fishmonger.

"Julia, for you I would recommend the shrimp; they're the size of my fist and are fresh off my boat. Or the sardines; they came in early this morning," Nikanor said genially.

Nikanor Albus and his four sons operated a successful fishing business, with ten boats in all. They provided a wide variety of fish, including eel, sea bass, and parrotfish, just to name a few of the forty-three species that inhabited the waters of the bay. And, of course, they offered the most delicate and more expensive red mullet, which only certain patrons could afford.

"That sounds wonderful. I'll take both," Julia said. "They'll be perfect appetizers for the party tonight. Nikanor, could you have them cleaned and wrapped? I'll pick them up on my way out."

"For you, anything," Nikanor responded, his grin revealing one missing front tooth. After bidding Nikanor a good day, Julia and her group continued through the market.

The tabernae, or shops, lined the market's walls, which were richly decorated with still-life paintings portraying the shops' many and varied wares, including chestnuts, flowers, baskets, birds, poultry, wine jars, breads, cakes, figs, grapes, fruits in jars. The shops themselves were all the same size and followed a consistent design. Each had a single room, a wide doorway and a window overhead to let light into an attic where the shop assistants lived above the shop.

There were twelve food stores occupying the north-facing side of the building; to help keep their goods protected from the strong sunlight and keep them fresh longer. Everything that was perishable had to be bought and eaten the same day because there was no means of keeping food fresh. Twelve more stores along the outside wall of the market opened on to the street.

Three rooms lined the rear wall of the central court. The one in the middle was a shrine, dedicated to the worship of the imperial family. The other two were where meat—butchered or alive—was sold and where sacrificial banquets took place.

As much as Dani and Daric were awed by the physical features of the market, they were impressed even more by the people, the sounds and the smells that filled the courtyard. There were the enticing aromas of drinks and cooked food. There were peddlers hawking their goods, such as exotic spices from India and Egypt, luxury silks from China, magnificent gem stones from Africa, and slaves from Gaul. There were jugglers, magicians, flame eaters and musicians adding to the cacophony. And olives, wine and grain, from the local agricultural estates and farms were being brought into the market to be sold.

Julia and her party passed one woman with her right hand cupped tightly against her jaw, searching desperately for someone who could help her with her raging toothache. They stepped over a man who had already had one too many drinks today, and around another leaning against a wall in the shade, who was suffering from a severe hangover.

They passed a few crowded stalls belonging to money-changers, where merchants and seamen were looking for coin in exchange for their goods. Another crowded shop distributed free grain to the public. Next to it, a cobbler's shop was busy with a family looking to buy shoes.

They encountered Neapolitans, Grecians, Athenians, Thessalians, Egyptians, Romans, Pompeians and Corinthians. All of them milling around the market, searching for something specific, whether it be food for the day's meals or something else, the market was where they would find what they were seeking.

After a few minutes, Julia turned to her right and led Dani and Daric into one of the market's several clothing shops. With Julia's help, they had soon picked out clothes suitable for their needs. After some serious haggling with the shop owner, they settled on a fair price. They paid him with money Julia had given them, knowing she would be reimbursed when Tobius returned from his errand.

With their new clothes in hand, Dani and Daric followed Julia out of the shop and set off to pick up the rest of the items they would need for the evening's party.

47

JULIA AND HER party walked out of the market and back through the Forum, the same way they had entered. Julia's slaves were laden with parcels, as they weaved their way through the growing throng of people. As they passed by a group of toga-clad men, Julia was just able to make out part of their conversation.

"And that's when Firmus ordered Primus to have the three-hundred-six fence poles he had previously moved taken over to Primigenius, until they settle the boundary dispute," Ennychus informed them. "And Primus was none too happy about the directive, either. I suspect he will have to go out to his estate tomorrow to make arrangements to have the poles delivered."

"Are you sure?" one of the toga-clad men asked.

"I was there! I witnessed the whole thing. I even signed the declaration as an official witness," Ennychus affirmed. Lucius Venidius Ennychus was a shrewd businessman, but a fair one. He had very little respect for Primus or for his dubious business dealings. As a result, on those rare occasions when things didn't go in Primus's favour, Ennychus took every opportunity to tell anyone who would listen that Primus wasn't all he appeared to be. Ennychus was determined that the good citizens of Herculaneum would see the real truth, not just what Primus wanted them to believe.

"Is that man over there talking about the guy we ran into earlier today?" Dani asked.

"Yeah, Primus, and he will not be thrilled that word is being circulated about his misfortune," Julia replied boldly, as they progressed through the Forum.

Julia's party passed another small group deep in conversation by the steps of the temple; the speaker was using exaggerated hand gestures to make his point. "I know we get tremors in this region. We've had them for as long as I can remember, but none as violent as they have been. And definitely not as frequent either."

"I agree," another man chimed in. "Maybe it's the giants under the mountain."

"Don't tell me you believe in that nonsense," another scoffed.

"There's always a kernel of truth to any legend," the second man declared. "When the battle of the giants of earth and the gods of heaven was fought, the gods forced the vanquished giants underground. The tremors and rumbling we've been experiencing are the giants' restlessness. They're preparing to rise again in revolt. Just the other day, I heard that a shepherd had seen giant-like creatures, in the form of smoke, rising from the mountain."

As Julia's entourage continued walking, Dani caught sight of a beggar out of the corner of her eye. He was sitting on the ground in the shade of a temple. He was holding out his hand, hoping for any pittance some passerby could spare. Lying at his side was his devoted dog. Dani stopped. She glanced at Julia, who nodded her consent and handed Dani some coins. Dani bent over and placed the sesterces in the beggar's hand.

"Thank you," he whispered, staring up blindly at Dani.

"I detest beggars. Let him pay for what he wants," Primus snarled, as he walked past, ensuring his voice was loud enough for those around to hear.

"Wasn't it Plautus who said: 'No one benefits a beggar by giving him food or drink. You merely lose what you give him and prolong his life of misery.'?" one of Primus's entourage quoted.

"But, wasn't it Seneca the Elder who said 'It is wrong not to give a hand to the fallen. This right is common to the whole human race.'?" Dani responded.

Primus stopped dead in his tracks. He spun and glared at Dani, who returned his cold glare, unflinching. Primus said nothing and continued on his way, seething within.

"Those who can't work are reduced to becoming beggars," Julia explained. "And unfortunately there are tens of thousands in the Roman Empire. The lucky ones manage to attach themselves to wealthy houses where household slaves dish out scraps to them. The not so lucky ones come here and hope someone with a kind heart and a few extra coins will help them out. I commend your kindness, but opposing Primus wasn't the smartest thing to do."

"I couldn't help it; he just rubs me the wrong way," Dani groaned.

"Me, too," Julia said softly as she smiled understandingly. "Come on, it's getting late and we have a party to get ready for."

48

JULIA'S SLAVE, TOBIUS, had hurried off to the gem-cutter's shop, as he had been instructed. He had been careful not to draw any attention to himself, for fear of being accosted or detained from his errand or, even worse, robbed. Tobius wasn't a large man, but he was very nimble as a result of his long years of running up and down staircases in servitude of his various masters. He had a much easier life now, and he didn't want to ever disappoint his mistress for fear she might sell him for someone younger than he.

Tobius ducked into the shop and was thankful that there were no other customers present. He wanted to transact his business and return to his regular duties; being an errand runner was making him nervous.

The gem-cutter was sitting behind a low stone counter. Arrayed on the wall behind him were numerous tools: chisels and files of differing sizes and tweezers or tongs with varying tips. A finger-shaped polishing stone was resting on the counter. To the gem-cutter's right, closest to the light streaming in through the doorway, was a stone grinding wheel and, below it, a pitcher of water, used in the grinding process. Most of the precious gems and valuable metals were locked in a strong box on the second floor where the gem-cutter lived with his teenage son. There was, however, a small container behind the counter containing fragments of old necklaces, bracelets and rings that would later be melted down, in the furnace out back, to make new pieces.

In front of the counter was a small brass chair where patrons could sit as they discussed their needs with the gem-cutter. In the back corner of the room, there was a little terracotta altar that bore the inscription 'Herculis'. Beside it, there were two marble busts. One was of Bacchus, god of wine. The other was of a man sporting an Augustan hairstyle and baring a striking resemblance to Primus, the gem-cutter's patron.

"Good day, citizen; I'll be with you in just a moment," the shopkeeper said cordially, without lifting his head. He remained focussed for several minutes on the delicate task of etching the image of a tortoise into an apple-green chrysoprase stone. "There that should do it," he announced, as he finally looked up to address his visitor.

"Tobius, I was just finishing the details on your mistress's ring, but I still have some work left to do before it's ready," Antigonus stated. "I know I promised her it would be ready before now, but I had other pressing matters that needed my immediate attention. Please apologize for me."

Antigonus Decimus was a slight man, with extremely steady hands and an excellent eye for detail. Julia Felix had commissioned him to make her a signet ring she could use for sealing documents. She had chosen the image of the tortoise, because tortoises were among the oldest living creatures and, therefore, she believed that they might be an omen of good luck. Besides, she had a tortoise, in her courtyard, which she treasured.

Tobius nervously looked over his shoulder before he sat down in the chair opposite Antigonus. He reached inside the folds of his tunic and extracted the precious items that had been entrusted to him.

"My mistress wishes to exchange these for coin," Tobius whispered. "She also said to make sure you give her a fair price." The last was said with stronger emphasis.

Antigonus picked up one of the gold cuffs. He turned it over slowly several times, examining it closely. He was in awe. He had never seen such delicate work before; it was exquisite. He saw a symbol which he thought could resemble the sun, but in the middle, instead of a round sphere, there was a square face or possibly a mask. He picked up the second gold cuff and found that it was identical to the first. Next, he picked up one of the two bands of braided gold, turning it over in his hands. *Exquisite. I can sell these just as they are,* he thought. *But the cuffs, I'll have to get rid of that strange image.*

Tobius suddenly jumped to his feet when he heard a sound from the rear of the shop.

"Relax, Tobius," Antigonus said. "It's just Rufinus."

Rufinus was Antigonus's teenage son, whom he had been raising on his own since his wife and their second child died during childbirth ten years ago. Antigonus's only desire was to teach his trade to his son, just as his father had taught him. It was good, honest and respectable work that had kept food on their table and clothes on their backs and had put a bit of coin in their pockets. Despite Antigonus's best efforts, Rufinus just wasn't interested in learning the trade. When Antigonus pressed him about what he would do for a living, the boy would just say, 'I've got it covered,' and then would storm out of the house. Antigonus was at a loss about what to do next.

"Hi, Tobius," Rufinus said heartily. "I'm going to the Forum, Father."

"Good, then you can get a chicken and some cabbage at the market. And be home before dinner time. We have to cook that bird if we want to eat tonight," Antigonus said.

"But, I was going to meet . . ."

"Be home before dinner," Antigonus repeated sternly. He thought Rufinus was wasting too much time at the Forum and he wasn't fond of the characters he was hanging out with either.

Rufinus huffed in frustration and left the shop.

"I'm sorry about that; he's really a good boy," Antigonus said, more for his benefit than anyone else's. "So, tell me, Tobius, where did you get this jewelry?"

"My mistress didn't say," Tobius replied bluntly. "A price?" Tobius pressed; he was eager to get this transaction finished.

Antigonus placed one piece of gold jewelry onto the bronze scale, which was to his left. He determined the weight of each piece and recorded the figures on a wax tablet. He quickly did the math. "I'll be right back," Antigonus said, picking up the gold jewelry and heading up the back stairs.

Antigonus entered his room and knelt by his strong box. Removing the key from around his neck, he unlocked it. He instantly noticed that the contents had been disturbed. *How can that be?* he wondered. *I have the only key.* Not wanting to detain Tobius any longer than necessary, Antigonus didn't take the time to determine whether anything was missing. Instead, he simply put the two gold cuffs in the box, and tucked the two braided bands of gold into the inside pocket of his tunic, the one he had made specifically to conceal items while in transit. He picked up his coin purse from inside the box and counted out several coins. After returning the purse to the box, he dropped the coins in a small leather pouch. He locked the box and, with the pouch in his hand, left his sparsely furnished room.

A few moments later, Antigonus was back in his shop. He handed the small pouch to Tobius.

"Tell your mistress that this is more than a fair price and that, if she has any more like these she wishes to sell, I'm buying," Antigonus said eagerly. He knew just the right person who would buy the bands of braided gold from him and, if there were more, he might be interested in those, too.

"And tell her the ring will be ready in two days," Antigonus shouted after the quickly-departing Tobius.

49

IMMEDIATELY UPON TOBIUS'S departure, Antigonus closed his shop and locked his door. He turned north and proceeded along via Herculia. When he turned left onto the main street, he narrowly missed a collision with Casus.

"Hey, watch where you're going," Antigonus growled. There was no reaction whatsoever from Casus, who sauntered along, oblivious to his surroundings. "Wonder what his problem is," Antigonus muttered to himself, as he continued on his way. Antigonus had never seen Casus looking so miserable. Even given Casus's past or the constant tormenting he'd been receiving thanks to Primus's goons. Whatever was troubling Casus, Antigonus wanted no part of it. He had his own problems to deal with.

After Casus had left the Basilica earlier that day, he had been spotted wandering aimlessly around town. No one could have known that all of his hopes and dreams had been destroyed the minute he had observed Firmus and Primus in conversation. What did Casus expect? Primus had the whole town eating out of his hands, why not Firmus, too?

Antigonus knew his exact destination. It was early enough in the day; he would still find his patron at his house. He crossed via Veneria and approached a large wooden door. He hammered twice and waited patiently; he knew his patron would reward him handsomely.

The door was pried open a couple of inches. The porter carefully assessed the caller.

"Clitus, I must speak with Primus immediately," Antigonus declared.

"This is not a good time," Clitus coldly informed him.

"He'll want to see what I have for him," Antigonus persisted.

Clitus opened the door wider and bid Antigonus to enter. "Wait here," Clitus directed. He went to inform his master he had another unexpected visitor. He was fervently hoping that this visit wouldn't take long; he knew how upset his master became when his daily routine was disrupted.

A few moments later, Primus appeared from the corridor that led to the open courtyard. "You're timing is questionable, Antigonus," Primus grumbled.

"I'm sorry, but I thought you'd like to know immediately," Antigonus replied meekly.

"Well, out with it then, and make it quick; I'm on my way to the baths," Primus snapped, as he perched on one of the lounges.

"Tobius, Julia Felix's slave, came by my shop just now to sell some jewelry."

"So?"

"The jewelry is like nothing I've ever seen before. The quality of the gold pieces and the craftsmanship are outstanding," Antigonus explained, as he reached into his pocket and pulled out the two braided bands of gold. "See for yourself," he said, as he handed the pieces to Primus.

Primus was no expert, but he had a good eye for quality. Antigonus was right. These were exquisite pieces. "Where did Tobius get these?" Primus asked abruptly, already knowing the answer.

"He didn't know or wouldn't say, I'm not sure which," Antigonus replied timidly.

"Well, I do know and you've just confirmed it," Primus sneered evilly. "And I'll take these as gifts for my wife and daughter. They'll look elegant wearing them, I have no doubt."

Primus spun around and walked out of the atrium, unceremoniously dismissing an embittered and empty-handed Antigonus, who let himself out.

50

RUFINUS DECIMUS TRAMPED along via Herculia, passing a few shops and grumbling to himself. "One of these days, I'm going to get away from that foolish old man." Rufinus was five-foot-eight, tall by most standards, and he was large in stature, the complete opposite of his father. Rufinus had never had much schooling because his father was going to teach him all he needed to know to take over the gem-cutting business that had been in the family for generations. But he had other plans.

Rufinus crossed the street and walked up a narrow alleyway. At the end of the alley, there was a staircase. He climbed the creaking wooden steps. At the top of the stairs, there was a single wooden door. He rapped on the door twice, then opened it and walked in.

"It's about time you showed your face. Where have you been?" Tiro snapped.

Rufinus was standing in the tablinum, or office, one of four rooms in the apartment of Lucius Cominius Tiro, Primus's debt collector. The ex-slave had done very well for himself. Besides the elaborate apartment which he owned, he also owned the three shops below. One was a tavern that served food and drink. The others were a dye shop and a dressmaker's shop.

Tiro's office was separate from his private living quarters, which consisted of the apartment's two front rooms overlooking the main street. The office was furnished with a large maple desk, where Tiro kept his records, along with those of Primus. There were four cushioned brass chairs and two brass lamp stands.

"I'm here now, aren't I?" Rufinus grunted. He had never cared for the man, but he was making a substantial living working for the weasel. Rufinus nodded to the two older men sitting in the brass chairs.

"I have a job for the three of you," Tiro announced.

"Hope it doesn't take long; my old man wants me home to cook dinner," Rufinus groaned. As he spoke, out of the corner of his eye, he caught the other two men snickering. He flashed them a spiteful glare, which quieted their merriment.

Publius and Calvus were both in their mid-thirties and had been working as enforcers for Tiro for several years. They hadn't taken kindly to Tiro's hiring of the young upstart. But they had needed the extra help after Marianus died. And, since Rufinus was bigger and stronger and able to do most of the heavy work, the two of them went along. They also found they enjoyed having a little fun at Rufinus's expense.

"It won't take long at all, if you do exactly as I say." Tiro's expression darkened.

51

"IF YOU'LL JUST sign here, Crescens, we'll be all set," Ennychus explained, sliding the loan agreement across the table.

"You can't imagine how grateful I am for this loan, Ennychus, and you're a much better person to do business with than Tiro," Volusius Crescens declared honestly.

"I wouldn't want to be indebted to him, either, or to Primus for that matter. I don't trust them," Ennychus said, as he accepted the signed document from Crescens, in exchange for a sum of coin in a leather pouch.

"Come, Crescens, let's have a drink in the courtyard and put business aside for a while," Ennychus suggested. He filed the loan agreement, and before leaving the office with Crescens, instructed one of his slaves to take the wine and glasses to the garden.

Lucius Venidius Ennychus's house was one of Herculaneum's more luxurious mansions. It was on the main street and had an enormous front entrance. On the right side of the entrance, there was a shop sign for the adjoining property, which just so happened to belong to Primus.

The entranceway or vestibule opened onto a rectangular atrium. Like most opulent Roman houses, there was a marble-lined impluvium, or pool, in the center, along with a wellhead with a fluted shaft made from a single block of white limestone. On the west side of the atrium were two bedrooms and a kitchen while on the east side there was a third bedroom and an alcove. At the rear of the atrium was Ennychus's large office.

Ennychus led the way to the courtyard which had colonnades on all four sides and a small garden in the center.

"Livia Acte! Venidia! Please come join us," Ennychus hollered, when he and Crescens reached the open courtyard and sat down on a couple of the lounges. The mist coming from a fountain in the middle of the garden seemed to lower the temperature of the stifling day by at least fifteen degrees.

Ennychus was an ex-slave who had been given his freedom before he had reached the age of thirty. However, an ex-slave had to be thirty to become a Roman citizen. But if ex-slaves got married, had a child, and declared that child before the local magistrate, they were given a certificate that said they now merit Roman citizenship. So, Ennychus had married Livia Acte, who was a freed slave like himself, and, on 24 July AD 60, she had given birth to a daughter whom they named Venidia. Exactly one year later, they had become Roman citizens.

"Well hello, Crescens," Livia Acte said, as she entered the garden and sat beside her husband. Crescens had stood when Livia Acte appeared. She was a stunning woman of forty, with long brown hair and swaying ringlets framing her delicate features. She wore a flowing crimson stola accented with elegant jewelry and large dangling earrings.

A moment later, a beautiful young lady of nineteen years entered the garden from the other side of the house. She was the spitting image of her mother and just as lovely. Again, Crescens stood. "I didn't know we were expecting company; I would have dressed for the occasion," Venidia said, as she sat gracefully on one of the lounges. Crescens thought she looked as if she were already dressed to meet guests, or perhaps to go out, in her sapphire colored dress and gold accoutrements.

* * *

After enjoying some light conversation, Ennychus escorted Crescens to the door. “Again, Ennychus, thank you. I’ll pay you back as soon as I’ve sold the clothes from the new shipment of silk I’m expecting from the Far East later this week.”

“You’re more than welcome, my friend,” Ennychus said, shaking his hand.

When Crescens had left and Ennychus was closing the door, a foot was suddenly wedged between the door and the jamb. There was a forceful push that propelled Ennychus backwards. The door swung open and three men entered.

“What do you want?” Ennychus inquired nervously, while regaining his balance and trying to put on brave front.

“We’ve been sent here to teach you that lending money in this town isn’t good for your health,” Publius said coldly, as he nodded to his fellow enforcers.

Rufinus slowly approached Ennychus, a malicious grin plastered across his face.

* * *

Livia Acte and Venidia were in the garden enjoying a cup of watered wine when they heard crashing sounds coming from inside the house. As they cautiously approached the atrium, they heard, “The next time, it will be your beautiful wife and daughter we’ll focus our attention on.” The door slammed shut. Then silence.

“Ennychus!” Livia Acte screamed, as she rushed to her husband’s side. His bloodied and beaten body was sprawled on the floor. Furniture had been overturned, clay lamps had been smashed, cushions had been torn, and marble busts had been shattered on the floor.

“Father!” Venidia screamed in horror. “Who did this to you?”

“Let it be, child, I don’t want any more trouble,” Ennychus moaned, as he tried to sit up.

"Get some help," Livia Acte told her daughter, who immediately left to get the house slaves to carry her father to his room, but not before overhearing what followed.

"They stole our money, too," Ennychus whispered despondently to his wife.

52

THE GUEST LIST for Julia's dinner consisted of the most prominent women of Herculaneum. As each woman arrived, she was escorted to the courtyard where she could enjoy a drink while awaiting the arrival of other guests.

"Your house is as beautiful as ever, Julia," Aquilina remarked.

"Why, thank you, my dear," Julia replied. Even though Julia didn't care for Aquilina's husband, Primus, she and Aquilina were close friends.

Aquilina wore a crimson dress with gold trim. Her auburn hair was elaborately coiffured. And to accentuate the gold trim of her dress, she wore an exaggerated amount of gold jewelry, including a band of braided gold around her head.

Julia had introduced Dani as one of her cousins and had explained that she was visiting for a short while before continuing on to Rome. And it hadn't gone unnoticed by Dani that Aquilina was wearing one of the gold bands that Dani and Daric had given to Julia. *Primus must have bought it for her,* Dani speculated.

Once all the guests had arrived, they were led to the interior dining room. The room's windows overlooked the formal garden to the north and the vegetable garden to the east. There were three brass lounges with overstuffed cushions and pillows for the diners' comfort. The lounges were arranged in a U-shape with a large rectangular marble table in the center. In the corners of the room, there were brass standards with suspended oil lanterns that provided the light.

Recognizing that all the dinner guests would be female, Julia had earlier in the day suggested to Daric that he dine at the private baths' tavern. He had willingly embraced the suggestion, relieved that he wouldn't have to dress up and sit for hours listening to idle gossip. After wishing Julia and Dani success in their efforts to enlist help in identifying the baby's mother, he had headed to the baths' tavern, taking Bear along with him.

While walking through the garden along the way Daric thought about the money Tobius had received from selling some of their jewelry. Even after reimbursing Julia for their new clothes, they seemed to have a fair amount left, although he didn't really understand the value of things in Herculaneum.

The ladies were in no hurry. They enjoyed the cordial atmosphere and the opportunity to catch up on the latest gossip, all the while savouring a fine array of delicious food. The first course had featured shrimp, sardines and olives. The second consisted of cold roasted duck with assorted vegetables, such as radishes, carrots, celery and cucumber. And, now, figs, grapes, cherries, plums and cheese were being consumed along with sweet Lyttian wine from Crete.

As Julia watched her guests, she was satisfied with the way the party was going and she didn't want to interrupt the conversations that were flowing easily among the ladies. But she would have to if the party was going to achieve its purpose.

Julia nodded to Nneka, who left quietly to carry out the errand that Julia had assigned to her. "Ladies," Julia spoke to get her guests' attention. After several seconds, she tried again, only a little louder. This time, the conversation subsided. The dining room was quiet. "The reason I've asked you here is that I need your help," Julia stated.

"And I thought it was to catch up on all the local gossip," Tactia replied jokingly. Tactia was the eldest of the group and was the wife of the duumvir, Firmus.

"That, too," Julia agreed warmly. Julia was about to continue, but remained silent when she saw Narissa enter the dining room, cradling a sleeping baby in her arms. Everyone looked at the slave as she handed the baby to Julia. "This baby was abandoned just outside town and I need your help in discovering who the mother is," Julia explained.

"By the gods, who would do that to their own child?" Aquilina asked in disgust.

"That's what we'd like to find out," Dani said, as she took the baby from Julia.

"What's wrong with her?" Tactia asked, thinking the baby had been abandoned because she was deformed.

"Absolutely nothing," Dani replied, as she handed the baby to Tactia. "She is perfect: ten toes, ten little fingers, and beautiful brown eyes."

"She's so small," Tactia remarked.

"She's only a day old; we determined she was born sometime mid-day yesterday," Julia supplied.

"The mother can't be any of our nobler citizens, because we would have known of the pregnancy," Aquilina asserted, as the baby was passed to her to have a closer look.

Julia loved Aquilina dearly, but Julia considered her a snob. In this case, however, Aquilina was right; they would have known about the pregnancy. The search for the baby's mother had just become a bit narrower.

Aquilina peered at the tiny bundle in her arms. She thought the baby's colouring looked familiar, but she wasn't sure. While she was still studying the infant, she opened her eyes. Aquilina drew a sharp breath, a breath that didn't go unnoticed by Dani. Aquilina would know those eyes anywhere and, now that she looked closer, the jawline could be from only one person. She quickly gave the baby to the next guest and sat back, quietly contemplating how to deal with this unexpected discovery.

"I think you should talk to Fuscus," Marcella suggested. "Her coloring looks almost Egyptian to me and doesn't Fuscus own an Egyptian slave?" Marcella was a buxom woman in her mid-forties and the wife of the other duumvir, Celus.

"That's as good a place as any to start," Julia said optimistically. She was eager to reunite mother and daughter. She also wanted to give the mother a piece of her mind.

Just as Julia finished her sentence, a tremor shook the house. The lanterns swung on their chains. It lasted only a few seconds, but everyone was ill at ease.

"These are happening much too often for my liking," Marcella said anxiously.

53

CASUS HAD BEEN wandering the streets of Herculaneum for hours; he had lost all track of time. When he finally snapped out of his dazed distraction, he realized he was on the west side of town. It was an area he usually had little reason to visit. For starters, it was the high-class neighbourhood; as a result, it was rarely necessary for Casus to be sent there to deal with disturbances. Also, most of the area was run by Primus, a man Casus wanted as little to do with as possible.

Casus noticed the slaves lighting the street torches and placing them back in their wall sconces. He hadn't realized that it was already dusk. He had to get back and check on Kallisto; he shouldn't have been gone this long. Casus headed east, back toward Alcimus's tavern, when he soon heard cheering and hollering coming from a bar on the corner. And an enticing smell of food reminded him he hadn't eaten all day.

What's the harm of stopping in for a quick bite to eat, he thought. *I won't stay long.*

On entering the bar, Casus walked up to the counter and ordered himself a drink. "What are you serving today?" he asked, as he accepted a mug of wine from the bar owner.

"We have lamb stew," the man behind the counter replied

hospitably.

"Great, I'll have some," Casus said, as he placed some coin on the counter. He took his drink and sat down at a table.

Another cheer erupted. He looked at a group of men at a table in the back of the bar. *So that's who's making all the noise,* he noted.

A homely looking barmaid brought over a large bowl of stew and a loaf of bread. She placed them on the table in front of him. "Enjoy," she said as she turned and left.

"Thanks," Casus said, as he dug into the stew, not appreciating until now how hungry he was. After a few mouthfuls, he realized there were more vegetables than lamb in the stew; he had found only two pieces of meat and the bowl was already half empty.

Casus reached for his wine and froze. The liquid in the mug was vibrating. Then he felt a tremor. "Not again," he mumbled. Seconds later the trembling stopped and the ripples in his mud disappeared.

After finishing his meal, Casus picked up his drink and walked toward the back of the room to see what all the excitement was about. Three men sat at a table playing dice. Two seemed to be a lot older than the third.

"At least we're not using our own money, eh, boys?" When Casus approached, the game and conversation stopped; all three men looked up at him.

"You going to just stand there and stare or are you going to play?" the young man asked.

"I'll play," Casus replied. He sat and the dice were immediately passed to him.

"The game's Ten," the young man informed him.

By Pollux, Casus cursed to himself, as he looked down at the three dice in his hand. He was the Banker, the roller. Casus pulled a coin from his purse and placed it on the table; they quickly covered his bet.

Casus picked up the beaker and placed the dice inside. He knew he was at a disadvantage being the roller. With three dice, the odds of the outcome of the roll being less than ten were slim. Any roll over ten meant he would lose the bet.

"Come on, Fortuna, be kind to me," Casus said, as he spilled the dice onto the table. There was a four and two ones. "Yes!" Casus exclaimed, as he raked in his winnings.

After a couple of hours, Casus had become a rich man. "Well, thank you, gentlemen, but I must be going. Maybe another time, eh?" he said, as he stood up. He raked the last of his winnings into his leather purse, tied it to his belt and left the bar.

A few minutes later, the three gentlemen, also stood up and left the bar.

Present Day—Friday

54

RICHARD APPROACHED THE gazebo, on the well-treed end of the private peninsula and overlooking the pristine waters of Lake Ontario. The windows were a specially treated glass, concealing the interior. Eddie had stayed close to Richard on the walk out to the gazebo, because he didn't want to provoke Richard, but mostly because he was a terrible judge of distance. He recalled that the perimeter collar would emit an electrical charge that would arrest his heart if he was over half a mile away from Richard. Eddie didn't want to find out the hard way if he had strayed too far. It would be the last thing he would ever do.

After keying in the digital access code, Richard opened the gazebo's door and crossed the threshold, followed closely by Eddie. It had been a long quiet walk, neither uttering a single word, until now.

"Doesn't look like much," Eddie said, referring to the sparse contents. He noted there were only two items in the room: a six-by-eight-foot computing island in the middle of the spacious room and, on the rear wall, a tinted projection surface.

"This is merely the surface," Richard muttered, walking toward the back of the room, behind the projection area. He flipped up a small concealed plate, the same colour as the walls. He inserted a USB key into the tiny, rectangular-shaped port. "This was the first virus you made for me, and it works like a charm." The virus was designed to infiltrate and override any existing security system before anyone knew anything had ever happened and without triggering any alarms or warnings in the system. Eddie had to admit, it was one of his more brilliant hacks.

A red light beside the port flashed on, followed immediately by a green light, and, then, a clicking sound. Eddie took a cautious step backwards. Parts of the wall and the floor started to move. A three-foot-wide piece of the wall rose upward, until the bottom edge was three feet above the floor. Simultaneously, a three-foot-wide section of the floor moved slowly back from the wall. The combined result was an opening which led downward.

"Whoa," Eddie muttered, as he moved toward the opening, his curiosity piqued. He saw a set of stairs going down to a lower level.

Richard reached around the opening in the wall and flipped on the light switch. He quickly descended the stairs, with Eddie close behind.

When Eddie reached the lower level, his breath caught. He moved farther into the room, taking in everything.

A central computer station, similar to the one on the upper level, sat in the center of the room. It appeared to be the control center for a bank of display screens that ran the entire length of one wall. In the far left corner, there was a five-by-five-foot square platform; he wouldn't even hazard a guess what it was for. Eddie didn't see a single piece of paper anywhere; no notes, no pens, no pencils, not even reference material. Absolutely everything was electronic.

Off to the left side of the computer station, there was a small metal table with an empty shelf underneath it. On top, sat three open and empty jewelry cases, each lined with blue velvet. *Strange,* Eddie thought. They all seemed to be out of place in here. Then Eddie noticed a comm lying between the cases.

"When you've finished gawking, I need you to remove the other virus from this console," Richard barked.

"All right," Eddie replied reluctantly, drawing his attention away from the smaller door at the far end of the room.

55

EDDIE APPROACHED THE central computer station. Locating the USB port, he inserted a key. It contained the codes to remove the virus he had previously created for Richard that temporarily disabled the system. *So that's what it was for,* Eddie thought. He still had no idea what Richard was up to, but he was slowly putting the pieces together; he would figure it out, eventually.

"That should do it," Eddie said, as he removed the key a few moments later.

"Great," Richard grunted impatiently, pushing Eddie aside as he stepped up to the console. Richard reached into his coat pocket, pulled out a glove, and slipped it on. Eddie recognized the glove. It was one he had fabricated a few days ago that contained someone's hand print; whose print, he had no clue.

Richard waved his right hand over the console. It immediately came to life.

On the square platform in the corner of the room, a faint light flickered for a moment before a 3-D hologram appeared.

"You did this! You corrupted my system!" the toga-clad hologram bellowed.

"Whoa!" Eddie exclaimed, as he jumped backwards, bumping into the small metal table. Eddie quickly grabbed the edge of the table and steadied it, before it could crash to the floor. Why was he so frightened? It was only an image after all, nothing to be afraid of, he reasoned.

"Yes, I did," Richard replied coldly, staring at the hologram.

"What logic is there in doing that?"

"It served my purpose," Richard snapped at the image. "And, by the way, you now work for me. Quinn is dead!"

Eddie had been watching the exchange closely, mesmerized by the floating image in the corner. Right away, he knew the hologram was an AI, a computer program. But what Eddie couldn't comprehend was the range of emotions it displayed: first outrage, and then shock and now despair upon hearing of Quinn's death. He wondered who or what Quinn was.

"I control this console; therefore, I control you," Richard said matter-of-factly. "And I need you to finish Quinn's work. I need you to complete the computations for forward time travel so you can bring the twins back. Didn't you say you were only a few hours from finishing?"

Twins back? Back from where? What twins? What's going on here? Eddie puzzled. He remembered what he had seen on the table. He glanced down and, then, up at Richard. Eddie slowly snaked his hand out, grasped the comm, and shoved it into his pocket while Richard was still occupied with the AI. Eddie wasn't sure what he was going to do with his new-found possession, but he would figure something out.

"That was before you violated me," the hologram replied harshly, his voice raw with emotion. The news of Quinn's death had hit him hard. Without Quinn, Hermes felt his life no longer had purpose. "And what I said, precisely, was that I was one hour and thirty-two minutes from completing my calculations. Now, I will need to scrub my system for any residual effects from your virus and recheck everything I've completed to date to ensure nothing is askew."

"Uh, what's that?" Eddie asked, pointing at the hologram. "Or should I say, who?"

"That's Hermes," Richard replied curtly. "Hermes, this is Eddie. You'll be working together."

Hermes vanished from the platform and materialized in front of Eddie, causing him to take a step backwards. Hermes looked Eddie up and down, scrutinizing him closely. He looked deeply into Eddie's sad jade-green eyes behind his thick black-framed glasses. Hermes's demeanor changed to one of compassion and concern. Hermes had never trusted Richard. When Quinn had confided in Richard and had asked for his help, Richard had shown his hand. Hermes had overheard Richard mumble about the platform, even though that was supposed to be the very first time Richard had set foot in the lower lab. But Eddie, he seemed different.

"Hi," Eddie said meekly.

"Hi."

"Okay, enough. It's time for you two to get to work," Richard barked.

"Even when I do finish the computations, we don't have the chronizium necessary to initiate time travel at the source," Hermes reminded Richard.

Then it's true, Eddie thought in utter amazement.

"The trip to New Zealand wasn't a complete loss," Richard jeered, pulling a chunk of the precious mineral from his pocket and showed it to Hermes in his open palm. There was no way Richard was going to give up possession of this rare mineral, not until the very last second. Besides, it was the only piece he had, and he had absolutely no intention of going back to that cave and Quinn's corpse to look for more, especially since there was no guarantee he would find any.

"I see," Hermes mumbled despondently. He tried to console himself with the thought that by completing the calculations he would be helping Quinn by reuniting the twins with their mother. That was the least he could do for the family, his family, as he had chosen to believe.

"So, let's get at it. But first, Eddie, get me those eyes and ears. Now!" Richard ordered. Then, just for the hell of it, he pressed a button in his coat pocket with his ungloved hand. Eddie dropped to his knees.

"All right," Eddie screeched, clutching his collar.

"Good boy," Richard chastised. "And I need you to keep an eye on him," referring to Hermes, who just glared at Richard's back as he walked to a chair.

Herculaneum—August 21, 79 AD

56

JULIA WAS UP at dawn. She wanted to get an early start on the day and her first stop would be the house of Marcus Nonius Fuscus. She was going to follow up on the suggestion by Marcella, from the previous night, that the mother might be one of Fuscus's slaves. When Dani had joined Julia in the dining room, she had asked to accompany her to see Fuscus. When they were ready to leave, Julia and Dani climbed into the litter and were whisked away by six slaves.

It was going to be another hot day; there wasn't a cloud in the sky. Julia chose not to draw the curtains on the litter; it would have been too stifling inside. Besides, they were out early enough that the streets were not yet crowded.

The litter bearers turned right onto via Mineria and came to an abrupt halt. "What the . . ." Julia's words caught in her throat when she saw that her slaves had almost trampled over a body lying crumpled in the street.

"Isn't that . . ." Dani started to say.

"Yes, it is," Julia confirmed, as she climbed out of the litter. Dani was close behind. She knelt down by the man's body and placed two fingers against his neck, checking for a pulse. "He's alive," she announced, even though from first appearances it was questionable. Dani saw blood on the back of the man's head and bruising on his arms and shoulders. *Looks like he took a good beating,* she thought.

"Get him into the litter; we'll take him back to my place," Julia ordered her slaves and then turned to Dani. "It's close and we can check the extent of his injuries there and, if need be, I'll send for the physician." Julia had watched Dani examine the baby and believed she could assess Casus's injuries and offer recommendations for his care.

"Be careful," Dani cautioned, as the slaves carefully picked up the injured man and gently placed him in the litter. She was worried that there might be some broken bones, ribs especially.

"I'd say this was a robbery," Julia asserted.

"His sword is missing; so is his dagger, his balteus and the pack he was wearing the last time we saw him," Dani stated grimly.

"And his purse is missing, too," Julia added, knowing that Casus always carried one on his belt.

"Who would want to take on Casus, given his size and background? Wouldn't that be a little risky?" Dani asked, curious why someone would want to attack a soldier, regardless of the valuables he might be carrying. *Besides, where would you sell his weapons?* she wondered.

"He was probably attacked from behind, unaware of what was happening, and most likely there was more than one attacker," Julia surmised.

Once Casus had been loaded into the litter, the slaves reversed their direction and headed back to Julia's house. Julia and Dani walked along behind the litter. Unfortunately, their mission for the morning would have to be postponed.

57

PRIMUS AWOKE IN a bitter mood this morning. He had to pay a visit to his vineyard, not because he wanted to, but because he had been ordered to and that was what had him so irritated.

After paying homage to the household gods, Primus met with his clients, as he did every morning. But somehow, this morning proceedings were more of a chore than a pleasure.

Festus, the innkeeper, walked through the atrium and approached the tablinum where Primus sat on his throne-like chair. Festus bowed and then raised his head. Primus remained silent. *This is not good,* Festus thought. *Hopefully, my news will lighten his day.*

"I've found the strangers," Festus said proudly. "They're staying at Julia Felix's house."

Primus waved a dismissive hand. "I already know that, you fool. Do you know how long they're staying?"

"No," Festus answered. His shoulders slumped at yet again disappointing his master.

"No matter," Primus grunted. He had a plan, and he needed Festus to start the ball rolling. "This is what I want you to do. You told me the other day that the young lady was parading through town inappropriately dressed."

"Well, yeah, I guess so, but she could have been dressed okay for where she comes from," Festus suggested timidly.

"I don't care where she comes from; she's here now," Primus snapped. "The foremost virtues of a woman are modesty and fidelity, not to provoke the lustful gaze of a man. Now, I want you to go and spread the word about how appalling it was for her to be parading around town and I want the citizens of the town to take their complaints to the aediles. Do you understand me?"

"Shouldn't they be going to the duumviri; they're the ones responsible for local squabbles?" Festus questioned hesitantly.

"I know that, but I have better control over the aediles and I need them to act quickly. That buffoon, Firmus, will drag this out for days, even weeks," Primus grumbled. "The aediles, do you understand?"

"Yes, Master," Festus replied humbly. He didn't have the slightest notion why he was being asked to do this, but he accepted nonetheless. He had no real choice. Festus bowed and showed himself out.

Primus grinned maliciously. *This day may not be so bad after all,* he thought, as he envisioned how his scheme would unfold. *Brilliant,* he mused. Being pleased with himself, he left his office and prepared for his trip.

58

MARCUS NONIUS FUSCUS stormed up the back staircase. When he reached the door at the top, he didn't knock; he just opened it and marched in. Close on his heels was aedile Marcus Rufellius Robia, whom Fuscus had insisted join him on this errand. This business ends here and now, Fuscus reflected firmly.

Fuscus was a respectable businessman in Herculaneum and had been a freedman for over fifteen years. He had learned a lot about treating slaves with kindness and respect; he had learned from his late master, Marcus Nonius Balbus, the town's benefactor and leading citizen.

Tiro was sitting at his desk reviewing some documents, as was his routine in the morning, after, of course, paying his respects to his patron, Primus.

"What's the meaning of this?" Tiro asked irritably.

Fuscus walked to the front of the desk, glaring down at Tiro for a moment, hoping to convey that he meant business. Fuscus lifted his hand and dropped a bag of coin on the desk, inches from Tiro.

"That is the six-hundred sesterces I borrowed from Primus, plus the interest I owe him. Now, I want my security deposit back," Fuscus demanded.

"Uh . . ." Tiro stammered.

"Pull out the agreement and mark it paid in full," Fuscus ordered. He looked over his shoulder at Robia, who was sitting in one of the cushioned brass chairs. He appeared totally disinterested and utterly inconvenienced.

"Robia, you bear witness to this transaction. My debt here is paid in full," Fuscus announced.

Robia looked at Tiro. Refusing to budge from his chair, he asked, "Has the debt been paid?"

Tiro reluctantly opened the bag and counted the brass coins. "Yes, the debt has been paid," he confirmed. Tiro knew Primus would not be pleased. He had made it clear to Tiro he was to refuse Fuscus's repayment of the loan, because Primus intended to keep the security deposit.

"What about my security deposit? What about Nais?" Fuscus demanded, glaring at Robia.

Robia had seen for himself how much Primus enjoyed Nais. If he could find a way to avoid being involved with his transaction, he might still have a chance of marrying Primus's daughter. But he saw no good—only trouble—coming his way.

"Tiro, mark the loan agreement paid in full and have Nais returned to Fuscus as soon as possible," Robia commanded. He extricated himself from the chair and approached the desk. He spun the agreement around, took the stylus from Tiro, and witnessed the transaction.

"I have other business to attend to," Robia announced, as he left the apartment.

"And my property?" Fuscus asked bitterly.

"Primus is out at his estate today. I will enquire tomorrow as to the disposition of your property," Tiro informed him.

Fuscus stormed out of the apartment. Why he had ever borrowed from Primus in the first place was beyond him. The next time he needed a loan, he would go to Ennychus.

59

PRIMUS HAD ORDERED Ferox to fetch the horses from the stable. He wanted to make this a quick trip, so only he and his bodyguard were making the trek into the country.

The two men passed through the gates of town and galloped along the road, past the lower pasturelands and small farmhouses. They travelled past dried-up river beds and parched fields while a haze of dust gathered in their wake. The mountain loomed ever more colossal the closer they got. The heat from the sun seemed almost merciless the higher they climbed.

Primus could see his country estate perched on the slope of the mountain, just below the ridge of the forest. The fertile soil around the mountain and the climate of the region provided ideal conditions for growing grapes.

Primus's property comprised a spacious four-bedroom villa, which he rarely used, a foreman's domus, or house, and a large ergastulum, or prison, where the slaves slept at night, shackled together. On his acreage, besides growing grapes, he had orchards of peach, fig, olive and almond trees. It wasn't uncommon to grow vines among the trees, which acted as natural trellises.

Primus and Ferox rode past two statues of Bacchus, god of wine, which announced the entranceway to the estate. As they cantered along the winding road toward the foreman's house, Primus saw the slaves already busy picking the plump purple fruit.

Primus easily spotted the stocky foreman among the skinny, half-starved slaves. He rode over to meet him. Fifty feet away from the foreman's house was a dried corpse hanging on a cross. His eyes had been pecked out by scavengers. Broken leg bones were poking through his paper thin skin, which had blackened from the sun. By the stench, Primus figured he had been hanging there for a few days.

The foreman saw a cloud of dust, but he couldn't identify the approaching riders. Only when they were about twenty yards away did he recognize them. His demeanor changed instantly; he sucked in his bulging gut, slicked back his hair, what little he had left, and brushed the dust off his tunic. He finished just as Primus reined in his horse in front of him.

"Master, what a pleasure. What brings you all the way out here?" Lycus asked. "Nothing wrong, I hope," he added with a nervous stutter, as his eyes wandered over to the rotting corpse.

Primus dismounted and surveyed the area. The slaves had stopped working the moment Primus's feet touched the ground. "Is it a holiday?" Primus asked sarcastically.

Lycus spun around and cracked his whip against the back of the nearest slave. "Back to work, the lot of you!" he bellowed.

"And I would suggest you take him down," Primus remarked, pointing to the corpse. "I think they have all learned the lesson you were trying to teach, whatever it was." Primus could have cared less what the slave had done to earn the most horrific form of torture ever devised by man. The slaves were his property to do with as he pleased.

Lycus barked, as he pointed to two nearby slaves, "You and you, get him down and drag him to the pit." They immediately jumped to obey his command.

"Can I get you a drink?" Lycus asked, fidgeting.

"Let me sample what you're making this year," Primus replied.

Lycus shouted for one of his house slaves to bring some wine.

Almost immediately, a slave came running out with a pitcher and three goblets. He poured the wine and passed the goblets around. Primus took a gulp, waited a moment, and then asked, "What grapes are we using?"

"This wine was made from Greco, Fiano, Aglianico, and Piedirosso grapes," Lycus answered, not offering an opinion on the taste; he knew Primus didn't care to hear any opinions unless had asked for them.

Ferox downed his wine; the day was hot and the ride out here had been dusty. He thrust out his goblet, which was quickly refilled. Not that his opinion mattered, but he thought the wine was superb, either that, or he was just very thirsty.

"What other grapes are we growing?" Primus asked, taking another gulp of wine and held out his goblet for a refill. *By the gods, it's like a furnace out here,* he moaned internally.

"The Caprettona and Falanghina aren't quite ready for picking yet, maybe in a week or two," Lycus informed him.

Suddenly there was a loud crash, the sound of breaking branches, and a blood-curdling scream. "Now what?" Lycus groaned, making his way over to see what the commotion was about.

It didn't take Lycus long to determine what had happened. One of the slaves had been up in the tree picking fruit. He had stepped on a weak branch which snapped under his weight. He had crashed to the ground, cracking his skull open when he landed. Lycus could see from the slave's twisted form he had probably broken his back, too.

Primus, too, came to investigate; after all, it was his property. One look and he knew. "Dispose of that," Primus said indifferently, referring to the man lying crippled and bloody on the ground. Lycus pointed to two men to drag the now unconscious, or possibly dead, man away.

"Go into town and buy a new slave, one younger and stronger, preferably Nubian," Primus instructed, as he wiped the perspiration from his brow. He needed to finish his business at the estate and get back to town where it would be much cooler with the fresh breezes blowing in off the bay. "And on your way into town, I need you to deliver three-hundred-six fence poles to Primigenius, the same ones I had you move."

Lycus nodded and started to organize the slaves to carry out the master's bidding. Meanwhile, Primus simply walked away. Without even a backward glance, he and Ferox mounted their horses and headed down the road by which they had arrived. Lycus hoped that future visits by Primus would be few and far between. Although he recognized that the estate belonged to Primus, he had come to treat it as his own business and he preferred to run it without interference from Primus.

60

THE SIGHT OF the baby at Julia's dinner party the previous night had raised some strong suspicions. There was no question in Aquilina's mind what had happened. It hadn't been hard for her to put two and two together. She knew exactly the last time she and her husband had been intimate. If she was no longer satisfying his needs, he had to be getting it elsewhere. Aquilina had waited patiently for her husband to leave on his trip to the estate this morning before she set out to confirm her suspicions.

Having had breakfast and bidding Primus farewell, Aquilina was sitting in the shade of an olive tree and enjoying a glass of honeyed wine in the open colonnaded courtyard. The fountain provided a fine spray of mist, which was refreshingly cool in the heat of the day. The gold finches were also enjoying the revitalizing vapor, as they darted from the branches, through the fountain, and back to their perches among the leaves, chirping merrily.

"You asked to see me, Domina?" Nais said meekly.

"Yes, sit, please," Aquilina said, indicating the seat next to her. Nais sat down, hesitantly.

"How long have you been with us, Nais?" Aquilina asked, knowing full well when Nais had arrived.

"About fifteen months," Nais answered to the best of her

knowledge. It was hard to keep track of time when the days seemed to blur together.

Aquilina figured that the timing was just about perfect. “And has my husband bedded you?” Aquilina asked bluntly, catching Nais by surprise.

* * *

Cominia Prima had heard voices in the garden. Thinking her mother had company, she had decided to join them, but the moment she heard her mother’s question she froze in her tracks. She snuck behind a column hidden in the shadows but well within hearing range of the conversation. She waited breathlessly for the answer.

Nais was in a very precarious position. She wouldn’t fare well, regardless of how she answered. She decided to appease the mistress. She answered, “No.”

“Look me in the eye, Nais, and tell me truthfully. I promise I won’t punish you; after all, you wouldn’t have had a choice in the matter,” Aquilina explained calmly.

Nais slowly raised her head. Tears were running down her cheeks. It was the answer Aquilina was expecting. “Now, answer me truthfully, did you just have a baby?”

“No,” Nais choked nervously. *How did she know? How could anyone know?*

Aquilina reached over and touched Nais’s breast: she flinched.

“Just as I thought; swollen and sore. Why did you lie to me?” Aquilina asked, with a hurt tone in her voice.

“I didn’t know what to say; it just came out,” Nais said sombrely.

“How on earth did you ever hide your pregnancy?” Aquilina asked, unable to comprehend how a slave could complete her tasks, especially toward the end of her term.

“I had help from the other slaves. They helped me with any heavy lifting toward the end,” Nais explained.

“Why did you leave your baby to die? Why did you deliver your baby in the graveyard and then abandon her there? How could you leave a child, a helpless newborn?" Aquilina's questions were getting louder with each one she asked. She was becoming enraged. "What if someone else had found her? They could have raised her as their own slave. Or even worse, she could have been purposely maimed or crippled as a child by a plebeian and sent out onto the streets as a beggar to earn whatever scraps were thrown her way."

"I know that giving birth as a slave means that my child is the property of my master, and I know how cruel my master can be. I would rather her go to Elysium than have to be subjected to that monster," Nais spat out, then cowered after realizing she was speaking about Aquilina's husband. "Forgive me," she pleaded, as she quickly got down on her knees.

"It's all right, my dear, please get up," Aquilina said, as she reached down to help Nais up. "I know exactly how demanding my husband can be."

"Now, tell me everything," Aquilina insisted, "and don't be afraid to tell me the truth."

Thirty minutes later, Aquilina had a clear and sordid picture of Nais's existence. So did Cominia Prima, who was appalled at her father's brutality and cruelty. Sure she had heard rumors, but she had refused to believe them. But now, she had heard it directly from Nais, someone she had grown to like, someone close to her own age, and someone she could converse with. *How could he? Nais isn't even his property; she's a security deposit,* she thought, totally disgusted by her father's behavior. Well, she would do something about that.

61

"DARIC!" DANI HOLLERED, as they entered Julia's house.

"What? What is it?" Daric asked, racing into the atrium in a panic, thinking something was wrong with his sister. Bear was right on his heels. *They shouldn't be back so soon*, he thought. Then he saw the slaves enter the house carrying a body.

"Take him to the empty room next to Narissa," Julia instructed the slaves, who carefully carried the still unconscious Casus.

"What happened to him?" Daric asked, following the procession through the atrium and across the courtyard.

"He was mugged," Dani informed him. "I'm not sure how serious his injuries are, but I know I could use your help to find out."

The slaves placed Casus on the bed and left. Nneka joined them; it was her duty to be available at all times for Julia; so when she had recognized her mistress's voice, she had set out to find her.

"Nneka, get some water and some clean rags, quickly," Julia ordered.

"And bring me the strongest wine you have and some honey," Dani shouted after the quickly disappearing Nneka.

"An odd time for a drink, don't you think?" Julia asked warily.

"It's used for treating wounds. Trust me," Dani assured her. "Daric, help me get him undressed. I need to check for any broken bones and possible internal bleeding."

"You two seem to know what you're doing and it wouldn't be appropriate for me to remain here, so I'll be out in the garden. Holler if you need anything. Come on, Bear, let's see if we can find that tortoise," Julia said, as she excused herself and left the sparsely furnished room with Bear trotting happily beside her.

Once Dani and Daric had removed Casus's jerkin, they could better assess his condition. Besides the laceration previously identified on the back of his skull, they discovered three fractured ribs on his left side and a stab wound on his left femur. "Will you look at all of those scars?" Daric stated, after he lost track when he was trying to counting them all.

"Just like Cilo told us," Dani remarked.

"You know, I feel kinda sorry for him. He kinda reminds me of me," Daric mumbled.

"What?" Dani exclaimed, wondering where Daric was coming from.

"You know, like Cilo said, Casus wanted to be a hero. He wanted to make a name for himself. He wanted to protect and support his family. But he always came up short, just like me. I'm the screw-up in a family of geniuses," Daric muttered miserably.

"Now, you listen to me," Dani stated assertively. "You are not, I repeat, not a screw-up. When we're faced with situations that test our strength and challenge our courage, we all have the opportunity to dig deep and discover what we're really truly made of. You, dear brother, haven't run away from trouble, but have faced it head on. And, on more than one occasion, you've saved our lives. So, in my book, that makes you a hero. So don't sell yourself short."

"Thanks, sis," Daric said shyly. *Maybe I'm not as much of a screw-up as I thought.* This little confession had pumped up his confidence and his self-esteem as well.

"Domina told me to stay and help you," Nneka said, returning with the requested items. She looked down at the battered body on the bed and shuddered.

"I'm going to need a needle and some thread," Dani informed

her. Nneka looked at her, puzzled. "The wound on his leg will need stitching, like sewing. I need a fine needle and thin, strong thread, like a cotton thread." Dani had just finished wrapping a rag around the stab wound for the time being. She wanted to clean, stitch and dress it all at once to minimize any chance of it becoming infected.

Nneka nodded in understanding and ran off.

"Daric, can you help me roll him gently over onto his right side? I want to check his head wound," Dani explained, as she positioned herself to assess his injury. "Perfect," she said, as she began to gently probe the wound. She reached over and pulled a wet rag out of the bucket of water and wiped away the blood. "Good, it's just superficial." She cleaned the wound and wrapped a strip of cloth around his head before Daric rolled him onto his back. "He may have a concussion, which would explain why he's still out. We'll need to keep an eye on him for the next twenty-four hours."

Nneka ran back into the room, carrying the needle and thread that Dani had requested. "That was fast," Dani said appreciatively.

"I'll go tell Julia we're just about finished in here," Daric offered, as he left the small chamber, making room for Nneka.

"Okay, now we need to stop this bleeding, but first we have to clean the wound," Dani stated, as she reached for the wine. She poured the wine into the wound, flushing it out. "We'll have to watch this wound for a while. If it shows signs of redness, swelling, heat or pain, it may be infected. But hopefully, that won't happen."

Dani reached for the honey. She dipped her fingers in the jar and applied a liberal amount of honey on the area of the wound. "The honey will help reduce the pain and any inflammation. It will also protect the wound from infection," she explained to Nneka.

Dani threaded the needle and carefully sutured the wound, leaving a length of thread at both ends. She didn't tie it off, so that, if the wound were to become infected, she would be able to pry open the gash and flush it out again. She wrapped the wound with a strip of cloth she had doused with wine, just for good measure. "We'll check the wound and change the dressing regularly," she told Nneka, who had been attentively taking in everything Dani had been doing and saying. Nneka picked up the needle, rags and bucket and headed back to the kitchen.

Dani was still perched on the side of the bed looking down at Casus when she saw him stir slightly. One groggy eye slowly opened, then the other, and he stared directly into the face of a goddess. “I must be in Elysium,” he mumbled and then slipped back into unconsciousness.

62

DARIC WALKED BACK into the room to check on Casus when another tremor hit. He grabbed the frame of the doorway to steady himself. "I hate this," he grumbled, when it ended a few seconds later. "Look, we're running out of time. We have three more days before the mountain blows its top," Daric stated uneasily.

"Don't you think I know that?" Dani snapped. She had been thinking long and hard about it. Maybe picking up the baby wasn't the smartest thing she had ever done.

"When we find the baby's mother, and it better be sooner rather than later, we say goodbye to Julia and disappear before the volcano erupts," Daric stated with conviction. He hated being so close to the mountain even though they had a means of escape: their travel bands.

"But what about all of these people?" Dani countered.

"We can't change history, remember?" Daric firmly reminded her.

"I know, but consider this. Only ten percent of the population of Herculaneum perished and only ten percent of Pompeii's, as well. So, something must have happened to indicate an evacuation was crucial," Dani explained.

"Go on," Daric encouraged.

"So, what if we say our family was originally from Sicily and that, throughout the generations, a story was passed down to help the citizens of Sicily recognize the signs of an imminent volcanic eruption? And that these tremors are the same signs. Maybe the people would pack up and leave on their own. We could warn the people without really altering the outcome."

"Ten percent, eh?" Daric thought for a moment. "But, that's not to say the remaining ninety percent of the citizens aren't still buried somewhere. Most of the public buildings in Herculaneum have yet to be excavated. Maybe some of them ran into the temples to pray to the gods for salvation. And what if more bodies are discovered in future excavations of Herculaneum?"

"It doesn't matter. We can work with what we and what history already knows," Dani asserted.

"I'm willing, if you are. I just hope we don't screw up our reality," Daric cautioned. "I hate jumping into these different time periods, knowing what's going to happen and being helpless to do anything about it."

"I agree." Dani smiled at her brother; they finally had a plan they could both live with.

63

AFTER MAKING SURE her father was resting peacefully, Venidia left the house and headed for the Basilica. She was determined to see that justice would be served. She walked along the main street, passing the house of her next door neighbour, Primus. A sign prominently displayed on its front door, read: 'Salve lucrum', or hail profit. She spat at the sign, then swiftly looked around to see whether anyone had witnessed her less-than-lady-like behavior. Thankfully, the street was deserted.

Venidia passed under the triumphal arches and across via Jupitinius. She continued on under the portico, or covered entranceway, and through the center door of the Basilica. She stood at the back of the long hall and looked toward the tribunal. The duumviri were seated on the raised dais. In front of them was a line of three people waiting to be heard. She moved forward and took her place in the line.

The longer Venidia had to wait, the more she fumed. She became more and more agitated as those ahead of her, one-by-one, approached the duumviri to seek resolutions to trivial squabbles between neighbours. Finally, after thirty minutes, it was her turn.

"What brings you here, Venidia?" Firmus asked cordially. He could tell she was troubled by her ridged posture. After all his years sitting in this chair, he had learned to read body language.

"My father was assaulted yesterday afternoon in his own house, by three men," Venidia stated firmly.

"How awful," Celus sputtered.

"Is he all right?" Firmus asked with true concern. He thought one elderly man against three assailants was hardly a fair fight. He also had his suspicions about who the perpetrators had been; the attack exhibited a familiar modus operandi. Before taking any action, however, he wanted to hear his suspicions confirmed first.

"He's banged up pretty badly, but he'll be fine," Venidia replied, appreciative of Firmus's concern for her father's well-being. "Not only did they beat him, but they destroyed several marble statues, ripped open cushions, overturned furniture, smashed clay lamps and stole his money."

"And do you know who did this?" Celus asked skeptically.

"Yes, I do," Venidia answered decisively. "It was Primus." She had overheard her parents' conversation about the assault on her father and knew who had ordered the attack.

Celus bolted upright in his seat. "You can't be serious?"

"I'm dead serious," Venidia said unwaveringly. "It wasn't Primus personally, of course; far be it for him to actually get his hands dirty. It was Tiro's enforcers. And Tiro takes his orders from Primus."

"How can you be so sure?" Celus asked. The last thing he wanted to do was haul Primus in on assault charges.

"My father recognized the men; they've been working for Tiro for years, except for young Rufinus, who just recently joined the group. They also threatened my father by telling him to get out of the money lending business; they told him it wouldn't be good for his health. And they threatened my mother and me, too. So, I ask you, who's the only other money lender in town?" Venidia asked brazenly.

Firmus had heard all the validation he needed. "I'll send Casus, as soon as I can find him, to order Primus and Tiro to appear before us, so we can hear what they have to say in their defense."

"Thank you," Venidia said respectfully. She bowed her head, then turned and walked out of the Basilica, but not before overhearing Celus ask, "Do you think that is wise?"

64

COMINIA PRIMA SNUCK out of the house, taking Andreas, a kitchen slave, with her, because, whenever respectable women went out, they were accompanied by one or more slaves. She took only Andreas because she didn't have far to go and she hoped to be back home before anyone even realized she had left.

Cominia rapped on the door of the house that belonged to Fuscus; she prayed to the gods that he was home. A moment later, a porter opened the front door.

"I've come to see Marcus Nonius Fuscus. I have urgent news," Cominia stated seriously.

The porter opened the door and gestured for them to enter. They walked along a narrow entranceway which opened onto the atrium. "Please, wait here," the porter instructed, as he left to inform his master he had a visitor.

While waiting, Cominia walked around the atrium, past marble-lined impluvium, or pool, marked out by a marble display table and an elegant fountain at its head. She walked to the table and admired the sculpted lion's head at the top of the legs and the clawed feet at the bottom.

At the rear of the atrium she noticed the tablinum, or office. It was separated from the atrium by an elegant wooden partition, which comprised a series of panels, which could be opened and closed at will. The partition served to reduce the broad opening leading from the office onto the courtyard.

Cominia heard footsteps approaching. “Well, this is an unexpected pleasure, Cominia,” Fuscus said amiably.

Marcus Nonius Fuscus was a tall thin man with warm friendly brown eyes. He had been a slave of the town’s benefactor, Marcus Nonius Balbus, but had long since obtained his freedom and Roman citizenship. Besides his house, he owned a few shops, three of which were on the north and west side of the house. He also had apartments which he rented out.

“Come, sit, and have a refreshment with me,” Fuscus said, motioning toward the courtyard.

“I can’t stay. I must get back before they realize I’m gone,” Cominia blurted out nervously. “I’ve come to convey some disturbing news.”

* * *

Fifteen minutes later, Cominia left and hurried back home, leaving a speechless, enraged, and remorseful man behind. Fuscus had never wanted to give Nais up as a security deposit, but Primus had insisted, even though he knew that Fuscus was a reputable man to do business with and that a security deposit was unnecessary.

Besides being angry with Primus, Fuscus was angry with himself. Why had he not tried much earlier to get Nais back? Why had he not enlisted the aediles’ help before now? Had he acted sooner, he might have saved Nais from the abuse and suffering inflicted by Primus. And how could Primus have done what he did? How could he have treated Nais as if she was his property? Nais was a security deposit only, not a slave for Primus to use and abuse.

As Fuscus’s anguished mind remained focussed on Nais and Primus and all that had transpired, a picture started to emerge. Everything made sense now. Fuscus finally understood why Primus had insisted on a security deposit, why Primus had requested

Nais, and why Primus had refused Fuscus's repayment. The reason was simple: Primus wanted Nais and had no intention of giving her up.

Fuscus committed himself to making things right. He resolved to start by ensuring that the proper authorities knew how Primus had refused to accept his repayment so he could keep Nais.

65

"HOW COULD YOU?" Aquilina screamed. "How could you abuse that poor child?"

"Hush, woman, you'll disturb the household," Primus snapped, annoyed at the trivial allegation.

"I don't care who hears. You had no right," she shrieked.

"Sure, I do. I can do whatever I want with my slaves."

"She's not your slave," Cominia Prima interjected, as she stepped into the room. "Nais is Fuscus's property, and you took advantage of her. She was a security deposit, one you had insisted on; one you used to threaten Fuscus. You told him his deal wouldn't be ratified if he didn't provide Nais as a security deposit."

"What would you know?" Primus grunted coldly at his daughter, as he poured himself another mug of wine.

"I know far more than you think, Father. I've become close with Nais over the fifteen months she's been here. I'm just sorry she didn't feel she could confide in me," Cominia said regretfully. "Maybe I could have put a stop to your abuse."

"Not likely," Primus snapped.

"Well, I have now!" Cominia said defiantly.

"What have you done?" Aquilina asked nervously.

"I spoke to Fuscus. I told him everything. I told him how

you repeatedly abused his property, and how you had got Nais pregnant."

"What?" Primus blurted out, spitting wine down the front of his toga.

"I hadn't got around to telling him that bit of news, yet," Aquilina disclosed calmly.

"How is it I didn't know?" Primus asked bitterly.

"She had help hiding it from all of us," Aquilina answered. "None of us knew."

"It doesn't matter. What does is that Nais is Fuscus's property; therefore, so is her child," Cominia stated matter-of-factly. "And Fuscus is going to the duumviri tomorrow to insist that you follow the repayment agreement that was witnessed by Robia earlier today. Nais is no longer your security deposit and she will be in my custody until she is returned to her owner," Cominia said curtly.

"How dare you tell me . . ." Primus started to say before being cut off.

"And in my custody, as well," Aquilina affirmed. "You'll need to buy your sex from now on," she added. Aquilina reached for her daughter's hand, and the two women left to tell Nais the good news.

"By Pollux," Primus spat.

Present Day—Friday

66

EDDIE HAD REMOTELY synced the surveillance camera mounted on the roof of the garage to one of the display screens in the array that covered the entire length of one wall in the lab. He had also fed the transmission from the planted audio devices in the house to a speaker in the corner of the lab.

Richard had made himself as comfortable as he could in one of the two chairs in the lab. While watching the feed from the surveillance camera, he was listening intently for any sound coming from the house, so he could track Sandra's movements. So far, she had awakened, run a shower, and made her way to the kitchen. Right now, it sounded as though she was pouring a liquid, likely making herself a cup of coffee. Richard took his eyes off the monitor for a moment and glanced at Eddie and Hermes. They were conversing over mathematical equations plastered across the wall. All those numbers just gave Richard a headache.

Richard's attention was abruptly switched to the surveillance monitor when the speaker picked up the doorbell. "Damn, I didn't see him drive in," he said to himself, feeling uneasy. Chief Bill

Brown was standing at the front door. The door soon opened and Sandra appeared. Richard turned up the volume on the speaker, but the conversation was out of range of the audio transmitters.

"Bill, what a pleasant surprise," Sandra said amiably. "Come on in. I just poured myself a coffee. Won't you join me?"

"I'd love to, thanks," the chief replied.

"Damn, what's going on in there?" Richard cursed. With "eyes" outside and "ears" inside, he wasn't getting the whole picture. He started picking up the conversation as they entered the kitchen. "Well, at least that's something," Richard mumbled.

"So, what brings you all the way out here, Bill?" Sandra asked, while she poured a fresh cup of coffee for her unexpected guest.

"A couple of things. But first, I wanted to see how you're doing," Bill replied. "Thanks," he added, as he took the offered cup. "That was one hell of a day at the crash site. I've never in my eighteen years as a cop seen anything like it."

"Yeah, and I never want to again," Sandra concurred, as she reflected on the devastation caused by the train derailment.

"That was a great interview you gave, by the way," Bill said kindly.

"I looked like hell," Sandra grunted, then took a sip of her coffee. "Bill, do they know how it happened? What caused the derailment?"

"The black box they recovered from the locomotive revealed that the train approached Blain's Bend at a higher-than-recommended speed. And the Rail Traffic Controller swears up and down that the signals changed by themselves. And as it turns out, he was right. Computer forensics affirmed that the Central Traffic Control System had been tampered with."

Eddie stopped what he was doing and cocked an attentive ear toward the speaker. Richard, meanwhile, was hanging on every word of the conversation.

"But why would someone do that?" Sandra asked fretfully. "Do they know who it was?"

"Unfortunately, that's where the trails goes cold," Bill replied despairingly. “Whoever hacked the system left no trail. They used a rat.”

“A what?”

“A RAT: a Remote Access Trojan, essentially a computer virus. The hacker had complete access to the Central Traffic Control System and changed the track signals. The locomotive engineers had no clue the system had been compromised, or that they were going too fast for that bend in the tracks. And the RAT was buried under so many layers of encryption that there’s no way it can be traced back to its origin,” Bill explained sombrely.

Eddie’s shoulders slumped in relief; it didn’t go unnoticed by Hermes. Neither did Richard’s deep sigh and relaxed posture. Something didn’t sit quite right with Hermes. He would have to dig for more details since he had been out of commission when everything Sandra and the chief were discussing had happened.

“That’s terrible. All those poor people, their families. I can’t imagine what they’re all going through: the loss, the life-changing injuries many suffered. It’s tragic,” Sandra said sadly. In fact, she could imagine what they were going through. She was still struggling with her own grief arising from the continuing absence of her children, the uncertainty of their return, and the death of her husband, a death she refused to believe. However, as the hands of time relentlessly move forward, her holding out for hope slowly continued to wane.

“They think it may have been a terrorist group, but no one’s claimed responsibility,” Bill resumed.

“None of it makes any sense,” Sandra insisted quietly.

“I know.”

Sandra got up and poured Bill another cup of coffee. “So, where’s Quinn?” Bill asked, taking the cup just as it slipped from Sandra’s hand.

Present Day—Thursday NZ

67

"MOUNT COOK IS claimed to be the first peak to be lit by the rising sun. And it's said that it shares this honor with Mount Hikurangi on the North Island," Jaclynn informed Quinn. They were standing on the deck of the Granity Pass Hut, ready to begin their trek back to civilization.

As promised, Jaclynn and Quinn were up at dawn and ready to leave within a half hour. Jaclynn took the lead as they left the hut. They followed the dry marble creek bed that wound around marble bluffs. "We'll be approaching The Staircase," Jaclynn informed Quinn. "It's a steep climb, but relatively easy."

"Lead the way," Quinn said eagerly, as he limped behind Jaclynn along the narrow trail, watching his footing.

The pair followed a track through the saddle. "That's Billies Knob, on your right," Jaclynn said, acting like a seasoned tour guide. They passed through a forest of beech trees and were making a gradual ascent. When they emerged into a clearing, Quinn had to pause for a moment to take in the spectacular view. "Beautiful, isn't it?" Jaclynn beamed.

On this clear, crisp morning, you could see for miles to the north and to the west. Rolling pastoral landscapes were dominated by the majestic mountains, range-upon-range of titanic pressure-fold ridges, stretching for as far as the eye could see. Wherever you looked, the eyes were guided upwards to the high ragged skyline. Sometimes there were dark forests up to the crests of their notched ridges; sometimes there were sparkling white caps of year-round snow. Some were single summits; others were bands of powerful peaks. Overall, mountains were the predominant feature of the landscape. And looking closely into their folds, there were crystal clear lakes reflecting the bulbous white clouds floating in the blue sky above.

"Wish I wasn't in such a hurry and could take the time to enjoy this," Quinn said regretfully. He was also sorry that he was depriving Jaclynn of this glorious opportunity to soak in Mother Nature's splendor. But he had no choice; they had to keep going.

Jaclynn could see the sadness in Quinn's eyes. "Hey, I've been here many times. It's one of my favorite treks. And I'll be back here again soon; not to worry."

"Thanks," Quinn replied contritely.

They followed the well-marked trail down until it joined with the Blue Creek Trail, which followed alongside the water's edge. "Hey, I know where we are now," Quinn announced, with relief in his voice. They were almost at their destination.

Quinn took the lead and headed for Blue Creek Resurgence. He was hoping to retrieve his clothes and, more importantly, his comm he had left in his pants pocket. He was disappointed, but hardly surprised, when he and Jaclynn found nothing there. Everything was gone.

It was another twenty minutes through beech forests, past old mining relics, before they came out at Courthouse Flat.

"I have a sat-phone in Samwise, if you need to call someone," Jaclynn offered, referring to her vintage pumpkin-orange Volkswagen camper van she had affectionately named.

"Great, thank you. And yes, I do need to make a call," Quinn said with a sense of urgency.

While navigating his way through the various caverns, Quinn had spent considerable time wondering what had motivated Richard to turn on him. What was Richard up to? It had eventually become quite apparent to him that Richard was after the travel bands. He had concluded that Richard was determined to right a wrong from his ancient past, the wrong Richard had shared with him on their flight to New Zealand.

Quinn desperately wanted to contact Sandra to let her know that he was all right and that he was coming home. He was concerned, however, about how Richard might react if he learned that he was alive. He was worried that Sandra's life could be put in jeopardy. After all, Richard had already left him for dead; there was no telling what else he might be capable of. It didn't take Quinn long to decide what he would do. He walked to Samwise and placed his one call.

Herculaneum—August 22, 79 AD

68

"GOOD MORNING," DARIC said when Casus finally opened his eyes. He had been drifting in and out of consciousness throughout the night. Dani, Nneka and Daric had taken turns making sure Casus's condition didn't deteriorate.

"Where am I?" Casus mumbled, as he tried to sit up and immediately realised that that wasn't a good idea.

"Hey, take it easy; you're safe here," Daric assured him, as he gently pushed on Casus's shoulder until he was lying back down.

"What happened?" Casus asked groggily as his hand went up to touch his aching head.

"We figured you were attacked," Daric replied.

"Where's my gear?" Casus asked, not seeing it anywhere in the small room.

"We also think you were robbed," Daric explained. He had hesitated to tell Casus about both events at the same time. He had thought Casus might find the bitter pill easier to swallow if he received it in pieces.

"Well, how's our patient this morning? Awake, I see," Dani

remarked pleasantly, as she entered the small room.

"No," Casus moaned.

"What's wrong?" Dani asked in alarm as she rushed over to the bed.

"I just told him he had been attacked and robbed. He didn't take it too well," Daric said.

"That was everything I had," Casus groaned. "My room doesn't have a strong box, so all my worldly possessions are in my pack." Then he remembered his weapons. "I'll never be able to replace my sword or dagger; they've been with me since I enlisted. They're priceless to me."

"I'm so sorry," Dani said sympathetically. "Do you remember what happened?"

Casus took a moment to look closely at the beautiful woman kneeling by his bed. "I saw you in Elysium," he mumbled.

"I'm sorry, but you never left this realm. You'll have to wait for another time." Dani smiled at him.

"What was I thinking? My place will be in Tartarus, not Elysium," Casus said reproachfully.

"That's not going to happen today," Dani told him. "Do you remember anything?"

"I was walking back to . . . Kallisto!" Casus yelled as he bolted upright and immediately wished he hadn't. "Ugh!" he moaned, clutching his ribs.

"Easy, you've got a couple busted ribs," Daric reprimanded, as he helped ease Casus back down.

"Kallisto?" Dani repeated.

"She's been sick; tired, throwing up, and overly emotional, even for her. I was on my way to check on her," Casus explained. "She works at Alcimus's tavern as a barmaid. She'll be wondering where I am. I have to go to her," Casus said, trying to sit up again.

"Look, I'll go and tell her what happened and, while I'm there, I'll see what I can do to help her," Dani offered.

"You?" Casus stammered. He looked confused.

"I'm the one who patched you up; so don't go judging a book by its cover," Dani snarled.

"Sorry," Casus mumbled. "I didn't know. Thank you."

"You're welcome. Now, lie here and rest. I'll be back before you know it," Dani stated, and then left Casus in Daric's care.

"Let me check your leg wound to make sure there's no infection," Daric said, as he reached down and started to unwrap the dressing.

69

"GOOD MORNING, JULIA," Dani called out when she saw her in the rear atrium.

"Good morning, Dani. How's your patient this morning?" Julia asked.

"He's awake and upset, naturally. He lost everything in that assault. But he should make a full recovery; at least we can be thankful about that. Daric will keep an eye on him until I get back; then I'll redress his wounds."

"Get back?"

"I have to go to Alcimus's tavern. Do you know where it is? I have a message for a woman named Kallisto. I told Casus I'd look in on her. I think she's someone special to him."

"Then you must take Tobius with you. It's not proper for a woman like you to go out without an escort," Julia informed her. "I'm going to head over to Fuscus's. He may be able to help us with our search. Hopefully, I'll be able to talk to his slave and get some answers."

"Okay. I'll meet you back here in a couple of hours; all being well with some good news."

Fifteen minutes later, Dani and Tobius left the house heading for Alcimus's tavern. She wore the pale blue stola, or dress, she had bought the day before; over it she wore a cream cloak called a palla. She wore a modest amount of jewelry: a gold necklace and her travel band, which she never took off.

Dani and Tobius walked down the main street, passed the Basilica, and turned right onto via Jupitinius. They made their way past the shrine to Hercules, located in the middle of the street and blocking any vehicular traffic. Even without the shrine, the street would have been too narrow to accommodate vehicles of any kind: chariots, carts, or wagons.

"Tobius, how long have you been with Julia?" Dani asked, trying to engage in some small talk. The silence was driving her crazy.

"Many years," Tobius answered.

The two of them took a left onto via Neptunia and proceeded another two blocks east to via Herculia.

"Have you been in Herculaneum long?" Dani tried again, hoping for a more informative answer.

"Many years," Tobius replied flatly.

So this is how it's going to be, Dani thought. *Hope it's not much farther.*

"This is the place," Tobius said, indicating the shop on the corner was Alcimus's tavern.

"Great," Dani remarked, a bit too enthusiastically. She walked into the tavern, with Tobius right behind her.

"Good morning. Are you looking to quench your thirst on this blistering day, or perhaps something to eat?" a middle-aged woman in an apron asked cordially.

"Actually, I'm looking for Kallisto," Dani replied. "I was told she works here."

"What's your interest in Kallisto?" the woman asked defensively.

"I have a message for her from Casus," Dani said calmly.

"Casus?" a voice asked from the back room. "Is he all right?" A woman appeared in a doorway, holding the hand of a young boy. She was a slender woman in her late twenties, with wavy chestnut hair and soft hazel eyes. The boy appeared to be five, maybe six, years old; his dog sitting obediently by his feet.

"He's fine," Dani assured her. "Is there someplace where we can talk?"

Kallisto looked imploringly at Nona, Alcimus's wife, who nodded her consent. "Come, Livius, you can help me in the kitchen."

"This way," Kallisto said, walking to the staircase.

"Is that your little boy?" Dani asked, as she climbed the stairs.

"No, he's Alcimus and Nona's boy. I'm teaching him how to read and write," Kallisto replied, as she led Dani into her room. Kallisto sat on the bed and offered the three-legged chair to Dani. The only other items in the room were a small brass table and a chest for storing clothes, with a pitcher and basin sitting on top.

"Who are you and how do you know Casus?" Kallisto asked guardedly. In this town, a person never knew who they could trust.

"I'm Dani. I'm staying at Julia Felix's house," Dani replied genially. The mention of Julia's name seemed to calm Kallisto.

"And Casus? Where is he?" Kallisto asked anxiously.

"He's at Julia's. He was assaulted and robbed . . ."

"By the gods! Is he all right?" Kallisto cried in alarm.

"He has a few broken ribs, a gash on the back of his head, and a stab wound in his left leg, but he'll be fine, trust me," Dani informed her, immediately noticing the tension ease in Kallisto's posture.

"I was wondering what had happened, and I feared the worst," Kallisto sobbed. "He's always been good to his word. He said he was coming back, but he never showed up."

"We found him unconscious on the street yesterday morning. His first thoughts were of you," Dani said, trying to console her.

"I don't know why I'm crying. I'm not usually this emotional," Kallisto explained. "Maybe I'm just overly tired."

Dani had been observing Kallisto carefully throughout their conversation. She had noted some subtle signs, besides what Casus had already told her. "This may seem like an unusual question, but are your breasts tender or swollen?"

"How do you know that?" Kallisto stammered.

"Because you're displaying signs of being pregnant," Dani replied quietly.

Kallisto looked at her dumbfounded. She just stared at her, speechless, for what seemed like an eternity. "Are you okay?" Dani asked, as she reached over for Kallisto's hand.

"I . . . I think so." Kallisto was doing a quick calculation in her head, praying that her results were right.

"I can give you a few easy remedies for morning sickness; your vomiting," Dani clarified, not knowing whether the term was even used in this time period.

"That would be great, thank you. And thank you for letting me know about Casus; I was really worried," Kallisto said warmly.

"My pleasure," Dani replied. At that moment, there was another tremor. This one seemed more pronounced than the others Dani had experienced.

"I hate these," Kallisto said a few seconds later, when the tremor had subsided.

"I think the tremors are a warning," Dani said bluntly.

"A warning for what?" Kallisto asked, her curiosity piqued.

"My family is originally from Sicily. My ancestors went through the eruption of Mount Aetna. Since then, my family has made sure that each generation knows how to read the warning signs, so we can leave the area in case it erupts again," Dani explained.

"Are you saying that Vesuvius is going to erupt?" Kallisto asked nervously.

"The signs would indicate so," Dani said, as seriously as she could. "I would prepare to leave and maybe spread the word to others as well. It's not safe to stay here."

Dani looked at Kallisto and instantly saw her face turn extremely pale. *Maybe I said too much,* Dani thought.

70

"HERE, I BROUGHT you some broth. See if you can drink a bit," Daric said. Casus started to sit up, but was clearly still in pain; with Daric's help, he managed to get upright. After several seconds, the pain had subsided, and he held out his hand and took the mug of broth from Daric. Meanwhile, Bear, who had arrived close behind Daric wandered around and thoroughly sniffed out the small room. She soon lay down in a corner where the heat was slightly less oppressive.

"That's good. Thanks. I didn't realize how hungry I was," Casus remarked, quickly draining the mug's contents. He handed the empty mug back to Daric.

"Well, I'm not surprised; you have eaten nothing in over a day. I'll get you some more," Daric said, as he stood up to leave.

"What? How long have I been here?" Casus asked anxiously.

"We found you yesterday morning. I would hazard a guess that you were attacked the previous night or very early that same morning," Daric explained. "And you slept all day yesterday."

"By the gods!" Casus moaned.

"Can you remember what happened?" Daric probed, wanting to help this man.

"Let's see. I left the Basilica . . ."

"What were you doing there?" Daric interrupted. He was curious to know the purpose of that particular institution.

"I went to talk to Tiberius Crassus Firmus, the duumvir, to ask for help getting my money back from Primus, the bastard. But when I arrived, the two of them were talking. I shouldn't have been surprised; Primus owns most of this town and the people who run it," Casus replied.

Daric remembered the story Cilo had told them about Casus sending his army wages to his family, only to find out they had died eight years earlier and that their owner had pocketed the money. Finally, Daric understood; it had been Primus who had owned Casus's mother and sister and who had kept Casus's money. Daric was developing an impression of Primus and it wasn't favourable. "Okay, so you said you left the Basilica; then what?"

"I don't know. I just wandered around lost in my own thoughts. I had plans for that money. But when I saw Primus and Firmus talking, my plans were completely destroyed."

"What plans?"

"I was going to use that money to buy Kallisto's freedom. Then I was going to ask her to marry me and, hopefully, we'd start a family someday," Casus explained. "A man without sons is a man without a future, my father always said. But none of that will happen, now. I even lost all the money I won at dice, which would have bought Kallisto's freedom, too. The gods know I've made a few mistakes; maybe they're punishing me."

"Back up a minute. Dice? You said you were wandering the streets. Where did you play dice?" Daric asked, trying to piece together Casus's day.

"I ended up in the west side of town," Casus recalled. "I was going back to Alcimus's to check on Kallisto and it was dark. I hadn't realized how late it was. I heard a ruckus in a nearby tavern and went in to investigate and grab a bite to eat. I remember a tremor hit as I reached for my wine."

Daric felt he was making progress. He now knew that Casus had been in the west end. And that Casus had been there about the same time as Daric had been eating at a shop attached to Julia's public baths and the girls had been at the dinner party. They had all felt the tremor.

"When I finished my meal, I walked over to see what all the noise was about. There were three men, two older, one younger, sitting at a table, in the back, playing dice. I joined them," Casus explained. He paused for a moment, grinning. "I won big. It was my lucky night."

"Not so lucky, I would say," Daric corrected. "So, let me guess: you collected your winnings and left and that was the last thing you can remember."

"You were there?" Casus asked angrily, his voice raised.

"No!" Daric replied firmly, but displaying an element of concern.

"Grrrr," Bear growled at the alarmed tone in Daric's voice. She jumped to her feet and rushed to his side. She took an aggressive stance and snarled menacingly at Casus.

"It's okay, Bear." Daric assured her, as he stroked her head. "Look, Casus. It's obvious. The three men you were playing dice with and had won money from didn't take kindly to you leaving the game before they had a chance to recover their losses. So they followed you outside and attacked you, taking back their money and everything of value you possessed."

"You think so?" Casus asked. Daric could see Casus digesting Daric's hypothesis.

"I can almost guarantee it. They were the only ones who knew you were carrying a lot of money. Why else would anyone attack a soldier carrying weapons unless there was a lot at stake?" Daric asked confidently, still stroking Bear's head as she rested by his feet. Bear had placed herself between him and Casus. "Do you know who these three men were?"

"Yeah, I know them," Casus growled, startling Bear. He didn't know their names, but he knew them by reputation: the enforcers. And he also knew they worked for Primus.

"Well, when you're up to it, we'll pay them a visit and get your belongings back. What do you say?" Daric suggested.

"I say, let's do it," Casus responded. He was about to get up when Daric gently pushed against his shoulder.

"Whoa, not so fast. You need more time to build up your strength before we go rushing off," Daric stated bluntly. "Let me go to the kitchen and get you some more broth. Or do you think you can eat something a bit more substantial?"

"I'm so hungry I could eat a boar," Casus claimed, as his stomach rumbled.

Daric headed to the kitchen to see what he could scrounge for Casus. Before he reached the doorway, the floor under his feet started to shake. He grabbed hold of the doorframe to steady himself. The trembling lasted only a few seconds, but Daric thought this tremor was more severe than any he had experienced so far.

"I hate when that happens," Casus mumbled uneasily.

"It's a warning," Daric stated soberly. "You know that mountain out there? Well, it's going to blow its top any day now."

"How do you know that?" Casus questioned warily.

"My ancestors experienced the eruption of Mount Aetna in Sicily over two hundred years ago and they passed down the warning signs through my family. These tremors are just the start," Daric warned. "Have you noticed how dry the riverbeds are?"

"Sure; that's because we haven't had any rain in weeks," Casus reasoned.

"Maybe, but it's one of the signs I'd heard about. I'm just saying that now would be a good time to take a little trip, is all."

71

PRIMUS THREW OPEN the large door and stormed down the long central aisle. He pushed past the group gathered around the dais and placed himself directly in front of Tiberius Crassus Firmus. "The three-hundred-six fence poles were delivered yesterday, before the end of day, to Marcus Nonius Primigenius, as you requested," Primus snorted. He couldn't bring himself to say ordered, because, in his world, he was the one giving orders, not taking them.

"Pardon me," Firmus apologized to the gathered crowd before addressing Primus. "Thank you," Firmus said to Primus, who started back up the aisle. "But I will see you here again tomorrow morning. We have a matter to discuss."

Primus stopped abruptly. He turned his head and gave Firmus a glacial stare which was totally lost on Firmus because he had already turned back to the business he was addressing before he had been so rudely interrupted.

"Just so I understand," Firmus resumed. "Petronia Justa, you claim that Petronius Stephanus owned your mother, Petronia Vitalis, and that you are his illegitimate daughter. The issue you bring before this court, however, is whether you were born a slave or you were born free, not whether you were legitimate or illegitimate."

"That is correct," Justa replied. "My mother was granted manumission prior to my birth. In other words, she was a freedwoman, making me free as well.

"That's not true," Calatoria Themis interrupted. "Vitalis was still my husband's slave when Justa was born, so that makes Justa a slave, too."

"I'm not a slave!" Justa asserted, her voice raised.

"Unfortunately, both Petronius Stephanus and Petronia Vitalis are no longer in this realm and can't provide clarification in this matter," Firmus said miserably.

"Justa, have you brought witnesses who can support your claim of being a free born woman?" Firmus asked.

"I have," Justa asserted. "I've brought members of Stephanus's household. And I've also brought some neighbors."

"Then, let's proceed. Present your first witness," Firmus instructed.

Primus's eyes narrowed as his anger grew. He had hoped to catch Firmus's attention and convey his displeasure, but Primus was being purposely ignored, irritating him further. Primus continued up the aisle and left the Basilica; he had other business to attend to today.

Ferox was leading the way. He couldn't hide his grin, so it was better he go ahead of Primus. It wasn't often that someone got under Primus's skin and Ferox was rather enjoying it.

72

PRIMUS DIDN'T HAVE far to go. He only had to cross via Jupitinius. Ferox stepped aside so Primus could open the front door of the Curia.

Primus yanked the door open and received a blast of angry voices, each shouting over the other, hoping to be heard. He walked down the narrow corridor and into the main hall. It was packed with people. Primus signalled to Ferox to plow through so that Primus could get closer to the front. He wanted to add his grievance to the rest of these disgruntled citizens. His standing in the town might be just enough for the aediles to take immediate action.

Ferox pushed several people out of the way, often receiving a steely glare or an indignant 'Hey!' in protest. But, as soon as the people saw Primus behind Ferox and realized who was being so assertive, their objections abruptly ended.

"What was she thinking, prancing through town half dressed?" one citizen shouted.

"I had to cover my son's eyes for fear her nudity might blind him," another announced.

"It was shameful, an utter disgrace, to walk about town dressed like that," a woman said.

"To parade through town with hardly anything on; it's not

right," another complained.

Marcus Rufellius Robia and Aulua Tetteius Severus had been listening to these complaints for an hour. As aediles, they were responsible for keeping the water flowing and the streets clean. They took care of the town's public buildings, the issuance of business licenses and the sponsoring of the town's events, like the Vulcanalia tomorrow night. It was the duumviri who were responsible for handling local squabbles, for keeping the peace. As a result, Robia and Severus were puzzled why all these people were here, in front of them, and not in front of the duumviri at the Basilica. Even if, as aediles, they could address the complaints being so loudly expressed, there wasn't much they could do: no one could identify the brazen young woman whom everyone was criticizing.

The crowd suddenly parted. Robia instantly recognized Ferox. Moments later, Primus emerged from the crowd.

"Primus, thank the gods. Maybe you can shed some light on all of this," Severus sputtered. "Why are these people here and not at the Basilica where they should be heard?"

"My only guess is that Firmus, in his own arrogant way, has sent them here for you to deal with, because he considers their complaints to be a matter beneath his station," Primus lied. He easily saw the discomfort in the two aediles; handling an angry crowd was definitely outside their area of expertise. He liked what he saw. He was sure he could manipulate the crowd and have it lead the aediles to the decision and outcome he was seeking.

"Well, that's just great. No one even knows who this woman is," Robia grunted.

Primus wanted to make sure his voice was heard above all the other complainants and he wasn't averse to shouting. He faced the crowd. "Citizens of Herculaneum!" he began, holding his arms in the air. He waited a few moments while the noise diminished. Then, he started to grandstand.

"We're all aware of the virtues that every one of us has valued most greatly in a woman for centuries. I'm speaking of her modesty and loyalty. But this woman, who goes by the name of Dani, has broken her sacred vow of modesty. She has brazenly provoked the lustful stares of our fellow men—our husbands, our sons, our nephews—as she defiantly strolled through our town. She has no respect for civility. What kind of example is she setting for our young women, I ask you?"

The crowd erupted in supportive hollers. Primus faced the flustered and increasingly uncomfortable aediles.

"What are we supposed to do?" Severus whispered to Primus, imploring him for his help. Primus grinned devilishly and turned to face the crowd, again.

"The aediles have asked me to bring this woman before you to answer for her indiscretions." The crowd cheered again. "We will have justice!" The crowd went wild. Somewhere from the back, a chant went up: "Primus. Primus. Primus." And it kept growing louder and louder.

Primus looked back once again at the stunned aediles and grinned. His job here was done. Now, on to the next step in his plan. Primus nodded to Ferox, who sliced a path through the chanting crowd.

Present Day—Friday

73

"SORRY, IT SLIPPED." Sandra said, hoping to cover her misstep, which almost caused the cup of hot coffee to land in Bill's lap.

"No problem, I've always had quick reflexes," Bill replied. Pausing for a moment to study Sandra. "Hey, are you all right? You don't look so good."

"Just a bit under the weather," Sandra lied. "I think I pushed myself too hard over the past few days, got a little run down, that's all."

"You need to take better care of yourself, Sandra," Bill said tenderly.

"I know and I will."

"So, is Quinn around?"

"Yes, but he's out in his lab, working as usual," Sandra lied again, choking back a sob that went unnoticed. *Why didn't I tell Bill that Quinn is dead?* she scolded herself. Maybe, because deep down in her heart, she didn't believe it to be true. *Not until I see for myself.* Sandra knew Quinn was very resourceful and, if there were the slightest chance he had survived the cave-in, he would do whatever it took to get out and to get back home. He knew what was at stake—their children.

"I won't disturb him, then," Bill said. "Are the twins back from their dive trip in the Caymans? That's the real reason I came here today, to close that case on the anonymous call the precinct received earlier this week."

Richard spun in his chair and barked, "Hermes, I need you to replicate Dani's voice and place a call to the house. Do it now!"

"What will you have Dani say?"

"I'll tell you what to say. Now, place that call," Richard snapped.

It took only a millisecond for Hermes to place the call.

Sandra's comm rang. "Excuse me for a second, Bill," she said, getting up from the table to have a little privacy as she answered her comm.

"Hi, Mom." Sandra's legs went out from under her.

Bill jumped up and rushed to Sandra's side. "Are you okay?"

"I guess I stood up too fast; got a little light-headed," Sandra replied awkwardly, as she slowly got to her feet and leaned against the kitchen island.

Bill noticed that Sandra's face had gone ghost white. "Sit for a minute." He helped Sandra to the table and guided her onto the padded bench, taking a seat right beside her.

"Oh, wait." Sandra remembered the call. "Hello?" she said tentatively into her comm.

"Hi, Mom." Dani's voice came over the comm once again.

"Dani, is that you? Where are you?" Sandra's voice stammered. Could her children be home, safe and sound? Was it possible?

"We're still at Uncle Richard's island," Dani's voice replied.

Sandra slumped dejectedly. As much as she wanted to believe her children were home, she knew they weren't. The call was a clever deception. She knew the facts. In order to put an end to Bill's questions when he had asked about Dani and Daric's whereabouts, she and Quinn had told him they were at Richard's island in the Caymans, even though Hermes had just recently told them that the twins were in 1692. So, there was no way that Dani, the real Dani, could have known about that ruse. Although Sandra couldn't tell who was behind the call or how they had timed it so perfectly, she smelled a rat. A very clever rat.

"Is that Dani? Can I speak with her?" Bill asked expectantly.

"Honey, I'm here with Bill Brown. He wants to talk to you," Sandra played along, as she moved closer to Bill so he could talk to Dani.

"Hi, Bill," Dani's voice announced, cheerfully.

"Hi, Dani," Bill replied. "How's the diving?"

"Well, that's the reason I called. Daric and I are going to stay until Sunday. The diving has been fantastic. Is that okay, Mom?"

"Sure, Honey. Call me when you land at the airport," Sandra said warily.

"Okay, bye." The connection went dead.

"Well, that closes that case," Bill declared. "I should be getting back. Thanks for the coffee, Sandra. I'll let myself out. You sit here for a bit longer; your color is just starting to return."

Bill kissed Sandra on the top of her head. "You take care of yourself, you hear." Ever since high school and their brief courtship, Bill had always had a soft spot for her.

"I'm feeling much better, Bill, really. Let me walk you out; the fresh air will do me good," Sandra insisted, as she got to her feet and made her way to the kitchen door.

"If you're sure?" Bill questioned one last time, as he walked toward the door.

"I'm the doctor, remember?" Sandra bantered, following him out of the kitchen.

"And a fine one at that," Bill observed, smiling warmly. He was worried about his dear friend. She didn't seem to be herself. Maybe there was a bug going around.

* * *

"Damn!" Richard grunted. "I can't hear a thing, now." He had to think of something, quickly. His eyes remained fixated on the surveillance camera's monitor.

74

SANDRA HAD ACCOMPANIED Bill out to his black, unmarked police SUV, when something caught Bills' eye, something that seemed out of place. He looked up and pointed. "Sandra, why did Quinn install a surveillance camera up there?"

Sandra paled again at the mention of Quinn's name, but she quickly composed herself. She looked at the garage roof and was shocked and surprised by what she saw, but her expression never changed, like that of a seasoned poker player. "He wants to keep an eye on the house when he's working in his lab, in case anyone comes calling." She was a bit concerned at how easily the lie had rolled off her tongue.

"Not a bad idea. Why don't you go back inside and rest for a while? It'll do you good."

"I will. And thanks for dropping by, Bill; give my love to Amy," Sandra mumbled.

"I'll touch base with you in a couple of days, maybe get you guys over for a barbeque," Bill said, as he climbed into the SUV and started the engine.

"Sounds great." Bill closed the door, waved, and drove down the tree-lined driveway.

Sandra stared at the camera mounted on the garage roof. It was pointed directly at the house.

"Shit, she's seen the camera," Richard cursed. "I'll be back shortly. Keep working,"

Sandra walked back into the house, trying to figure out how the camera had mysteriously appeared on her roof. Dani and Daric certainly hadn't put it there; they were lost God knows where or when in the past. Nor had Quinn put it there; he had been gone since Tuesday morning. And she knew it wasn't there during the past two days; if it had been, she would have noticed it when she had come home from work. So, it must have been installed recently. But by whom? The only other visitor she had had at the house was yesterday and that was Richard. His name suddenly left a sour taste in her mouth. *But why would he do that?* she wondered.

Herculaneum—August 22, 79 AD

75

A FEW HOURS later, Daric entered Casus's room to relieve Nneka. Casus was awake and sitting on the edge of the bed.

"Well, you look much better," Daric said pleasantly. He nodded at Nneka, who left the room to attend to her other duties. "How do you feel?"

"Besides an unbearable headache, not bad. I've had much worse," Casus replied.

"Are you up for a little walk?" Daric asked, wondering just how strong Casus might be.

"Actually, I'm up for a little justice," Casus grunted, as he stood up. He retrieved his brown leather jerkin off the chest and proceeded to dress himself before Daric interrupted him.

"Hang on a second. Let me bind those ribs; you'll find it a little more comfortable," Daric suggested. "I'll be right back."

Daric ran across the courtyard and up the back stairs, into his room. He located the cloak he had received from Manco Inca and tore long strips off it. He had already ripped it earlier, so it wasn't in any shape to wear out in public. And the strips of cloth would be long enough to wrap around Casus's frame.

After Daric had wrapped Casus's ribs and Casus had finished dressing, they left Julia's house and headed west. Casus knew exactly where to go. They walked along the main street until they reached via Herculia where they turned right. Directly behind the first shop, there was a wooden staircase. They swiftly ascended.

Casus didn't stop when he reached the top, or bother to knock. He threw open the door and stormed in, with Daric close behind.

"What's the meaning of this?" Tiro demanded, taken aback by the forceful entry.

"I've come to collect what's mine," Casus said, as he approached Publius, who was sitting in a chair. Casus towered over the cringing figure of one of Tiro's enforcers.

"Look, we only wanted our money back," Publius admitted sheepishly.

"You mean the money I won fair and square. And what about my belongings?" Casus asked, as he reached for the scruff of Publius's tunic.

"That was all Rufinus's idea. We didn't want any part of that," Calvus interjected to support his long-time friend. He had known from the start that attacking Casus was a bad idea; they should have just left him alone.

Casus released Publius and turned on Rufinus. He walked to where Rufinus was standing, looking defiant and brazen.

"Explain yourselves!" Tiro demanded irritably. No one was sure where Tiro was directing his question: at his own men or at the two intruders, so Daric responded.

"Your men here assaulted Casus. They acted like a bunch of cowards," Daric spat. "They struck him on the head from behind and then beat him when he was down. They stole everything he possessed, except for what he's wearing. And I'd like to know why someone would want to stab an unconscious man. What's the point?"

"That was Rufinus, too. He wanted to see how sharp the gladius was," Calvus offered.

"You stabbed me with my own sword?" Casus growled.

Rufinus glared coldly at the two cowards; he had thought they were his friends, and that they would have had his back. Evidently he'd been wrong. Then he stared belligerently at Casus as if to challenge him. Rufinus knew Casus wasn't one-hundred percent, and he was confident he could beat the big guy. Rufinus took a step forward and was immediately intercepted by Daric.

"Don't even think about it," Daric threatened. Casus might not be up to the challenge, but Daric was, and he had several inches and pounds on the young Rufinus. Daric knew it wouldn't have been a fair fight, but he was standing by Casus.

"I want my money back, now," Casus barked. "All of it!"

Publius and Calvus quickly handed over their leather pouches, without even bothering to count out their share of the take. Rufinus reluctantly followed their lead. The three of them would be lucky to lose only their purses in the deal.

"Now, where's my gear?" Casus demanded as he scowled at Rufinus.

"It's at my place," Rufinus confessed grudgingly.

"Let's go," Casus ordered. "I'm going to have a few words with your father, as well," Casus added. "Now move," he ordered, giving Rufinus a firm shove toward the door.

"And Tiro, you and your men will be making a visit to the courts soon to answer to assault charges. Good day," Daric announced, as he followed Casus out the door.

"You idiots!" Tiro bellowed at his two remaining men. "Primus will have my hide for this."

76

"NO, A LITTLE higher; that's the spot," Dani said, when Kallisto found the right pressure point. "When you start to feel nauseous or you think you might vomit, just apply pressure there," Dani went on, indicating the point on the palmar side of the wrist, "and the nausea should go away. And the next time Nona goes to the market, get her to pick up some fresh ginger for you. Cut off a piece about the size of your little finger. Then make some weak black tea, add the ginger and a spoonful of honey and let it steep for about five minutes. That should help, too."

"You're very kind. Thank you, Dani," Kallisto said appreciatively. She was feeling much better.

"I had better get back, before they start to worry. Take care and remember the warnings I told you about and do what you can," Dani cautioned. She knew Kallisto couldn't just pack up and leave; as a slave, she didn't have that type of freedom. Dani hoped that Kallisto could convince Alcimus to take his family and slaves on a trip away from the region.

"I will," Kallisto assured her.

Dani walked down the stairs and met with a patiently waiting Tobius. "Okay, we can go back now," Dani told him, as they walked out of Alcimus's tavern. She paused on the street for a moment.

"Can we go a different route this time?" she asked, hoping to see more of the town.

"Domina would not wish it. We must get back, now," Tobius said nervously. They had been gone far too long, and he was anxious to get back. He had spotted two men loitering on the opposite side of the street. He knew these men. "Come."

"Hang on a sec," Dani said, as she walked over to the public fountain on the corner. There were several slaves with large pitchers or jugs, fetching water from the mouth of Neptune. The slaves quickly moved out of her way when she approached the fountain. "No, please. I'll wait my turn."

While Dani waited until they had finished, she looked up the street to the north. She saw Vesuvius looming in the distance. There wasn't a cloud in the sky, but there appeared to be a small one above the mountain's peak. She looked south over the bay where many fishing boats dotted the tranquil sea. A few large ships had their sails furled; there wasn't a breath of wind to be had. She could just make out the splashing white water as the oars struck the glistening surface, slowly propelling the ships forward. They appeared to be heading to mouth of the bay.

When it was her turn, Dani walked to the fountain, cupped her hands and took a drink of water. It wasn't cold, but it was thirst quenching. She repeated the process three more times. It was another blistering hot day.

"Come, please," Tobius said anxiously, heading back the way they had come. They walked along via Neptunia, turning right onto via Jupitinius. All the while, Tobius kept glancing over this right shoulder, watching the two men who were following them. He stepped up his pace, but not enough to cause Dani to question his actions.

Dani and Tobius were just approaching the shrine of Hercules and about to turn left onto the main street when Primus stepped out in front of them, blocking their progress. The two men behind closed the gap and boxed them in.

"Well, hello there. Dani, isn't it?" Primus said caustically.

"Hey!" Dani exclaimed as her arms were seized. "Let go of me!"

"I'm afraid we can't do that. Cause, you're under arrest," Primus informed her.

"For what?"

"For parading through town half-dressed and disturbing the peace," Primus stated coldly.

"Seriously! Do I look half-dressed to you?" Dani retorted.

Primus was soaking in the beauty standing before him: the tall slim physique, the elaborately styled hair with its rare honey blond colour, and her azure eyes burning with anger. He had to admit that she was now dressed more appropriately, displaying her status in this society, one of the more noble and wealthy.

"Not today, my dear. But the day you arrived in our humble little town you caused quite a stir," Primus said deprecatingly. He nodded at Tiro's two men, whom he had commissioned for this little enterprise. He would have preferred to use only Rufinus, but Rufinus hadn't been available, according to Tiro. When Primus had pressed him for details, Tiro had been vague, saying it was a family matter, whatever that meant. So Primus took Tiro's other enforcers.

Publius and Calvus tightened their grip on Dani's arms as they hauled her away. "Wait! Stop!" Dani protested.

"Do you know what they do to people who disturb the peace?" Publius hotly whispered in her ear. "They tie them to a stake and whip them."

"Run along now," Primus instructed Tobius, who had been standing by, helpless to intervene. Tobius took off up the main street, racing back to his mistress.

77

UNBEKNOWNST TO DARIC, Dani had been only one block south when he and Casus had turned the corner onto via Herculia, missing Tobius and Dani by mere seconds as they headed west on their way back to Julia's.

"Are there no patrols or forces in town to prevent crimes?" Daric asked Casus, as they escorted Rufinus along via Herculia to Antigonus's shop, which was just down the street. Casus was eager to finish his business with Rufinus, so he could go see Kallisto. She was only a few doors down from Antigonus.

"That's really my job," Casus replied, as he limped along, the ache in his leg intensifying with every step he took. "In the bigger cities, there would be soldiers assigned to discourage people from committing crimes. Their presence and the rather harsh punishments keep the crime rate down."

"What about the crime against you? How do you handle that?" Daric asked.

"When a crime is committed against a Roman, it's the victim's job to catch the criminal and bring the culprit up before the magistrates to be tried. And I'll do that. The government can't help people catch criminals; they can only help stop crimes from happening."

"They aren't doing a very good job, are they?" Daric scoffed.

"I guess not, especially when you look at Primus and what he's been able to get away with, and right under the noses of the town's officials," Casus grunted.

Rufinus had been silent the whole time. When they approached Antigonus's shop, that's when he started to beg. "I'll bring out your stuff. You don't need to go in; you can wait here."

"I think not," Casus replied coldly.

"Come on, you don't need to bother my father about this. It's all settled. No hard feelings," Rufinus said optimistically.

"Sorry, kid, not this time," Casus said, pushing Rufinus through the shop's entrance.

"Casus, what brings you here?" Antigonus asked nervously, as he noticed another man he didn't recognize enter behind Rufinus. He knew his son had been in trouble before and he sensed that Casus's presence wasn't a good sign.

Casus explained the whole situation to Antigonus; he felt sorry for the old man, having to deal with such a defiant son all on his own. Antigonus promptly ordered Rufinus to give back everything he had stolen.

Rufinus left the room. Soon after, he returned with an armful of things. He deposited them on the shop's counter in front of Casus. Casus went through the pile, item by item. When he was finished, he looked at Antigonus. "Everything's here," he said.

A look of something like relief spilled over Antigonus's face, as if he had been fearing a different, more difficult outcome. He ordered Rufinus to return to his room. Antigonus would deal with him later.

"Good luck," Casus said, as he and Daric walked out of the shop.

"I'm going to check on Kallisto," Casus informed Daric. "She's just at the next corner. Do you think you can find your way back? I know you're new to town."

"Yes, that won't be a problem," Daric assured him. The streets were laid out in a grid. It wouldn't be hard to retrace his steps, especially since they had made only one turn, and that had been down this street.

Casus extended his arm. “Thanks for everything. If I can repay the favour, let me know.”

Daric grasped the proffered arm, remembering his greeting with Cilo. “You’re more than welcome. Remember to check that leg and change the dressing. You don’t want it to get infected.”

“I will,” Casus promised, as he turned south and limped down the street.

Daric pondered for a moment, watching Casus. He realized that this ‘Uncle Richard’ was actually a good guy, for once. He had become a little tired of ‘Uncle Richard’ trying to kill them. Daric turned north and headed up via Herculia, with the mountain on the horizon ahead of him. He hung a left onto the main street. He hoped Julia had had some luck locating the baby’s mother. He was getting nervous and their time was running out.

Present Day—Friday

78

RICHARD LET HIMSELF into the Delaney house through the kitchen door and unobtrusively made his way into the living room. He found Sandra stretched out on the sofa with her arm draped over her eyes. He approached quietly, watching the gentle rise and fall of her chest. He could watch her for hours, but . . .

"Sandra," Richard said in a hushed tone, trying not to startle her. He failed.

She bolted up, glaring at the intruder. "Richard, I'm sorry; I didn't hear you come in."

"I arrived a few hours ago," Richard clarified, as he sat down beside her. "When I didn't see you downstairs, I assumed you were still asleep. I didn't want to disturb you."

"That's very thoughtful of you," Sandra replied, as she leaned back and waited for her heart to stop pounding. When she had composed herself, she turned to face Richard.

"Did you install the surveillance camera?" Sandra asked. It wasn't a question per se, but an accusation.

"Yes, for a couple of reasons," Richard replied. "It was a way for me to help protect you, like I just did with that nosy police chief."

"What do you mean?" Sandra asked suspiciously.

"I could see on a monitor in Quinn's lab he had arrived," Richard explained. But he didn't disclose the whole truth; he wanted to keep an ace up his sleeve. "I remembered that he was coming back here on Friday to talk to the twins. Since we both know that is still impossible, I came up with a plan. I asked Hermes . . ."

"He's back?" Sandra blurted out incredulously.

"Why yes. The friend I told you about was able to eradicate the virus."

"That means you can finish Quinn's work. That means you can bring my children home."

"That's the plan," Richard acknowledged calmly.

"Oh, Richard." Sandra sighed as she threw herself into Richard's arms and held him tight. "I don't know how I'll ever be able to thank you."

Richard held onto Sandra until she pulled back; he was reluctant to release the shapely body he had long dreamt of holding and caressing. Sandra's tear-filled eyes stared warmly into Richard's for a moment. Then Richard leaned in and kissed Sandra, his right hand behind her head, his left hand in the middle of her back. He took the risk. In his delusional mind, he didn't think he would get a better opportunity to let Sandra know that he still loved her. She would be forever grateful to him for bringing her children home. Quinn would soon be a distant memory. He would shower her with jewellery, take her wherever she wanted to go. Fiji. Bora Bora. French Polynesia. The Galapagos. Madagascar. All the places he would love to share with her, in the best accommodations money could buy and with their own personal staff to attend to their every whim. He could feel her tremble with excitement. Richard, however, had become so lost in his own thoughts about what he and Sandra would have together that he didn't realize that Sandra was squirming to break free.

"Richard, please don't," Sandra stammered, pushing him away. Once freed from his embrace, she sprang from the sofa to put some much-needed distance between the two of them.

"But, I thought," Richard said uncomfortably.

"Richard . . ." Sandra tried to explain, but was quickly cut off.

"Maybe you just need some more time," he suggested hopefully. "I can wait."

Their eyes met and held. She couldn't help but notice how dark and distant Richard's eyes looked, not like Quinn's, warm and captivating. And Richard's raspy voice was in stark contrast to Quinn's deep and soothing. As for personality, Richard's was aloof and self-centered, so different from Quinn's quiet and charming with just the right touch of playfulness she had fallen in love with so many years ago. She had often invited Richard to family functions, but only because of his friendship with Quinn. The two men, she knew, were completely different, like night is to day. There had never been a choice for her. There never would be.

"Richard, I fell in love once and there will only ever be one man in my life. I could never love another," Sandra said softly.

Sandra could see Richard was about to interject, so she quickly added, "I know you said he was dead, but I'm having a hard time accepting that right now."

Richard looked at Sandra. She suddenly lowered her eyes; she couldn't meet his gaze. His face reddened, not from embarrassment, but from rage and anger. His eyes were cold and hard. He got up from the sofa and stormed out of the house. He didn't take rejection well. He had always got whatever he desired even if he had had to use whatever means were at his disposal. But this was different. This wasn't just a rejection; this was a failure in his mind. And he vowed he would never allow failure to be associated with the name Case ever again!

"She should have been mine," Richard seethed, as he made his way back to the gazebo. "She would have been better off with me. And she would have been with me if Quinn hadn't entered the picture. I'm glad he's dead!"

Although he was still furious, Richard realized, sadly, that Sandra would never love him, not the way he desired, not the way she looked at Quinn; not with the warmth and light that filled her very soul whenever Quinn was near. Richard had seen it—the look, the warmth, the light—a million times, and he knew it would never be directed at him.

"So be it," Richard growled. "Soon, I'll be able to traverse the boundaries of time. I'll have my choice of exotic women throughout history. Who knows, maybe a wife from the future could prove to be exciting. And why be limited to one?"

Richard picked up his pace toward the gazebo. He accepted, however reluctantly, that Sandra would never be his. Now, he would have to change his plans.

Herculaneum—August 22, 79 AD

79

BEFORE PRIMUS RETURNED to the house to prepare for his daily visit to the baths, Aquilina and Cominia Prima took the opportunity to leave, with Nais.

"Again, I'm so sorry for what you've had to endure," said Aquilina, offering her apology to Nais once again.

"At least you're away from that monster, now," Cominia spat, still furious with her father. Not only had he assaulted Nais, he had spurned his own wife of twenty-two years.

"Where are we going?" Nais asked nervously, uncertain of what the two ladies wanted with her. She didn't believe that they wanted to do her harm; after all, they had kept her isolated from Primus all night.

"We're taking you back to where you belong," Aquilina said softly.

* * *

Fuscus and Julia were sitting in the small colonnaded garden. The elegant fountain feature in the middle was providing a pleasant cooling effect on such a scorching day.

"Yes, I have an Egyptian slave; her name is Nais. Or maybe I should say; Primus has her," Fuscus explained bitterly to Julia. "Primus's daughter, Cominia Prima, came by to see me late yesterday," he continued. "She told me that Primus had repeatedly forced himself on Nais and that she had just recently given birth."

"That's it," Julia said excitedly. "Nais has to be the baby's mother; it's just too much of a coincidence."

"Well, of course . . ."

"No, no, you don't understand," Julia interrupted. "I have a baby at my place. Two people found her abandoned outside town, in the cemetery."

"That would be my child," Nais confessed quietly. She, along with Aquilina and Cominia Prima had been let into the house and shown to the garden by the porter.

"Nais," Fuscus shouted, as he quickly got up and walked over to embrace her. "I'm so sorry. I never meant for any of this to happen."

"It's no one's fault but my husband's," Aquilina acknowledged sadly. "Once we found out what had been going on, we kept Nais with us; today was the first opportunity we had to return her to her rightful owner."

"Thank you," Fuscus said gratefully.

"My baby?" Nais asked Julia, her voice conveying a mixture of fear and hope.

"She's fine. She's being well cared for, but I'm sure she'll be a lot happier when she's reunited with you," Julia said warmly.

"Forgive me; I didn't see I had any other choice," Nais confessed despondently.

"Forgiveness is something you must give to yourself," Julia pronounced. "I'll have the baby brought to you as soon as possible. You take good care of her and yourself."

"I . . ."

"We will," Fuscus interjected.

80

THEY DRAGGED DANI through the entrance of the Forum and then behind the Temple of Augustus.

"Why are you doing this?" Dani pleaded, as she continued to struggle with the vise-like grip that held her so securely.

Publius unlocked a door while Calvus continued to battle Dani's protesting resistance. *She's a feisty one, I'll give her that,* Calvus thought.

When the door opened, it revealed a small barren room. Publius and Calvus dragged their unwilling prisoner toward the back where a set of shackles was bolted to the rear wall.

"Look, this really isn't necessary. I'm sure I can straighten out this misunderstanding," Dani persisted, remaining as calm as she could. "As you can see, I've adapted to your ways. I didn't know any better when I arrived. I'm not trying to cause any trouble. Please, believe me," Dani begged. She continued to resist as best she could, but they easily overpowered her.

"I can see that," Primus said callously, as he walked into the small dark room, with Ferox remaining in the entranceway. "But the damage has been done. The town folk want justice."

"What are you going to do?" Dani asked nervously.

"Well, my dear, that all depends on you," Primus grinned

malevolently.

Publius and Calvus strapped the shackles around Dani's wrists and locked them. They handed the key to Primus and left, leaving Dani alone in the room with Primus.

Primus held the key up in front of his face, slowly turning it around, taunting Dani.

"What do you want?" Dani demanded bluntly.

"It seems to me that you possess a great deal of wealth . . ." Primus stated, before he was quickly interrupted.

"So, that's what this is all about: money!" Dani barked. "You have no intention of bringing me in front of the magistrates. This is for ransom; that's all this is. Fine, if that's what you want, then let me go and I'll give you what I have."

"My, aren't we easily swayed? Too easily, I'd say. I've got to believe that you have more wealth than what you've brought here," Primus responded.

"Don't be ridiculous. Where would I have more?" Dani snapped.

"You tell me? What about that man with you? How wealthy is he? And is he willing to buy your freedom?" Primus probed.

"He's my brother and I'm offering you all we have. Just let me go and I'll take you to it," Dani implored.

"Let me think about this. You seem much too eager to part with your wealth. I need to understand why, because, frankly, it doesn't make any sense to me, unless, as I said, you have more elsewhere," Primus reasoned aloud. "But first, let me relieve you of that little trinket."

"No!" Dani yelled as she tried to pull away from Primus's reach; the shackles made her range of movement very limited. *Think quick.* "It won't come off," Dani lied. "It was a gift from the Greek god, Hephaestus, crafted by his own hands from his forge beneath Mount Aetna. See the 'H'? You wouldn't want to anger the god of fire, now would you?"

Primus most certainly didn't want to anger the god of fire, especially not for the piece of jewelry Dani was wearing. He considered it to be nothing more than an everyday bobble. He figured she had others that were worth just as much or more, maybe much more. Primus turned and walked out of the room.

"Wait! Please! You can't leave me here! I'll give you my fortune, just don't leave me here!" Dani shouted. Her voice, however, was drowned out by the slamming of the door.

Ferox had left the cell with Primus; it was his job to accompany Primus back to the Primus's house. The two men walked in silence, with Ferox thinking about what he had just witnessed. Holding an innocent woman hostage didn't sit well with him, but what could he do? Furthermore, it appeared that the gods had favored her, and Ferox had no desire to do anything that might anger the gods, any god. He was still deep in thought when he and Primus reached their destination. He would wait until he was called upon again.

Dani was terrified. She was locked in a dark room, somewhere in Herculaneum and Daric had no idea she was even missing. And in two days, Mount Vesuvius would erupt. They were running out of time.

81

"HEY, JULIA! WE got Casus's belongings back," Daric shouted cheerfully, as he entered Julia's house.

"Eeeheeeheee," Bear screamed, as she ran to greet Daric. It was a loud, high-pitched scream that Shiba Inus were known for.

"Yeah, I missed you, too, Bear," Daric said, as he gave her a big hug. "Were you being a good girl?" he asked, as he scratched behind her ears. She was obviously enjoying the attention.

"Daric! Dani's been taken!" Julia shouted, running along the corridor.

"What? Where? When?" Daric fired back.

"I don't know. Tobius escorted Dani to Alcimus's tavern to see Kallisto, and, on their way back, they were being followed. It wasn't until they were near the Forum that she was grabbed and hauled away."

"Who grabbed her?" Daric demanded.

"Primus and two of his buffoons," Julia snorted.

"I'm going after her! We're running out of time." Daric spun around to leave.

"Daric, wait! Where are you going? You have no idea where to start looking and neither do I. We can't just confront Primus and demand he tell us where she is; that will get us nowhere. He's too powerful in this town for us to go up against head on," Julia pointed out grimly.

"I have to find her. We're running out of time," Daric said, on the verge of unraveling.

"You mentioned you're running out of time, twice. What's going on, Daric?" Julia could see panic in Daric's face.

"Our family was originally from Sicily and experienced the eruption of Mount Aetna. We've learned to read the warning signs when we see them," Daric explained, pulling himself back together. He had to keep a level head. "Those tremors we've been having, they're the precursor to an eruption. And it could happen any day now. Once I find Dani, we're getting as far away from here as possible, and I suggest you get packed and take your people away from here, too." All the time he had been speaking, he had been reprimanding himself for not telling her sooner, after all she had done for them.

"You can't be serious?" Julia asked, horrified. *Vesuvius erupting. Is that even possible? It's been dormant for over 1500 years. Why now?*

"I'm deadly serious," Daric assured her.

"Okay, let's say you're right. If Primus has Dani, then he must want something, but, until we can figure out what that is, our hands are tied," Julia observed. "But I have an idea."

While Julia and Daric had been talking, Tobius had walked into the atrium, his head hung low, blaming himself for Dani's abduction. "Domina, I am sorry I have failed you."

"Tobius, like I told you earlier, you couldn't have done anything. The best thing you could have done was to come right back here and report what had happened. And you did that," Julia said hurriedly. She wanted to get back to outlining her plan to Daric.

"Daric, you've crossed paths with Primus only once and you were dressed in one of my slave's tunics," Julia recalled.

"Yeah, so?" Daric replied hesitantly.

"Primus doesn't know who you are. Every day around this time, Primus goes to the baths, like most of the town's male population.

That's where they all catch up on the news, make business deals, and talk politics. If we want to know what's happening around town, that's where we have to be. Primus prefers the Central Baths, because that's where the more noble male population bathe, and it's closer to where he lives."

"I wish to help," Tobius said, as forcefully as he could. Tobius was well-aware that, as a slave, he had to be careful about what he said and how he said it; he couldn't afford to violate the parameters applicable to people in his station in society.

"So, let me get this straight: you're telling me to go have a bath?" Daric asked disbelievingly. He was astonished by Julia's seeming lack of urgency about recovering Dani and, even more, about getting away from Vesuvius. He had hoped that his remarks about Vesuvius would have prompted serious concern and swift action.

"Yes," Julia affirmed. "You must take Cyrus with you. All respectable citizens take their personal slaves to the baths to attend them. The fact that you're only taking one can be easily explained, since you've just arrived in town."

Julia turned toward Tobius. He hadn't moved. He looked hurt. "I'm sorry, Tobius, but your presence would only raise Primus's suspicions. You can replace Cyrus, until he returns," she added, almost as an afterthought. Her words made Tobius feel better as he headed off to tell Cyrus to report to Julia.

"The baths?" Daric asked quietly. He was hoping to bring Julia's attention back to her idea that he needed to go the baths. He was also hoping that his voice hadn't revealed his skepticism about her idea.

"If you get there before Primus, try to blend in, look inconspicuous," Julia instructed. "Then when he arrives, casually make your way closer so you can eavesdrop on his conversation. If I know him, and I do know him for the arrogant idiot he is, he'll want to share his entire day with his supporters."

"You're sure this is the only way?"

"It's the only way to get the information we need. And the quickest way, too. I'll meet you back here and, then, we'll figure out our next move," Julia said confidently.

"Okay, let's do it," Daric agreed, before turning and making his way out of the atrium. He still had misgivings about Julia's plan, but it was the only one they had and he was prepared to give it his best shot. He would keep his fingers crossed and hope it worked.

Julia lingered in the atrium for a few minutes, identifying and prioritizing what she had to do while Daric was at the baths. For starters, she would deliver the baby to her rightful mother. Then, she would share the latest news, about Vesuvius's possible eruption, with Fuscus and his people. And, finally, she would see about pulling her prized possessions together. She had lots to do and not a lot of time to do it.

82

DARIC, DRESSED IN a simple white toga, was being escorted to the Central Baths by Cyrus, who was carrying all the necessary bath equipment.

As they neared the baths, Cyrus explained to Daric that the Central Baths were divided into men's and women's baths, each with separate entrances. With the men's baths, there were two entrances: one off via Veneria and the other off via Jupitinius. Daric and Cyrus used the via Jupitinius to enter the bathing complex.

Both entrances opened onto a spacious recreational area, surrounded by covered porticoes. In the central portion of the area, Daric noted four young men playing catch with something that resembled a heavy medicine ball; another three were exercising using a set of weights. Clusters of older men sat on benches playing board games, some in heated discussions, some playing dice, and some simply relaxing or reading. Among them wandered vendors offering drinks and snacks.

The actual men's baths were entered directly off the northwest corner of the recreational area. Cyrus turned to his left, gesturing for Daric to follow. They walked past the latrine with its shiny marble seats and through a long narrow room lit by a small window. At the end of the room was a doorkeeper sitting at a small table.

Cyrus paid him the requisite small fee and ushered Daric into the first room, the apodyterium, or change room.

The change room's vaulted ceiling was decorated with stucco. The floor was paved with irregular fragments of stone or marble chips, inserted into the beaten earth floor. On the north wall, a small arched recess contained a marble water basin, with alternating streaks of green and white. The basin was for patrons to wash themselves prior to entering the inner rooms of the baths. Running along the walls was a shelf with divided stalls or slots for the bathers' clothing.

Cyrus placed the bathing equipment on one of the shelves and helped Daric undress. Cyrus explained to Daric that he was to use the basin to remove any surface dirt. Once Daric had finished, Cyrus handed him a loose robe supplied by the baths. Then he led Daric toward the next room on their right.

"Wait, what's in there?" Daric asked, as he poked his head through another doorway.

"That's the frigidarium, the last stop in the baths," Cyrus informed him. "A plunge in the cold pool closes the pores. We'll be back here later."

The entrance to the frigidarium was on the west wall of the change room. The circular cold room had a domed ceiling and was accessed from a small lobby. Directly from the entrance, two steps led down to the plunge pool. The circular pool was painted blue-green. The dome was pale blue and was decorated with fish and other marine animals.

"We must hurry," Cyrus announced, as he directed Daric into the room on their right.

The tepidarium was forty feet long by twenty feet wide. The vaulted stucco ceiling was adorned with coffering and medallions portraying subjects relating to the gods and mythology. The floor had a fine mosaic, depicting a triton surrounded by dolphins. The room was lit by a window at the top of the south wall. On all four sides, there were benches above which were stalls for bathers' clothing and bathing supplies, such as oils and utensils. The room was heated by hot air beneath the floor and in ducts in the walls. The room was considered the vapor-bath where bathers could clean their pores through sweating, like a sauna.

Cyrus removed Daric's robe, placed it in one stall, and began the cleaning process. He started by opening a flask and rubbing olive oil over Daric's toned body. Then Cyrus unfastened a curved strigil from the metal handle holding the assorted bathing equipment and proceeded to scrape oil, sweat and dirt from Daric's skin.

Daric wasn't sure what to make of the whole cleaning process. He preferred the privacy of his own shower and a good bar of soap. But then again, when in Rome . . . or more specifically Herculaneum, he figured it would be best to just go with the flow. So, he stood with his arms held out from his sides as Cyrus ran different sizes of strigils over the different parts of his body. Meanwhile, Daric checked out the other patrons in the tepidarium. Five men were all in various stages of receiving the same treatment from their attendants. There was a sixth man lying on one bench, where his attendant appeared to be using tweezers to pluck the hair from the man's body, causing him to twitch from time to time. And so far there was no sign of Primus. *Sure hope Julia is right or this could all end up being a huge waste of time,* Daric thought.

When Cyrus had scraped Daric's body thoroughly, he retrieved the robe from its stall and draped it over Daric's shoulders. He gathered up the bathing equipment and led Daric toward a small door near the center of the east wall. They passed through the door into the caldarium.

The caldarium, or hot room, measured forty-one feet by twenty-one feet and was lit by a window on its southern side above a recess. The recess was decorated with stucco and contained a water basin. On the opposite side, a large rectangular tank was raised on two steps and filled with hot water. It had a bench seat allowing a dozen bathers to sit in the heated water.

Cyrus again removed Daric's robe and nodded to the large tank. Daric walked up the two steps, sat on the edge, and swung his legs around. *Damn that's hot,* he realized as soon as his feet touched the water. He gradually eased himself into the tank. A satisfied moan escaped his lips unexpectedly. The four bathers already in the tank were watching him discreetly.

"I haven't seen you around here before," one of them said. Daric felt as though the man was sizing him up. He was right.

"I've just arrived in town," Daric replied, keeping his conversation friendly but limited. He closed his eyes and rested his head on the edge of the tank. Before long, he could hear the other bathers stirring and eventually leaving the tank and, then, the caldarium.

Soon afterwards there was a commotion in the otherwise quiet room. Daric slowly tilted his head and pried open one eye. He saw three men enter with their accompanying slaves. One slave stood out among the others. He was walking in front of a distinguished looking man, whom the other two seemed to be following.

Daric glanced at Cyrus who nodded confirming Daric's assumption. After all, Daric had only seen Primus once before.

Daric slowly laid his head back on the edge of the tank and closed his eyes, displaying a totally relaxed posture. He listened carefully. He heard them enter the water. He pried one eye open, just enough to see the newcomers clustered together. He closed it again, quickly. Daric turned his head slightly to the side to help conceal his face. He had met one on the men earlier today and wanted to remain inconspicuous. Thankfully, they appeared to be unaware of or indifferent to his presence.

83

"WHAT WERE YOU thinking, Tiro?" Primus growled in a low voice. "I told you I never, under any circumstances, wanted you to accept that loan repayment from Fuscus. I intended on keeping his slave, and now that she's had a child, I'll keep it, too, after I have someone find it."

"He had no choice, Primus. Fuscus brought me along to be his witness," Robia said.

"By Pollux," Primus swore, disappointed that he would finally be forced to give up his sex slave.

"I have some other news you best hear from me," Tiro started reluctantly.

"Go on," Primus grunted. "How could this day get any worse?"

"My enforcers roughed up Ennychus as you ordered, but they also trashed his place and stole his money."

"What?" Primus barked, a little louder this time.

Robia quickly glanced at the other bather. He showed no sign of having heard Primus's outburst. *Must be sleeping,* he thought.

"I didn't tell them to do that," Tiro replied, obviously trying to shift the blame to others. "I told them specifically to rough him up, that's all. That young Rufinus took it too far."

"I think I'll have to have a little talk with that boy, to let him know that he works for me."

"There's more. After they roughed up Ennychus, they went to a tavern and played dice with the loot they had stolen, only to lose it all to that has-been soldier. Then, to make matters worse, Rufinus attacked him and stole the money back, plus his personal belongings."

"What?" Primus exclaimed.

"Casus and another guy showed up at my place. Casus demanded the return of his money and his belongings," Tiro added.

"I wonder if that's what Firmus wants to see me about tomorrow. And you and your goons will probably be brought up on charges." He paused for a minute, before continuing. "I'm sick and tired of having to answer to Firmus. It seems like I'm being told to report to him every day on one thing or another. First, it's the stupid fence poles; next my daughter tells me Fuscus is going to see Firmus about his slave, and now the assault on Ennychus. What's next? Is Casus pressing charges, too? I'm sick and tired of it. I need to make all this disappear."

Primus stood up and climbed out of the tank; Tiro and Robia followed. While putting on their robes, Tiro asked casually, "Publius told me you had him and Calvus snatch a young woman and lock her in the Temple of . . ."

"That goes no further than right here," Primus snapped. "I don't need Firmus sticking his big nose into my dealings. Do you understand?"

Tiro and Robia nodded. "What are you planning on doing with her?" Robia asked.

"It didn't take much to persuade the aediles to let me handle the enraged mob who was easily appeased by a promise that I would arrest her on charges of decadence and immorality. After all, it was I who got the mob all riled up in the first place." Primus stared coldly at Robia, who cowered in embarrassment. Primus knew he had the young aedile right where he wanted him, completely under his control.

"But instead of taking her to court, I'm holding her for ransom.

I plan on making a substantial sum of money," Primus continued, all the while grinning sinisterly. "I'll force her brother to pay a fortune for her release. Severus and his fellow town officials are expecting the money to go into the town's coffers, but they'll be deeply disappointed, when it gets buried in a few of my businesses. Let's call it a fee for services rendered, shall we?" Primus concluded, staring brazenly at Robia before walking out of the room.

Present Day—Friday

84

"IT'S HERMES, RIGHT?" Eddie asked hesitantly. He was determined to learn as much about this fascinating new technology as he could while Richard was gone.

"That is correct," Hermes replied. "And you are?"

"Edward Jonathan Keys. Just call me Eddie."

"That collar you have on; did Mr. Case give you that?" Hermes asked, having his suspicions.

"He snapped it around my neck and I can't find the clasp to remove it," Eddie explained, as his hands roamed over the metal ring, once again in vain.

"I can help you with that. I just have to hook it up to a degausser," Hermes responded.

"A what?"

"A degausser will neutralize the magnetic field by encircling the collar with a conductor carrying electrical currents. Quite simple really; we just have to build it."

"Great, with what?" Eddie groaned, as he scanned the sparse lab.

"You must get the supplies from the garage. I'll give you a list of what we'll need."

"You're not like any computer I've ever seen."

"I am a second generation cognitive computer. I am designed to mimic humans. I learn. I sense. I adapt. I am not programed like other computers; I am much more efficient."

"So I can see," Eddie said in awe. "Why the name Hermes? Is it an acronym for something?"

"No." Hermes smiled at the memory of receiving his name from Quinn. It was a special moment for him, as an artificial intelligence, to be given a proper name like a sentient being. "The professor gave me the name Hermes, after the messenger of the gods, also known as the god of travellers."

"The professor?" Eddie questioned.

"Professor Quinn Delaney. This is his laboratory. Or was." He hung his head, remembering that his creator and companion for over ten years, was now dead.

"Hermes, I'm sorry," Eddie said empathetically, before remembering he was conversing with a machine. Eddie pressed on with his questioning. He was still trying to figure out what Richard was up to. "Can you tell me what you were working on?"

"The professor and I have been working on Einstein's theories. It's taken us years, but we finally did it," Hermes said announced.

"Did what?"

"We proved that time travel is possible, and we created a device to attest to that."

"So, Richard was right!" Eddie exclaimed. "He can bring my parents back!" Part of Eddie had never believed Richard's claim that he could travel back in time and prevent the accident that had killed Eddie's parents. But Eddie had had nothing to lose and everything to gain by believing Richard's claim, so he had agreed to help with his plan, whatever it was. He had never been privy to the plan; he had been given only specific instructions to carry out including one that continued to haunt his sleepless nights. He still had no idea what Richard's overall plan entailed and he no longer cared. He would finally be reunited with his parents, after all these years. He could hardly wait.

"No, he can't," Hermes said bluntly, interrupting Eddie's joyful thoughts of being with his parents again.

"What do you mean? I thought you said time travel was possible?" Eddie stammered.

"Well, first and foremost, the travel devices, or bands, as we call them, are not here. They're in Herculaneum in AD 79," Hermes explained. "And second, time cannot be altered. What has happened in the past will always remain the same; it cannot be changed."

"Why not?"

"Many physicists who have examined the concept of time travel refer to a principle called self-consistency. It states that the only solution to the laws of physics is those that are globally self-consistent. That is, paradoxes can't happen," Hermes recited from his vast knowledge, giving little consideration to a layman's inability to comprehend what he had just said.

"Paradoxes?" Eddie queried, somewhat confused.

"A paradox, according to the dictionary definition, is something that seems self-contradictory or absurd, but in reality, expresses a possible truth," Hermes explained, spewing forth information that was slightly over Eddie's head. Hermes considered Eddie's puzzled expression and offered a simpler explanation.

"A very widely used example of a paradox is a boy who travels back in time and kills his own grandfather. Or there's the other example, which I actually prefer, of a mad scientist who travels back in time and shoots himself in the past before he assembles the gun in the future."

"What's with all the killing?" Eddie wondered aloud.

"These examples illustrate a violation of the fundamental rule that governs the entire universe: namely, that causes happen before effects, not the other way around. The mad scientist cannot shoot himself in the past when the gun he would have used had not been assembled yet. Nor can the boy kill his grandfather, since he—the boy—already exists means that he had failed. Therefore, both instances are logically impossible; in other words, they're nonsense."

"But what about my parents?" Eddie persisted. He was still cautiously optimistic.

"To put it simply, their accident had repercussions. It was a link in a series of events. To change one link would impact the other events in the chain and, therefore, would violate the principle of self-consistency. It can't happen. The past cannot be changed," Hermes concluded, seeing how distraught Eddie was. "I'm sorry, Eddie."

"I knew it sounded impossible, but I was . . ." Eddie stopped and choked back a sob. "The accident happened so long ago I hardly remember what my parents looked like."

"I can help you there," Hermes offered encouragingly.

"How?"

"I pulled a picture of your parents from an old newspaper article. Look at the monitor, Eddie, and watch." Hermes projected the newspaper picture and slowly, before Eddie's eyes, the grainy black-and-white picture turned into a clear, vibrantly colored image.

"That's them!" As Eddie watched the monitor closely, Hermes used an age-progression application to show how Eddie's parents would have gradually aged over the years had they lived. Eddie could hardly believe what he was seeing; his faded memory of his parents was being brought back before his very eyes. He watched, in disbelief, as his parents continued to age, right up to the ages they would have been today. They looked so happy. A tear rolled silently down his cheek.

While Eddie remained fixated by the display on the screen, Hermes was busy executing another task.

Herculaneum—August 22, 79 AD

85

DARIC COULD BARELY control his fury. He wanted to grab Primus by the scruff of his neck and hold his head under water until he told him where Dani was being held. But, as he lay there, listening to the men's conversation, he figured out why one slave stood out from all the others. It was because of his size and his build; he had to be a bodyguard. Daric thought it prudent not to make an aggressive move against Primus right here, right now.

So, he waited for what seemed like an eternity for Primus and his group to leave the baths. When they finally did, Daric quickly dressed and rushed back to Julia's, Cyrus running to keep up with him.

Daric barged into the house. "Julia!" he yelled.

Bear came running when she heard Daric's voice, screaming in joy at his return. She hated being left behind.

"Back here," Julia hollered from deep within the house. Daric followed the direction of her call. He found her in the smaller dining room next to her bedroom. There was a small feast laid out before her. "Come, eat something. You must be . . ."

"Julia, they've got Dani," Daric interrupted. "Primus has her locked in a room under a temple, but I don't know which one."

"At least we now know that Primus is behind this. And the fact that Cyrus also witnessed his confession will work in our favor," Julia said encouragingly, as she gestured for Daric to join her. "What else did you learn?"

"It seems that Firmus, whoever he is, has been rubbing Primus the wrong way." He reached for a shrimp. He had to admit it, he was hungry.

"He's one of the magistrates in town and, unfortunately, the only town official not under Primus's control, not that Primus hasn't tried to persuade him," Julia explained.

"Well, based on what I could hear, Firmus instructed Primus to move some fence poles, don't ask me what that means, because I haven't got a clue. Then this guy Tiro told Primus that his men assaulted Ennychus just as Primus had ordered, but they went too far. And these were the same guys who attacked Casus, the ones Casus and I visited earlier today. Primus was worried Casus might report the attack and robbery to Firmus. Then Primus's own daughter told him she went to Fuscus about a loan and some kind of security deposit and that, as a result, Fuscus is going to talk to Firmus. It got really confusing after that. But I made sure I kept the bit about Dani perfectly clear. And what he wants is our money. He thinks we're filthy rich, and he wants what we have. He's holding her for ransom, plain and simple," Daric growled.

"Okay, we've got some leverage here we can work with, but we'll need Casus's help." She reached for another piece of sea bass.

"You have a plan, don't you?" Daric ventured a guess, as he took a gulp of wine.

"I do and Primus will not like it, which makes it all the better." She handed a small piece of fish to Bear, who had been sitting patiently waiting for some table scraps.

"Tobius, run over to Alcimus's tavern and ask Casus to please join us; we have an errand that requires his help," Julia ordered.

While they waited for Casus to join them, Julia filled Daric in on the events of her day. Her main news was that she had found the baby's mother and that the mother and baby had been reunited.

86

CASUS SHOVED THE door hard, pushing Clitus backwards as the group barged into Primus's house. They didn't have to ask where Primus was; it was dinner time. Julia had been to the house on many occasions and knew exactly where to go.

Just as Julia, Daric and Casus entered the dining room, Primus's chef, using a large kitchen knife, sliced open the belly of the roasted wild boar resting in the middle of the table. Half a dozen live thrushes immediately took flight from the cavity, looking for the closest escape. During the commotion, Ferox had rushed forward to protect Primus from the unannounced intrusion.

"Easy," Casus said, as he placed his hand against Ferox's chest, halting his forward progress. "We're just here to talk." Ferox backed down. He knew Casus and respected the man, regardless of what the rest of the town might think.

"What's the meaning of this?" Primus growled indignantly.

Julia looked apologetically at Aquilina and Cominia for interrupting their meal. She recognized Aquilina's sister, Procilla, and her niece, Gaia, whom Julia had assumed were visiting from Rome. She knew the other diners quite well: the two aediles, Robia and Severus, and the duumvir, Celus. The other duumvir, Firmus, was noticeably absent.

Daric ignored everyone at the table and focused on Primus. "You kidnapped my sister!" he seethed.

"What?" Aquilina flinched.

"I arrested her, as instructed by the aediles; isn't that right, Severus?" Primus replied.

"That's correct," Severus answered obediently.

"You were at the baths earlier today. I remember seeing you in the caldarium," Robia said, recognizing the young man standing before them.

Primus cringed when he recalled what might have been divulged in front of this stranger.

"Yes, I was. And I know you have no intention of turning my sister over to the magistrates. You explicitly stated you are holding her in order to exchange her for money," Daric asserted.

"Primus?" Aquilina interjected uneasily.

"Quiet, woman, this is none of your business," Primus snapped irritably. He looked at the women around the table and saw the loathing in their eyes. *A houseful of angry women for the rest of the summer, great.* But then again, what did he care? It was his business dealings that allowed them to enjoy their current lifestyle and all the fringe benefits that came with it; they had no right to object or complain.

"And what if I am? Are you willing to pay for her release?" Primus taunted.

"How could you?" Cominia spat out in disgust, as she got up and stormed out of the room. Aquilina glared at Primus with an equal measure of contempt and quickly left the room, taking Procilla and Gaia with her.

"We have something much better than money," Daric stated directly. "We know that you ordered Tiro to have his enforcers rough up Ennychus. And we also know that they trashed his house and stole his money."

"I . . ." Primus started to object, prompting Julia to immediately raise her right hand to silence him. Then she continued on from where Daric had been interrupted.

"We also know that those same men assaulted and robbed Casus, here. And, then, there's the matter with Fuscus, where you refused to accept repayment of a loan from him on more than one occasion, just so you could continue to abuse his slave, Nais, whom Fuscus had given you as a security deposit, the slave you specifically demanded. So that's assault, battery, theft and, now you've added abduction and bribery to those charges."

"So you see, Primus, we can play this game, too," Julia scoffed. "You will release Dani or we'll go directly to Firmus with our evidence."

"You have no evidence," Primus snapped.

"But, we do," Julia rebutted.

Primus stared at Julia and the young man with her, trying to gauge whether or not they were bluffing. Julia's hazel eyes were set, her expression firm. The young man was too enraged to be bluffing. Primus judged that they might well have enough information to cause him some serious trouble.

"Fine," Primus relented, for now. He had another idea, which would still let this little ransom deal work to his advantage. "I have to see Firmus first thing in the morning. After that, I'll release her."

"What about right now!" Daric growled, slamming his palms on the table in front of Primus. He leaned in so he was only inches away from Primus's face.

"I said in the morning," Primus replied coldly, looking up from the bracelet he had noticed on the young man's right wrist. It was the same as Dani's, a gift from Hephaestus.

"If she is harmed in any way, I'll . . ." Daric threatened.

"I'll kill him for you," Casus eagerly offered.

Present Day—Thursday NZ

87

UPON ARRIVING AT Jaclynn's orange Volkswagen van, Quinn had used her sat-phone to make a single phone call, a call that would set the wheels in motion to get him back to Sandra. Since that call, Jaclynn had driven like a NASCAR driver to get them from Courthouse Flat to Tapawera. Finally, she brought the van to a stop in front of the auto repair garage that served the small town. After thanking Jaclynn for all her help, Quinn wished her well.

When Jim saw Quinn get out of the van, he ran outside to greet his old pal. "Okay, Quinn, we're all set . . . hey, buddy, are you all right? You look like hell, and what's with the limp?" His excitement quickly turned to concern when he noticed Quinn's bloody and tattered appearance and awkward gait.

Quinn greeted his old friend, retired Lieutenant Colonel James (Jim) Hicks, the same friend he had visited when he and Richard had first arrived in New Zealand. Jim was a few years older than Quinn, with a sinewy physique and a slightly receding hairline. "It's a long story," Quinn replied. He didn't want to get into all the details. "And we're in a hurry."

"Okay," Jim responded. "In that case, everything's been arranged and we're ready to go." The two men climbed into Jim's Chevy truck and sped out of town, leaving a cloud of dust in their wake. Five minutes later, Jim turned off the main road and pulled up beside an old steel hangar. Jim jumped out of the truck, followed closely by a hobbling Quinn.

After unlocking the hangar door, Jim said, "Quinn, give me a hand." Quinn grasped one of the rusted metal handles and slid back the large steel door, while Jim slid back the other. When Quinn looked inside the spacious hangar, he saw a Harrier Jump Jet sitting in the center. "Where in the world did you get that?" Quinn asked as he looked thunderstruck at Jim.

"Just so happens, that at the end of 2010, the Brits announced they were scrapping their Harriers as part of the coalition spending cuts. So, I went to an abandoned military base and, there, in a big hangar, under a single light bulb, this beauty sat. So I bought her."

"But why a Harrier?" Quinn questioned, still trying to get his head around the aircraft in front of him.

"I wanted to preserve a valuable piece of history. Besides, this aircraft is the only subsonic jet capable of vertical short takeoff and landing operations. It took me and a bunch of my buddies thirteen months to refurbish her, but, now, she soars like an eagle," Jim said proudly.

"I guess all your hours of flying as a test pilot for the Marine Corps paid off," Quinn said, as he limped slowly around the beautiful plane.

"It took some doing, but I'm licensed to fly her. So, let's get going, but only after you put this on," Jim said, handing Quinn a flight suit. "You'll look kind of daffy flying in dive gear."

"Yeah, I guess you're right," Quinn responded with a chuckle. He took the flight suit and draped it over the back of an old chair near one side of the hangar. After taking the mineral sample from the utility pocket of his drysuit and placing it on the seat of the chair, he slipped off the lacerated drysuit, folded it roughly, and pitched it into a nearby garbage bin; it had served him well, but was no longer worth keeping. He started to unstrap his dive knife from his right leg, but changed his mind; it was safe and out of sight and might still come in handy. He put on the flight suit and tucked the mineral sample carefully into one of the suit's several pockets. Quinn looked at his two diver computers on his wrists and remembered he didn't have his comm.

"You wouldn't by any chance have a spare comm, would you?" Quinn asked hopefully. "I seem to have misplaced mine." He felt naked without his comm. He hadn't realized how dependent upon it he had become

"Top left-hand drawer of the office desk. Always keep an extra, just in case."

Quinn pulled a vintage-looking comm from the desk drawer and turned it on. He quickly entered his personal code, which instantly transferred all his personal information from his other comm to this one. He tightened the comm around his wrist, thinking of the possibilities if only Hermes were functional. He would be able to call Hermes and see what was happening at home. He might even get a secret message to Sandra. Unfortunately, however, Hermes had been out of commission when he and Richard had left for New Zealand. That was something else Quinn would have to rectify before getting his kids back.

While Jim and Quinn pulled the aircraft out of the hangar and performed the pre-flight routine, Jim cheerfully offered details about Harrier aircraft in general and about his in particular. He explained that single-seater Harriers had originally been designed for air strikes, reconnaissance and fighter roles. His plane, however, was a two-seater that had been built in 1979 as a trainer. Because it was a trainer, it could accommodate a student and an instructor, or a pilot and a passenger, one behind the other, with both cockpits having full flight controls. It was fifty-six feet long, had a wingspan of just over twenty-five feet, and could reach a maximum speed of seven-hundred-thirty-five miles per hour. It was powered by a single Rolls-Royce Pegasus turbofan engine with two intakes and four vectorable nozzles, giving it the ability to take off and land vertically. There were two landing gear on the fuselage and two outrigger landing gear under the wings. The four wing and three fuselage pylons would normally be used for carrying weapons, but, were now being used to carry four very large, three-hundred-thirty-gallon external fuel tanks. The tanks made the aircraft heavy, but would allow it to go a long, long way. The range would be even greater if the winds were with them. And, at the altitude at which Jim and Quinn were likely to be cruising, there would probably be a tail wind for their whole flight.

After completing the pre-flight checks, Jim and Quinn closed the hangar doors and climbed into the Harrier. A few minutes later, Jim had the aircraft moving down the runway where, even with its heavy fuel load, it would have to do a rolling takeoff. Soon it was airborne and Quinn was on his way home.

Quinn reflected on the past few hours. He had known that Jim had a lot of connections, but what Jim had accomplished seemed unimaginable. Quinn had no idea how he had managed to make all the essential arrangements and connections on such short notice, but he had.

Regardless of how Jim had pulled everything together, Quinn was very grateful. He recognized that, without a passport, wallet or a change of clothes, he could never have travelled on a commercial airline. He had only one option. It had to be a private jet with military connections, especially considering where Jim would have to land.

88

ONCE JIM HAD taken the Harrier to a comfortable cruising altitude, he could no longer contain his curiosity; he had to know. “Okay, Quinn, it’s time you answered a few questions; such as, what the hell is going on? Do you know how many strings I had to pull to arrange this little trip? I had to call in every favor I had and then some. So, what gives? Why the rush to get home?” Then it hit him.

“Oh my god, it’s not Sandra or the twins, is it?” Jim asked anxiously.

Despite the noise produced by the aircraft, Quinn had no trouble hearing his friend’s questions; the words were delivered clearly in his helmet through the Harrier’s communication system. But he wasn’t quite sure how to answer. After a brief pause, he said, “Sort of.”

“What the hell is that supposed to mean?”

“It’s kind of a long and somewhat unbelievable story.”

“We’ve got plenty of time. Besides, with all the external fuel we’re carrying, we won’t be stopping for fuel for at least five hours, so spill,” Jim urged.

Jim will never believe this, Quinn thought. He started to tell his old pal his incredible story, beginning with his miraculous invention, followed by his children's journey through time, and ending with the deception of a long-time friend who had left him for dead. During the entire relating of Quinn's tale, Jim uttered not a sound. Except for the sound of Jim's breathing, which came to Quinn through the communication system, Quinn would have thought he was all alone in the Harrier, flying in the azure skies high above the Pacific Ocean.

"Uh, Jim, you still there?" Quinn asked warily.

"Are you pulling my leg? How stupid do you think I am?" Jim asked in disbelief. "I know I live in some small back-water town, but, seriously, time travel?"

Just then, Quinn's borrowed comm went off. He activated it.

"Professor?"

"Hermes, is that you? How is this possible? Are you all right?" Quinn fired his questions in quick succession.

"Professor, I was told you were dead," Hermes moaned sombrely.

Quinn could hear the quiver in Hermes's voice, a clear indication of how the news of Quinn's demise had affected him. The sentiment touched Quinn. "Let's keep it that way for now. Tell no one, not even Sandra," Quinn stated unequivocally.

Jim overheard every piece of the conversation, but waited for a break before he interjected.

"Listen, Hermes. Richard is trying to get the travel bands. We can't let that happen. Do whatever you can to stall him for as long as possible," Quinn instructed his faithful companion. "Jim, what's our ETA?"

"Huh," Jim stammered, caught off guard. He took a moment to check his flight instruments before responding. "We have three more fuel stops. Depending upon how quickly we can get fueled and back in the air, we should be there by Saturday morning."

"How are you travelling, Professor?" Hermes inquired.

"By Harrier Jump Jet," Quinn replied, glancing out the aircraft's domed canopy at the cloudless sky.

"Then, I agree with Jim's calculations," Hermes stated, after having run the numbers himself.

"Gee, thanks," Jim grumbled. "Who the hell is that guy, Quinn?"

"Oh, that's Hermes, my artificial intelligence," Quinn quipped.

"You're what?"

"I'll explain later. Hermes, where are Dani and Daric?"

"They are currently in Herculaneum, August 22, AD 79, to be precise."

"Are they in any immediate danger?" Quinn asked nervously.

"Not at the present time, Professor. But in a few days, they will be," Hermes said.

"How so?"

"On August 24, AD 79, at approximately 1:00 PM, Mount Vesuvius will start erupting."

"Dani will know what to do. As long as they're together, they'll be fine," Quinn stated confidently. "Hermes, complete the calculations to bring Dani and Daric back home. I have the chronizium we need . . ."

"Professor, Mr. Case also has a sample of chronizium," Hermes disclosed.

"Great; all the more reason to stall him. If he gets his hands on those travel bands, Lord knows what will happen," Quinn spat out angrily.

Herculaneum—August 23, 79 AD

89

IT HAD BEEN a long, cold night, in a dark and barren room. With her hands shackled to the wall, Dani had very little movement. She wasn't even able to lie down, not that she wanted to, especially not after having heard the scurry of tiny claws across the stone floor. She noticed that the sky was gradually brightening, and the birds were starting to sing. The only light she had came in through a small east-facing window. A new day was dawning. And Vesuvius was one day closer to erupting.

Dani berated herself all night. She was responsible for putting she and Daric in this predicament in the first place. *Why did I have to pick up that baby? Why couldn't I have just left things well enough alone?* She had been running those questions through her mind over and over and, every time, she had come back with the same answer: *I couldn't live with myself if I'd turned my back on that poor baby.*

However, Dani's immediate concern was Daric. She figured he'd know by now that something was wrong. She also knew how he could behave when he felt helpless, not to mention frightened.

She feared that he would act without thinking and would get them both into more trouble than they already were. She needed Daric to remain level-headed, if she had any hope of getting out of her wretched little cell. Unfortunately, she realized, Daric had no idea where she was and, with little more than a day left, they were running out of time. Dani didn't want to think about the possible repercussions of them not being together when Vesuvius erupted. She remembered the exact time when the mountain blew its top and exactly how long they would have until they would suffer the same fate as everyone else who was left in Herculaneum. She prayed that word was spreading around town and that people were leaving, but from where she was, she had no idea what was happening outside her four stone walls.

Suddenly the floor started to vibrate. Dani clung onto the chains holding her to the wall until the tremor subsided a few moments later. She thought they were getting a little more intense, and she was certain they were lasting longer. She yanked on her chains, hoping the last tremor might have loosened their attachment to the wall, just as she had done after every tremor that had occurred throughout the night. The results were the same: the shackles were securely fastened. She had no other option but to sit and wait, wishing it wouldn't be much longer.

Just then, Dani heard the lock turn, and the door swung open.

90

"YOU'RE AWAKE," CASUS remarked, as he bent and kissed Kallisto, who was still lying in bed.

"And just where have you been so early this morning?" she asked warily, as she sat up. It wasn't like Casus to be up before dawn. He was definitely not a morning person, especially since he was usually up half the night gambling or carrying out some business for the duumviri.

Casus sat on the edge of Kallisto's bed. He reached for her slender hand and held it tenderly in his big, callused paws.

"We had some business to attend to," Casus said vaguely.

"We?" Kallisto asked uneasily.

"Alcimus and I went to see the duumviri as soon as the Basilica opened this morning," Casus answered. Casus could see the worried look in her eyes and felt it best not to delay his news. He released Kallisto's hand and reached into his jerkin and pulled out a piece of papyrus. He handed it to Kallisto.

Kallisto unrolled the document and read it. Tears flowed down her cheeks. Her watery eyes glanced up at Casus in disbelief.

"I had enough money, finally, to buy your freedom from Alcimus; you're now a freewoman," Casus said softly. "You no longer work for Alcimus, but if you'd like to go on teaching Livius how to read and write, I told Alcimus it would be for a fee from now . . ."

Casus couldn't get the last word out, as Kallisto hurled herself upon him. She hugged him so fiercely he could barely breathe, or stifle the moan of pain from his three fractured ribs, but there was no way he would let his discomfort spoil this moment.

Kallisto pulled back. She stared bleary eyed at Casus. "How am I ever going to repay you?" she asked, still struggling to accept the fact she was now a freewoman.

"Well, for starters, would you consider being my wife?" Casus ask nervously. "I know I have my faults, but we'll start fresh, we can move to Pompeii. No one will know us there; they'll just see a hardworking couple. I can start my own business as a carpenter and maybe, just maybe, we could start a family."

Kallisto looked into Casus's warm brown eyes and saw all her dreams were coming true. All she had ever wanted was to have a normal life, a caring and loving husband, and a few children to complete her. She had been born a slave and had known no other life than the one she was currently living, the one of servitude. Some masters had been much harsher than Alcimus, so, when she had been asked to fill in for the girls, she had felt she shouldn't complain, not that it would have done her any good. She really liked Nona and, even though Livius was challenging, she enjoyed his carefree attitude and his bright optimistic ways of looking at things. She found him to be a bright light in her otherwise dreary world.

Kallisto noticed Casus's face was suddenly pale; she was instantly alarmed. And then she recalled she hadn't answered his question. "By the gods, breathe," she said. "Yes! Yes, I'll be your wife!"

Casus exhaled, collapsing into Kallisto's lap. He hadn't realized that he had been holding his breath. Kallisto lifted his face up, so that she was looking into his twinkling eyes. "I'm pregnant," she announced, not knowing how to say it any other way.

"Are you sure?" Casus asked hesitantly. Could he hope?

"Yes, I'm sure. Even Dani agreed. That's why I've been sick

lately. I think she called it morning sickness, even though I'm sick throughout the entire day," Kallisto explained, waiting for the ultimate question.

"Is it . . ."

Kallisto looked in Casus's eyes, and without blinking, said with conviction, "Yes, it's yours."

Casus fell back into Kallisto's lap, his arms around her waist as he wept happy tears into her tunic. It was all he had ever wanted. And if the gods were on his side, the baby would be a boy to carry on his family name.

91

AS THE CELL door swung open, a stream of light penetrated the otherwise dismal room. Dani recognized the man standing in the doorway. He was one of the men who had grabbed her yesterday.

Publius approached the back of the room and placed a loaf of bread and a pitcher of water by Dani's feet. He turned to leave, without uttering a word.

"Wait!" Dani pleaded. Publius stopped and turned. "Thanks for the food. But I can't reach it." She feigned a stunted reach. If she really had to, she could have reached the food, but she wanted something else. "If you could remove just one of my shackles, then I'd be able to feed myself. I'll still be chained to the wall, so what harm would there be? I'm just a simple, weak woman completely at your mercy," she added, playing on his male superiority and ego.

Publius shrugged. She wasn't going anywhere; so why not? It was a simple request. He reached for her right wrist and unlocked the shackle. "There," he grunted. "Enjoy your meal."

Publius turned and walked away. "Wait! When am I getting out of here?" Dani shouted after him. But the door had locked and Publius was gone.

"Great, the fact they're feeding me can only mean I'll be here for a while. But not if I can help it," Dani sneered, as she reached up with her right hand and pulled out a hairpin, her honey blond locks cascaded down around her shoulders.

"Not so smart after all, eh, Publius? Simple, weak woman, my ass," Dani growled, as she started to pick the lock of the cuff attached to her left wrist. She paused every once in a while to have a small bite of bread and a sip of water. Even though her little room had been like the inside of a refrigerator last night, cold and dark, it was turning into an oven today. She could feel the temperature rising and it was still early in the day. She had no doubt her cell would be unbearably hot come the afternoon. *Best to save the water,* she thought.

92

PRIMUS WALKED UNDER the portico, under the arch with the marble statue of an emperor riding in a four-horse chariot, and threw open the center door. He walked down the long colonnaded central aisle and stood in front of the raised dais beneath the curved vaulted ceiling. Ferox followed dutifully behind.

"I expected you earlier than now," Firmus remarked coldly. He noted it was close to the noon hour and, therefore, business for the day would soon be halted, because of the festival this evening.

"I'm here now. So, what's the matter you need to discuss with me?" Primus asked irritably. Today was the third time in four days he'd been called before the magistrates and it was pissing him off. Primus had purposely waited until the close of business, knowing that Dani's brother and Julia wouldn't be able to see Firmus until tomorrow morning, at the earliest, and by then they would no longer have any leverage over him, if everything went according to plan.

"Tiro had his enforcers assault Lucius Venidius Ennychus. In addition, they trashed his home and stole his money," Firmus stated directly.

"What's that got to do with me?" Primus demanded coldly, as he peered up at the weak-minded Celus, who physically cringed under Primus's stare.

"Tiro works for you; therefore, he is your responsibility," Firmus stated firmly.

"I suggest you haul Tiro and his enforcers in here and charge them for Ennychus's assault; it has nothing to do with me," Primus said confidently.

"Really? Then why was Ennychus threatened? Why was he told that lending money in this town was not good for his health, when you just happen to be the only other moneylender in town? Not particularly caring for the competition, Primus?" Firmus taunted.

"That's no proof I was behind the assault or the robbery," Primus said adamantly. *Firmus was grasping at straws. He has no hard evidence I ordered the attack,* he thought.

"It is as far as I'm concerned," Firmus shot back. "I'll see you, Tiro, and his enforcers in here first thing tomorrow to answer to the charges brought before this court by Venidia. You'll be ordered to pay for the damage to Ennychus's house and property and to return the money that Tiro's enforcers stole."

Primus glared at Firmus, who simply ignored him as he got up from his seat and departed though the side door. Celus just shrugged his shoulders at Primus, as if to say my hands are tied, and then followed Firmus out of the Basilica.

Primus was infuriated. He wasn't going to take this any longer. "When we get back to my place, I want you to bring Rufinus to me," Primus barked at Ferox as they walked back up the aisle and out the front door, running right into Daric.

"Where's my sister?" Daric demanded. He had been anxiously waiting outside for them to exit. "You said she would be released today."

"I said, today; I didn't say when," Primus grunted.

Daric rushed Primus, but Ferox stepped between them, pushing back against Daric's chest, blocking his advance. Primus, meanwhile, continued down the main street, across via Jupitinius, turned right, and entered his house.

Only after Primus had disappeared behind closed doors did

Ferox step back from Daric and leave to carry out Primus's order to fetch Rufinus. Ferox felt sorry for the lad. He hadn't harmed Primus in any way, yet, by the pained look on his face, he was going through Tartarus worrying about his sister. Ferox would, too, if the sandal were on the other foot.

93

DARIC MADE HIS way back to Julia's house, pondering. *Why was Primus stalling? There had to be a reason. Was it still all about the money? It had to be.*

Julia was waiting anxiously by the door, hoping to greet Dani. She was disappointed when only Daric arrived. "What happened?" Julia asked miserably. She couldn't imagine what Dani was going through: a young woman locked up somewhere, all alone in a strange town, not knowing whether anyone was looking to help her. The mere thought sent shivers down Julia's spine.

"Primus said he'd release her today, he didn't say when," Daric reported dejectedly.

"I don't like it; he's up to something," Julia speculated.

"That's exactly what I thought. But I'm not waiting around to find out what. I'll find Dani. How hard can it be? We know she's in a temple; we just have to figure out which one."

"And then break her out, somehow," Julia added. "You do realize that there are six temples scattered from one end of town to the other. It will take hours . . ."

"I don't care how long it takes. I'm going to find her," Daric declared forcefully.

And as if to punctuate Daric's determination, there was another tremor and a sudden crash out in the garden.

"Roo," Bear whined pathetically, as she huddled by Daric's feet.

"It's okay Bear. It'll stop in a second," Daric said soothingly, as he bent down and held her to his body. It was if he were trying to protect her from the unseen forces of nature. Or from the gods, as the people of Herculaneum would have had him believe.

After the tremor ended, Daric said, "It's all over, Bear." He scratched behind her ear as he released her and stood up. Then he and Julia investigated the source of the crashing sound. They found that one of the terracotta tiles had slid off the roof and shattered on the ground.

"The tremors are getting stronger and more frequent," Julia remarked. Dani and Daric were right. It was time to start thinking about leaving town for a safer haven, at least until after the eruption was over.

"I know they are; that's why I have to find Dani," Daric said, going to his room. When he returned, he had Bear's makeshift collar and leash. "I know she's no tracking dog, but she has a great sense of smell and sharper ears than mine. I'm hoping together, we'll find Dani." Bear's ears perked up upon hearing one of her favorite human's names. "You ready, girl?" Daric asked.

"Roooooo!" was Bear's enthusiastic reply, which Daric took as meaning yes.

"Wait! At least take Tobius with you," Julia urged. "He knows where the temples are. It may save you some time."

"Thanks," Daric said gratefully. "What are you going to do?"

"I'm going to the festival . . ."

"What?"

"The Vulcanalia. It's held annually, on the twenty-third of August, when we honor Vulcan, the god of fire, who brings warmth and light into every Roman's life. It also marks the end of our long summer nights. The days get shorter and the nights longer. Everyone in town gathers to make sacrifices to the god Vulcan, who's believed to have his furnace under the mountain."

"Makes sense; maybe that's where the word volcano comes

from," Daric mumbled.

"Volcano?" Julia didn't recognize the word.

"Eruption," Daric explained. He was totally blown away by the fact that, even living so close to Vesuvius, Julia didn't know the meaning of volcano.

"That's why I'm going," Julia resumed, explaining her reason for attending the festival at such a dire time. "I want to warn as many people as I can that they should leave town immediately."

"Good idea. With any luck, we'll all meet back here later," Daric said, as he followed Tobius through the rear atrium and out the thick wooden door that opened onto via Mineria.

94

"GO OVER TO the Basilica and get me every single document that bears my name and bring it back here," Primus ordered, as he sat upon his throne-like chair on the raised platform in his tablinum.

"What if someone sees me?" Robia asked nervously. He held a prominent position in the town, a position he had worked hard to attain with, of course, help from Primus. He didn't want to throw it all away on some fool's errand.

"Don't be ridiculous. Everyone's either getting ready or already on their way to the festival. The streets at that end of town will be deserted."

"Can't you send someone else, one of your slaves perhaps?" What did he have to lose by trying to get Primus to change his mind? He had everything to lose if he were ever caught.

"I'm sending you," Primus said firmly. It was clear he wasn't going to tolerate further discussion on the matter. "The Basilica is already closed and you know where all the legal documents are kept. Don't disappoint me."

Robia, with his head hung in defeat, left Primus's office and set off to do as he had been instructed. Primus's last words and the warning they carried had been perfectly clear. As Robia was leaving the house, he almost bumped into Rufinus and Ferox. They were obviously in a hurry as they barely acknowledged Robia's presence.

"It's about time," Primus barked, as Rufinus and Ferox entered his office.

"Blame my father; he refused to let me come. He needed a little persuading," Rufinus sneered, as he looked back at Ferox.

Sometimes I hate this job; actually most days, Ferox thought. He wanted to believe he'd applied enough persuasion to fulfil Primus's orders, but not enough to seriously hurt Antigonus.

"I have a little job for you and you will do exactly as I tell you." Primus snarled as he leaned forward for emphasis.

"Just tell me what you need doing and consider it done," Rufinus answered cockily.

"You're going to the Vulcanalia tonight and you're going to sit on the right-hand aisle at the top of the section that leads down to the dignitaries' seating," Primus jeered evilly.

95

"JULIA SAID YOU know where all the temples are in town," Daric said to Tobius, as they left the house to start their search for Dani.

"Yes," Tobius replied. Everyone who lives in Herculaneum knows where the temples are.

"Great, we know she's in one of them; we just need to figure out which one. So, let's start at the exact place where she was grabbed. Can you take me there?"

"Yes," Tobius replied, as he headed east along the main street.

"Can you list all the temples for me and tell me where they are in town? I want to try to approach our search logically."

"Two blocks over, next to the theatre on via Jupitinius, is the Temple of Hercules. And south, down by the Suburban Baths, there are two smaller temples: the Temple of Venus and the Temple of the Four Gods, dedicated to Vulcan, Neptune, Mercury and Minerva. At the far eastern end of town near the Palaestra, is the Temple of Magna Mater. And, at the Forum, there's the Temple of Augustus and the Capitolium, which is the Temple to Jupiter." Tobius walked under one of the triumphal arches, turned down via Jupitinius, took a few paces and then stopped. "It was here," he said, pointing to the shrine in the middle of the street displaying a statue of Hercules.

"What are the closest temples to this location?" Daric asked, scanning the area. Bear was sitting patiently by his feet.

"The Temple of Hercules is close by, on the corner of via Jupitinius and via Neptunia."

"Show me," Daric encouraged. He didn't want to have to search every temple in town, but he would if he had to.

Tobius walked a block farther south along via Jupitinius and stopped in front of a temple. The temple itself was forty-eight feet in diameter, encircled by a colonnade comprising twenty fluted Corinthian columns, each thirty-five feet high. At the front, five marble steps led to a central doorway, flanked on each side by two rectangular windows.

Daric looked at the impressive structure and then surveyed the surrounding area. "Which way did you come when you returned to Julia's after visiting Kallisto?"

"That way," Tobius replied, pointing east down via Neptunia.

"If they had wanted to take her to this temple, why wouldn't they have grabbed her here instead of at the end of the street? I'm sure they wouldn't have wanted everyone to witness what they were doing or to hear her protests, which, I guarantee, would have awakened the dead. So, I would think they would've grabbed her close to the temple where they wanted to stash her."

"What temples are closest to the shrine?" Daric asked, directing his question to Tobius.

"The Capitolium is right inside the entrance to the Forum, across the street from the shrine and . . ."

"Let's go," Daric interrupted and hurried back up the street toward the shrine with Bear in tow. Tobius was bringing up the rear.

96

DANI HAD BEEN working for what seemed like the entire day. As she had expected, the cell had become unbearably hot and stuffy, even more so since little air seemed to enter or leave the room. She had been sweating like the proverbial pig, while trying to stretch out her limited supply of water. Despite her efforts, the jug was now empty, and she was parched.

Dani stopped what she was doing and looked up at the cell's tiny window, with its silvery spider web glistening with the last rays of the sun. She noted the sun had begun to set and the bird songs had diminished. *Crap,* she thought, *I've been picking at this lock all day and I'm still stuck in these damned cuffs.*

Dani's fingers were cramped and sore. Her bone hairpin was down to almost nothing after several pieces had broken off during her futile attempts to pick the lock on her shackle. "If Daric were here, he'd have had this lock open in a flash," she muttered. Just at that instant, the shackle fell from her left wrist and into her lap. "Well, I'll be," she said in amazement. "I did it." She slowly got up and stretched out her stiff legs. "Now, it's time to get out of here, before one of those goons comes back."

Dani made her way over to the door and examined the lock. The door and lock were too thick for the tiny remnants of her hairpin to do any good. So, she resorted to her next best tool. "Help! Someone! Help me! Please!" Dani yelled as loudly as she could, praying that someone would hear her, as she banged her fists on the heavy wooden door.

* * *

Daric and Tobius were standing at the base of the Temple of Jupiter. It was dedicated to the Capitoline triad of Jupiter, Juno and Minerva, and dominated the south side of the Forum. The temple stood on a podium that stood ten feet high. The temple housed vaulted rooms, accessed from a side door. Six freestanding columns stood across the front of the temple, with another five standing down each side. The temple's front staircase was divided into two flights to provide a central platform on which an altar could be set.

Bear tilted her head and listened. After a moment, she yowled, "Rooooo!" and took off, dragging Daric behind her.

"Hey, Bear, wait up!" Daric bellowed, as he struggled behind the racing canine. "Did you hear something?"

Bear was running deeper into the Forum and heading toward another structure that looked just like the Capitolium, but smaller. "Tobius, what's that building?" Daric yelled over his shoulder.

"That's the Temple of Augustus," Tobius answered, panting, doing his best to keep up.

Bear ran around the corner of the temple and stopped at a heavy wooden door. "Rooooo!"

"Bear, is that you?" Dani cried out. It had to be; she didn't know of any other animal who could make that sound.

"Rooooo!"

"Dani!" Daric yelled, as he turned the corner and stopped next to a very excited Bear. "Dani!"

"In here!" Dani replied, her voice strained from all the yelling she had been doing.

"Rooooo!" Bear yowled again.

"We'll have you out in a minute," Daric promised, not having the foggiest idea how he would open the door. “Any ideas?” he asked Tobius, who shrugged and almost immediately dashed off without saying a word

“Well, that’s great,” Daric moaned after the fast-disappearing Tobius. “Now, what?”

“Get me out of here!” Dani shouted impatiently.

“I’m trying. I just need to figure out how. Give me a sec, will ya?” Daric shouted back. He was looking around for anything that might be handy to pick, or if necessary, break the lock.

After finding nothing in the immediate area that could help him, he remembered the market and the merchants, who sold everything under the sun. Maybe one of them could help him. “I’ll be right back,” Daric shouted at the door, and, then, with Bear beside him, ran toward the market.

“Don’t leave me!” Dani yelled, but no one was there to hear her. “Daric? Daric?,” she called again. There was no answer, just silence. “Great, just great.” She sighed.

A few moments later, Dani heard something in the lock. The door swung open, and she saw a frail elderly man, whom she didn’t recognize, standing in the doorway. He was grinning at her and holding a key. Then she recognized Tobius standing just behind the old man. She ran to him and threw her arms around his neck, exclaiming, “Thank you. Thank you.”

“I’ve got it,” Daric yelled, as he raced around the corner, clutching a large stone, only to see Dani standing outside the temple with Tobius and another man.

“Eeeheeeheee,” Bear screamed and ran to Dani, who wrapped Bear in an affectionate embrace.

“This is Spurius Subinus,” explained Tobius, sounding rather pleased. “He’s the porter at the Curia, just across the street. Subinus works for the aediles and, since the aediles are responsible for all the public buildings, including the temples, I figured he would have a key.”

“Thank you, Subinus,” Dani said gratefully, with a gleaming smile that truly made Subinus’s day.

"My pleasure," Subinus replied. Unable to contain his curiosity, he asked, "What were you doing in there in the first place?"

"It's a long story" Tobius jumped in. "Thanks, again, Subinus. Maybe you'd best be getting back in case someone calls at the Curia."

With that, Subinus went back to the Curia, even though it was closed because of the Vulcanalia.

"Let's get out of here, before someone sees us," Dani urged, feeling decidedly uneasy.

The three of them exited the Forum and turned right onto the main street. As they walked under one of the triumphal arches, they caught sight of Robia, one of the aediles, leaving the Basilica, his arms laden with documents. *Wonder what that's all about,* Daric pondered. *Isn't the Basilica supposed to be closed?*

Present Day—Friday

97

RICHARD FUMED AS he stormed along the shoreline path that led to the gazebo on the tip of the peninsula. A host of thoughts raced chaotically through his mind; with every step, his anger intensified. It was like throwing fuel onto a raging fire. *How could Sandra refuse me? For Christ's sake, I'm going to reunite her with her children. Isn't that enough for her to be forever indebted to me, grateful even? What's wrong with her? She says she could only ever love one man! Stupid woman! He's dead! She loved me once. Why can't she love me again?*

Suddenly, Richard came to an abrupt halt. He looked out over the lake, as the gentle waves rolled gracefully upon the sandy beach. A solitary loon dove below the surface, looking for its next meal. Richard wasn't seeing the natural beauty before him; his mind was centered elsewhere. Slowly, a wicked grin emerged. He had an idea: a wickedly, wonderful idea. He turned and retraced his steps, but, instead of going into the house, he veered to the right and entered the garage.

Richard flipped on the interior lights. He was focused on

finding one specific item in the large three-car garage. He recalled watching an episode on a television drama series; it had described the perfect crime. Richard knew what he needed, and he was certain Quinn would have it. He was also pretty sure he knew exactly where to find it.

Richard approached the dive lockers along the back wall of the garage. "Strange," he muttered. "I don't recall that door being dented." He shrugged it off and opened the locker door. "Ah hah," he sneered, as a reached for the item he had been seeking. "Perfect."

Richard slipped the small vial into his jacket pocket. He had to keep it concealed so he could use it covertly. Sandra, after all, was a medical professional. His scheme had to be executed with precision. One slip-up and . . . he didn't want to think about the alternative. This had to work; it had to look like an accident, but he would see this through one way or the other, consoled by the weight of his semi-automatic, 45-caliber handgun in his coat pocket. Richard turned off the lights, closed the garage door, and headed for the house. He entered through the kitchen door and made his way into the living room.

Sandra was slouched on the sofa, her head resting against its back. Her eyes were closed, but fresh tears stained her cheeks.

"Sandra, I'm sorry," Richard said softly. He sat at the far end of the sofa, leaving as much space between them as possible. He didn't want to upset her, again.

Sandra wiped away her tears as she slowly sat up. She faced Richard. Her red rimmed-eyes and flushed cheeks only made him desire her all the more. Then he snapped out of it; berating himself for his momentary weakness. He needed to get on with it.

"Sandra, I never should have kissed you like that," he whispered. "It was wrong. I was wrong. What we may have had once is long past. I should never have presumed you could still have feelings for me." He hung his head in shame. *I should have been in the theatre,* he thought, proud of his performance.

"Richard . . ." Sandra began, but was interrupted.

"Sandra, there's no excuse for what I did. And on top of that, you're in mourning. What kind of beast would take advantage of a woman when she's so vulnerable?" His penitence act was working.

Sandra studied Richard closely. It wasn't like him to admit any kind of fault. He always seemed to find someone else to shoulder the blame; it was never him. But he seemed genuinely contrite, Sandra was rather surprised.

"It's okay, Richard. Let's just pretend it never happened." She reached out her hand, lightly touching Richard's as a sign of forgiveness.

"Thank you." He softly clasped Sandra's outstretched hand. "I'd hate for my transgression to ruin our friendship. I value what we have and I don't want that to change."

"Me too," Sandra said half-heartedly. She had only ever tolerated Richard because he and Quinn had been friends since high school. She hadn't wanted to interfere with their long-time fraternal bond.

"Great. Let me pour us a drink, so we can toast our friendship." Richard didn't wait for a response. He popped up from the sofa and walked behind the bar. He reached for two highball glasses and set them on the countertop. "Scotch on the rocks, right?" he asked, as he stooped to retrieve a bottle from the shelf under the bar.

"That'll be fine." Sandra just wanted to lie down. She was emotionally exhausted. Losing Quinn was weighing heavily on her heart. She didn't want to face life without him.

Richard took one of the glasses and bent down to get the ice cubes from the mini-fridge. While his hands were concealed behind the bar, he pulled the small vial from his jacket and poured its contents into the glass. Quickly stuffing the vial back inside his jacket, he dropped a handful of ice into the glass. When he stood up to retrieve the second glass, Sandra was standing directly in front of him, on the other side of the bar.

"Oh, you startled me," he blurted, placing his free hand over his pounding heart. He was holding his breath, waiting for the first words to cross Sandra's lips. They would dictate his next move.

"I wanted to make sure you found everything you needed,"

Sandra said amiably.

"Oh, not a problem. This isn't my first rodeo, you know." He picked up the bottle of scotch, poured two ounces into the glass, and, then, handed the drink to Sandra. "There you go."

"Thanks." Sandra took the glass and returned to the sofa. After adding a handful of ice into his glass, Richard quickly poured his drink and joined her.

"Here's to our treasured friendship; may it flourish and grow," Richard announced, clinking glass rims with Sandra.

Sandra took a sip of her drink. Richard watched closely, as he took a large gulp. He waited a few seconds; nothing. *It worked. Sandra didn't suspect a thing. It's a perfect plan. That colorless, odorless and tasteless liquid was just what I needed,* he thought. A few moments of awkward silence passed, then out of the blue . . .

"Here's to you and here's to me, best of friends we'll always be. If by chance we disagree, screw you, here's to me," Sandra recited, giggling like a little schoolgirl. "That's a toast my dear mom used to say at parties. Cute isn't it?" Drinking this early in the day and having nothing in her stomach were making her a little light-headed and giddy.

"You look tired. Why don't you go and lie down for a while?" Richard suggested nervously. He had never seen Sandra this tipsy after only one drink. Was it the result of what he had put in her drink? "I'm going to go back out to the lab and continue working on getting Dani and Daric home. I'll drop by later to see how you're doing and I'll fix us a bite to eat."

"I am a little tired. I think I will go and lie down for a while," Sandra mumbled, as she stood up. There was a slight lean to her posture as she made her way over to the staircase. She turned, glanced at Richard for a second, and then ascended the stairs.

Richard waited until he heard the bedroom door close, before letting himself out. "Well, that worked perfectly. A few more doses and that problem will be taken care of. Now, back to the real reason I'm here," Richard muttered as he headed for Quinn's lab and the task at hand.

Herculaneum—August 23, 79 AD

98

SINCE TOBIUS WAS out with Daric looking for Dani, Julia had Cyrus and Nneka escort her to the Vulcanalia. Unlike some of the other affluent citizens of Herculaneum, she was never one for pomp and circumstance. She saw no need to be accompanied by a large retinue of slaves or to flash her wealth or flaunt her status in the society. She believed more in letting her actions and deeds speak for themselves.

Julia and her escorts walked leisurely along the main street, under the light of the full moon. A large number of slaves hurried past them, hunched over under the weight of bundles of wood they were delivering for the sacrificial bonfire blazing in the center of the amphitheatre's arena. She also observed families with carts laden with all their worldly belongings, heading out of town through the east gate near Festus's inn. She recognized a two-wheeled cart drawn by two donkeys belonging to the baker. There was another cart behind his, this one four-wheeled and carrying the owner of the dye shop and his family. *So, some people are heeding the warnings and are leaving town; that's good,* she thought.

"Wait, what did Daric say about leaving?" Julia wondered aloud. Almost immediately, she yelled after the baker, "Sextus, don't go east; head west."

"I'm going to Pompeii," Sextus shouted back, over his shoulder.

"No don't. Go toward Neapolis or even Misenum; trust me," Julia called as loudly as she could. Sextus acknowledged her instructions by nodding; he had no reason to doubt or question the learned woman.

As Julia and her escorts neared the amphitheater, every inn, tavern and bar was open and anxiously accommodating all the people who were festival bound. The businesses on the west end of town were already closed for the festival, because everyone was heading eastward toward the festival.

The amphitheater was on the north side of the main street and at the most easterly corner of Herculaneum, overlooking the bay and right next to the Palaestra, or gymnasium. It was an impressive structure that could hold up to five-thousand people and was used exclusively for sports and town events, such as the Vulcanalia. If citizens wanted to attend gladiatorial contests and spectacles involving wild beasts, they had to go to the neighboring city of Pompeii. Posters advertising these games could be found on the walls of the amphitheater.

The amphitheater's arena was located twenty feet below the ground level. The earth that had been excavated to create the arena had been used to build the ramparts. The ramparts were supported on all sides by a continuous sustaining wall, which followed the oval shape of the arena and ran under the middle seating section.

Seating in the amphitheater was arranged based on social status. Public access to the amphitheater was by way of four stairways: two double and two single, built against the exterior wall and providing access to the upper tiered seating area. Access to the middle and lower tiered seating was by way of two corridors that led to a ringed passageway. A double staircase system sorted out those whose seats were in the middle section from those in the lower section. The lower tiered seating was reserved for persons of rank such as councillors, the duumviri and the sponsors of the games or spectacles.

From either end of the amphitheater, two tunnels led directly into the arena. A bronze statue stood just inside the entrances to each tunnel. The arena itself was ringed by a wall over six-and-a half-feet high and painted with scenes of sporting events.

The upper portion of the wall around the amphitheater included two rows of stone rings. The rings held poles that could support a large linen awning to protect spectators from the elements. No such awning would be required this evening.

Arriving at the amphitheater, Julia and her escorts entered the south corridor and went down several flights of steps to the lower tier seating. They located her seat, two rows behind those reserved for the town's dignitaries. When Julia was comfortably seated, Cyrus and Nneka sat on the floor near her.

Julia cast an eye over the arena and the nearby seats. Consistent with a widely accepted superstition, citizens were filing past a blazing bonfire in the middle of the arena, tossing live fish into the flames as a sacrifice to Vulcan; a hissing sound and a pop immediately followed each toss. While Julia had never believed in the superstition and had no intention of offering a sacrifice, many, maybe most, of the citizens were believers. Seemingly endless streams of citizens entered the arena through both the north and south tunnels and forming two slowly moving lines, one on each side of the bonfire. She had been right; the place was packed.

99

AS JULIA CONTINUED to observe the activities in the arena, Primus and his large entourage filed into the two rows of seats directly in front of her. Among the ladies in the entourage were Primus's wife and daughter, Aquilina and Cominia. There was also Aquilina's sister, Procilla, and Procilla's daughter, Gaia. They settled into their seats in the tiered row just below Julia.

This is perfect, Julia thought. She wanted to tell Aquilina what she had learned about her husband's questionable business dealings. She also wanted to warn her about Vesuvius.

Procilla turned around to acknowledge Julia's presence and said, "Beautiful evening, isn't it?" She was dressed in her finest for the festival, as were all the affluent women of the town. Their silk dresses and pallas were bright and colorful. Their hair was coiffed in elaborate styles. Their fine accoutrements, made of gold and silver and accented with rubies, pearls, sapphire and emeralds, included rings, headbands, necklaces, bracelets, ankle bands and earrings. Even little four-year-old Gaia was wearing a tiny pair of silver earrings.

"That it is," Julia replied pleasantly, as she admired Procilla's two gold snake-headed bracelets. She also noted the gold-braided headbands Aquilina and Cominia were wearing, the ones they had worn to her dinner party the other night. She leaned forward and whispered just loud enough to be heard. "Aquilina, I need to tell you some things that aren't very pleasant, but I believe you have a right to know."

Primus was aware of a conversation going on behind him, but, because of the noise in the amphitheater, he couldn't make out what was being said. Curious to know who was doing all the talking, he turned and saw Julia conversing with his wife. He scowled at her, but Julia took no notice. Before turning back to attend to his own affairs, Primus surveyed the long stairway to his right, especially up toward the distant rows at the back of the dignitaries' seating area.

100

A LONE FIGURE was sitting at the top of the dignitaries' seating area, just below the entranceway/exit to the lower section, next to the stairway that Primus had recently surveyed from below. His head was concealed by a cowl that was part of his cloak and was drawn up over his head. His identity was all but obscured.

Rufinus had determined exactly where to sit in the amphitheater during the Vulcanalia. He had arrived early to claim his preferred seat before the crowds started to file in for the ceremony. He talked to no one, not that anyone would have approached such an inhospitable-looking individual. He simply sat and bided his time, waiting patiently for just the right moment.

After all the official speeches had been delivered, the crowds started to disperse. Firmus, always the gentleman, was the last to leave the dignitaries' section. He made his way up the long stairway. Just as Firmus reached the top of the stairway, there was another tremor. He reached out to steady himself and was grabbed by a hooded stranger.

Grateful for the help, Firmus looked into the obscured face of the stranger who had helped steady him. But he saw only two menacing eyes before he was shoved forcefully backwards. He lost his balance and tumbled down the long stone stairway, over the upper edge of the arena wall and onto the arena floor six-and-a half-feet below his previously occupied seat. His body lay in a crumpled, unmoving heap. Blood ran from his ears and nose. His open eyes were unblinking, frozen in their last state of utter shock and terror.

Primus had been standing at the entranceway at the top of the dignitaries' seating area, the upper part of the same stairs that Firmus had just tumbled down. Primus had silently watched as his order was carried out. *What a shame; but at least that's one problem taken care of,* he mused. After taking one final look at the arena below, he left the amphitheater.

Casus was sitting in the same area as the hooded figure, just on the other side of the same aisle and two rows higher up. He had witnessed the entire accident. Or should he say murder?

* * *

Julia and her escorts, along with Aquilina and the female members of her family, had all left the amphitheater earlier and were walking home, when the ground started to shake. The group held onto each other, steadying themselves until the tremor stopped. "I hate when that happens," Procilla claimed.

Aquilina had been quiet for some time, deep in thought. She had heard everything that Julia had told her, and somehow it had not surprised her. She knew her husband was abusive; she had lived with his temper for twenty-two years. She had witnessed his cruel mistreatment of his slaves. Aquilina especially remembered Casus's family: they had often been malnourished and sickly, but Primus had never lifted a finger to help them. He had stood by and watched them slowly die. And, in his business dealings, she had heard rumours he hadn't always been honest and above board; at times he had been immoral and ruthless.

Aquilina turned to Julia and said, "I heard what you said and I know he's not a good man, but he's all I have. When I married him, I said it would be for life, through good and bad. I'm old school, Julia; I'm loyal to the core. Wives are required to be devoted, retiring and faithful. And that's me. I always thought there was nothing I could do, but perhaps, now, I can try to help those that he's wronged. At least that'll be something; but I can't leave him."

101

TOBIUS QUICKLY LED Dani and Daric back to Julia's house. Along the way, they spotted several groups of people, families mostly, who were leaving town through the west gate. Dani was hopeful; people were actually taking the warnings about the eruption seriously. Even so, she knew there was still much that needed be done.

When they arrived at Julia's, Dani's first priority was to have a bath and put on clean clothes. After having spent over twenty-four hours freezing and then sweating in a small, dark, dirty room, she felt grubby. Her stola was filthy. Her skin felt as though it was crawling with the tiny night creatures that had shared her accommodations. Her second priority was to get something to eat; she was famished.

After a rejuvenating bath, Dani dressed in fresh clothes and went downstairs to join Daric. Tobius had arranged for some food to be served in the small dining room next to Julia's bedroom, where Julia and Daric had met the previous night.

Dani found Daric sitting on one of the couches; she stretched out on the other one. They were alone, except for Bear, who was taking a small morsel of bread from Daric's fingers. Dani took a mouthful of wine and savoured it, briefly, before swallowing. She reached for the round loaf of bread, but her hand stopped in mid-reach. She had noticed a stamp on the bread; it read: Celer. "Why would anyone want to stamp a loaf of bread?" she asked, as she pulled off a piece and popped it into her mouth. "Maybe it's the bakery where it's from; it's really good."

"Will you forget about the bread," Daric snapped impatiently. "Let's get out of here."

"What about the baby? We have to find the mother," Dani said around a mouthful of food.

"Done. She's already back with her mother. Now, can we go?"

"That's great. Who's the mother?" Dani asked.

"Does it matter? You don't know her," Daric grunted. "Finish up and let's go."

"Go where?" Dani snapped back. "What makes you think we'll end up in a better situation? We jumped from a civil war into a natural disaster. We have no idea where we'll wind up next. Not to mention, we jumped . . ." Dani froze in mid-sentence. Tobius had just walked in, carrying a platter of roasted chicken with vegetables. He placed it carefully on the table in front of her.

"Thank you, Tobius," Dani said, warmly. She watched Tobius's cheeks redden, as he walked away.

When Tobius was safely out of the dining room, Dani turned back to Daric. "As I was saying, we jumped from 1537 to 79. Who knows where we could end up next or what kind of trouble we could be get ourselves into?"

"We'll definitely find out tomorrow when we're forced to leave, won't we?" Daric countered, barely able to conceal his sarcasm.

"Not if we escape with the others," Dani suggested. "Look, we know Dad is working to bring us home. It could be a matter of days before that happens. Except for Vesuvius, we're safe here. We have friends here. And what about Julia, or Casus and Kallisto; we have to make sure they get to safety. Oh, did I mention Kallisto's pregnant, with Casus's baby? She has to survive or Uncle Richard may not exist when we get back."

"I don't like being this close to something that's more powerful than a thousand nuclear bombs," Daric moaned, stroking Bear's head. She had been lying quietly beside him, accepting any and every morsel handed her way.

"We still have time. We can still help evacuate the town, but there's no room for error. We must stick together at all times," Dani cautioned.

Although Dani had said she and Daric might escape with others from Herculaneum, she had no intention of taking up valuable space in one of the boats needed to save the citizens of Herculaneum. She realized that, when the time came, she and Daric would be forced to rely on their travel bands to escape certain death, just as Daric had claimed. Until then, however, they would have a bit more time to help others.

"Dani! Thank the gods, you're safe," Julia exclaimed, rushing in and throwing her arms around her.

Present Day—Friday

102

"UGH!" EDDIE SCREAMED, as he fell to his knees, clutching the collar around his neck.

"What the hell are you doing?" Richard roared. "I'm gone for an hour and you decide to watch TV?"

"I wasn't watching TV," retorted Eddie. "Hermes was showing me what my parents would have looked like had they still been alive today."

"Isn't that just special," Richard mocked.

"He also told me you can't change the past, that you can't go back in time and save my parents, like you promised."

"Well, there's only one way to find out, isn't there? And that will never happen unless you finish your work," Richard snapped, focussing his glare on the hologram. "You're supposed to be a super computer. What's taking so long?"

"I'm still running diagnostics on my system to ensure it is clean of the intrusive virus you planted," Hermes replied calmly. He then turned his back to Richard. Facing Eddie, Hermes mouthed the words, 'Help me.'

Eddie was surprised by Hermes's request. He understood the message, but not the reason behind it. He decided to play along. "My virus penetrated deep into the programming," Eddie explained to Richard. "You wanted the best; I delivered the best. It'll take more time to complete the diagnostics to ensure that all systems are functioning normally."

"And then I must recheck all the computations that the professor and I had completed to date. Only after I have ensured they have not been compromised can we can finish the calculations for forward time travel," Hermes added.

"All right, all right," Richard barked. He had a headache, and he wasn't interested in the intricate details or lame excuses. "Don't just stand there, get to it," Richard ordered, then walked to the chair, sat down, and watched the monitor that was hooked up to the surveillance camera aimed at the house.

After a few hours of sitting, Richard had grown restless and impatient. He stood up abruptly, propelling his chair backwards against the wall. "Okay, what's taking so long?" he demanded.

Hermes and Eddie had been huddled over the console, conferring. Eddie took a deep breath, and said, "This is taking longer than I thought it would."

"Why?" Richard snapped at Hermes.

"As I previously informed you, the intrusive nature of the virus has penetrated deep into my systems, all of them. However, I have been able to verify that the virus has been successfully eradicated from seventy-seven percent of my programming. It will take more time before I can verify that the entire network has been restored to my satisfaction."

Richard looked at his watch; it was getting late, and he had other matters to contend with. He reached into his pocket and pulled out the collar control mechanism.

"No, don't," Eddie pleaded. "I'm doing the best I can."

Richard looked at Eddie, sneered, and pushed the button, just for the hell of it. "I know. I wanted to remind you who's the boss." He watched Eddie fall to the ground, writhing in pain.

"I'll leave you two to finish your work. I have other matters to attend to. I'll be back in the morning, and you had better be ready to bring the twins home," Richard announced.

"Wait! You can't leave without me. What about the collar?" Eddie said nervously, knowing the perimeter collar had boundary restrictions.

"I've turned it off, for now. I know you won't wander off, because if you're not here when I return in the morning, I'll turn this little device back on and . . ." Richard was interrupted.

"I get the picture," Eddie grunted, as he got to his feet.

"Good. I'll be back first thing in the morning. Don't disappoint me." Richard stared at Eddie; then he turned his piercing gaze toward Hermes. He held it for a moment, before he walked up the stairs and left the gazebo.

"I've got to get out of here. That guy is crazy," Eddie muttered in a panic, as he headed for the stairs.

"Eddie, wait, please. Running away is not going to solve your problems. In fact, according to Mr. Case, it could get you killed. I know you're in a tough situation right now, but I think, if we work together, we can help each other," Hermes said sympathetically.

"You did say you could help me get this collar off, right?" Eddie asked optimistically, as he stopped at the bottom of the stairs. Maybe he could delay his departure a little while longer, at least until they could remove the collar. Then he could take off.

"I did . . . and I will. But first, let's run some diagnostics to check whether my systems are up to par. Then, I'll fill you in on my plan. Besides, we have to make sure Mr. Case has left the estate before we can tackle removing that collar."

103

"EDDIE, WE NEED to slow our progress," Hermes announced, about an hour after Richard's departure from the lab.

"What?" Eddie mumbled, his mind elsewhere. He had been slowly putting together bits and pieces from the past several days; it was as if he had been assembling a jigsaw puzzle without knowing what the final image was supposed to be. While he had managed to fit together many pieces and complete part of the puzzle, the image that gradually emerged was one Eddie could never have imagined.

First, the security override virus that Eddie had developed and placed in a USB key, Richard had used to override the lab's security system and to gain access. Then, while in the lab, Richard had extracted finger prints; Quinn's whole hand prints to be precise, from material Eddie had provided for Richard. Eddie had later used these stolen prints to fabricate gloves, which Richard had used to activate the computer console. Next, there was the virus that Eddie had developed to incapacitate Hermes. Eddie could only surmise that the virus had been used to keep Hermes from warning Quinn of Richard's infiltration.

Eddie had also figured out the part of the puzzle where only Richard and Quinn would go to New Zealand to search for the rare mineral called chronizium. When Sandra had unexpectedly insisted on joining them, Richard had had to stop her from doing so. For that reason, and no other, he had asked Eddie to hack into the Central Traffic Control System and cause a Fastrax commuter train to derail, a derailment that left one-hundred-eleven passengers dead and hundreds more injured. With Sandra busy caring for the injured at a local hospital, Richard and Quinn had gone to New Zealand. When they had finally located the mineral, Richard had returned home, leaving behind the corpse of the oblivious professor in some obscure underwater cave.

The rest of the puzzle was still something of a mystery that Eddie was struggling to figure out. He had lots of pieces to work with, but he was still unsure where they fit into the picture, or whether they fit into it at all. For example, he had the snippets of a conversation he had overheard from the bugs planted in the house. He had heard the police chief and Sandra talking in the kitchen about the train derailment. He had heard the fake phone call from Dani saying she and Daric, whom he assumed were the twins, were still at Uncle Richard's island. Dani's reference to Richard as 'uncle' had both alarmed and confused Eddie, since it would mean that Richard and Quinn were related. Eddie couldn't fathom how Richard could purposely harm his own family, and for what? Personal gain? It was inconceivable to Eddie. If he still had any family, which he didn't, Eddie would do everything within his power to protect them

Eddie had also heard the police chief tell Sandra that the case was now closed. Eddie didn't know what case the chief was referring to; he would have to delve into that piece of the puzzle later. About thirty minutes later, Eddie had heard broken fragments of a conversation between Richard and Sandra. While Eddie desperately wished he could have observed what was going on, he didn't need a magic mirror to know what had transpired. Richard had got too up-close and personal with Sandra, who had snubbed his advances. Shortly after, there had been an apology, an out-of-the-blue about-face apology, and, then, all had been forgiven. Eddie was sure he was missing something; Richard hadn't sounded like his usual narcissistic self. Something was amiss. Eddie would have to investigate this peculiarity, too.

Even though there were still parts of the image that Eddie didn't understand, there was one thing about which he was certain. After all the planning, scheming, and deception Richard had carried out to get control of the time travel device, he would use whatever means were necessary to achieve his goal. There would be no stopping him.

"Eddie, did you hear me?" Hermes asked, trying again to get Eddie's attention.

"Uh, sorry, what?" Eddie muttered, being pulled back to the here and now.

"I said, we need to slow down our progress."

"Why? We're almost finished. You said another fifteen minutes, tops," Eddie grumbled. He was eager to get the final calculations completed so they could work on getting his collar off.

"The professor asked me to stall . . ."

"What did you say?" Eddie stammered.

Herculaneum—August 24, 79 AD

104

DANI, DARIC AND Julia had spent most of the night discussing and planning the evacuation of Herculaneum. Dani knew it was too late for anyone to leave town on foot and be out of harm's way when Vesuvius blew its top.

During their discussions, Daric had suggested that Casus could be helpful with the evacuation. As a result, Casus and Kallisto had been brought to Julia's, where Julia had explained the plan. Casus and Kallisto, without hesitation, offered to help in whatever way they could. In the course of the next hour or so, the plan was refined and agreed upon. At sunrise, everyone would start at the northern edge of the town and they would gradually work their way southward. As they moved through town, they'd deliver the same message to everyone they found: head south to the boat sheds and spread word of the evacuation as quickly as possible.

When night had finally turned to dawn, Dani noticed how unnervingly silent it was. There were no birds singing in the garden this morning, no high-pitched chirping of the goldfinches she had enjoyed every morning since they had arrived. *This can't be good,* she thought. *Maybe they knew enough to leave the area.*

Dani peered out her bedroom window and noticed the cloud that had so long been lingering over the crest of Vesuvius had disappeared. The sky was a brilliant blue. The sun was slowly rising from the east, in the promise of being another extremely hot day. A gentle breeze fanned the odors from the fragrant plants of the garden, sweeping them throughout the house.

Dani and Daric were wearing tunics; they had agreed that the shorter garment afforded more freedom of movement than the ankle-length dress or long toga. They joined Julia, Kallisto and Casus in the dining room for a quick bite before heading out. Kallisto had also chosen the shorter tunic. Casus had on his full military gear and Julia was wearing an emerald-green stola.

"As I was saying, we won't have enough boats for everyone," Casus repeated for the benefit of the new arrivals. "Even if we cram as many in as possible, there still won't be enough."

"I'll send Cyrus to the market to talk to Nikanor Albus, the fishmonger. He has a fleet of ten fishing boats we could load up with people, but we must reach him before the boats head out for their morning catch," Julia suggested.

"Let me go," Kallisto offered. "It'll make me feel useful." Receiving an affirmative nod from Julia, she immediately headed out the door.

"Even with Nikanor's boats and all the private yachts in the harbor, there's still won't be enough to evacuate everyone," Casus groaned.

"I saw a couple of trade ships in the harbor yesterday. If they're still here, they'll hold hundreds of people," Tobius mentioned, as he put down a plate of cheese, dates, figs and grapes on the table.

"If the ships are still here, I can stop them from leaving. I'll tell them it's by order of the town magistrates," Casus suggested, realizing that one trade ship could save close to five hundred people. He didn't wait around for any discussion on the matter; he just took off running.

A moment later, Julia exclaimed excitedly, "Misenum! The

Roman Navy is stationed at Misenum, just across the bay. They'll have plenty of ships to help with the evacuation. And I happen to be a close friend with Admiral Gaius Plinius."

Dani sat and stared into space, dumbfounded. *Gaius Plinius,* she repeated in her mind. Then it clicked. That name. *Pliny the Elder, which means that Cilo, Gaius Caecilius Cilo is Pliny the Younger; the guy who documented the eruption of Vesuvius first-hand. Well, I'll be.*

"Dani?" Daric repeated louder this time, snapping her out of her stupor.

"Sorry, what?"

"I said, since you're technically a fugitive, you'll have to remain here at the house."

"I am *not* staying here," Dani said defiantly, as she glared at her brother. "The more of us involved in spreading the word, the sooner we'll be done. Besides, dressed like this, I'll easily blend in with the crowds. Hardly a woman of wealth and reputation, if you know what I mean."

Suddenly there was another tremor. They grabbed onto whatever was within arm's reach to steady themselves. They heard several loud crashes out in the garden, as well as shouting in the streets.

"Roo," Bear moaned pathetically, huddled by Daric's feet.

"It's okay, Bear, it'll pass soon," Daric reassured her, just as the tremors ceased.

"They're getting more severe and they're definitely lasting longer," Dani remarked, praying that Cilo, or Pliny the Younger as history knew him, was accurate with his timing of the events that were about to unfold today, because their lives depended on it.

"Julia, you need to get to Misenum as quickly as possible," Dani said, her voice carrying more than a hint of urgency.

"Primus has a yacht at the pier; it will be the fastest boat there. As soon as we can get it loaded with people, we'll set off for Misenum," Julia replied.

"Great. Let's start getting people down to the boats. We'll load as many as we can and send them out of here; then we'll wait for the navy to pick up the rest," Daric stated concisely.

Dani, Daric and Julia, accompanied by Tobius and Nneka, left the dining room. They passed through the atrium to the front of the house. Tobius opened the door. As Julia and her escorts were stepping into the street, Daric grabbed Dani's arm to hold her back. "We'll be right there," he shouted after the others. "Go ahead. We'll catch up with you."

Daric lifted the key from around his neck and placed it around Dani's. "When we're finished, I want you to come back here and get Bear and our valuables out of the strong box."

"What do we want with that stuff?" Dani asked curiously, and a bit irritated. She was anxious to get on with the evacuation.

"We may be able to give it to someone or use it ourselves, depending on where we end up next. It can't hurt to have something to barter with," Daric explained. "Let's go."

The Seventh Hour (after sunrise)

105

THE SUN HAD just passed its zenith and was starting its downward journey. The wind was out of the northwest, blowing toward Pompeii. Julia and Dani had returned to Julia's house to gather their belongings before heading to the boats. Daric, meanwhile, had headed for the beach to give Casus a hand with the evacuation.

The group had spent most of the morning urging people down to the boat sheds. They had had some success, but not enough. Many of the citizens of Herculaneum had been reluctant to abandon their lands, their houses and, especially, their profitable businesses. Herculaneum was an integral part of the flourishing trade that existed around the Bay of Neapolis, the best natural harbor in Italy. The citizens had weathered many earthquakes, including the devastating one in AD 62. They felt that the threat associated with the tremors would pass. They planned to carry on with their daily routines until . . .

The ground shook violently. Only a few seconds later, there was a colossal thunderous boom. The sounds of crashing roof tiles could be heard over the shrieking women, crying children, and barking dogs.

Dani ran up the stairs to her room, threw back the wooden shutters, and trembled in terror. The top of Vesuvius had been torn open by a force greater than ten megatons of TNT. A huge dark grey blast cloud was billowing up into the sky, while tremendous forked lightning bolts flashed, going tens of thousands of feet into the air.

"We're out of time," Dani muttered, as she watched the dark cloud rise, higher and higher. *'How did Pliny put it? 'A cloud was ascending, the appearance of which I cannot give you a more exact description of than by likening it to that of a pine tree, for it shot up to a great height in the form of a very tall trunk, which spread itself out at the top into branches; occasioned, I imagine, either by a sudden gust of air that impelled it, the force of which decreased as it advanced upwards, or the cloud itself being pressed back again by its own weight, expanded in the manner I have mentioned; it appeared sometimes bright and sometimes dark and spotted, according as it was either more or less impregnated with earth and cinders,'* Dani recalled precisely.

A sudden blast of hot air raced through the town. It blew doors open. It rattled shutters, slamming many of them closed. Dani stepped back just in time to avoid getting her hands caught when the shutters on her window crashed shut. *Shock wave,* she reckoned

"Dani!" Julia yelled from downstairs.

"Coming, give me a sec," Dani shouted back, as she ran into Daric's room. She removed the key that Daric had given her that morning. Dani unlocked the strong box and dumped its contents onto what was left of Daric's cape. She tied it up carefully, so that nothing would fall out. Finally, she grabbed Bear's collar and leash and headed downstairs.

"What about the horses?" Tobius asked anxiously.

"Release them. They'll find their own way out of danger," Julia answered. She watched as Tobius and Cyrus ran out to the stables.

"Okay, I'm ready," Dani said, as she joined Julia in the atrium. She knelt and slipped on Bear's collar and attached the leash. "It's okay, Bear," she whispered, trying to assure her quivering pet. "You should've left before now," Dani remarked to Julia, as she stood up.

"I know. Let's go, and pray that we're not too late," Julia replied, as she ran out the door.

Dani with Bear in tow and Julia with her slaves ran past the marble statue of the horse-drawn chariot, which had sat above the entrance to the Basilica, but was now lying shattered in pieces on the ground. They hurried past the bronze statue of Hercules, who had toppled off its pedestal. They heard dogs barking and howling all over town. They saw chaos in the streets, as people finally realized the danger they were in.

* * *

On the outskirts of town, on the slopes of Vesuvius, a foreman bellowed, "You need to move faster than that!" Lycus cracked his whip on the back of a slave who just didn't seem to be working hard enough.

Just as the whip snapped, there was a tremendous explosion which seemed to resonate directly over their heads. Everyone stopped what they were doing and stared up at the slumbering giant who seemed to have awakened.

The shockwave from the explosion rolled down the side of the mountain and swept past them. As it passed, it knocked Lycus clear off his feet and threw him against a tree, impaling him on one of the tree's broken branches. It was the same tree that had taken the life of a slave three days earlier.

The slaves didn't hesitate. They ripped the keys off Lycus's bleeding corpse and ran to the large ergastulum and unshackled their fellow slaves. As soon as they had freed everyone, they went through the estate's villa and the foreman's house, scavenging whatever supplies they could carry, then they ran for their lives.

As the slaves fled from the estate, they came across Proculus, Primus's neighbor, fleeing in wagons with his slaves. Proculus graciously offered Primus's weaker and older slaves a ride who gratefully accepted his generosity. The able-bodied slaves hurried along beside the wagons as they moved on as quickly as possible toward Neapolis, five miles to the east of Vesuvius.

Present Day—Friday

106

"THE PROFESSOR ISN'T dead. I talked to him a little while ago," Hermes revealed. "He said Mr. Case is trying to acquire our time travel device. He told me to do whatever it takes to stall him."

"He's still alive! Well, that's good news, finally. Where is he now?" Eddie asked anxiously, hoping his nightmare would soon end.

"The professor is on his way home. He should arrive by morning. Our task is to stall until then," Hermes stated. "But I'm afraid I'm not very good at deception; it goes against my nature."

"I've got you covered; not to worry," Eddie assured Hermes. After all, Eddie had been cheating, lying and stealing for most of his adult life. Eddie pondered for a moment. If they needed to slow down their progress, he had the perfect distraction. Now would be an ideal opportunity for him to get more information to help fill in the missing pieces to his puzzle.

"Okay, let's take a break," Eddie suggested, as he took the chair previously occupied by Richard. "So, Hermes, this time travel device, how does it work exactly?" Eddie probed.

"Have you ever heard of wormholes?" Hermes asked.

"Sure, everyone has. They're found in outer space," Eddie responded proudly.

"Actually, wormholes exist all around us. They're virtual tunnels through time, shortcuts between two points," Hermes explained.

"Then why can't I see them?"

"They're smaller than a molecule, even smaller than an atom. They exist in a place called the quantum foam," Hermes revealed, as he looked at Eddie for comprehension.

"The time travel device the professor and I invented consists of bands. You wear one on each wrist. In the simplest terms, when the bands touch, the chronizium particles imbedded in the bands react to generate sufficient energy to capture a wormhole from the quantum foam. The wormhole expands and pulls the traveller through the opening and along a tunnel in time to the other end where it collapses upon the traveller's exit."

"Whoa! That's amazing! And it really works?" Eddie asked, astounded.

"Of course, it works," Hermes replied, irritated and offended by Eddie's doubt.

"Where are the bands now?" Eddie asked. He could hardly contain his excitement.

"Right now, they are with Dani and Daric, in Herculaneum, on August 24, AD 79."

"Seriously?" Eddie exclaimed "They're in AD 79? How do you know where they are? Or when, for that matter?"

"There is a chronometer built into the bands; it registers time. There is also a directional finder, similar to a GPS; it registers longitude and latitude. I use the coordinates to pinpoint a location using topographical information from that era," Hermes explained simply.

"So, can Dani and Daric go wherever they want? How do they move from one time and place to another?" Eddie asked, still trying to deal with the idea of actually travelling through time. Imagine being on the bridge of the Titanic when it hit the iceberg or walking on the moon with Neil Armstrong. Or what about going one-hundred or even two-hundred years into the future? What marvels awaited humankind in the next few millennia? The endless possibilities running through his mind were interrupted by Hermes's reply.

"I leveraged the research that Dr. Bin He did years ago at the University of Minnesota. Dr. He created an electroencephalography or EEG-based, non-invasive brain-computer interface. This interface allows the user to interact with the computer system using thought only. The EEG records and decodes a particular brainwave, called the sensorimotor rhythms or SMRS; the SMRS communicates with the computer. The computer, in turn, reads the SMRS as an executable command or, more specifically in this case, as a different spatial location," Hermes disclosed, matter-of-factly.

"That's unreal!"

"The only problem is that the bands were designed to be worn by one person, not two," Hermes continued. "Dani and Daric each wear one band. We have theorized that the stronger of the two brainwaves has been dictating the travel destinations. The professor sent Bear, the family dog, back in time with a message in her collar to inform the twins on how the travel bands work. We know Bear arrived safely, but we're still uncertain whether Dani and Daric can control their travels. I was out of commission on their last jump through time."

"That's truly unbelievable," Eddie uttered incredulously.

"But factual, I assure you," Hermes replied.

Eddie realized how dangerous this kind of technology would be in the wrong hands, Richard's hands. He had to come up with a way to stop him. "Look, I have an idea," Eddie said. "Let's finish the calculations for forward time travel, so, when the time is right, we can bring Dani and Daric home. I'll think of something to tell Richard to distract him, hopefully until the professor gets here, which better be soon."

"Okay," Hermes replied. He had grown rather fond of Eddie in the short time they had been together. Eddie was great with figures and computers, he had integrity, and Hermes admired his courage to stand up to Richard. The kid was okay in Hermes's mind.

Herculaneum—August 24, 79 AD
The Seventh Hour (after sunrise)

107

CASUS DASHED OUT of Julia's house and ran along the main street and, then, turned south down via Veneria. All the while, he was praying Tobius was right, that there were trade ships in the harbor. They could save the lives of thousands of people. He garnered a fair number of curious stares from citizens who were going about their usual business, as if it were any other day. But Casus knew that today would prove to be like no other.

"Get down to the beach. We need to evacuate the town," Casus yelled as loudly as he could. He was gasping for breath, but not missing a step in his race to the pier. "Get down to the beach. We're evacuating the town," he repeated as many times as he could.

Casus stopped and stood on top of the terraces just outside of the southern town walls, with the Temple of Venus to his right and the monument to Marcus Nonius Balbus to his left, next to the Suburban Baths. He looked down at the pier. The trade ships were still there, but he would have to hurry. It looked as though they were almost finished loading their cargo.

The trade ships were Roman corbitas, full-bodied wooden sailing vessels with a length of one hundred-and-eighty feet and a beam of forty-two feet. When their red rectangular sails were unfurled, the single large mainsail on a mast amidships was fifteen-hundred square feet; the two raffees, or triangular-shaped topsails, above the yard together, equaled three-hundred-twenty-five. One smaller mast, looking like a bowsprit, had a small square sail; the artemon or foresail, which was one-hundred-eighty-five square feet. Two steering oars, one on each quarter, were handled by one or two helmsmen, who sometimes stood on the roof of the ship's cabin, located near the vessel's stern. In strong winds and high seas, as many as four men were required on each oar to control the vessel. The aftercastle was decorated with a large elegant white swan's head. A corbita was capable of carrying up to two-thousand tons of cargo, the equivalent of forty-thousand amphorae.

Casus raced down the stairs that lead to the beach and then onto the pier. He ran up to a man who appeared to be directing the loading of one of the ships. "Are you in charge here?" Casus asked. He was trying hard to sound like he wasn't out of breath, but it was a losing battle; he was sadly out of shape, and his busted ribs were making themselves known, too.

"Yeah, I'm the captain," the older man replied gruffly. His sea-weathered face aged him beyond his years, but his physique spoke of the long voyages and the hard work involved with managing a trade vessel.

"By order of the magistrates, I command you to empty your cargo holds immediately," Casus said, as officially as he could muster.

"To Hades I will," the captain replied.

"Your name, citizen," Casus demanded.

"Pontius. Gaius Pontius. And you are?"

"Richardus Barak Casus, aide to the duumviri, Tiberius Crassius Firmus . . ." Casus paused for only a second recalling Firmus's death last night and, then, continued. ". . . and Arlus Marius Celus.

On their orders, I again command you to immediately empty your holds." He stood as tall as he could, with his right hand clasping the ornately decorated capulus, or knobbed hilt, of his gladius, for emphasis. "We're evacuating the town and we need your ships."

Pontius knew the duumviri, and he had had previous business dealings with Celus. If they needed his ship, who was he to argue. But then again, he still wanted to get paid, regardless of what he was hauling. "I'd be happy to oblige, once you get permission from Volusius Crescens. He's the one who's paid for this shipment. I take my orders from him."

"You've got to be joking. The magistrates' orders take precedence over everyone else's; so, empty that ship, now!" Casus barked.

Casus had barely finished issuing his command to Pontius, when the wooden pier beneath their feet shifted violently. Moments later, there was a thunderous explosion. Pontius and Casus looked north toward Vesuvius. Their eyes widened in terror. A gigantic dark grey cloud was spewing out of the mouth of Vesuvius, straight up into the sky, climbing higher and higher by the second. Brilliant flashes of lightning were scattered within the ever expanding cloud. The flashes occurred more and more often as the cloud climbed relentlessly higher.

Pontius and Casus stared at each other for only a second before Pontius yelled, "Empty the holds, now!"

Pontius's crew had just finished loading the holds. After that terrifying explosion and watching what looked like a very dark storm cloud growing in the distance, they were ready to do anything to get away from here as soon as possible. They began to throw overboard hundreds of amphorae containing wine, olive oil and grain–all originally destined to be traded for exotic spices in India and for fine silk in the Far East. Everyone's only concern now was to make as much space as possible available for the fleeing townspeople; their lives depended on it.

"What about those ships?" Casus asked, pointing to the ships tied to the other side of the pier.

"Those ships belong to my brother, Marcus Quintus," Pontius

said. “Marcus, empty your holds, quickly!” Pontius shouted to his brother. Marcus raised a hand, acknowledging the order. He never questioned it; the reason was all too obvious. The horror he was witnessing to the north, was much too close for his comfort. The sooner he got out of here the better.

One of the first citizens to reach the beach had been Volusius Crescens. As soon as he had heard about the evacuation, he had run to the pier to stop the ships from sailing, knowing that the sea was their only means of escaping the impending catastrophe. He was ecstatic to see that Casus had already started unloading the ships.

“Casus, how can I ever thank you?” Crescens asked sincerely. “You may have just saved thousands of lives.”

“Can you make sure these ships get fully loaded before they set sail?” Casus asked Crescens. “I have to see to the loading of the other boats.” Casus recognized it was Crescens’s merchandise that was being discarded and that Crescens was going to lose a fortune.

“I’ll make sure they’re full, Casus, and thank you for taking charge down here,” Crescens acknowledged appreciatively.

Casus nodded modestly, before running off the pier and down the beach. He was heading for Kallisto; he had previously spotted her in the distance waving her arms beside a man whom Casus couldn’t make out at this distance.

The Seventh Hour (after sunrise)

108

AFTER LEAVING JULIA'S, Kallisto found Nikanor at the Macellum, or market, just where she thought he would be. After explaining their dire situation, Nikanor wasted no time heading down to the beach, with Kallisto hot on his heels. As they were running through town, down toward the bay, the ground started to shake. Nikanor quickly reached out to grab Kallisto, saving her from a nasty fall. Then there was a tremendous roar. They peered to the north and saw an enormous dark cloud rising above Vesuvius. *Dani was right*, Kallisto thought. *I hope we're not too late.*

Nikanor and Kallisto raced to the beach; dodging red tiles that had slid off roofs and shattered on the paved roads below. Three of the columns of the Temple of Hercules had toppled over and broken into a hundred pieces, transforming the street into an almost impassable obstacle course. People were starting to gather in the streets. A palpable sense of panic was building.

When Nikanor and Kallisto finally arrived at the beach, Nikanor spotted seven of his ten fishing boats already out in the bay. He cursed his aged body; he hadn't been fast enough to stop them before they had launched this morning.

Nikanor stood on the shore and waved his arms like a maniac, trying to catch the attention of his sons and their crew. Kallisto joined in, trying to signal the boats, hoping they would return to shore. Moments later, Casus was standing beside her, signalling as well. After a few minutes, Nikanor spotted some encouraging signs. “They're pulling in the nets. They must have seen our signals,” he said excitedly.

“Maybe. Or maybe the fact that Vesuvius just blew its top made them think it was time to come back to shore,” Kallisto suggested

“Nikanor, I need you to get as many people as you can onto your fishing boats. I know they're not big, but each one should be able to hold ten people at least,” Casus said hopefully.

“If I toss out the holding bins, I can push it to fifteen. Don't worry, Casus, I'll get the boats loaded and under sail in no time,” Nikanor promised.

“Thanks,” Casus said. He grabbed Kallisto's hand and ran with her up the beach and onto one of the docks.

Two men approached Nikanor. One of them announced, “We need to get on a boat; we can pay for our passage.”

Nikanor recognized the two men as being Publius and Calvus, two of Tiro's enforcers. He despised both men; he had heard about the despicable things they had done. But he also knew from whom they took their orders. He slowly looked them over, sizing them up. Nikanor had never been one to turn his back on someone in need, and he wasn't about to do so now. But he would get payback on behalf of the individuals these two had wronged over the years. Besides, he could always use two strong backs on the oars and for handling the sails.

Nikanor stuck out his hand to accept payment from Publius and Calvus.

The Seventh Hour (after sunrise)

109

"BY THE GODS! What was that?" Primus roared.

"It's Vesuvius; it's erupting, just like Julia warned us," Aquilina said. She was terrified. "We have to leave, now! Cominia! Procilla! Grab Gaia and let's go."

Aquilina wasn't concerned for worldly possessions; she feared for her life and for the lives of her family. "Everyone down to the docks," she shouted, hoping that every person in the house, including the slaves, would hear her.

Primus was too busy packing to worry about his family. He was focussed on emptying his strong box. He hastily removed his valuables and stuffed them into leather satchels, which he would soon burden two of his slaves with. "Ferox, make sure those two stay right with us. I don't want them getting any ideas and wandering off." There was little chance that any slave would wander off, since a runaway slave could be executed when found.

"Master, what about the horses?" Ferox asked, as he stood watching Primus gather up all he held dear in life: his wealth.

"Leave them. What do I care? I'll buy more," Primus scoffed.

His attention never deviated from his packing.

Ferox seethed at what he had just heard; *how callous and heartless could a man be?* Ferox, however, could do nothing about it, a fact that enraged him even more.

Unbeknownst to Primus or the ever vigilant Ferox, Cominia had overheard Primus's cold-blooded remark and was taking matters into her own hands. She dashed through the courtyard and entered a small stable at the back. She untethered the four horses, including her favorite bay Maremmano mare. Cominia wrapped her arms around the mare's muscular neck. Then she cupped her muzzle and looked her right in the eye. "You know I'd take you with me, if I could," she said, as she felt her mare nod as if she understood exactly what Cominia was saying. "I need you to run as far away from here as you can." She rubbed her mare's forehead and kissed her nose. "Be safe; maybe, one day, we'll be together again. If not, I hope you find a gentle owner." Choking back a sob, she swatted her horse on the rump, and watched as she bolted from the stable, the other three horses close behind. The breed was recognized for its strength and ability to adapt to bad weather and rough terrain; she had to believe they would make it to safety. She had to. Cominia left the stable and went back into the house.

Ferox spotted Cominia entering the tablinum on her way through to the atrium, where her mother was gathering the family. Ferox looked imploringly at her. She nodded back in acknowledgement. Ferox let out a deep sigh.

"Let's go," Primus ordered. He ran out of the house with his left foot first. He didn't realize his mistake or frankly he didn't care. Primus was burdened with the thought he might have been the cause of the eruption. It was he, after all, who kidnapped Hephaestus's chosen one, Dani. Maybe the god was angry with him and was seeking revenge. Whatever the reason, he was getting as far away from that mountain as he could.

"Get out of my way!" Primus hollered, as he shoved an old beggar aside. The beggar was flung against the wall, hitting his head, and slumping in a heap on the ground, motionless.

Ferox looked back at the old man. He couldn't tell whether he was alive or dead. He shot an icy cold stare at Primus's back. That was the final straw; Ferox wasn't going to tolerate any more of Primus's cruelty and violence. *To Hades with him.* From now on, Ferox would be running for his own life; he would make sure he was no longer bound to Primus. Just how he would achieve his freedom wasn't clear, but unusual circumstances can present exceptional opportunities, as he had learned firsthand in the gladiator arena.

Present Day—Friday

110

THE SUN HAD set two hours prior to Richard's parking his black Audi Q7 SUV in the Delaneys' driveway. He exited the car, but instead of heading toward the house, he entered the garage. He flipped on the light and made his way to the dive lockers. Opening Quinn's locker, Richard pulled a vial off the top shelf and stuffed it into his jacket pocket. He closed the locker door, turned off the light, and left the garage. The whole side trip took less than two minutes.

Richard returned to his car and opened the passenger door. He reached in and pulled out a wicker picnic basket. Slamming the door, Richard walked to the house and entered through the kitchen door. "You're up," Richard remarked, when he saw Sandra standing at the kitchen sink. "How are you feeling?"

Sandra had been lost in thought, gazing out the large window that overlooked the manicured lawn and provided a panoramic view of the water. "A little sluggish, but for the life of me I don't know why," Sandra replied, as she turned away from the calming tranquility of the gentle waves rolling onto the sandy beach. She faced Richard and asked inquisitively, "What were you doing in the garage?"

Richard had been caught. He had to think fast. "I was just returning the thermal gloves Quinn lent me for our dive," he lied. He waited a moment; then breathed a sigh of relief when his lie seemed to have satisfied Sandra's curiosity. He raised his basket. "As promised, I brought dinner. Maybe, if you eat something, you'll feel better."

"You're probably right."

A few hours earlier, Richard had called Vashti Barinov, his cook and housekeeper, and had told her to prepare one of his favorite dinners. He had specified he wanted it to go.

Richard placed the basket on the kitchen's center island and began to take out its contents. He pulled out a sterling silver cloche-covered platter. Then he removed a bottle of wine, one he had carefully selected from his extensive wine cellar. This particular bottle was a 2009 Cabernet Sauvignon from the Chateau Montelena Estate. Next came a crystal dish containing a salad of mixed greens, tossed lightly with a balsamic dressing. And last, for dessert, homemade truffles. After checking that he had missed nothing in the basket, Richard took a second to admire the array of items on the counter. He then lifted the cloche. The room immediately filled with the delectable aroma of a classic English dish: Beef Wellington.

"That smells wonderful," Sandra admitted, reluctantly. "I'll set the table. Why don't you pour the wine?"

Everything was unfolding just as Richard had planned. He took the bottle into the living room and set it on the bar. He pulled two large crystal wine glasses from the rack, not the everyday glasses, but the good ones, and placed them on the bar. This was a special occasion in his mind: the elegant meal, the expensive wine, all shared with the love of his life, whom he would never possess. All his hard work was about to pay off in a little over twelve hours. Now, it was time to celebrate.

Once Richard had pulled the cork, he set the bottle down to

let the wine breathe for a few minutes. "I'm pretty sure I can bring Dani and Daric back home tomorrow," Richard announced, as he withdrew the small vial from his jacket pocket.

"Really?" Sandra blurted excitedly, as she rushed into the living room. "Are you certain?"

Richard froze, his hands still below the bar, out of sight. He hadn't expected Sandra would burst into the room upon hearing his news about her children. He should have. This oversight could have been disastrous for him. He vowed he would review the rest of his plan in minute detail. He was too close to achieving his goal to be derailed by another stupid mistake.

"Yes. Hermes and my associate will work all night, if need be, to make sure we can initiate forward time travel. I'll bring Dani and Daric home tomorrow, I promise."

"That would be incredible," Sandra said euphorically. Then her demeanour abruptly changed. Her head bent forward. Her shoulders slumped. "I wish Quinn could be here . . ." She turned her back to Richard, trying to hide the few tears that had trickled down her cheeks.

While thoughts of Quinn and her children distracted Sandra, Richard quickly poured some liquid from the vial into Sandra's glass before pouring wine into both glasses. After noting one last time which was Sandra's glass and which was his, he picked up the glasses and walked around the bar.

"So do I," Richard said sombrely, as he handed the glass in his right hand to Sandra. Even though he was ambidextrous, he preferred to keep that to himself. He never knew when it could become useful. He always preferred to use his right hand when conducting business, and, in this case, he needed to make sure he kept the correct glass for himself.

Richard and Sandra walked back into the kitchen together. Richard was disappointed, to say the least. He had been hoping the dining room table would have been elegantly set with the good china and silverware, with candles lit, to offer the proper atmosphere to accompany the elegant meal he had provided. But he would have to settle for casual dining at the family's kitchen table with its padded wooden benches. *Oh, well,* he thought. *Come tomorrow . . .* He raised his glass.

"Here's to tomorrow and all that it will deliver." Richard clinked glasses with Sandra.

"To tomorrow," Sandra repeated before taking a sip of her wine. "Now, let's eat before this delicious meal gets cold."

Herculaneum—August 24, 79 AD

111

RUFINUS WATCHED AS the panicking citizens of Herculaneum, from all segments of society, hurried toward the harbor. Some citizens, the wealthier class, were being carried on litters, but most were on foot. Rufinus looked up at Vesuvius, as it continued to spew dark grey smoke and ash high into the air. The mountain was over four and a half miles away. He looked back down toward the bay and the crowded beach and grumbled, "Cowards."

Rufinus headed back to his father's gem-cutter shop. As he was passing the house of Volusius Crescens, the merchant, he noted that the front door was wide open. He looked up and down the deserted street. "Easy pickings," he muttered, as he stepped across the threshold and into the house.

Rufinus made his way through the house, room by room. He picked up and took as many valuables as he could carry. In his mind, the town was his for the taking. Everyone was fleeing with only the few valuables they could carry and leaving behind vast quantities of varied treasures from which he could choose.

Rufinus resumed walking back to his father's shop. He intended to drop off his ill-gotten loot in his room before heading out again to collect more.

"Rufinus, thank the gods you're here. We have to leave immediately, come quickly," Antigonus said fretfully.

"I'm not going anywhere, old man," Rufinus grunted, as he pushed past his father and hurried toward his room.

Antigonus had a pack slung over his shoulder. It contained the tools of his trade, tools that had been passed down through generations. It also contained his collection of precious metals and stones. He was prepared to start a new business wherever he went, but it would all be meaningless if his son wasn't with him.

"Rufinus, I beg of you, come with me; it's not safe to stay here," Antigonus pleaded, when his son had returned.

"That mountain is over four miles away; we're perfectly safe here. I'm not going anywhere. If you want to run away with the rest of the cowards, go right ahead. You'll know where to find me when you realize what a big mistake you've all made," Rufinus declared conceitedly. He left his father's shop and set out once again on via Herculia. It would lead him to the more prestigious villas on the main street where the pickings would be exceptional.

Antigonus stood on the street and watched his only son walk away. Antigonus had failed somehow in raising his son. If only his wife had survived, maybe it would have been different. With his head hung low and his shoulders slumped, Antigonus turned and trudged off in the direction opposite to that taken by his son, not knowing whether he would ever see him again.

112

IT HAD TAKEN a while, but Casus had talked to the all trade ship captains. They knew what they had to do. Casus had also assigning captains to all the other seaworthy boats in the harbor around Herculaneum. Their job was to supervise the loading of their designated boats, to ensure they were fully loaded with people before sailing to a safer haven. Now, he had to deal with only one more boat: the yacht belonging to Primus.

Casus moved toward the yacht. Along the way, he noted approvingly of Daric and Kallisto, who were busy overseeing the loading of the smaller pleasure boats. Most of the boats in the harbor belonged to the wealthier citizens of the town, including the town's magistrates, who were hastily boarding with their families. Everything appeared to be proceeding well.

Just as Casus reached the dock where Primus's private yacht was moored, he saw Primus running toward the dock. Right behind him were Ferox and two slaves, who were heavily burdened.

Primus charged onto the dock. Almost immediately, he was stopped dead in his tracks. Casus was blocking his way.

Casus had no intention of letting Primus go any further. He put a hand on Primus's chest and stared at him. "I know what you did," he said coldly. "You had Firmus murdered. And we have witnesses.

So, I suggest you wait for the next boat." Casus glared at Primus, hoping that the threat would unsettle him, but it didn't seem to faze him in the least.

"Get out of my way. It's my boat," Primus shouted indignantly. When Casus stood firm, Primus turned to Ferox as if to say, do something.

Ferox took a step toward Casus, who had planted himself, preparing for a fight. Then the strangest thing happened. Ferox turned, stood beside Casus, and said to Primus, "The last thing I want to do right now is hurt you. But it's on my list. So, I suggest you do as he says, and wait." To emphasize his message, Ferox gave Primus a not-so-gentle shove. *That's for the old beggar,* Ferox mused, as he watched Primus stumble backwards and land on his back on the sand.

Casus stared at Ferox for only a moment before extending his hand. "I've wanted to do that for years," Ferox said simply.

"That's my ship," Primus protested pathetically.

"And we've commissioned it, because it's the fastest one around. It's going to sail to Misenum to get the navy to help with the evacuation," Casus explained, more to Ferox than to Primus.

"I'm sending the larger ships with most of the residents to Ostia, where they can get further passage up the Tiber River to Rome, if they so choose," Casus continued.

"That makes sense. There'll be more rooms there to accommodate the evacuees until it's safe for them to return home," Ferox concurred.

113

JULIA, DANI AND Bear had finally arrived at the beach along with the rest of Primus's family. Julia saw that all the vessels were being boarded by the residents of Herculaneum; it was an extremely efficient and orderly process.

Julia spotted Fuscus with his family and slaves, including Nais and the baby, boarding one of the trade ships. Nikanor's fishing fleet was already out in the bay, well underway. Being smaller boats, they would take longer to reach the far shore. She looked at another large ship and spotted Ennychus, being helped aboard by his wife, Livia Acte and his daughter, Venidia. He was still suffering from the beating by Tiro's enforcers. Petronia Justa was helping Calatoria Themis board another ship, putting aside their differences for the sake of survival.

Julia had just noticed Primus sitting on the beach. She looked at Casus, who just shrugged his shoulders. "We're ready to board, when you are," Casus told Julia.

Casus gestured for people to board the yacht. The first person to go aboard was Julia, who was on an urgent mission to meet with the admiral in Misenum and beg for his help. Next, there were the two aediles, Robia and Severus.

"I'm not leaving without you," Kallisto stated firmly.

"Think of our baby. I beg of you, please, get on board," Casus pleaded with his stubborn fiancée, praying that their child wouldn't be so obstinate. "I'm going to be right behind you, as soon as the rescue ships arrive from Misenum."

"You promise? Because I don't know what I'd do without you," Kallisto sobbed.

"I promise. I just need to finish up here and, then, I'll be right behind you. But you have to go now and send those ships back!" Casus urged.

Kallisto planted a passionate kiss on Casus's lips, then reluctantly turned and boarded the yacht.

Cominia was helped aboard next. Once aboard, she turned to help her mother, who was still standing next to her father on the beach.

"Mother, please, hurry," Cominia begged. She no longer felt any loyalty or respect for her father. Not one bit. But she was worried about her mother.

Julia sensed that Cominia was desperate. "Aquilina, there's still room," Julia cried out, urging her friend to flee with them.

"I'm sorry, Cominia. I can't leave," Aquilina replied, tears rolling down her cheeks as she looked sadly at her daughter. She shifted her eyes toward Julia. "Like I said before, Julia, my place is beside my husband."

Primus was still sitting on the sand, close to the bow of his yacht, mere feet away from a means of escaping Vesuvius's wrath. He had heard what Aquilina said. He looked at her, standing resolutely next to him. In his eyes, she was still a vision of beauty, just like the day he had met her. She had always been a woman of class and distinction. They were traits that had prompted him to marry her in the first place; standing by his side, she would make him look regal, contributing to his being all the more revered and admired.

"Procilla, take Gaia and go, please," Aquilina begged her sister.

"I'm not leaving you," Procilla responded adamantly. "I'll board the next boat with you and, then, we'll both sail away to safety.

Until then, I'll wait, while you wait."

"But, what about your family, your husband and your other daughters? You have to get back to them. I'll never forgive myself if something should happen to you and Gaia," Aquilina stated fretfully.

"We'll be fine," Procilla said unconvincingly, placing her hands on Gaia's tiny shoulders. Gaia was using both her hands to pull grapes off their stems and pop them into her mouth. She didn't understand what was happening, but she was always up for a boat ride.

Aquilina shouted from the beach to her friend, "Julia, go now, go swiftly to get help."

The yacht was about to cast off its mooring lines when Primus yelled, "Wait!" He ran onto the dock, only to be blocked from getting any closer to his yacht by Ferox and Casus.

"Cominia, please take our valuables with you. The next boats may be much smaller. The fewer possessions taken on board would mean the more people it will carry," Primus explained.

Ferox stared into the cold hard face he had served for years. He wouldn't have believed what he was seeing, if he hadn't witnessed it firsthand. There seemed to be some compassion there. Primus looked beseechingly at Ferox and said, "Go with Cominia. Protect her."

While this exchange had been taking place, Dani had quietly walked on board and handed a bundle to Kallisto. "We want you to have this," Dani said. "It's just a few trinkets you might be able to sell to get what you need for the baby. Let's just call it a wedding gift." Dani leaned down and kissed Kallisto's head. "Be safe," she said, as she left the vessel.

Ferox looked at Casus, who nodded in agreement. Ferox boarded the yacht, the lines were cast off, and the yacht lurched forward.

* * *

The grey ash cloud had eclipsed the sun, sending the town into darkness well before dusk. Torches had been lit to help with the final boarding of the boats.

All the vessels, large and small had been loaded to capacity and then some. Antigonus had walked along the pier and would be the last to board the one remaining trade ship. Before setting foot on the ship's deck, he turned his bruised face and peered back to the terrace above the boat sheds one more time, hoping to locate his son; once again, he had been disappointed. Antigonus hung his head and stepped onto the ship's deck and found a place to sit as the lines were released and the last ship left the pier.

Dani and Daric watched, with Casus, as the last ship left Herculaneum's harbor. The three of them had argued with their friends and loved ones over their decisions to remain behind and their friends had reluctantly accepted their motives. Casus felt an obligation to his home town to see that everyone got to safety. Dani and Daric remained behind to help Casus and added the lame excuse that Bear hated the water. They told their friends they would escape on horseback. Even though Bear really did hate the water, only Dani and Daric knew the real truth.

Present Day—Friday

114

EDDIE HAD HEARD a car pull into the driveway, then a car door slam and approaching footsteps. Eddie needed to hide, but where? He panned his flashlight around the four-car garage, frantically seeking a space large enough to conceal him.

Eddie's light revealed two of the Delaneys' cars. He quickly threw out the idea of hiding in one of them; the doors would probably be locked. His light moved on until it shone on the cabin cruiser. Again, not a good idea; he would need to get a ladder to climb inside, after, of course, having taken the time to unzip the boat's canvas cover. The light next hit the space beside the cruiser. The space had been used during the winter to store Daric's boat, which Quinn had recently launched for Daric to use while he was home.

Eddie redirected his light to one of the end walls; all he could see were two kayaks mounted on the wall. As he moved his light along the back wall, he spotted a large set of storage lockers. *Perfect,* he thought. He opened one of the doors and squeezed inside. It was a tight fit, but not all that uncomfortable. Hopefully, he wouldn't have to hide there for long.

Eddie saw the interior light of the garage come on through the vents in the locker door. He heard footsteps approaching. They were getting closer. They were getting too close. They stopped in front of the locker. *Oh, shit,* Eddie thought. *This can't be good.*

Eddie heard a metallic creaking as the dented locker door opened. A few seconds later it creaked again as it closed. The sound of footsteps faded as they receded. The light went out. The door slammed shut. Eddie didn't move a muscle. He heard the closing of a car door outside the garage, but he didn't hear the car's engine start or the car drive away. Whoever had entered the garage was staying at the Delaneys' for a while.

Eddie waited another ten minutes before he opened the locker door and slowly uncoiled his aching body. He winced when he tried to stretch out his cramped legs and stiff neck. He knew he should get what he came for and get out quickly, but his curiosity got the best of him. Eddie turned on his flashlight and opened the locker that the visitor had accessed; he saw only a few pieces of dive equipment. He opened another locker; it was packed with top-of-the-line dive equipment, as was the third one. Then he inspected the locker he had occupied. "Huh," Eddie muttered. He knew he was taking a huge risk. He had stayed too long. He needed to get out, now.

Eddie checked the list of items Hermes had told him to collect. He needed to find only two more items, and that only took a few minutes. He put everything into an empty bag he had found in the locker. Eddie moved cautiously to the garage door, being careful not to make a sound. He pried the door open and peered into the darkness. So far as he could see, the coast was clear. He took a deep breath, grasped the bag securely, and raced as quietly as he could across the dark yard, back to the gazebo.

"What took you so long?" Hermes asked when Eddie entered the lab.

"I had company," Eddie panted.

"That must have been Mr. Case," Hermes surmised. "I heard his voice over the speaker."

"What would he be doing in the garage? And why did he go to the lockers?"

"Oh, he told Dr. Delaney he was returning the dive gloves he had borrowed from the professor," Hermes answered.

It sounded like a reasonable explanation, but something didn't sit right with Eddie. Questions started running through his mind. *Where's all the other dive equipment? Why did Richard return only the gloves? If they were cave diving in New Zealand in April . . .* Then it hit him, the missing items from the locker Richard accessed; the thermal wear, the dive mask. Eddie looked down at the bag holding the items he had brought from the garage. It was a small square bag with the word Predator printed in gold lettering across the front; it would have contained a dive mask. *So where are those items? Why hasn't Richard returned those, too? Wait! There were no gloves in that locker! What was Richard up to? Was he covering for something else?*

"Did you get the items I asked for?" Hermes asked, interrupting Eddie's musings.

"Yeah," Eddie replied. He opened the bag and pulled out the items Hermes had requested: a coil, a transformer, a plastic box, two electrical cords, four wire nuts and electrical tape. "Now what?"

"I'll walk you through the steps to build a degausser," Hermes replied. "Then, you can get rid of that perimeter collar."

And finally get away from that maniac, Eddie reflected.

Herculaneum—August 24, 79 AD

115

SPURIUS SUBINUS WAS terrified. Why was Vulcan so angry? he wondered. Like many others in Herculaneum, Subinus had made his way down south to the boat sheds. When he had reached the upper landing and had peered down at the beach, he realized that all the boats had already sailed. But there were still hundreds of people gathered there, anxiously waiting to be rescued. His shoulders slumped and, with his head hung low, he retraced his steps back up the street.

As Subinus trudged wearily back to his quarters in the Curia, he was philosophical. His had been a long life. Although it hadn't been particularly noteworthy, it had been one he could be proud of; he was, after all, working for the aediles. Although he feared what Vulcan might have in store for him and Herculaneum, he wasn't prepared to put himself ahead of others. If more evacuation ships were to arrive, he would gladly give his space in favor of a younger man, one who was just starting his journey through life. In his mind, it was the right thing to do, especially since he had no family–he was alone.

Subinus finally arrived at the Curia. He entered through the side door, crawled into his bed, and prayed to the gods that Vesuvius would soon rest.

* * *

Primus dusted the sand from his toga as he watched his yacht slowly fade into the distance. He walked back to the beach and stood in front of his wife. "Aquilina, there's a place I know that will provide you with the best protection. Come with me," Primus said. He tenderly clasped his wife's hand and led her down the beach, with Procilla and Gaia right behind. The little girl was still munching on a bunch of grapes, as she was dragged along by her mother. They came to one of the boat sheds further down the beach. "In here," Primus said as he walked inside. "At the very back, there's a small niche where you can take shelter. It's the most protected place down here," Primus assured them.

"How do you know about this place?" Procilla asked suspiciously.

"Let's just say that, occasionally, I've used this little hiding place to store some merchandise," Primus admitted vaguely.

* * *

Marcus Livius Alcimus and his family were among the last to arrive at the boat sheds. *We're too late,* he thought, after noticing all the boats had already sailed. If they hadn't wasted so much time trying to calm his son's dog, Titan, they might have been able to get onto one of the last boats.

"Help should be coming soon," Casus tried to assure Alcimus. "Why don't you find some place in one of the boat sheds to take shelter from this stuff," he suggested. As he spoke, he held out his hand, palm side up, and started to collect the falling ash that was dropping like a fine mist. "I'm keeping watch for the rescue ships that are coming from Misenum." *Soon, I hope,* he prayed.

* * *

"Festus, they said we should leave," Agatha pleaded for what seemed like the umpteenth time.

"I'm not going anywhere. I've worked too hard and too long to get this business and I'm not going to walk away from it simply because some slave tells me to. What makes you think his word is any better than mine?" Festus barked.

"But everyone's already headed to the beach; it's our only way out of here. I think we should go, too, or at least check it out and see what's happening," Agatha pressed nervously.

"What about our customers?" Festus grunted, wondering where his usual patrons were.

"We have had no customers since Vesuvius blew; that should tell you something," Agatha stated bluntly. "Now, let's lock up and go see what's happening."

"All right," Festus agreed, giving in reluctantly. He walked out from behind the counter and locked the door behind them. He and Agatha hurried along via Herculia until they reached the terraces at the southern end of town. They peered at the beach. Hundreds of people roamed about, but there was only one boat in sight; it was overturned farther down the beach.

Festus and Agatha spotted Casus standing at the end of the pier, waving a torch. They approached him.

"Casus, what's happening?" Festus asked nervously. Maybe Agatha was right, maybe they should have come down sooner.

"We've sent for help. We're just waiting for the navy at Misenum, to send boats to evacuate the rest of us," Casus informed them. "Why don't you take some shelter in one of the boat sheds with the others? I'll let you know when the boats arrive."

"What about that boat?" Festus asked, pointing to the one down the beach.

"I've already checked it; it's not seaworthy," Casus told them.

With that, Festus and Agatha walked off the pier and found a place to sit in one of the boat sheds while they waited for the navy to come to their rescue. They didn't realize how many others were waiting as well: there had to be at least three-hundred, if not more.

116

AS THE FLOTILLA left Herculaneum's harbor and sailed across the Bay of Neapolis, the passengers on board the vessels saw a different perspective of the phenomenon happening back on shore.

The top of Vesuvius had disappeared completely; it no longer had a defined peak. The dark ash cloud had risen directly above the mountain and appeared to be climbing. Forked lightning flashed sporadically amidst the cloud, making it seem like a vicious thunderstorm, except that the lightning was fiery red, not white. The winds were blowing from the northwest. They propelled the ash cloud toward Pompeii, flattening out along the top as it drifted away from the mountain. From this distance, it was impossible to make out Pompeii; no lights could penetrate the darkness that surrounded the city.

In contrast, looking back at Herculaneum, the passengers could still see their town and the numerous lights on the beach. There might still be hope.

"I'm afraid," Kallisto murmured, as she sat on the deck, with her arms wrapped around her knees drawn to her chest. The sound of the sails' cables flapping against the mast, only added to Kallisto's distress.

"It'll be all right; look!" Julia said excitedly, pointing toward the mouth of the bay.

Kallisto sat up and beamed. There was a whole fleet of ships heading toward the coast, heading toward Herculaneum. Either word had somehow reached the admiral of the navy or he had seen the catastrophe and had launched a rescue mission.

"They'll be fine, I know they will," Julia said reassuringly, but she had to admit she was worried, too.

Kallisto hugged Julia, seated to her left on the deck. After a few moments, Kallisto, let go. She rested her back against the side of the yacht. She glanced encouragingly at Cominia, who was to her right. The awning above them was flapping slightly in the wind.

Kallisto reached for the parcel Dani had given her. She was curious to see what was inside. She placed it in front of her and opened it carefully. "By the gods," she blurted.

Cominia glanced over and smiled. "You have a small fortune there," she observed.

Inside the parcel were two large exquisitely crafted gold pins, four bands of braided gold and two gold necklaces.

Kallisto looked at Julia, who smiled happily at the mother-to-be. "Nice wedding gift, I must say," Julia remarked.

Herculaneum—August 25, 79 AD

117

TELLING TIME HAD become extremely difficult; when Vesuvius had erupted around 1 PM, day had almost instantly turned to night. Dani didn't know how much time had passed since then, which meant she had no idea how much time they had left. She prayed that Cilo a.k.a. Pliny the Younger had his facts right when he recorded that the dark column above Vesuvius had collapsed at 2 AM and not any sooner. When that happened, they would have only mere minutes after the collapse to escape certain death, so she stuck right next to Daric.

Dani joined Daric walking along the beach with Bear. Men clustered along the shoreline holding torches, desperately waiting for the rescue boats to arrive. They saw families huddled in the boat sheds; most of the children asleep on their mothers' laps. *That's good,* Dani thought, *they won't ever know what happened.* Most of the town's people who were still waiting to be evacuated seemed to have lacked status or wealth. Or maybe they had simply chosen to leave their valuables behind when they fled their homes.

From her knowledge of history, Dani knew that Herculaneum

was experiencing a different kind of disaster than Pompeii. The wind was blowing debris from the volcano toward Pompeii which was being pummeled with ash and pumice and had been now for hours. Herculaneum, by comparison, was getting away relatively unscathed, with only a fine film of falling ash. If it hadn't been for the calm and orderly evacuation, thousands of citizens would surely have perished here. History never changed, it just unfolded as it was supposed to. And in 1982, over three-hundred skeletons were found, right down here, along the shore, in and around the boat sheds.

The last ship had left the harbor at Herculaneum hours ago. With a bit of luck, everyone on board would be safe from harm by now. As for those who remained, Dani's heart ached. She knew that this disaster would resonate from the ancient to the modern world; that the bones of these people would become a frozen moment of a real population, a time capsule, and the best example of how a Roman town really worked. Herculaneum, once the playground for the rich where the inhabitants would have a glass of wine while they watched the sun set over the bay, would soon be buried under eighty feet of ash that would eventually turn to solid rock.

Daric saw Casus standing at the end of the pier where he had been stationed for hours now, watching for any shapes emerging out of the darkness. From time-to-time, he would wave his torch, hoping to signal any unseen vessel that happened to be near. Casus, given the chance to escape, had stayed, to wait on the beach with the rest of the town's inhabitants until the very end. Extraordinary times sometimes created extraordinary people, and the current version of "Uncle Richard" was a prime example. Daric noticed a figure approaching Casus from behind.

"I need to get on the first boat that arrives," Primus said to Casus, as he handed him a small pouch of coins. "It's all the money I have on me, and it's yours."

Casus tucked the pouch into his belt. "I'll see what I can do," he replied, never committing one way or the other.

As Primus walked back to the beach, a few other men

approached Casus. It seemed to Daric they were all looking to Casus for instructions.

"What are we going to do?" Tiro asked, nervously. He had dallied too long before heading to the boats. He had stayed behind to make sure that Primus's documents were safely locked up, but Primus hadn't said so much as 'thank you' for his efforts.

"I'll keep signaling. Why don't you guys hunker down somewhere? Hopefully we'll be rescued come morning, if not sooner," Casus suggested confidently.

A few moments later, there was a tremendous rumble. Bear took off down the beach; the leash slipping through Daric's hand.

"Bear, no!" Daric yelled, as he gave chase.

"Daric!" Dani hollered after him. They had just run out of time. She took off after Daric. They couldn't be separated now; it would mean certain death if they couldn't touch bands within the next few minutes.

"Take shelter!" Casus shouted.

Everyone on the beach heard something, but they couldn't see the mountain. There was a sense of panic, as everyone ran for shelter. Disaster was about to rain down upon them.

The vertical column of gas and steam that had continued to expand upwards to a height of approximately twenty miles could no longer support its own weight. It collapsed onto itself, entering its most destructive phase. The collapse of the eruption column produced pyroclastic density currents: lethal clouds of ash and gas. Within a matter of minutes, the poisonous mass came barreling down the mountain at hurricane speeds.

"Daric! Wait! We're out of time!" Dani yelled as loudly as she could. Daric had always been a faster sprinter, and Bear was even faster. Bear had long since disappeared into the darkness beyond. The roar of the collapse had frightened her, and she reacted instinctively–flight.

Daric stopped running. He looked back at Dani. There had to be the distance of at least two football fields separating them. Daric recalled what Dani had said: once the column collapsed, they would have only a few minutes before the turbulent avalanche of death would reach them. Panic suddenly gripped him. What had he done?

"Keep running," he yelled, as he took off toward her. They were trying desperately to close the gap between them. But could they close it in time?

The billowing super-heated gases, mixed with a dense cloud of fine ash, raced toward the town of Herculaneum in great swirling torrents. It passed over the town's outer walls, passed Festus's inn, passed the amphitheatre, picking up speed as it descended toward the bay, instantly vaporizing flesh as it went.

Damn, Daric cursed himself, as the sound of the raging death wave approached. His lungs felt like they were about to explode, as he put everything he had into increasing his speed. He realized they would never reach each other in time, and it was entirely his fault. He had just killed them both.

"I'm sorry!"

Then everything went dark.

Present Day—Saturday

118

DURING LAST NIGHT, Hermes and Eddie had finished the computations for forward time travel. If they had had the chronizium, they could have brought Dani and Daric back to the present and could have kept the travel bands out of Richard's nefarious clutches. Unfortunately, Richard had had the chronizium in his possession. As a result, Eddie and Hermes had been trying to devise another plan to prevent Richard from stealing Quinn's invention.

"Where's the professor? I thought you said he would be here today," Eddie ranted. He was getting frustrated, because he was running out of viable ideas for thwarting Richard's plan.

"He will be," Hermes replied and then paused. "He's still en route; ETA is just over an hour from now, so we need to keep stalling."

"And how do you suggest we do that, given Richard will be back any minute?" Eddie sputtered uneasily.

"I thought you said you were good at deceptions. I was relying on you for an answer," Hermes stated uncomfortably.

"Relying on Eddie for what?" Richard grunted, as he took the last step down into the lab. He had caught only part of the conversation.

"Uh . . ." Hermes stammered nervously, unsure how much of their conversation Richard had overheard.

"Hermes was relying on me to recheck the computations for forward time travel. We want to be one-hundred percent sure we have them correct or we could lose Dani and Daric in time forever," Eddie replied, fabricating a plausible excuse.

"I told you I wanted everything done by the time I returned," Richard growled while he reached into his pocket. He pulled out the collar control mechanism and pushed the button. Eddie didn't fall to his knees screaming. He pushed the button again and got the same effect: nothing. Richard glared at Eddie and noticed the collar was missing.

"Where is it?" Richard barked.

"It fell off," Eddie replied coldly. "Then I destroyed it."

Richard threw the control device across the room. It shattered into tiny pieces when it smashed against the wall. *No matter,* he thought.

"I don't need that to control you," Richard snapped. "You have thirty minutes to finish your work. Any longer and Sandra will be dead. The antidote won't work any longer."

"What have you done?" Eddie raged.

"I poisoned her," Richard jeered. "When I realized you two were taking too long, I thought I'd provide a little incentive. So, get going. You're wasting time!"

Richard had no antidote, because there was none. He also had no idea how long Sandra had. All he knew was that Sandra was running out of time. The only way Sandra would survive would be with immediate medical attention, which would never happen, so far as Richard was concerned. She hadn't looked at all well when he checked in on her this morning.

"All right," Eddie snapped angrily. "Give us a couple of minutes to make sure everything is set. And we'll need the chronizium to make this work."

"I'll give it to you when you're finally ready to flip the switch, so to speak," Richard snarled, as he checked the time on his comm.

"You now have twenty-eight minutes."

"I know!" Eddie growled. He was angry. And he was more determined than ever to follow through on a decision he had made during the night. Finally free of Richard's control, Eddie felt he owed it to the Delaneys to make sure Richard didn't succeed with his plan. Having been forced to do Richard's bidding, he was already responsible for killing one-hundred-eleven people and injuring hundreds more. He didn't want three more deaths on his conscience, as he had explained to Hermes when he had told him about Richard lies and deception. Hermes had reacted sympathetically, vowing with Eddie to stop Richard at all costs.

"Okay, Hermes, let's get to it," Eddie said. His anger had subsided only slightly.

* * *

For the next ten minutes, Hermes and Eddie conferred in hushed voices. Meanwhile, Richard fumed in the corner chair. To pass the time, he inattentively watched the surveillance camera monitor.

Eddie noticed that Hermes had gone quiet. "What is it?" Eddie whispered.

"The professor is almost here. I told him we couldn't stall any longer; Dr. Delaney's life was at stake," Hermes whispered.

"That's great." Eddie's enthusiastic remark didn't go by unnoticed.

"What's great?" Richard asked, as he left his chair and walked over to the console.

"Uh, we're ready to initiate forward time travel," Hermes announced.

"We need the chronizium," Eddie said, extending his hand.

Richard pulled the rare mineral from his pocket and handed it to Eddie. "With fifteen minutes to spare."

"What about the antidote?" Eddie snapped irritably.

"Only after the twins are back," Richard said coldly. "Now, get on with it."

Part VII

. . . When Time Ended

Present Day—Saturday

119

EDDIE COULD SWEAR he was looking at a Greek goddess. The young lady sprawled on the floor was the most beautiful woman he had ever seen, even under the fine layer of ash that covered her from head to toe. With her delicate features and slim athletic physique, Eddie believed she could have been Artemis herself. Her Roman name was Diana, not that far off of the young lady's real name. The young man sprawled beside her could have been a Greek god as well, maybe Artemis's twin brother, Apollo. And their clothes supported that idea. Eddie realized just then that they were in fact twins

"It worked!" Richard exclaimed, as he rushed to Dani's side.

"Uncle Richard?" Dani mumbled when she recognized a familiar voice, while waiting for her vision to clear.

"Thank goodness you're finally home," Richard said, as he knelt beside Dani's prone form. "Let's get this thing off. We don't want to lose you again." Richard reached for Dani's left arm and quickly removed the travel band.

"Where's Daric?" Dani asked anxiously.

"Right here," Daric answered groggily, as he sat up and glanced around. "Hey, we're back home; this is Dad's lab. Whoa, who is that?" Daric had spotted a toga-clad character and was hoping the stranger hadn't travelled back through time with them.

"That's your dad's artificial intelligence, Hermes," Richard explained indifferently.

"Really? Way to go, Dad," Daric said enthusiastically. He had always been fascinated with technology and was eager to learn more about this AI.

"Where's Dad?" Dani asked uneasily, as she got to her feet. She was looking around the sparsely furnished lower lab when she noticed a young man standing by the computer console. He wore navy blue pants and an indigo long-sleeve Henley shirt under a navy blazer. He was shaking his head, as discreetly as possible. He looked very nervous and Dani wondered why.

Eddie was trying to warn the strangely dressed newcomers that they were in danger, but to no avail.

"He's not here," Richard replied bluntly. He was in the same room as the travel bands and he didn't want to waste any more time on trivial conversation.

"Well, that's obvious," Daric stated curtly.

Richard sensed by Daric's tone that something had changed. Daric wasn't usually this brazen or flippant.

"Daric, let's get that band off you, too," Richard suggested calmly, as he walked toward him.

"Answer the question, Uncle Richard," Daric insisted. "Where's Dad?"

Richard detoured toward the metal table and placed Dani's travel band into one of the velvet-lined cases. He would have to deal with a couple of matters first. Richard turned around. He was holding a gun pointed directly at Dani.

"He's dead!" Richard pronounced.

A gasp came from Dani, then a low moaning. "No." She sank to her knees.

"I don't believe you," Daric said defiantly.

"Where's Mom?" Dani uttered, barely holding back a sob.

"She could be dead now, too, for all I know," Richard grunted.

"Wait, what about the antidote you promised?" Eddie chimed in, afraid to move a muscle, now that Richard had a gun pointed at Dani.

"I lied. There isn't one," Richard sneered. "Now, I'll tell you one more time: remove that band and place it on the table. Eddie, give him a hand."

Daric had no choice but to comply. He watched as the young man, small in stature, walked toward him. He had no idea what these two were doing in his dad's lab, but he didn't have to be a genius to know they were trouble. His first concern, however, was Dani's safety, so he needed to keep a level head.

"I recognize that gun," Daric said contemptuously, as he unfastened the travel band and placed it in the velvet-lined case, as he had been told to do.

"How could you possibly know this gun?" Richard asked warily. It had been locked in a safe for years.

"It was the gun one of your ancestors, probably your great-grandfather, used to try to kill me in 1939." Daric shot him an icy glare. "He was the one responsible for sabotaging Amelia Earhart's world flight and, for all intents and purposes, the one responsible for her death."

Richard had received the gun from his father, who had said it had belonged to his father. But how did Daric know that? Could what he was saying be true? *No matter,* Richard thought. He was so close to seeing his plan come to fruition; he couldn't allow himself to be distracted by Daric's petty comments. He had to stay focussed on his plan. Nothing else mattered.

Bear suddenly appeared, momentarily distracting Richard. Daric saw an opportunity, but, before he could challenge Richard, Eddie grabbed his arm and stopped him. Daric gawked at Eddie, who just shook his head a tad. He was trying to warn Daric to stand down.

120

JIM HICKS MANOEUVRED the Harrier Jump Jet over the tennis courts. He hovered there for a few moments to blow away all the loose debris that could get sucked into the engine and, then, gently set the aircraft down. The Delaneys hadn't used their tennis courts in years. The kids had lost interest in the game and Sandra and Quinn had turned their attention to pickleball.

Quinn had suggested the courts as a possible landing site for several reasons. They were large enough to accommodate the jet. Their nets and fences had been removed long ago; as a result, Jim would be able to find the courts easily and set the jet down right in the middle. They were located almost a mile from the lab, far enough, Quinn hoped, that the loud Pegasus engine wouldn't alert Richard to their arrival. Most important of all, the abandoned tennis courts were solid concrete and in good condition.

No sooner had the Harrier's wheels touched down, then Quinn pushed open his canopy, unbuckled his restraints, and climbed out of his seat, preparing to jump to the ground.

Jim yelled, "Hang on a sec!"

Quinn froze. With one hand on the edge of the open canopy, he stared down at Jim. "What?" They both knew that time was of the essence.

"Wait until I shut down the engine or you'll be nothing but mincemeat," Jim cautioned. After what seemed like an eternity to Quinn, but was actually closer to thirty seconds, Jim shouted, "All clear."

Quinn jumped to the ground, ignoring the boarding steps that were available. It was a nine-foot drop to the concrete courts. And his left ankle screamed on impact.

"I'll be right behind you, once I secure the plane," Jim hollered down to Quinn.

"No! Go to the house and find Sandra," Quinn yelled over his shoulder, as he started for the gazebo on the far side of the peninsula. He was sure Richard would be there.

Quinn was going as fast as he could. He wished he could go faster, but he wasn't as young as he used to be and he was still feeling the painful effects of his twisted ankle he had suffered in New Zealand. He forced himself to ignore the pain and increase his pace. He was being driven by the last communication he had received from Hermes that said time was running out and they couldn't stall Richard any longer. Richard had poisoned Sandra to get Hermes's cooperation. Hermes was about to initiate forward time travel to bring Dani and Daric home to the present day. Once the twins got home, Quinn realized, Richard would get his hands on the travel bands. He couldn't let that happen. He had to run faster.

When Quinn arrived at the gazebo, he stopped to catch his breath. As urgent as the situation was, he recognized that he needed to rest, at least briefly.

After barely a minute, Quinn crept inside the gazebo and made his way to the back wall. When he reached the stairs leading to the lower lab, he stopped. There was no indication that his presence had been detected. Only muffled voices were coming from below. He immediately recognized Richard's grating tone, which triggered his rage. Then he caught one of the sweetest sounds. It was pure music to his ears: it was Dani's voice. He was ecstatic. *It worked. They were able to bring my children home,* Quinn rejoiced, relieved.

121

"WHY ARE YOU doing this?" Dani asked.

"These travel bands are mine now," Richard announced with a malicious smile.

"What are you going to do with them?" *How could this be happening? What went on while we were gone?* Dani wondered.

"I need to right an injustice done to my family," Richard said. "I need history to correct itself and play out the way it was supposed to, before one of my ancestors was accused of a crime he didn't commit."

"As I see it, your family tree is chock full of traitors and murderers. When your family went diving into the gene pool, they neglected to get any morals, any decency. Lack of ethics seems to be an inherited trait," Daric shot back. He was referring to Richard's ancestors whom Dani and he had met during their travels. "And the apple didn't fall far from the tree, did it?"

"Enough talk. Now move." Richard waggled the gun and jerked his head in the direction of the rear emergency exit door. "Eddie, get them inside."

Eddie went to the rear door of the emergency escape tunnel and waited beside it. He was stalling as long as possible. There was no way he was going to drag anyone through that door. If Richard wanted Dani and Daric inside, he would have to do it himself.

Bear sensed the tension in the room and instinctively knew the cause. She approached Richard from the side. Baring her teeth, she issued a deep guttural growl.

Richard was in no mood to deal with a snarling dog. He swung his arm and pointed the gun at Bear.

"No! Please!" Dani screamed, as she lunged at Bear, throwing her arms around the dog's neck. Richard flung the barrel of gun upwards, just mere seconds from pulling the trigger.

"Damn you," Richard cursed. Had the gun discharged, and the bullet struck Dani, the drowning wouldn't be considered accidental; it would have been a homicide. He figured he could have buried the dog's carcass in some remote location or dumped it into the lake; no one would have been the wiser. Disposing of human bodies without them eventually being missed, well, that was a completely different problem. No, the bodies had to be found, and it had to look accidental or an investigation would be ongoing until the truth finally came out. No, an accident was still the best plan.

"Take the damn dog with you, now!" Richard barked.

Dani picked up Bear and walked to the emergency exit. She could feel Bear's growling vibrations on her arms.

Eddie caught movement out of the corner of his eye. It was on the surveillance monitor. Someone had just run into the house. *That must be the professor,* Eddie thought. Thankfully, Richard's back was to the monitor, and he remained unaware.

"You don't need to do this," Dani pleaded, as she was roughly shoved through the door.

Daric turned on Richard and was about to charge him, but found the cold barrel of Richard's gun pressed against his forehead

"Don't even think about it," Richard snarled. "Now, get in."

Daric knew he couldn't compete with a loaded gun and, therefore, reluctantly went through the rear door. He was almost knocked over when Eddie was also pushed inside. The door slammed behind him. "Hey!" Eddie shouted at the door.

"Eddie, I hereby terminate our partnership," Richard announced through the sealed door. "This will look like a simple accident. No one will ever suspect murder," Richard jeered, pocketing his gun as he walked over to the computer console.

"Open the inner hatch and, then, open the outer door just a half an inch," Richard instructed Hermes. Richard had closed the inner hatch when he left the lab nine days ago and it needed to be open for his plan to succeed. He didn't want the outer door opened completely, because they could swim out of the tunnel into the lake just as he had done. Opening the outer door only slightly would trap them inside while the tunnel gradually filled with water.

"I can't do that; they'll drown," Hermes protested.

"That's the idea," Richard grinned. "Now, do as I said."

Hermes hesitated. Richard glanced over at the door's control panel; it still showed a green light. "Do it, now!" Richard snapped.

"I can't," Hermes resolutely objected. He knew the professor was on his way; he just hoped he would arrive in time.

"You can't refuse me!" Richard growled. Hermes did not budge. "Fine, I'll do it myself." Richard hadn't fully grasped Hermes's abilities as a cognitive computer. He had assumed that Hermes had to execute all commands given to him. Richard opened the inner hatch and the outer door by just a fraction. He turned back to the door's control panel; a moment later, a red light flashed on, indicating the lab door was sealed and the outer door was open. The tunnel was slowly filling with water. It would not be the rushing flood that Richard had experienced. The end result was all that mattered; they would all drown.

Richard glanced over his shoulder at Hermes. He gave him a stone-cold glare and hit the console again. Hermes vanished.

"Now for the bands," Richard said, as he walked over to the small metal table. He picked up one band from the velvet-lined case. He fastened it around his left wrist. He twisted his arm in the air, taking a moment to admire his new bling.

As Richard reached for the second band, his arm was seized. He was abruptly spun around. He was facing his worst nightmare.

"You're supposed to be dead!" Richard blurted, staring into the hard, determined eyes of his old friend.

"Far from it, no thanks to you," Quinn grunted, as he wrestled Richard for possession of the second travel band. He could get his hand firmly locked around the band, but Richard's hold was like a vise. Quinn tried twisting his wrist to wrench the band free, but Richard reached up with his left hand to add some extra leverage. The bands suddenly touched.

122

"HEY! LET US out of here," Daric yelled, banging on the locked door of the pitch dark room.

Dani had put Bear down and had been running her hands along the walls, when she found a switch. She flipped it, turning on a red emergency light above the doorframe.

"Don't waste your time; it's electronically sealed," Eddie sighed.

Daric spun around to confront Eddie. "And who the hell are you?" Daric barked, as he pushed him back against the wall of their small compartment.

"Daric, don't," Dani cautioned. "He's stuck in here, too."

"I tried to warn you," Eddie said apologetically.

"Warn us about what?" Dani asked.

"Richard. He'll stop at nothing to get what he wants," Eddie said. "And he wants those travel bands."

"Well, that's apparent," Daric agreed. "But why kill us in the process? Why not just take them and leave? And what did he do to our parents?"

"Relax." Eddie raised his hands to discourage Daric from advancing on him. "Your dad is alive and on his way here. I saw him run into the house just before I got pushed in here. He looked kind of like a balding football player."

"Our dad doesn't look like that," Dani said pointedly. "He's over six feet tall with wavy hair . . ."

"Who was it, then?" Eddie responded. "It doesn't really matter. Hermes said your dad would be here at any moment."

"That's good," Daric observed, "'cause this chamber just sprang a leak."

"How do you know?" Dani asked.

"Because my feet are wet," Daric explained.

"That's not a good sign. If the water keeps rising, we could end up drowning in here," Dani observed.

"I think that's the idea: to make our deaths look like an accident. Richard was never going to shoot you," Eddie volunteered.

"Then, why did you stop me?" Daric questioned. "I could have taken the gun from him and, then, we wouldn't be in this mess."

"I'm just saying that Richard wasn't planning on shooting anyone, but if push came to shove, he wouldn't have hesitated to put a bullet between your eyes."

"How can you be so sure?" Dani asked.

"Because he forced me to cause a train derailment that killed one-hundred-eleven people and injured hundreds more, just to keep your mom from taking that trip to New Zealand with your dad," Eddie said. "I had no choice."

"Oh my god," Dani uttered.

"We'll address that later. For now, we need to deal with the water that's slowly filling this room. You, come with me," Daric directed, poking Eddie in the chest. "Let's go explore our options."

Daric and Eddie made their way farther back in the narrow compartment, when they came upon a steep staircase which looked more like a hastily built ladder set at about a sixty-five-degree angle.

"After you," Eddie urged. The light Dani had turned on by the door didn't penetrate this deep into the compartment. Eddie had no intentions of leading the way into the unknown.

Daric climbed tentatively up the wet stairs, using the handrails on either side to steady and guide him. *Now we know where the water's coming from,* he thought, when his foot slipped off one of the narrow stairs.

Daric advanced slowly and deliberately in the darkness. He paused occasionally and ran his hands over the rock surfaces around him. Like the air, the surfaces were cold and damp. He cautiously moved up another two stairs. He reached into what seemed to be an open space and groped around hesitantly in the dark. At about the level of his waist, he felt a slimy flat surface in front of and beside him. As he explored the surface as far as his arms would allow, he began to think the surface might be some kind of floor. Daric clambered up the last of the stairs and crawled carefully onto the surface. It felt solid. He stood up cautiously. He reached out, once again, and tried to get a sense of how big the space might be. He touched something; it felt like a switch. Daric took a deep breath. *Here goes,* he thought, as he pushed whatever it was he had just discovered. Almost immediately, there was light; a string of grime-covered overhead lights ran the length of a horizontal tunnel carved out of stone, about thirty feet long, heading out to what Daric believed was the lake. *That would explain where the water was coming from.*

At Daric's feet was the edge of a circular manhole. A metal collar ran around the top edge. Attached to one side of the collar was a round cover leaning back against the nearby wall, like a hatch cover on a submarine. Daric peered down the hole. "Come on up," he said to Eddie.

"What's happening up there?" Dani hollered from the chamber below.

Eddie popped his head up through the hatch. "Whoa!" Eddie exclaimed at what he beheld, as he pulled his body up through the opening and stood beside Daric.

"We found a light switch . . ."

"So I noticed."

While Dani and Daric were conversing, Eddie was looking at two hooks screwed into the wall, above the light switch. One was empty. A snorkel hung from the other. *I wonder where the mask went.* Eddie pondered a moment. He also noticed a peculiar looking red button.

"There's a long tunnel I'm guessing goes out toward the lake. I'm going to check it out," Daric shouted down the hatch.

"Be careful," Dani cautioned from below.

"Hey, don't leave me here," Eddie stammered, as he hurried to catch up to Daric.

When they got to the end of the tunnel, Daric and Eddie were confronted by a small metal door open about a half-inch. There was no sign of a latch, key hole or handle on the door. There was, however, a steady flow of water running around its open edge and into the tunnel.

Daric put his shoulder against the door and was about to push it open, when Eddie yanked his tunic, pulling him away, which caused him to fall back against the tunnel's wall.

"What did you do that for?" Daric snapped.

"Because, if you'd pushed on that door and, if by chance, you'd opened it, there would have been a flash flood in here," Eddie explained calmly. "We'd have been knocked senseless, if not crushed against the walls. And Dani and Bear on the lower level would have drowned in a matter of minutes."

"You got any better ideas, Einstein?" Daric snorted. As much as he was angry at Eddie, he knew Eddie was right; he could have killed them all. He had just been trying to find a way out. He had thought that, if he could nudge the door open, they could swim to safety, get a jump on Uncle Richard, and make him pay for what he had done. The only problem was he had let his emotions get the best of him. He hadn't taken the time to think through the whole scenario, something he failed to do on a regular basis. *You'd think by now, you'd know better,* Daric chided himself.

Eddie ignored Daric's snarky comment. "I'm assuming the door is electronically controlled, because I don't see any handles or levers that we could use to try to pull it closed. Closing it would at least stop the tunnel from flooding any further," Eddie explained. "And I don't see any switches or buttons along the walls, either.

Let's go back and check the other end of the tunnel again," Eddie suggested, recalling a red button he had noticed under the snorkel.

"Hey, that's it!" Daric said excitedly. "Let's go back down the stairs and close the hatch behind us. It will stop the water from filling the lower level. And you did say help was on the way?"

"I did," Eddie replied, as he followed Daric back down the tunnel. "But I don't know how soon help will get here and closing the hatch will cut off our oxygen. I think our best bet is to . . ."

"Bear!" Dani screamed.

"Dani, what's wrong?" Daric asked anxiously, as he ran back to the hatch.

"It's Bear; she just vanished out of my arms," Dani said, dumbfounded.

Unknown

123

THE VEIL OF darkness slowly receded. Quinn's first rational thought was that he was no longer in his lab. He was lying in a small glade on the edge of an evergreen forest. The early morning dew still glistened on the blades of grass. The foliage of the forest was so dense he could barely see past the first line of trees. Shadows danced in the distance, as the light breeze gently tousled the overhanging tree boughs.

Quinn had no idea where he was, or when. He carefully got to his feet and looked around for Richard. As he turned, a solid object struck him on the side of the head, knocking him to the ground. His ears were ringing and stars were flashing before his eyes.

"Give me the band," Richard screamed, as he towered over Quinn's prone form, holding a large tree branch, poised to strike another blow.

Quinn shook his aching head, trying to clear his senses. Had he heard correctly? Did Richard have only one travel band? The other must have fallen out of their hands during the struggle.

Without waiting for a reply, Richard pounced on top of Quinn and started to beat him with the branch. "Give it to me!" Richard screamed.

Bear, who had been dragged into the past when the travel bands had touched, came barreling out of the shadows. She launched herself at Richard, going for the arm holding the branch. Seeing her out of the corner of his eye, Richard turned and swung the branch, catching Bear across her mid-section. She flew backward through the air and landed hard on the ground about fifteen feet away. She uttered a weak whimper and lay there motionless.

"You, heartless bastard!" Quinn growled, just as the branch was once again heading for his head. He reached up and latched onto Richard's arm as the branch descended, blocking the blow. With his free hand, Quinn reached toward his ankle and pulled his dive knife from its sheath. As he raised it to strike, Richard switched the branch to his other hand and swung it around, smashing it against Quinn's wrist. The blow knocked the knife clear out of Quinn's hand and it fell out of reach.

Quinn caught Richard's arm as the next attack came at him. Quinn quickly realized that Richard possessed the same strength in both arms. He twisted Richard's arm with all his might. Finally, Richard was forced to relinquish his grip on his makeshift club. Quinn arched his back and bucked, throwing Richard's body off to one side.

Quinn sprang to his feet and immediately put some distance between himself and the madman. He used the sleeve of his flight suit to wipe away blood that was trickling down his forehead and into his eyes, causing his vision to blur.

Having retrieved the branch, Richard got to his feet. He glared treacherously at Quinn.

"Richard, listen to me," Quinn pleaded, making sure he kept a sufficient distance between them. "Like I told you before, you can't go back in time and change history. It just can't be done."

"There's only one way to be sure, now isn't there?" Richard taunted. "My family's legacy has been branded with labels such as traitor, coward, zealot, murderer, thief and deserter. Your family has had the distinction of being labeled pioneers. Your family has always been at least one step in front of everyone else, from the exploration of new worlds to inventions to benefit humankind. And now, even your wife's research into the use of nanotechnology is rewriting medicine as we know it. I'm sure your kids would have followed in their parents' footsteps, too."

"They will," Quinn asserted proudly.

"I'm afraid your legacy ends here, old friend," Richard jeered, as they continued to circle. "Because, by the time I get back, they'll all be dead. And it will look like an accident, of course. I can't have any loose ends, now can I?"

Richard had been closely watching Quinn as the two of them circled around the small glade. He had noticed something. Every time Quinn put any pressure on his left leg, he grimaced. *A weakness,* Richard thought, one he could definitely exploit. He had a knack for identifying an opposition's weakness. It had served him well in his business dealings.

"Leave them out of this," Quinn growled. "This is between you and me."

"That's right, old friend, and I win this round." Richard took a secure hold of the branch and lunged forward.

Quinn was ready for the attack this time. He raised his arms to protect his head, but this time Richard swung at his left leg. The outcome wasn't what Richard had been looking for. Richard had assumed that Quinn had injured his leg, but it was Quinn's left ankle that had been sprained. Richard's strike was, therefore, too high to do the damage he had been hoping for.

Quinn took the blow. It jarred his ankle, but he didn't buckle. The fanatical swing of the branch, however, had pulled Richard off balance. Quinn saw his opportunity to launch his own offensive. And he took it. He planted his good foot and kicked out with the other, hitting Richard square in the chest, knocking him to the ground.

Richard landed hard. He quickly rolled onto his back. He slid his hand into his jacket pocket and pulled out his gun. Richard stared down the barrel with Quinn clearly in his sights.

As soon as Richard had fallen to the ground, Quinn had picked up the branch and was already swinging it toward Richard's head. It landed with a sickening sound just as a shot rang out. Richard lay motionless.

Quinn dropped the branch and grabbed his left arm; it felt as if someone had stabbed him with a hot poker. After a moment or two, he cautiously removed his hand and examined the wound. The bullet had just grazed his arm; the bleeding was minimal. *That was too close,* Quinn thought.

Quinn bent over Richard and checked for a pulse. He hadn't killed him with the blow.

Quinn removed the travel band from Richard's wrist and strapped it onto his own. He ran over and knelt on the ground beside Bear. There was a large cut in Bear's side that was bleeding profusely, but Quinn had no way of knowing whether Bear had suffered any internal injuries. "Hang in there, Bear. I'll get us both back home."

Quinn started to search for the second band. *It has to be here somewhere.* He needed both of them, if he was ever going to get back home. On his hands and knees, Quinn raked his fingers through every inch of the small clearing. Just as he was losing all hope of finding it, his hand stumbled across something cold and hard. "Finally," Quinn muttered, as he clutched the metal band. Once on his feet, Quinn fastened the travel band around his other wrist.

"No!" Richard screamed, as he launched himself at Quinn, in utter desperation. He needed those travel bands. He had to have them!

Quinn quickly stepped aside, as Richard flew past. Richard spun around and was ready to rush Quinn again.

Quinn noticed the crazed look in Richard's cold dark eyes. It terrified him. With no further hesitation, Quinn put his two wrists together and disappeared.

"No!" was the last Quinn would ever hear from Richard.

But just before Quinn vanished, he caught something directly behind Richard at the edge of the clearing. He had seen a horse and rider emerge from the forest. The rider had looked like a medieval knight. He had been wearing a surcoat draped over his body armour and tied at the waist with a belt. The dark red surcoat had been emblazoned with three golden lions. Quinn had realized Richard had got exactly what he wanted: to go back to the 1100s. At the same time, Quinn knew Richard could never alter history. He had only guaranteed himself a front-row seat to the inevitable as it would unfold.

Present Day—Saturday

124

QUINN FOUND HIMSELF lying on the floor of his lower lab. He immediately tapped the comm on his wrist. "Hermes!" he hollered, his voice resonating off the barren walls of the lower lab.

"I'm on it, Professor," Hermes replied eagerly. He had already sealed the outer door and activated the pumps to drain the water from the tunnel and from the lower chamber.

"Are my children okay?" Quinn asked anxiously, as he got to his feet. He promptly removed the travel bands and placed them on the metal table. He didn't want to chance accidentally travelling anywhere right now.

"See for yourself, Professor," Hermes announced cheerfully, just as the seal indicator turned green and the door swung open. Rivulets of water trickled out of the chamber. Then Dani emerged. She rushed into her father's arms, tears of joy streaming down her cheeks.

Daric was close behind, followed by Eddie. Quinn wrapped his arms around both his children, reluctant to let go of either of them. He had never been one-hundred-percent sure he would ever see his children again. And here they were, home, safe and sound.

"What happened to you?" Eddie asked, a hint of concern in his voice. He had noticed the congealed blood on Quinn's face and the red stain on the arm of his flight suit.

Before Quinn could answer the stranger in his lab, Bear suddenly materialized in the far corner of the lab. She uttered a pathetic whimper.

"Bear!" Dani hollered, as she ran to her side. "What happened?"

"Richard attacked her," Quinn snapped. "I didn't have time to help her; everything happened so fast."

Dani ripped a strip of fabric off the bottom of her tunic and placed it against Bear's wound, trying to stem the bleeding.

"Where is Uncle Richard?" Daric fumed. "I have a score to settle with him."

Daric was kneeling beside Dani, helping her check on Bear. He gently stroked Bear's head. "It's going to be okay, Bear," Daric said tenderly, as he reached down and removed the bands from Bear's legs. He also removed her collar and leash.

"We won't be seeing Uncle Richard ever again," Quinn grunted.

"I, for one, am glad. But we do have a problem," Eddie interrupted.

"Who are you?" Quinn asked bluntly.

"Professor, Eddie is correct," Hermes jumped in. "Mr. Case has poisoned Dr. Delaney and we're not sure with what," Hermes added fretfully.

Quinn didn't hesitate; he was up the stairs and dashing for the house, as quickly as his injured ankle would take him.

"Dani, I'll get Bear; you go with Dad. We'll be right behind you," Daric said, as he placed the two small bands on the table with the others and returning to Bear's side.

"Keep pressure on her wound," Dani advised, before racing up the stairs and disappearing from sight.

"Come on, Bear. Easy does it," Daric said, while he gently picked her up in his arms; a tiny whine escaped Bear's lips.

While Eddie and Daric were making their way to the house,

Daric continued to comfort Bear. Eddie was at a loss for what to do; he didn't know how he could help. Feeling insignificant, he shoved his hands into his pants pockets. His right hand touched something he had forgotten was there. He pulled it out and said, "I found this on the table in the lab the other day."

"Hey, that's mine," Daric said when he recognized his comm. "My hands are kind of full right now. Can you snap it on my wrist?" Eddie was happy to oblige.

* * *

Upon arriving at the house, Quinn charged through the front door. He found Sandra on the living room floor, Jim on his knees beside her. "I found her like this," Jim said anxiously.

Sandra's lips were a bluish color; so were her fingernails. Sandra was having trouble breathing and, when he touched her hand, it was like ice. "Hang in there, honey. We'll get you some help."

"Jim, Sandra's been poisoned. I don't know how much time we have. We need to get her to a hospital, fast. Can you get the Harrier ready?" Quinn asked hopefully. It was an unusual request. He wasn't sure whether Jim would agree to fly his jet into the city or whether he would, or could, land on a hospital's helipad.

"On it," Jim answered without hesitation.

Dani knelt beside her mom. Her appearance terrified Dani. Her mom looked close to death.

Quinn ran to the kitchen, yanked open a drawer, and pulled out a sharp knife. He raced back into the living room and returned to Sandra's side. Taking her hand, he made a small cut on her pinky finger and placed a drop of blood on his comm.

"Hermes, analyse this blood. We need to determine the toxin in Sandra's system. Call me the minute you know anything. Seconds could mean the difference between life and death," Quinn instructed his trusted partner.

"Got it, Professor." The tiny hologram that had appeared on Quinn's comm vanished.

Quinn carefully lifted Sandra into his arms and headed for the door.

"Mom doesn't look very good," Dani said fearfully, as she held open the front door.

"I know," Quinn replied. "Dani, can you search the house and see if you can find out what Richard used to poison your mom?"

"I'll do my best." Dani ran upstairs to begin her search. She knew there wasn't much time.

Quinn was walking along the pathway when he saw Daric approach the house.

"Mom?" Daric whispered nervously, when he saw his mom's unconscious body cradled in his dad's arms.

"Daric, get the ladder out of the garage and take it to the tennis courts," Quinn hollered.

"Okay!" Daric replied. "Eddie, take Bear, will ya?" Daric placed Bear in Eddie's arms. "Keep pressure on that wound."

"I got her," Eddie acknowledged. "Aren't you a pretty girl?" Eddie cooed, as he passed through the front door and made his way to the kitchen. The flimsy piece of fabric that was serving as a makeshift bandage had become saturated with Bear's blood; he needed to find some towels. Maybe he could tie them around Bear to help keep constant pressure on the wound.

Daric entered the garage. Moments later, he emerged with a six-foot extension ladder flung over his shoulder. He sprinted to the courts, passing his dad along the way.

125

JIM HICKS WAS already in the cockpit performing his pre-flight checks when he saw Daric arriving with a ladder. “Place it against the fuselage directly behind me,” Jim instructed.

Out of the corner of his eye, Jim caught sight of Quinn cradling Sandra in his arms as he made his way to the plane. Quinn’s gait reminded Jim of a speed-walker: he was trying to move as fast as possible with his injured ankle. “Put her in back, Quinn, and strap her in. Where’s the closest hospital with a helipad?”

After checking once again that the ladder was firmly in place, Daric positioned himself where he could hold it steady. With some difficulty, Quinn carried Sandra up the ladder and, as gently as he could, manoeuvred her into the rear cockpit. “Mount Albert; it’s Sandra’s hospital,” Quinn informed him, as he fastened her restraints. “I wish I could come with you,” Quinn said miserably, as he softly stroked Sandra’s cold cheek. *I can’t lose you.* Quinn prayed.

Quinn closed the rear canopy and jumped from the ladder. Once on the ground, he grabbed the ladder, threw it well clear of the Harrier, checked that Daric was out of harm’s way, and gave Jim a thumbs up.

“I’ll make sure she receives only the best care, don’t you worry none,” Jim assured Quinn. “Now stand clear,” Jim shouted, as he closed his canopy. He pressed the starter button to start the gas turbine starter known as GTS, used to start the Harrier's main Rolls Royce Pegasus engine. He checked his instruments. As the Pegasus spooled up to an ear-piercing idle, the auxiliary air doors were being sucked in. The jet was now like a gigantic vacuum cleaner, sucking up anything in its path, including Quinn and Daric, if they weren't careful.

As soon as Jim had a stabilized idle and his NAV equipment had aligned, he selected the water injection for about one-thousand-pounds of additional thrust. He made a final check to ensure that Quinn and Daric were well clear of the hot jet blast and, then, lowered the nozzles to the eighty-one-degree hover stop for a vertical takeoff. He slammed the throttle full forward. Within six seconds, the Pegasus was at full power, producing nearly twenty-two-thousand-pounds of pure thrust and spewing out heat hot enough to melt asphalt, a fact that Quinn had known when he chose the tennis courts and their concrete surface as a landing site. Within fifty seconds from when Jim had first pressed the starter button, the Harrier had lifted off vertically.

Once the Harrier was clear of the surrounding trees, Jim eased the nozzle lever forward to transition to forward flight. In no time, the Harrier had become a conventional jet, travelling at over four-hundred-knots to the hospital. The same hospital he had visited when Sandra gave birth to the twins.

As soon as Quinn and Daric saw the Harrier rise from the ground, they ran toward the house. Quinn was busy giving Jim directions to the hospital over his comm. Not far behind, Daric was on his comm to the hospital.

"A Harrier Jump Jet will be coming in from the west," Daric announced.

"Only authorized air-ambulances are permitted to use the helipad," the dispatcher replied mechanically.

"This is an emergency," Daric persisted. His voice conveyed the urgency he was feeling.

"All incoming flights to the hospital are emergencies," the

dispatcher replied, in the same mechanical manner. Daric was in no mood for a smart-ass answer.

"I don't care about your rules," Daric barked, not backing down. "Clear the area! Because it's going to land, with or without your permission! That flight is carrying Dr. Sandra Delaney; she's been poisoned . . ."

"Dr. Delaney?" The dispatcher's tone changed considerably.

"Yes, and it should arrive there shortly." Daric's harsh tone had softened when he realized the dispatcher seemed to know his mother.

"Do you know what type of poison she was exposed to?" the dispatcher asked, sounding concerned.

"No, but my dad is trying to run an analysis of her blood." Daric paused to catch his breath. "If we find out anything, we'll let you know."

"We'll have the trauma team ready," the dispatcher announced before cutting off the communication.

Quinn had reached the driveway and immediately headed for Richard's SUV, knowing Richard never locked any of his vehicles and always left the keys in the ignition. Richard's theory was that his vehicles should be ready to move when he was.

"Hey, wait for us!" Dani yelled, as she ran from the house. Dani had been searching the house, looking for anything Richard might have used to poison her mom. She had come up empty. She was about to search the garage when she spotted her dad and Daric heading for Richard's car. "Come on, Eddie; bring Bear," Dani yelled.

While Dani had been frantically going through the house, Eddie had grabbed some towels from the kitchen and was applying pressure to Bear's laceration, trying to staunch the bleeding. When he heard Dani's yell, he carefully lifted Bear up in his arms and headed for the SUV.

Quinn was out of breath and his ankle felt like it was on fire by the time he got to the SUV. He got in behind the wheel. Daric slid into the front passenger seat. Moments later, Dani and Eddie, carrying Bear, climbed into the back seat.

126

QUINN HIT THE accelerator and tore down the driveway, spewing a rooster tail of gravel in his wake.

"Are you two all right?" Quinn asked anxiously. Everything had happened so fast, he had never had a moment to check on his two kids, until now.

"We're fine, just a tad wet, is all," Daric replied, watching the trees zip past as the SUV sped down the long lane and onto the main road.

Eddie noticed Dani shivering a bit. He pulled off his blazer, being careful not to disturb Bear. "Lean forward," Eddie murmured to Dani. She complied and Eddie draped his blazer over her shoulders.

"Thanks," Dani sighed.

Those eyes. Eddie thought he was sinking deep into those beautiful azure pools.

"Professor," Hermes called over the SUV's speaker system. "I've analyzed Dr. Delaney's blood and found traces of tetrahydrozoline." Hermes had taken advantage of the advances in toxicogenomics, bioinformatics, systems biology, epigenetics, and computational toxicology. These scientific advances had transformed toxicity testing from a system based on whole-animal testing to one founded on in vitro methods that evaluates changes in biologic processes using cells, cell lines, or cellular components of human origin.

"What's that?" Daric asked.

"Tetrahydrozoline is a form of a medicine called imidazoline, which is found in over-the-counter eye drops and nasal sprays. Its main purpose is the constriction of blood vessels and, thereby, to relieve the redness of the eye caused by minor ocular irritants," Hermes explained.

"I have Visine in my dive locker in the garage," Quinn remarked.

"That would explain why Richard went into the garage," Eddie blurted out. "I heard him in there. He opened the locker beside the one I was hiding in."

"Hiding in?" Dani repeated hesitantly.

"I agree," Hermes continued. "Dr. Delaney questioned why Mr. Case went into the garage and he told her he was returning some borrowed thermal dive gloves."

"I knew there was something suspicious about his answer. I didn't think it made any sense at the time. Now I know," Eddie groaned. "He purposely lied to her!"

"But how did Sandra ingest the Visine without her knowing?" Quinn asked, while he navigated a right turn.

"Tetrahydrozoline is colorless, odorless and tasteless. Mr. Case could have easily slipped the poison into a drink and Dr. Delaney would never have been the wiser," Hermes revealed.

"Hermes, call Jim and tell him about the poison. If they know what the toxin is, they'll have a better chance of saving her life," Quinn said urgently. "Oh, wait! Use my voice, Hermes. The last thing I want to do is distract Jim while he's flying."

"Consider it done, Professor," Hermes acknowledged.

"Now, young man, who are you, and what are you doing here?" Quinn asked guardedly.

"It's kind of a long story," Eddie said. He was reluctant to say anything, but somewhere deep inside, he felt he owed the Delaneys an explanation. In fact, he felt he owed an explanation to all the people whose lives he had destroyed. And for what? A promise that was never kept.

"You have fifteen minutes to explain," Quinn insisted, as he looked intently at Eddie through the rear-view mirror. There was something about the young man that didn't sit right with Quinn. He tapped his comm to record whatever Eddie was about to disclose.

Eddie went through the sordid details: how Richard had snatched him off the street and kept him locked up for months; how Richard had forced him into bypassing security systems; how Richard had manipulated Eddie into developing a RAT, a Remote Access Trojan, essentially a computer virus; how the virus had been used to hack into the Central Traffic Control System and cause a commuter train to derail, killing one-hundred-eleven people.

As Quinn listened to Eddie's story, he couldn't help but be impressed at how intellectual and resourceful the young man was. As Eddie continued to tell his story, he shifted the focus to the reason he was involved with Richard.

"I lost my parents in a car accident when I was five years old. I've been bounced between foster homes my entire life." Eddie was fighting desperately to hold back the tears that were rolling down his cheeks. "I would have done anything to get them back, to have the life every other kid had. Richard promised he could bring them back. He said he could go back in time and make sure my parents weren't killed in that car accident. I just had to agree to do whatever he wanted, no questions asked. When I look back on it now, I can't believe how selfish I was. I destroyed so many lives, and for what?"

Eddie was inconsolable. He sat sobbing with his head in his hands. Quinn watched in the rear-view mirror. *That poor kid,* he thought. And all because Richard wanted those travel bands. Quinn was mortified that Richard had gone to such lengths. Daric was speechless. And Dani just looked dolefully at a grieving Eddie.

If Richard could go to those extremes to get what he so dearly coveted, maybe my invention is too dangerous to have around, Quinn mused. *If word were to get out, anyone could attempt to get them. Look what it did to my family. I put their lives at risk, and Sandra is still fighting for hers.*

Quinn turned the SUV onto Medical Drive. They were only minutes from the hospital.

"What about Richard? What happened to him?" Daric asked reluctantly, as he turned to look at his father, noticing for the first time the blood on his right temple. His hatred for Uncle Richard was growing by the minute.

"We fought; I won. Richard is, to my best recollection, confronting Richard the Lionheart," Quinn said coldly. "He got exactly what he wanted. But I'm afraid he'll never get the outcome he went to all this trouble to bring about."

"Wait! How do we explain his disappearance," Dani asked. "Surely, he'll be missed."

"I don't know," Quinn admitted irritably.

Hermes had caught and recorded the entire exchange.

127

JIM HICKS HOVERED the Harrier over the big red 'H' painted on the hospital's roof, and then gently set the aircraft on the helipad. He immediately shut down the engine and threw open his hinged canopy. "All clear," he called to the waiting trauma team. "I need some help up here and bring a ladder!"

As promised, the trauma team had been waiting on the roof. On hearing Jim's request, a member of the team promptly disappeared and returned moments later with a ladder. It was more of a small stepladder, not what Jim had in mind, but it would have to do; there was no time to find another one.

Jim extricated himself from the cockpit and set the small ladder by the rear canopy. Jim climbed the ladder, threw open the rear canopy, and unstrapped Sandra. Jim shouted to the team, "I'll climb in and hand her over the side to you guys. You'll have to get up on the ladder and hold her, as I lower her down. Whatever you do, don't drop her!"

It took four people to get Sandra out of the cockpit and safely down to the ground. Two members of the team had positioned the gurney by the aircraft to receive Sandra. She was like a limp dishrag and could provide no help at all; she was pure dead weight.

"Vital signs, stat and what's her O2 saturation?" the emergency room doctor shouted, as Sandra was being placed on the gurney.

"Where are you taking her?" Jim yelled down.

"To the ICU, fifth floor," an attending doctor hollered over his shoulder as they rushed Sandra away.

"I'll follow just as soon as I get the brakes set and the ejection seats secured," Jim called back. "We don't want anyone getting killed if one of these gets tripped."

"No! Get that thing off my helipad," the ER doctor shouted. "She's in good hands; we've got her from here."

Jim knew the doctor was right. Leaving the Harrier on the helipad while he checked on Sandra's condition would prevent other incoming air-ambulances from accessing the hospital. He would call Quinn later to see how Sandra was doing. Besides, he had to begin his return flight home soon, while all his 'connections' were still available to him.

"She's tachycardic–rate is 120, temp is 34C–BP is soft 80/50, pupils are pinpoint, lips are dusky. Be prepared to intubate–give a 500cc bolus of normal saline now and start a propofol infusion at 50 micrograms. Let's move, people!!" the ER doctor barked, just as he had so many times before. "I want a tox screen. We need to sink an NG tube and instill activated charcoal," the ER doctor directed.

"It would help if we knew what she had ingested," a nurse said, as they waited for the elevator. "Hang in there, Sandra," she whispered, as she rubbed Sandra's cold hand, noticing her fingers, like her lips, were a dusky color.

"Wait, it was tetrahydrozoline," Jim shouted from the cockpit to the waiting team, remembering what Quinn had told him during his flight to the hospital. He also remembered that the only treatment for the tetrahydrozoline poisoning was immediate medical attention. What Jim didn't know was that it was actually Hermes who had determined the source of the poison and who had made the call.

"That helps, thanks," the ER doctor hollered back. At that moment, Sandra's blood pressure bottomed out and the ER doctor could be heard shouting orders. "Get some phenylephrine and mix some Levophed; let's keep her systolic BP greater than 100. I need the RT to intubate; has she had that bolus of saline yet??"

The trauma team and gurney disappeared behind the elevator door.

128

QUINN PULLED THE SUV into Sandra's designated parking spot at the hospital. The four doors flew open, and the Delaneys ran to the hospital's emergency entrance, followed closely by Eddie, who had offered to carry Bear. He appreciated that the family needed to get to Sandra as quickly as possible.

"She's in ICU, fifth floor," one of the nurses said, when she recognized the family. She was taken aback by their appearance, wondering what on earth had happened to the Delaney family.

"Thanks," Daric said, as he followed his dad to the stairwell. They were not wasting time waiting for an elevator.

The fifth floor stairwell door flew open moments later. Quinn ran to the nurse's station. "Where is she?" he panted.

Before a nurse had a chance to answer Quinn's question, an ICU doctor appeared halfway down the hallway to Quinn's left. "Quinn, over here," the doctor called out. Dr. Diane Cole had been working at Mount Albert hospital almost as long as Sandra had been. Over the years, the two doctors had established a great working relationship; unlike other hospitals that were departmentally divided and extremely competitive.

Dr. Cole was hardly prepared for the scene that came rushing toward her. Leading the group was Quinn, wearing a filthy, torn and bloodied flight suit, with blood caked on his face and favouring his left ankle. Right behind him were two dust-covered, blood-spattered, tunic-clad twenty-year-olds who looked as though they had just walked off a movie set. And bringing up the rear was another young man carrying a bundle in his arms. Eddie, who had decided he was not going to climb five flights of stairs while carrying twenty-three pounds of dog, had just arrived by elevator and was hurrying down the hallway. When he reached the group, he stopped and glanced down at his charge; blood had begun to seep through the towels wrapped about Bear's wound. To Dr. Cole, he was the only normal looking person in the group, and even that was a bit of a stretch, given the blood stains on his shirt and pants.

"How is she?" Quinn asked anxiously, as his children and Eddie waited nervously.

"Sandra's critical, but stable," Dr. Cole replied as calmly as she could. She wanted to ease the family's distress, but she would not whitewash Sandra's condition. "We have her sedated on propofol and analgesics. The next twenty-four hours will be critical."

"Diane, I have to see her," Quinn pleaded.

"Okay, but only a few minutes," Diane consented. She held open the door to Sandra's room. After the family had entered the room, she looked at Eddie and pointed, "You, come with me."

A nurse was standing beside Sandra's bed taking blood samples. There were hoses, tubes and wires everywhere. Dani's breath had caught when she beheld her mother. She had never seen her in such a vulnerable state.

Quinn dragged a chair to the side the bed and sat down. He reached for Sandra's hand and raised it to his lips; he kissed it gently. "She doesn't look so good," Quinn mumbled, as he reluctantly took his eyes off his wife and glanced up at the nurse.

"Neither do you," the ICU nurse replied candidly.

"Who would have thought Visine eye drops could do this?" Dani remarked.

"I remember a movie a while ago where one of the characters, in an act of retribution, spiked someone's drink with Visine, causing the character to experience violent diarrhea," Daric recalled. "But this is nothing like that."

"Visine poisoning is no laughing matter," the nurse said firmly. "We had a case here a few years back, shortly after that movie aired, where some idiot tried that same prank. That idiot is now in jail."

The nurse assessed the neuro vitals and ventilator settings and announced, "That's enough for now, everyone; time to give Sandra some time to rest."

Quinn leaned over and placed a tender kiss on Sandra's forehead. Dani and Daric did the same, telling their mom they would be back soon.

Dr. Diane Cole had returned and was waiting outside Sandra's room. "Whose blood is that?" Diane asked, pointing at the twins.

"Bear's," Dani and Daric replied in unison. They peered at each other and, for the first time in their lives, didn't utter their catch phrase: twin-thing.

"You two can wait here," Diane said, indicating the chairs by the nurses' station. "I'll come back and get you shortly. I want to check out your dad first. Quinn, come with me," Diane said, as she led the way down the hall.

"Wait! Where's Bear?" Dani asked fearfully.

"And where's Eddie?" Daric added.

"They're fine. They're with me," Diane said calmly, as she opened a door, two rooms down from Sandra's, and waited as Quinn limped inside.

Eddie was next to the bed, gently stroking Bear's soft fur. "Is she going to be okay?" Quinn asked, as he approached the bed. He peered nervously down at another frail member of his family.

"We took some precautionary x-rays, just to make sure there was no internal damage," Diane replied, as a nurse stuck a needle into Bear's thigh, while Eddie tried to comfort her. "She has a deep laceration that will need stitching. We've just put some lidocaine in the wound. Once it takes effect, say in five to ten minutes, we'll clean and suture the wound. But right now, let's take a look at you. Hop up here," Diane said, indicating the other end of the bed, as she pulled over a surgical tray laden with instruments and some gauze and bandages.

"Now, what on earth happened to you?" Diane asked, as she looked at the cut and bruising above Quinn's right eye and the blood on the left arm of Quinn's flight suit.

Quinn wasn't sure how to reply. He could say he had twisted his ankle. If he were to say that, it wouldn't be far from the truth. But, what about his head and his arm? Did his arm injury look like a bullet wound? Would it have to be reported to the authorities?

Diane noticed Quinn's hesitation. "I'm asking only as a family friend, not as a physician," she clarified softly.

"I was working on some new cribbing along the shoreline when I slipped on a rock, twisting my ankle. When I fell, I cut my arm on the metal screening and hit my head on one of the rocks. Pretty clumsy of me, eh?" Quinn replied, hoping that his creative explanation would satisfy Diane's curiosity.

"Well, that would explain the state you're in, except I don't recall any type of rock that has bark in its composition," Diane stated bluntly, as she pulled a splinter from his head wound with a pair of tweezers. "And since when do you do yard work in a flight suit?"

Quinn's reaction was clearly one of unease, but Diane didn't press him; she wasn't there to interrogate him. She did, however, need to know one thing. "Can you tell me what happened to Sandra?" Diane asked as she stared hard into Quinn's soft blue eyes. She wouldn't be easily fooled by some fabricated story when it came to Sandra.

"Honestly, Diane, I don't know," Quinn said regretfully. "When I went into the house, I found Sandra on the living room floor." And that was the honest truth.

"I guess I'll have to wait and ask Sandra," Diane conceded. She wouldn't get any more information out of Quinn. He was near total exhaustion and Diane wasn't sure how he was still holding himself upright.

After Diane had cleaned Quinn's wounds and had concluded sutures weren't needed, she bandaged him up. "I'll order a set of x-rays for your ankle to make sure it's only a soft tissue injury and not broken bones."

"I think it's just a sprain. I don't need any x-rays," Quinn mumbled.

"Humor me, will ya?" Diane retorted. She paused for a moment to observe Quinn. Her heart ached for him. It was going to be a very long twenty-four hours. She would do whatever she could to make them all as comfortable as possible. It was the least she could do.

"Quinn, why don't you rest in here for a while? I'll tell Dani and Daric to join you. It will give you all a little privacy," Diane said comfortingly. "I'll check back on you in a couple hours."

"Thanks," Quinn replied, fighting to keep his eyes open.

"Oh, one more thing."

"Yeah?"

"What on earth are they wearing?" Diane asked. Her curiosity had finally gotten the better of her.

"They were about to go to a themed party," Quinn lied.

"That explains it," Diane said, as she let the door close behind her. *Seriously?* she thought, *at this time of year?* She was not convinced.

129

A FEW HOURS later, Dr. Diane Cole went to check on the Delaney family. She opened the door to Room 503 and unobtrusively took in the silent scene. Quinn was lying on his back on the floor, with Dani and Daric curled up on either side of him, their arms possessively draped over his chest. They were sound asleep. Diane couldn't help wondering what the Delaney family had gotten themselves into to be so exhausted this early in the day.

Diane glanced at the bed. Eddie was curled up with a sedated Bear; they were the only ones in the room who looked comfortable. She had brought them all a set of scrubs to put on in place of the filthy, torn flight suit, the out-of-place tunics, and the blood-soaked shirt and pants. Diane had stopped by to inform Quinn about his x-ray results, but she didn't have the heart to disturb them. She would come back later. She had rounds to complete and the first patient she would look in on was Sandra.

Dr. Cole walked down the hall and opened the door to Room 501. A nurse was assessing the neuro vitals and jotting down the reading on Sandra's chart. "Update, please," Dr. Cole ordered, as she took the chart and examined the recorded vitals.

"She regained consciousness a while ago. After we extubated her, she asked where she was," the nurse replied.

"Diane?" Sandra asked weakly, having recognized her friend's voice.

Diane reached for Sandra's hand and held it gently. She noticed it was much warmer than earlier in the day. The change was a good sign. "Can you tell me your name?"

"Don't give me that crap," Sandra retorted groggily. "I know the drill: name, date and place."

"Just following routine," Diane replied, smiling warmly. The questions were standard procedure and were used to test a patient's level of awareness.

"Then, how about: how are you feeling?" Diane asked, skipping the other two standard questions. There was no doubt in her mind that Sandra was very aware of her surroundings.

"Like hell. What am I doing here?" Sandra rasped hoarsely.

"You ingested some poison," Diane informed her. "Can you tell me how that happened?"

Sandra knew the procedures for suspected poisonings, stabbings, and gunshot wounds. She knew there would be an investigation. She also knew she had to prevent it until she had answers to her own questions first.

"How did I get here?" Sandra asked, purposely ignoring Diane's question. Sandra was doing her best to stall until she could come up with an appropriate response.

"You were flown in here by Harrier jet, as I understand it. I think the pilot was a friend of Quinn's . . ."

"Quinn?" Sandra tried to sit up, but was quickly restrained.

"Hey, take it easy," Diane said, trying to calm Sandra down to prevent any tubes from being pulled out. "He's fine. He's in another room resting with the twins." She could see tears welling up in Sandra's eyes and couldn't, for the life of her, understand the reason behind them.

"Why don't you just rest a bit and I'll come back and see you later?" Diane suggested, thinking Sandra could use the extra time to rest and pull herself together. She had never seen Sandra so emotional before. What had happened to the strong, even-tempered, always-under-control professional she knew?

Sandra just nodded. She turned her head away from the door, because she could no longer hold back the flood of tears. *Diane must think I've gone nuts,* she thought. But those eight words, *He's in another room resting with the twins,* were the most glorious words she had ever heard. Her family was finally all back home. Now, all she had to do was get well enough to be with them.

130

"THE X-RAYS SHOWED nothing's broken, but you'll need to ice that ankle and keep that leg elevated for at least twenty-four hours. In other words, Quinn, you need to take it easy for a day or two," Dr. Diane Cole instructed.

"That shouldn't be too hard, since I'll be in here visiting Sandra, now should it?" Quinn replied eagerly. He had learned a few minutes earlier from Diane that Sandra would make a full recovery, but would spend the next nine days in hospital.

"I guess not," Diane agreed, smiling softly. "And if you're having headaches, take some Advil or Tylenol. Watch for any swelling or drainage around that wound," Diane cautioned, as she gently probed the area in question.

"If the headaches persist or you're feeling drowsy, you may have suffered a concussion. And if you have a fever, I need you to see me right away. Do you understand?" Diane asked bluntly. She could tell Quinn's attention was elsewhere.

"Yeah," Quinn replied absent mindedly.

"We also prescribed some antibiotics for Bear," Diane continued. "You'll need to take her to your vet and have them put on a 'cone-of-shame' so she doesn't lick her stitches."

"Okay, okay. Can I see my wife now?" Quinn asked impatiently.

"Hop on," Diane said, gesturing to the wheelchair she was standing behind. Diane wheeled Quinn into Room 501 and pushed the chair up next to the bed. Sandra appeared to be resting comfortably. Quinn noticed Sandra had been extubated. Some IV medications had been discontinued. And her vital signs were now stable. Even so, they were keeping a close watch on her neuro status. Diane checked Sandra's chart and, then, left the two of them alone.

Quinn pulled himself out of the wheelchair and sat on the edge of Sandra's bed. Even in her current condition, Quinn was looking at the most beautiful woman he had ever seen. He gently took her hand, lifted it to his lips and kissed it. Then he kissed her on the forehead. When he pulled back, he could see Sandra's eyes flutter open.

"Quinn?" Sandra croaked.

"The one and only," Quinn answered with a grin.

"Dani and Daric?"

"Home safe and sound," Quinn announced, as he wiped a tear from Sandra's cheek.

"I want to see them," Sandra stated emphatically.

"In a few minutes. I wanted to talk to you alone, first," Quinn replied candidly. "Richard poisoned you with tetrahydrozoline."

"Why?"

"My guess is he didn't want to leave any witnesses," Quinn said acidly. "He tried to drown Dani and Daric . . ."

"Are they okay?" Sandra asked, alarmed.

"Yes, they're fine," Quinn assured her. "I think he wanted our deaths to not raise any suspicions. Yours would have looked like a suicide and Dani and Daric's like accidental drownings. And my body would probably never have been found in that underwater cave."

"Why would Richard want to kill us?" Sandra probed, aghast at what Quinn was telling her.

"Because he wanted the travel bands," Quinn grunted. "He said he had to go back in time and right an injustice done to his family."

"Where is Richard now?" Sandra asked bluntly. She was enraged. *How could he harm my children?*

"Relax," Quinn whispered, as he gently squeezed Sandra's hand. "He's right where he wanted to be, back in 1189." Any doubts he had had earlier about Richard's whereabouts were gone. Hermes had told him exactly where Richard was. Richard would eventually witness his family's disgrace and Quinn knew, whatever Richard tried to do, the outcome would be the same. "We won't be bothered by him ever again." He reached down and wiped another tear from Sandra's cheek. "It's a shame he'll never pay for derailing that commuter train."

"What? You're not saying . . ."

"Richard caused the train derailment to keep you from going to New Zealand; the narcissistic maniac," Quinn snapped angrily. "He was planning to kill me while he and I were in New Zealand. If you had been with us, he would have had to kill you, too and that wasn't part of his plan. At least not then."

"All those poor people," Sandra said sadly while reflecting on that horrific day. "All those senseless deaths at the hands of one crazy, self-absorbed lunatic," she added in a barely audible whisper.

"You're right," Quinn acknowledged quietly. "But right now we need to focus on fabricating a story about your poisoning. We don't want the authorities to start an investigation," Quinn explained, trying to direct Sandra's attention back to the matters at hand.

"I agree. Diane already asked me what happened," Sandra said nervously. "I just skirted around her question with a question of my own. But she won't be put off for long."

"Maybe you could tell her you went into the medicine cabinet during the night. You didn't bother turning on the light and you grabbed the Visine by mistake," Quinn offered.

"It's not a great excuse, but it's plausible," Sandra said thoughtfully. She smiled a disarming smile. Quinn leaned in and planted a tender kiss on her lips.

"I thought I was going to lose you," Quinn whispered hoarsely.

"And Richard told me you were dead. But I refused to believe him," Sandra rasped back. "What about Richard? What's going to happen when people start missing him? How do we explain his disappearance?"

"We're working on something," Quinn answered encouragingly. "We just need to nail down some details first and make sure everyone involved is onboard. Don't you worry about it; you just focus on getting well." Quinn smiled lovingly and leaned in to kiss his wife again.

Present Day—Two Weeks Later

131

SANDRA WAS HOME from the hospital, fully recovered. The story that Quinn and she had concocted regarding the poisoning worked; there would be no investigation.

Dani and Daric had gone back to university to finish up the semester. They would be home in just under a month's time.

Quinn had been spending a considerable amount of time either in his lab or over at Richard's place. He and Eddie had been working on something, along with Hermes. Today, however, they were in Quinn's lower lab.

"Hermes?" Quinn called sombrely, as he activated the computer console. Eddie was standing at the end of the console, waiting to receive instructions.

"Yes, Professor," Hermes replied, as he appeared on the platform in the corner. "Oh, hello, Eddie."

"Hi, Hermes," Eddie acknowledged. "Thanks again, for all your help over the past few weeks. You sure made everything fit together nicely."

"My pleasure, Eddie," Hermes answered, grinning all the while.

"Hermes, come over here," Quinn said. "I have something I need to explain to you."

Hermes immediately materialized beside Quinn. It was a position he was quite familiar with. It was his place of honor, where he had hovered while they had worked together over the years. Today, Hermes noticed something peculiar; his companions looked as though their best friend had just died.

"Professor, is everything all right?" Hermes asked anxiously.

"Yes. Well, actually, no," Quinn stammered. "I don't know how to thank you for saving my family. You warned me about Richard, you finished the computations to bring my children back home, and you determined the poison that Sandra had been given, which saved her life. I don't know how I'll ever be able to repay you. I am in your debt," Quinn said sincerely.

"Professor, I feel that they are my family too and I would do anything to protect them," Hermes announced.

"Would you?" Quinn asked frankly.

"Without hesitation," Hermes said insistently.

"Well, that's what I want to talk to you about," Quinn stated. "You know the lengths that Richard went to in order to get possession of the travel bands."

"Of course I do," Hermes replied.

"And you know that he put my family's lives in danger," Quinn continued.

"*Our* family," Hermes corrected. "And, yes, I know he tried to kill you all, unsuccessfully I might add."

Quinn took a moment to compose himself. This was one of the hardest things he had ever had to do. Eddie could see Quinn was conflicted, yet determined to see this through; he had no choice.

"Hermes, I'm going to destroy the travel bands . . ."

"But, Professor, we worked for years to prove Einstein was right. Professor, you deserve the recognition . . ."

"That's the problem, Hermes. If the world ever found out I possess the ability to travel through time, who knows how many lunatics we'd have at our door trying to get their hands on the bands, just the way Richard did. And who knows what lengths they'd go to. I almost lost my family, our family, once. I don't want to put them at risk ever again," Quinn said resolutely.

"I see your point, Professor. It's a shame the world will never know all that you've accomplished," Hermes conceded.

"All we've accomplished, my friend." Quinn smiled at his faithful companion and partner.

"Unfortunately, not only the bands, but all of our research must be destroyed." Quinn paused for a moment, waiting to see whether Hermes would comprehend the full implication of what he had just said.

"Are you saying what I think you're saying?" Hermes asked nervously.

"I'm afraid so," Quinn mumbled. "I can't have any of this—the bands, the research or anything else—falling into the wrong hands."

"But, Professor . . ."

"Hermes, you said you'd do anything to protect our family. I can't think of any other way of protecting them than to destroy everything we have built together over the past ten years. I'm so sorry." Quinn could feel a lump form in his throat. Terminating Hermes's programming, in essence, ending Hermes's life—was a hell of a way to reward a true friend for having saved the Delaney family. He was sick about his decision, but he could see no other way.

Hermes hung his head. "I understand, Professor."

"I'm so sorry, my friend," Quinn said, as he nodded to Eddie.

Eddie had a tear running down his cheek as he inserted a USB key into the console, immediately uploading a virus to eradicate Hermes's programming. Eddie had come to really appreciate the AI and would have loved to have been able to work with him some more. They had accomplished so much over the past two weeks. Eddie could only imagine what they could have achieved over the next few years. Eddie considered Hermes a true friend.

Hermes glanced at Quinn, one last time; a faint smile crossed his lips. “It has been a pleasure working with you, Professor.” Then the hologram blinked twice and vanished.

“You, too, my friend,” Quinn said to the empty space beside him.

Quinn headed for the stairs, right behind Eddie. He turned off the lights. He would seal the door to the lower lab from above.

A tiny blue light flickered on the console beside the USB port, flickered again and then went out.

Present Day—Six Months Later

Epilogue

IN THE MONTHS following Richard Barak Case's disappearance, the world didn't know he was even missing, let alone dead. As far as they were concerned, he was still making an impact on hundreds of lives.

Thanks to his technical expertise and to the previous help received from Hermes and Quinn, Eddie had effectively taken Richard's place. He had already acquired Richard's fingerprints and retina scan and, consequently, had gained access to all of Richard's financial holdings and assets.

Richard had always been somewhat of a recluse; he had been rarely seen out and about in the community. As a result, Eddie could conduct business remotely without raising suspicions. After having secured Harry Bennett's allegiance, Eddie had taken over Richard's mansion. During his discussions with Harry, he had explained that Harry was free to leave, since Richard no longer held any sway over him. Eddie had also explained that he wanted to employ Harry as his second-in-command for the estate. With no other place to go, Harry had gladly accepted Eddie's offer.

Eddie had also retained Vashti Barinov as his housekeeper and personal chef. In addition, he had brought Vashti's family over from Russia, the family Richard had denied her for years. He had set up the Barinovs in one of the small farm houses on the estate and had asked them to get the farm up and running again, to bring it back to being self-sufficient. Since the Barinvos had been farmers in Russia, they were perfect for the job and only too eager to help. Reviving the farm had been a major undertaking. The vast refrigeration plant, the cow barns, the slaughter house and the smoke house had all been resurrected. The three silos had been refurbished, and each was ready to hold one hundred tons of grain come the winter. The water reserve tank had been cleaned out and refilled. The old horse stable and the nearby bridge had been reinforced and the stable now housed eight beautiful Clydesdale horses. Eddie was partial to the big majestic animals and the Barinovs had promised not to overwork them on the farm.

The large barracks out by the estate's greenhouse now housed eighty gardeners. All of them were homeless people whom Eddie had pulled off the streets and to whom the Barinovs had taught the basics of gardening and farming. Now, in addition to having a roof over their heads, they had three square meals a day and a decent wage to boot.

The west wing of the mansion had been transformed into a residence for gifted youth. With Quinn's help, the youth participated in an education and research program linked to the Perimeter Institute. It was named after its benefactor, The RBC Institute of Academics, and its motto was 'Looking toward the Future'.

Eddie had compensated all the victims of the train derailment. He had set up trust funds for the children of parents who had been killed in the accident, ensuring that no child ever went without the best education money could buy. As for the derailment itself, the authorities had carried out an extensive investigation and had concluded that it was an attack carried out by a terrorist organization.

All of Eddie's charitable acts had been carried out under Richard's name. As a result, they may have earned Richard the recognition he had so desperately desired. Over the years, his family legacy and philanthropic deeds would be recorded in the annals of time and would portray him as a genuine saint.

* * *

As had become part of the normal routine over the past few months, Quinn arrived home late, again. Bear greeted him excitedly at the door. “Arrrooo,” Bear called out.

“Shhhush, Bear, you’ll wake the house,” Quinn said, as he bent down to give his four-legged family member a rub behind the ears. He ran his hand down Bear’s sides. He could just feel under her fur the scar from her injury. Other than the scar, Bear was back to normal. She couldn’t have been happier, having her whole family back under one roof.

“Come on, it’s time for bed,” Quinn whispered, as he turned off the light and left the kitchen. He walked into the living room, stepped behind the bar, and poured himself a scotch neat. He took a sip and closed his eyes for a moment. All seemed to be right with his world. His children were home and helping run the gifted youth program at Richard’s estate. And, thankfully, there were no residual effects from Sandra’s poisoning.

Quinn took his drink and climbed the stairs, quietly opening the bedroom door. The light on his bedside table was on low and there were smouldering embers in the fireplace. He knew he should have been home sooner. Sandra loved to snuggle in bed with the fireplace going, watching the flames dance and the shadows flicker on the walls.

Bear had wandered into the bedroom behind Quinn and went to her usual bedtime place; curling up on the small foam bed in front of the fireplace.

Making as little noise as possible, Quinn went into the bathroom, closed the door and turned on the light. He took another sip of scotch before placing it on the vanity, as he got ready for bed. He hung his clothes on the back of the door, as he had done many times before. He picked up his glass, turned off the light, opened the door, and made his way silently toward the bed.

As soon as Quinn sat on the bed, Sandra felt the mattress shift under his weight. She rolled over and glanced at him lovingly. She reached up and seized Quinn's glass, stealing a sip. "Mmmm."

"Give me that," Quinn teased, as he snatched his glass back and quickly emptied the contents. He placed the glass on the bedside table. Then he crawled over to Sandra, straddling her slender body. He leaned in and kissed her passionately.

"Mmmm," Sandra moaned, enjoying the attention. But part of her mind was elsewhere. She had a question that had been bothering her for weeks and she was eager to know the answer, even if now wasn't the ideal time to ask.

"Quinn," Sandra whispered in his ear, as he nibbled her neck.

"Hmm."

"If you had kept the travel bands, what would you have done?" Sandra asked softly.

Quinn leaned on his elbow and looked amorously into his wife's soft hazel eyes. He reached over to the bedside table, turned off the light, and, then, leaned down and whispered in her ear. "I'd go back in time and fall in love with you all over again."

THE END

Author's Notes
Part VI

I chose Herculaneum as the location of my story, gambling that readers would not be as familiar with this town as they would be with Pompeii. I wanted to keep Vesuvius undisclosed for as long as possible.

Finding information about Herculaneum posed several challenges. One was the fact that, compared to its sister city of Pompeii, there was not a lot of material available in relation to it. My biggest obstacle, however, was that Herculaneum, for the most part, is still buried under the current city of Ercolano.

The Decumanus Maximus is the main street and the heart of every Roman town. In Herculaneum, it was also the northern edge of the excavation work. As a result, the northern half of the town is still buried, unexplored and unknown. To fill the informational void, I drew on my imagination and on details gleaned in relation to Pompeii: the Forum, the Macellum or public market, the amphitheater, the colosseum, and the numerous temples. I hope I did the town justice.

While Pompeii was blanketed in ash and pumice pebbles, Herculaneum was covered in a fine, hot dust of pyroclastic surges and flows, resulting in the preservation of organic materials, such as wood, food, cloth and papyrus. The eighty-foot depth of this covering at Herculaneum preserved a significant number of the town's buildings, including their upper floors. Accordingly, the story includes a lot of details about Roman/Herculaneum architecture, about how the ancient Romans lived, and about their diet, their homes and their public buildings.

Having established the story's location, I had to consider what I wanted to convey, what kind of story I wanted to tell. In the end, I remembered watching a BBC documentary called the Hero of Herculaneum and being inspired by the documentary's central character, a lone soldier. I now had my protagonist, Richardus Barak Casus, and I wanted to tell his story. But I also wanted to tell the story of some of the victims of Vesuvius and what their lives might have been like almost 2000 years ago.

In 1982, during a new phase of excavation by the ancient seashore, researchers discovered over 300 skeletons in and around boat sheds, the largest concentration of the population found to date. I used information that the researchers gleaned from the skeletons and from documents found in the town to put life back into the residents of Herculaneum.

One of the residents was skeleton ERC26. He had been a soldier (Casus), who was around thirty-seven years of age and who, at five-foot-eight, was well above the local average height. That he was a soldier was inferred from the sword he carried. The signs of his calling could also be seen in the remains of a stab wound on his left femur and in the absence of three front teeth.

A skeleton of a mother (Nona) was discovered clutching her child (Livius), who was embracing his pet dog (Titan). Another skeleton (Spurius Subinus) was found lying in a bed in the Curia.

Three exceptionally well-preserved skeletons were revealed in a niche at the back of one of the vaults: two women in their forties (Aquilina and Procilla) and a small child (Gaia). Tiny silver earrings were found on either side of the child's skull; grape seeds were found in her ribcage.

Lucius Cominius Primus was a real resident who had a boundary dispute with a neighbor regarding 306 fence poles. He had also taken a slave as security against a loan. Whether he was as villainous as I have portrayed him, I don't know, but I needed an antagonist for my story and he fit the bill.

Julia Felix was an actual character of 79 AD, albeit she lived in Pompeii rather than in Herculaneum. I borrowed her and her story of opening her villa's baths to the public and renting her rooms to those who had had their homes destroyed during the earthquake of 62 AD.

Herculaneum offered a detailed glimpse into the private lives of an ancient world. Like a time capsule, if you will, it conveyed what life would have been like in an idyllic town on a peninsula overlooking the placid waters of the Bay of Naples. Until all hell broke loose.

I would be remiss if I did not acknowledge the debt of gratitude I owe to those who have dedicated so much of their time and effort to researching, analysing and documenting Herculaneum and its inhabitants. I have tried to honor their work by adhering to historical facts, while at the same time interweaving my characters—the Delaneys, Richard Barak Case and others—into the fabric of history.

We all travel through time when we get lost in a good book or movie. Sometimes we step into the past and experience what life might have been like; sometimes we jump into the future and let our imagination take us on a wild ride. Wherever you choose to travel, be safe and enjoy the journey.

I hope you enjoyed this one . . . ***Until Next Time***.

Bibliography

1. Time Travel

- Gott, J. Richard. *Time Travel in Einstein's Universe: The Physical Possibilities of Travel Through Time.* Mariner Books, 2002.
- Kaku, Michio. *Physics of the Impossible: A Scientific Exploration into the World of Phasers, Force Fields, Teleportation, and Time Travel.* Doubleday, 2008.
- Magueijo, Jaao. *Faster Than the Speed of Light: The Story of a Scientific Speculation.* Basic Books, 2003.
- Nahin, Paul J. *Time Travel: A Writer's Guide to the Real Science of Plausible Time Travel.* Johns Hopkins Univ Pr; Revised ed. edition, 2011.

2. Herculaneum

- Aldrete, Gregory S. *Daily Life in the Roman City: Rome, Pompeii and Ostia.* University of Oklahoma Press. 2009
- Ameary, Colin and Curran, Brian Jr. *The Lost World of Pompeii.* Frances Lincoln Ltd. 2002
- Cooley, Alison E. and M.C.L. *Pompeii and Herculaneum: A Source Book.* Routledge. 2013
- De Albentiis, Emidio. *Secrets of Pompeii: Everyday Life in Ancient Rome.* J. Paul Getty Museum. 2009
- Garland, Robert. *The Great Courses: The Other Side of History—Daily Life in the Ancient World.*
- Grant, Michael. *Cities of Vesuvius—Pompeii and*

Herculaneum. Phoenix Press. 2005

- Sigurdsson, Haraldur and Cashdollar, Stanford and Sparks, Stephen R. J. *The Eruption of Vesuvius in A. D. 79: Reconstruction from Historical and Volcanological Evidence.* American Journal of Archaeology, Vol. 86, No. 1 (Jan., 1982), pp. 39-51
- Wallace-Hadrill, Andrew. *Herculaneum: Past and Future.* Frances Lincoln Ltd. 2002
- Documentaries/Specials:
  - *Pompeii: The Mystery of People Frozen in Time.* Discovery. 2013
  - *The Other Pompeii: Life and Death in Herculaneum.* BBC. 2013
  - *The Last Day Pompeii.* BBC. 2003
  - *Out of the Ashes Recovering the Lost Library of Herculaneum.* PBS.
  - *The Hero of Herculaneum: from the Mummies Alive Series.* Smithsonian Channel
- Website:
  - *AD79 Destruction and Rediscovery.* https://sites.google.com/site/ad79eruption/herculaneum-1

3. **Present Day Storyline**
   - *Castles of the Underworld.* NZonscreen, 1991

Acknowledgements

I can't say it enough; thank you Hugh Willis for your valuable feedback and encouraging words. You stuck with me through all three books. How? I don't know, because I'm sure I must have driven you crazy at times with my writing. I do apologize, again, and again. And I am so glad you found the journey enjoyable! I was thrilled to have you along.

For technical assistance, I'd like to thank Diane Cole, Registered Nurse in the Neuro/Trauma Intensive Care Unit at St. Michaels Hospital who, aside from being one of my golf buddies, was also my on-call medical and poisonous substances expert. And thank you to Dr. Susan McMillen, Doctor of Veterinary Medicine, who provided her expertise for treating Bear.

I'd also like to acknowledge retired US Marine Corps aviator, Lieutenant Colonel Art Nalls, for his eagerness and enthusiasm in providing his expertise with the technical aspects of the Harrier Jump Jet. Actually, it was Art's personal story I caught on a YouTube video that inspired the Harrier sequence. He holds the celebrated distinction of being the first and so far the only person in the world to privately own and operate a Harrier Jump Jet. Thank you, Art, for letting me share part of your story.

And I'd like to give a special shout-out to my former Annandale curling team, Charlie Quinn, Peggy Delaney and Sandy Riddell. Thank you for letting me borrow your names.

Hopefully, throughout the three books I've covered everyone who has joined me on this incredible journey and I pray I didn't overlook anyone.